Stephen King • Dave Barry
Amy Tan • Ridley Pearson

FEATURING SPECIAL GUESTS

Warren Zevon • Tess Gerritsen

APPEARING

May 8

8pm BANGOR AUDITORIUM

TICKETS AVAILABLE AT

Bangor Civic Center Box Office 990-4444

TicketMaster 775-3331

All Proceeds to Benefit

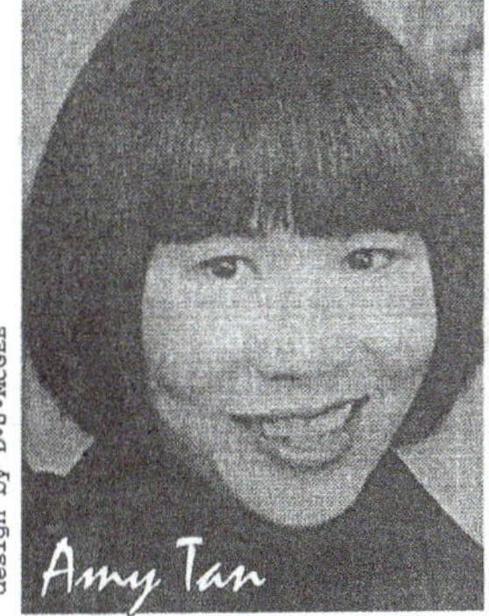

The street is no place for a child.

design by D•J•McGEE

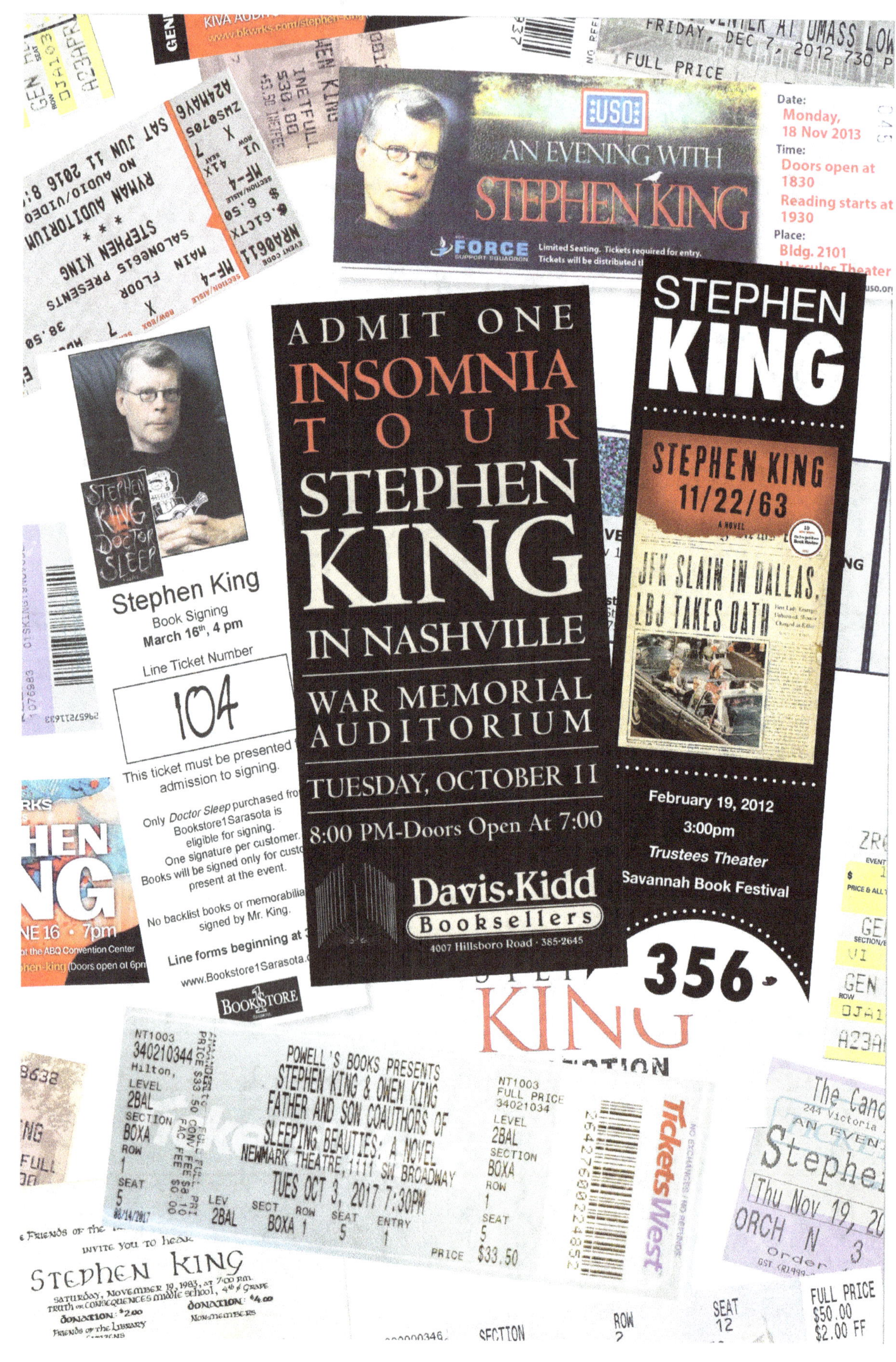

FRIDAY, DEC 7, 2012 730 P
FULL PRICE
USO
AN EVENING WITH
STEPHEN KING
FORCE SUPPORT SQUADRON
Limited Seating. Tickets required for entry.
Date:
Monday, 18 Nov 2013
Time:
Doors open at 1830
Reading starts at 1930
Place:
Bldg. 2101
STEPHEN KING PRESENTS
RYMAN AUDITORIUM
ON AUDIO/VIDEO
SAT JUN 11 2016
MAIN FLOOR
Stephen King
Book Signing
March 16th, 4 pm
Line Ticket Number
104
This ticket must be presented for admission to signing.
Only Doctor Sleep purchased from Bookstore1Sarasota is eligible for signing.
One signature per customer.
Books will be signed only for customers present at the event.
No backlist books or memorabilia signed by Mr. King.
Line forms beginning at
www.Bookstore1Sarasota.
BOOKSTORE
ADMIT ONE
INSOMNIA TOUR
STEPHEN KING
IN NASHVILLE
WAR MEMORIAL AUDITORIUM
TUESDAY, OCTOBER 11
8:00 PM-Doors Open At 7:00
Davis-Kidd Booksellers
4007 Hillsboro Road · 385-2645
STEPHEN KING
STEPHEN KING
11/22/63
JFK SLAIN IN DALLAS, LBJ TAKES OATH
February 19, 2012
3:00pm
Trustees Theater
Savannah Book Festival
356
KING
at the ABQ Convention Center
POWELL'S BOOKS PRESENTS
STEPHEN KING & OWEN KING
FATHER AND SON COAUTHORS OF
SLEEPING BEAUTIES: A NOVEL
NEWMARK THEATRE, 1111 SW BROADWAY
TUES OCT 3, 2017 7:30PM
NT1003
FULL PRICE
LEVEL 2BAL
SECTION BOXA
ROW 1
SEAT 5
PRICE $33.50
TicketsWest
Friends of the Library invite you to hear
STEPHEN KING
Saturday, November 19, 1983, at 7:00 p.m.
DONATION: $2.00
DONATION: $4.00
Thu Nov 19, 20
ORCH N 3
FULL PRICE
$50.00
$2.00 FF

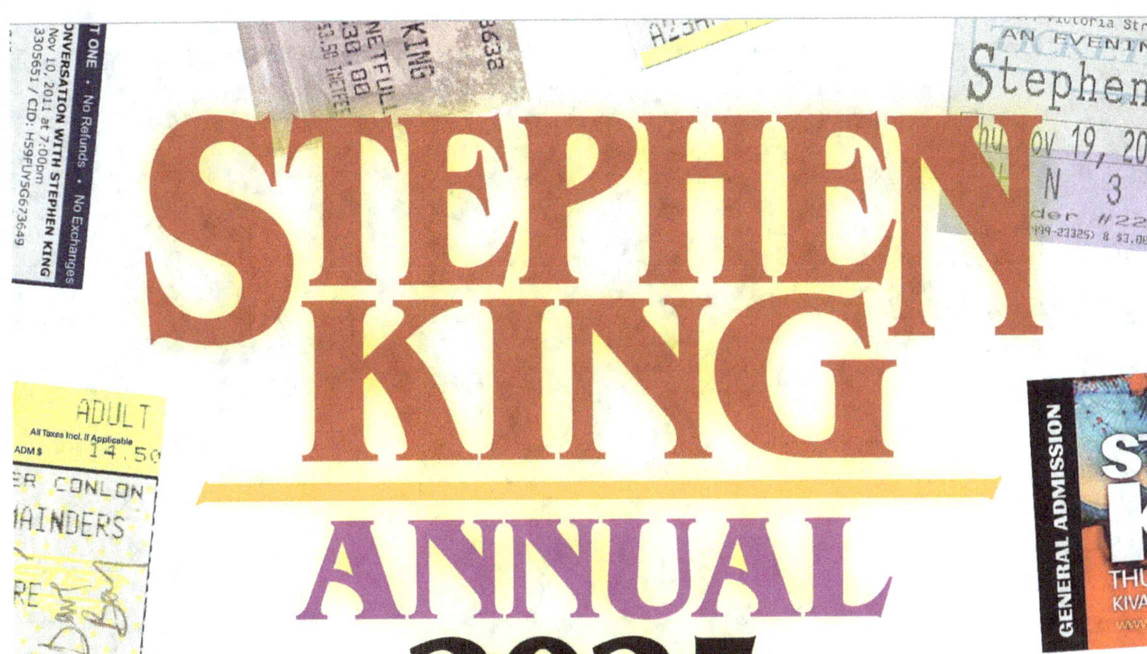

STEPHEN KING ANNUAL

-2025-

STEPHEN KING ON TOUR

Written and Edited by Dave Hinchberger

Cover and Interior Art by Glenn Chadbourne

OVERLOOK CONNECTION PRESS

The Mason Award
STEPHEN KING

TABLE OF CONTENTS

All The World's *His* Stage: Stephen King On Tour

In 2016 I had a discussion with my son, Ian, about Stephen King's then upcoming US tour for his novel, *End of Watch*. He asked "how does Stephen King go on a tour and appear at the Ryman theater in Nashville? Don't authors usually appear at bookstores?" Valid questions, from the uninitiated. How many authors fill up a venue that holds thousands of folks? This certainly isn't the norm, but I got it… how was he on tour, playing in large venues, as an *author*?

But then, we're talking about the one… and only… Stephen King.

Stephen King has been in a unique position for decades now. As he describes it he became "the Great Pumpkin" of the horror field somewhere back in the '70's, when many of the *heads of horror* had gone on to the great beyond. Alfred Hitchcock, Rod Serling, et al, and suddenly he was "the man" of the genre they'd previously embodied. Even though he writes in all genres, that's what the world has come to know him as, a *horror* writer (folks are still surprised when I tell them *The Shawshank Redemption* is by him). Fine, but as a writer the man is certainly prolific. He steadfastly writes up to five hours every morning. This is his self-imposed daily regimen at his *job*. This amount of creativity, along with a growing audience, six decades in the making, from book, film, and TV, has created an immense following.

So, "yeah," I told him, "Stephen King sold out the Ryman Auditorium in 5 minutes, but he's had a lifetime of readers to get to this point." I said "we're not just talking about any author, but a man who has had the good fortune of being able to write a story, publish, and have an expecting audience waiting for it. Then his readers clamor for more, constantly (thus his affectionate tag for his readers, 'Constant Reader'), on the hunt for more of King's work. Now they get the chance to see him in person, the event is announced and *boom*, he sells out."

Upon leaving the Ryman Auditorium that night in Nashville, my wife having just seen Stephen King speak for the first time, said, "I never imagined that Stephen King would be so funny. I mean honey, he was funny!"

He's been speaking to audiences for over forty years, he's had time to hone his engagement with the crowd. Many authors aren't comfortable speaking to large crowds, and I think Stephen King is a unique example of this kind of event. He's been at this a long time. And his audience has grown from addressing a bookstore audience to literally thousands in one sitting. He's also had the advantage of knowing that when he steps out on that stage, he's immediately loved by his readers. I was with Harlan Ellison once when a woman came up and got her book signed and when walking away with her husband, she began crying. Meeting your hero can be personally gratifying and, surprising. Authors usually recognize they can have quite an effect on their readers. Especially when they've reached millions of people, like Stephen King has.

The first time I met Stephen King was at his office, in Bangor, Maine, July 1989. We had stopped by to take the King Assistants out for lunch. He showed up, surprising us all as he wasn't expected that afternoon. I was surprised! Again, meeting one of your hero's can give you a jolt, especially when it's unexpected. That was a moment I'll share another time, but what a grand afternoon it was.

The anticipation at these events to see Stephen King in person is somewhat akin to watching our favorite rock stars come out on stage. If anyone is a rock star in this world, it's Stephen King. I have never seen such adulation that I've seen with the audience responding to this author. Being in, and around, the music business for 20 years, I should know, as I've seen this response at many a backstage with fans and bands. I have been selling books for over 40 years and I've attended many bookstore events, and I've never seen anything quite like how an audience responds when seeing Stephen King.

We have fans, who've told us their stories within this Annual, who've seen and met Stephen King from all over the world, and in unexpected places that even I was surprised to learn from compiling this edition. We've had Constant Readers who could barely speak upon meeting him to one fan who keeps her photo of them together in her treasure chest of jewelry. This was in case there's a fire, she'd grab that box first!

Hey, I get it. I think most King fans do. Stephen King readers have an intimate connection with him. His fiction has gotten under our skin, made us crawl, made us smile, made us cry, and taken us within many facets of whatever community he's created in his stories. Readers relate to his fiction, and thus, they relate to the creator himself. It's a known fact that his fiction feels as if you could stop by and just take him out for lunch. I offered this invitation in a letter back in 1986 when I sent him albums from our current releases when I worked at Polygram Records. I said something like "hey, would you like to have lunch or dinner when I'm up your way someday?" Little did I know that many folks have offered this idea. Not surprised. He gets personal, he gets "under your skin," it's that… connection.

So, meeting Stephen King feels like you've met up with an old friend. In a sense you have. He recognizes this and I've always felt he appreciates his readers as much as humanly possible. These tours, sometime signings, sometime just a talk, has helped keep him stay connected to his readers.

Stephen King didn't tour for every book release. If he had he'd be on that forever tour that would come during his annual book release. Early in his career he did have book signings in areas near where he lived. Whether it be home in Bangor, summer/winter homes such as his Florida residence. He's appeared in some different venues over the decades, as you'll see in the chronological timeline at the bottom of the pages.

Creating this year's Annual, and reading all the stories from King fans to see their favorite author one thing is clear: you have all made great strides to get to Stephen King appearances. You've taken buses, planes, trains and almost any form of transportation to take you hundreds, thousands, of miles to get to your event with Stephen King. We had to travel for our last jaunt to see Steve in Nashville, at the Ryman Auditorium in 2016. That trip is four hours one way, and we spent two nights there. We had friends in from St. Louis to attend (5 hours one way). You (we), will travel far and wide to hear the man speak, and maybe he'll read a story or two, all to catch his 1-1/2-hour event. Always worth it. It's obvious he enjoys seeing everyone as much as the audience does seeing him. A rare gift when people get together, and all because one man, an informed man, could tell us his personal stories. That's a special moment we have all gravitated to.

Most have not been able to see Stephen King in person. I'm hoping that by anyone reading these shared stories within, from fellow fans, Constant Readers all, that you can feel the sense of their excitement and adventures seeing Stephen King live.

I'd like to offer a special *Thank You* to Bryan McAllister (who creates these *Annuals* for us) for this year's unique edition. He took on the gargantuan task of putting together the illustrated timeline you see at the bottom of each page with King tours, along with current happenings during those decades. I applaud your idea and taking the time to implement it. I know this was a personal endeavor for you and it looks magnificent, Bryan.

I've had this idea to look back at the history of Stephen King, touring the US and the world. What an informative and delightful undertaking this edition has been. Thanks to the generous contributions of fans who attended and reported on King's events as well as our regular contributors who offer their unique moments within. A heartfelt thank you to ultimate King fan, Glen Reitz, who supplied so many event photos, event items, and articles. Glen your efforts are appreciated, my friend.

JOIN US for the 2026 Annual and 2026 Calendar releases (now up at StephenKingCatalog.com) as we take a tour of the sewers… of Derry! With Pennywise as our guide, we'll be gettin' jiggy… with *IT*! Novel, films, merchandise, More!

Until next time… exit, stage left… *kiddies*.

– Dave Hinchberger

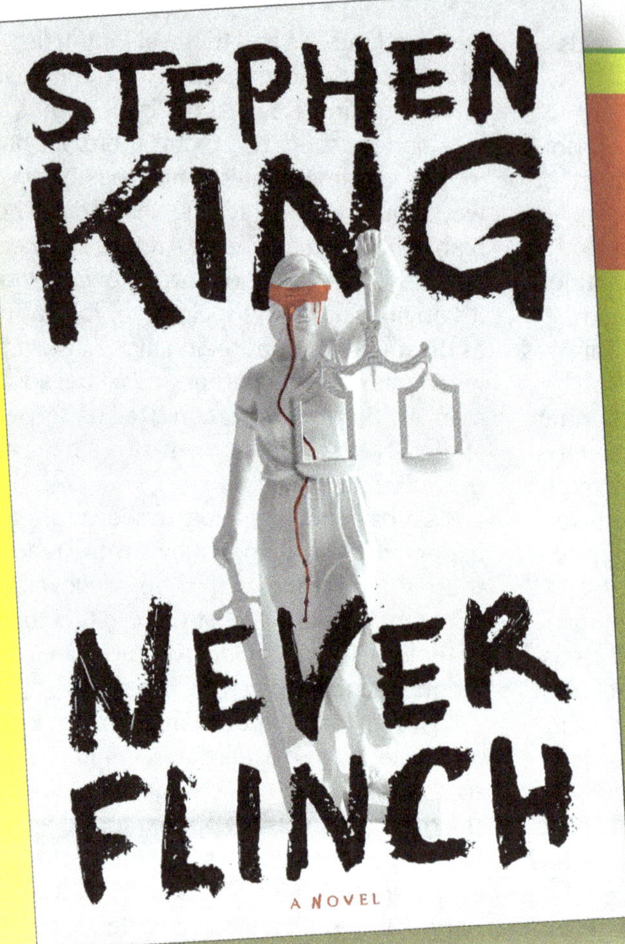

Release Date:
May 27th, 2025

Never Flinch is Stephen King's New Novel!

From master storyteller Stephen King comes an extraordinary new novel with intertwining storylines — one about a killer on a diabolical revenge mission, and another about a vigilante targeting a feminist celebrity speaker — featuring the beloved Holly Gibney and a dynamic new cast of characters.

Unique Exclusives from StephenKingCatalog.com

- First Printing hardcover with Exclusive Glenn Chadbourne wraparound cover
- First Printing hardcover with Exclusive slipcase
- First Printing hardcover Remarqued by Glenn Chadbourne, Slipcased
- Red & Silver Slipcases available separately (see on website)
- Includes an Acid-Free Book cover placed on every book purchased!

You can see all details and order at StephenKingCatalog.com

Pre-order from Stephen KingCatalog.com and you will receive:

- **FREE** bookplate of Stephen King, with art currently featured here by Cortney Skinner with all pre-order purchases!
- **Acid-Free Book Cover** placed on your copy with every purchase.
- **First Printing guaranteed!** We analyze every book to make sure it is As New before sending out.
- **Shipped in a well-packed box for complete Protection.**

Visit **StephenKingCatalog.com** to pre-order and read complete details

The First Time I Met Stephen King

by Bev Vincent

In January 1988, *The Tommyknockers* was in the #1 position on the *NY Times* bestseller list, and I had been reading Stephen King's novels for almost a decade. I lived in Halifax, Nova Scotia for most of the 1980s, maybe 400 miles from Bangor (a city I'd visited often as a child), but I never thought I'd get the chance to meet him in person.

The ink on my Ph. D. diploma wasn't yet dry when I moved to College Station for four months. I arrived in Texas shortly after the Black Monday stock market crash in October '87 and was promptly set upon by fire ants—an encounter that almost made me head straight back to Canada.

I don't remember how I learned King was going to have a signing in Houston, about 100 miles away. King had recently published *The Ideal Genuine Man (IGM)* by Don Robertson through his Philtrum Press (which had previously published the limited edition of *The Eyes of the Dragon* and the three installments of *The Plant*) and he was appearing with Robertson to promote the book.

Without a car, I spent those four months in College Station walking everywhere I needed to go. However, I'd arrived from from Houston on a Greyhound bus, so I knew I could get there that way. After filing for the day off from work, I took a taxi to the rudimentary bus station and waited at a picnic table for the bus to arrive. I have a distinct memory of hearing the staticky call of grackles in the trees as I waited. I brought my copy of *The Tommyknockers* with me—the only King book I had in Texas—hoping to get it signed.

The trip into Houston took over two hours. From the Greyhound station, I walked over four miles to the River Oaks Bookstore on West Gray. I don't remember anything particular about that journey, but I was later told by people in line that I'd passed through some iffy neighborhoods. Naïve Canadian that I was, it never occurred to me there were parts of the city that might be dangerous in the middle of the day.

Stephen King
appearing at
River Oaks Bookstore
1987 W. Gray
Friday, January 29
5-7
Mr. Stephen King
is accompanying
Don Robertson
with his new book
"The Ideal, Genuine Man"
published by Stephen King's press Philtrum

"Don Robertson was and is one of the three writers who influenced me as a young man who was trying to become a novelist."
Stephen King

(Stephen King will only autograph Don Robertson's book.)

April 16, 1974
University of Maine Bookstore
Oxford, Maine
Carrie

May 11, 1974
Bookland, Promenade Mall
Lewiston, Maine
Carrie

When I arrived, a line had already formed outside the bookstore. At some point we were informed King would only be signing *IGM*, which had people (including me) leaving the queue to buy a copy. One unconfirmed source puts the number of attendees at over 700.

The signing was scheduled for 5-7 pm, which had many worried it would end before everyone made it inside, but King announced he would keep going as long as there were people with copies of *IGM* in line. As seven o'clock approached, people who didn't have a copy were asked to leave the line.

I don't remember how long I waited, but it felt like hours. Long enough to have interesting conversations with the people around me. Someone asked what King's signature looked like, so I pulled out my copy of *The Tommyknockers*, which has a simulated autograph on the hardcover. One guy I talked with offered to drive me to the bus station after the signing, sparing me a long walk across the city in the dark!

The upper level of the store had a railing looking down on the ground floor. King and Robertson were seated there at a table, so we could see them from downstairs once we were inside. I recall King excusing himself to go to the bathroom at one point, loudly announcing, "Everything came out all right!" when he returned.

A store employee was taking photographs when customers reached the table, but I didn't have the foresight to arrange for one, so I'm not in any pictures of the event. I don't recall much about the few seconds I got to spend with the authors, but I still have that signed/ personalized copy in my collection.

This was one of only two events King attended in support of *IGM*, one in Cleveland on January 28, 1988, Don Robertson's hometown, and the one in Houston, where *IGM* is set, the following evening. The Houston signing was written up by William R. Wilson in the March 1988 issue of *Castle Rock*, along with

Stephen King and Don Robertson, River Oaks Bookstore, Houston, Texas. Jan. 29th, 1988. (all photos)

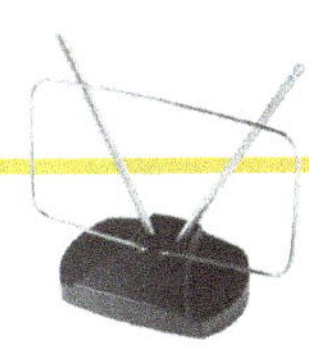

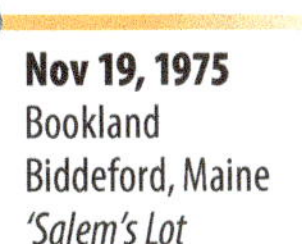

Nov 17, 1975
Bookland, Promenade Mall
Lewiston, Maine
'Salem's Lot

Nov 19, 1975
Bookland
Biddeford, Maine
'Salem's Lot

a companion piece about the Cleveland event, which was held in a restaurant with attendance limited to 200 people.

King and Roberts appeared at a luncheon at the Westin Galleria on the day of the Houston signing. King described Robertson as one of his three chief influences, along with Richard Matheson and John D. MacDonald. He and Robertson connected after Robertson found several references to his work in King's novels. When King inquired if Robertson had written anything lately, he received three unpublished novels in response. He felt strongly enough about *IGM* that he decided to publish it himself, although he confessed that his inexperience had made him underestimate the costs involved.

Robertson published two more novels after *IGM: Barb* in 1988 and *Prisoners of Twilight* in 1989, ten years before he died of cancer. Sadly, many of his novels are out of print. However, an Italian publisher recently translated *IGM*, as well as *Praise the Human Season* and *Julie*, a previously unpublished novel.

As for the River Oaks Bookstore, it remained a Houston landmark until it closed at the end of 2020, a victim of online bookstores and the pandemic. In an interview with the *Houston Chronicle*, co-founder Jeanne Jard cited two memorable events from the bookstore's 47-year history. John Grisham arrived at the store unannounced with a trunk full of copies of his first novel, *A Time to Kill*, published by a small press. The owner at the time agreed to let him do a signing, which around 30 people attended. The other event Jard mentioned was the incredibly well-attended King/Robertson signing, with people lined up down the street and around the corner.

1970s

Nov 21, 1975
Bookland
Brunswick, Maine
'Salem's Lot

Nov 24, 1975
Bookland
Portland, Maine
'Salem's Lot

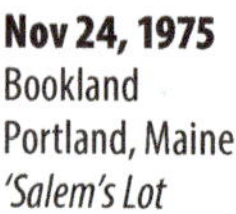

Do the Collapse

by **Kevin Quigley**

In my defense, I was twenty-two.

You have to understand the time period, too. Picture it: 1998. The internet is still sort of new. I don't have my own computer at home because I'm broke as hell. I'm part of an online group of Stephen King aficionados called SKEMERs (an acronym of Stephen King EMailERs, which seems so quaint and antique now), a text-based newsletter-like friend group I access at the Quincy Public Library. The concept of online friendships is new and only slightly terrifying. Right now, a fellow I know only through monochromatic letters floating on a dark screen is barreling toward my efficiency apartment all the way from Virginia. His name is Bob and he's ostensibly going to pick me up and drive me up to Bangor, Maine, to a Stephen King book signing at "The Stephen King Store," Betts Books. My friend Tracey assures me that, instead of that plan, Bob is going to arrive with an ax and chop me into pieces the second I fall asleep. The springs of my used double bed will squeal into the night against the metal of the blade, underscoring my own agonizing and hellish shrieks of pain and terror.

When Bob arrives, he looks like an accountant (That's what he wants you to think!!! my internal Tracey cries) and is immediately genial and kind. Our sleep is without incident – my limbs completely intact – and as dawn bubbles into the late November sky, we bundle up into his small, sensible car. Maybe not an accountant; maybe, perhaps, an actuary. Bob is the very definition of mild-mannered, and my earlier worry in these daylight hours feels so mislaid. Tracey and I had even worked out that thing where we had a code word for danger so that if I called her on the phone in the middle of the night, I could alert her to the ongoing predicament by saying, "Yosemite." The logic of figuring out how to work "Yosemite" into normal conversation, perhaps while Bob's vorpal blade went snicker-snack into my back, was a part of the plan we had not quite ironed out.

It's late November in New England; we get the windows up, we blast the heat, we roll out of Quincy, Massachusetts on the way to Bangor. Bob slides a tape into the deck. I expect some Christopher Cross. I expect Michael McDonald. In short, I expect yacht rock in the days before that term had ever been invented. Instead, shrieking power cords and screaming vocals erupt from every speaker, slamming the inside of the car with jangling noise I can barely process. This was *Tomcattin'*, an album by the heavy metal band Blackfoot, and I realize that I have made many errors in judgment (and also, I listen to Barenaked Ladies and Billy Joel; I have *always* been the mild-mannered one here). Bob flicks the devil horns at me and laughs in way not dissimilar to that of a demon on his throne of priest skulls. Maine awaits us.

It's getting on dusk by the time we pull up in front of Betts. I've been here before. Sure. Of course I have. As far as my SKEMERs buddies and I know, it is the only Stephen King bookstore in the world, and thus a sort of Downeast Mecca for King obsessives. The year before, my little group had had the good fortune to snag the first copies of Wizard & Glass anywhere in the country. (I specifically had had the outrageous fortune of helping deliver a couple boxes of the new hardcovers to Stephen King's office, but the man wasn't in at the time. Often, you don't know you're

Jan 30, 1977
Belk Books
Charlotte, North Carolina
'Salem's Lot

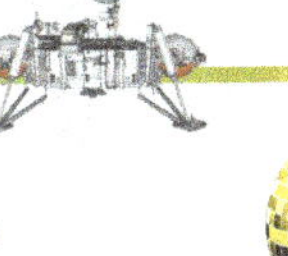

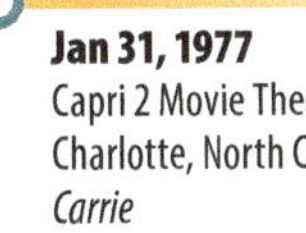

Jan 31, 1977
Capri 2 Movie Theater
Charlotte, North Carolina
Carrie

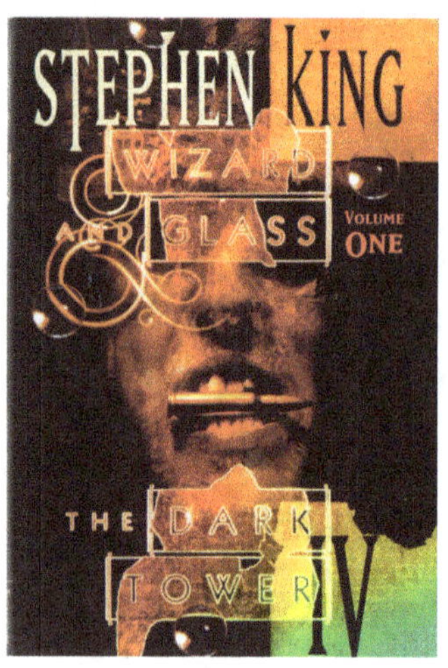

in the middle of one of the best moments of your life until much later, when it sticks out as a needle spike on a chart of memories; that was one I knew at the time.)

In the time I'd been visiting the store, Betts had supplied me with limited editions, rare hardcovers, gentlemen's magazines that confused my father, who was finally coming to grips with the fact that his son was gay. Now: they would supply me with Stephen King himself. And I was nervous.

I'd met King once before. Back when I was in high school, my mother worked at a radio station that had invited King's all-writer rock band, the Rock Bottom Remainders, in for an interview before they went to play a local club. Mom's producer didn't know anything about them and had asked me to write the interview questions, which were then read on air. Talk about outrageous fortune. My first and only interview with Stephen King, and I'd done it by proxy. I was only seventeen, and when my mother literally pushed me in the path of King in the lobby to sign my copy of *It*, I turned scarlet and murmured and stuttered through the whole experience. Let me tell you: the path from fanboy to monographer is a short but crucial one. The critical eye you need to write cogently and convincingly about your favorite subject develops over time. At seventeen, I was still new, and still unable to reconcile Stephen King the concept with Stephen King the person. That would change.

But not just yet.

A line had formed by the time Bob and I joined it, and it's mostly outside. As the dusk comes down, folks huddle together, breath visible, teeth a little chattery. The fine folks at Betts hand out cookies and cocoa to keep us warm and fed. It's a good thing, too; I'd been so nervous about meeting King later that I haven't really eaten much today. I don't want to get up to the table where he's signing books and be all weird or creepy or, worse, boring. I'd read up on all the questions King hates hearing: "What scares you?" "Where do you get your ideas?" "NEW *DARK TOWER* WHEN?" I'm determined not to be one of those people, and even more determined that when I get there, I won't be able to say word one, because of my now rampant anxiety and terror that I'm going to be the nuttiest nut in the fan parade.

Fortunately, several other SKEMERs are in line with us, including semi-famous writer (and, by this point, friend) George Beahm, on hand to take pictures of the event for a new book on King. My pal Jay, who I'd never met in person because this is the way the internet is going to keep working, notices how visibly nervous I am and decides to help me out. "You should ask him about characters in a non-*Dark Tower* book."

I grab him by the arm, atavistically staring. "Jay, that's a *great idea*." More and more, it seems like Tracey should have been trying to protect everyone else from me. But I seize on Jay's idea ferociously. I could ask him about Jack from *The Talisman*. I could ask him about Ben and Mark and what really happened in the town of *'Salem's Lot*. This concept is entirely original and no one has ever done it before, and King will be so impressed that I'm asking this question

Feb 7, 1977
Waldenbooks, Maine Mall
South Portland, Maine
The Shining

March 31, 1977
Hasting's Former Hall, UMO
Orono, Maine
'Salem's Lot
Lecture, unsure if books were signed

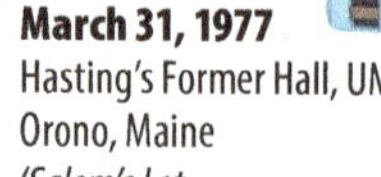

April 13, 1977
Hauck Auditorium, UMO
Orono, Maine - *The Shining*
Lecture, unsure if books were signed

that everything will be easy and awesome. How am I to know that he gets this question all the time? How am I to know that by 1998, he's as sick of it as "Where do you get your ideas?" I have decided that I am original and breezy and *not* weird.

"I'm going to ask him about Alan and Polly!" I shout, just an excitable boy. Several people look around, brows knitting in consternation as they hunch deeper into their jacket collars. There's a reason for my *Needful Things* focus, though. When I was fifteen, I had my first

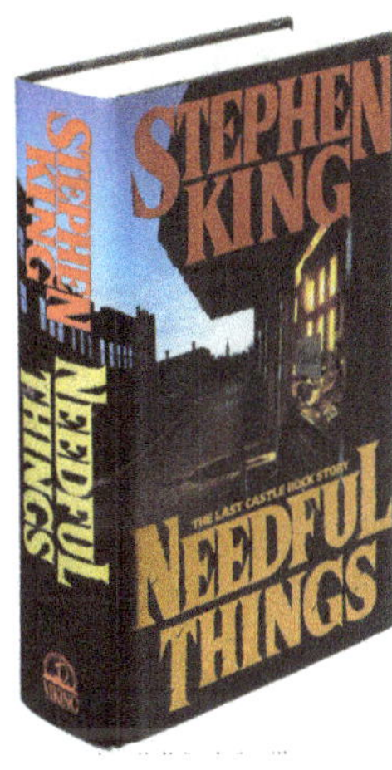

job – a paper route deep in the suburbs. I'd owned a few Stephen King hardcovers, but they were either inherited from my uncle Doug (*It*, *The Eyes of the Dragon*) or given to me at Christmas (*The Stand: Complete & Uncut*, *Four Past Midnight*). In October 1991, for the first time ever, I was going to be able to buy my own Stephen King hardcover. On release day, I marched straight into Infinity Books – my local indie bookstore at which I would later end up working – handed my earned money over, and took home *Needful Things*. We all have our own rites of passage, and when you grow up a little poor, you recognize these milestones. I vowed then I would never wait for the new Stephen King to come out in paperback. You worry, when you're young and feel trapped by circumstances and geography, that you'll never find a way out, that you'll never get to a place where success and a brighter future are achievable goals. The winding path toward those goals could be paved, I realized, with Stephen King hardcovers. Maybe it sounds silly or grandiose, but buying *Needful Things* with my own money had represented that path for me, three years before I struck out on my own, seven years before this chilly night, on which I have my brand-new copy of *Bag of Bones* tucked under my arm.

The line progresses apace. I'm also carrying *Misery* and *The Dark Half*, because Stephen King writing on writing is my jam, and because the actual *On Writing* is still a few years in the future. When Bob and Jay and George and I finally hit the warmth of the store, my face tingles and my hands regain feeling; I'm wearing a thin winter jacket I bought at a secondhand store because I prioritize books over comfort. As usual, I'm astounded at the riches on display. Classic copies of *Fantasy & Science Fiction* magazine with *Gunslinger* stories inside. Rare as hell Philtrum Press copies of *Eyes of the Dragon* and *The Plant*, published by Stephen King himself. And, dream of dreams, the sumptuous limited edition of the uncut *The Stand*, with its gilt-edged pages, its red silk endpapers, the black wooden box it rests in when not being pored over. This printing of King's tale of dark Christianity is so Biblical, I had tried to convince my friend Sarah the year before that the words of Mother Abigail were in red. "*Really!?*" she'd exulted, and was sorely disappointed when she found out I was lying. Cardinal sins everywhere.

We're closing in. I can see King near the back of the store, signing books and laughing

Aug 26, 1977
Magic Lantern Theater
Bridgton, Maine - *Carrie*
Even though this is the cycle for *The Shining*, this was at a *Carrie* event.

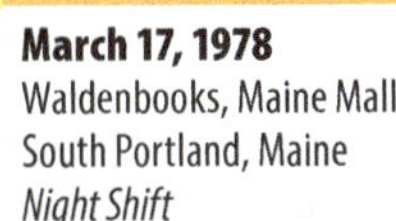

March 17, 1978
Waldenbooks, Maine Mall
South Portland, Maine
Night Shift
Guessing at the book being signed

and joking with people as *if this is some sort of normal situation.*

"Jay! Bob! I am going to go mental!"

They're finding my predicament extremely amusing. Jay says, "Just remember: Alan and Polly. That's all you have to keep in mind. You'll be fine." Jay does *not* understand. I am *not* going to be fine. My neurons and electrons are zigging and zagging so fast I'm pretty sure I am about to legitimately explode. Bits of me will shower all over the old copies of *Castle Rock* newsletter, which is a real shame. It's this image that is capering through my mind when I find myself thrust forward, and I'm face to face with Stephen King.

Twenty-two. I have spent most of my private life either reading Stephen King or reading *about* Stephen King. 70% of my high school essays had been about Stephen King, to the point where my teachers had to tell me to stop. The person standing in front of King right now is not the writer who will write several well-received books on the man, is not the relatively well-adjusted human man who has discovered other interests and written books on *them*, is not capable of any sort of higher thought. We are trapped in the full seize of a fan facing his hero, and that fan is completely unable to move.

"Hey, how are you doing?" Stephen King asks, like a regular, normal person would. A sound emits from me that … is audible? Is it a squeak? Is it an attempt to breathe? "Have you read *Bag of Bones* yet? I think it's a good one."

Of *course* it's a good one, I want to say. I have a *lot* of thoughts on *Bag of Bones*. Later, I will tell them all to Bob. Right now, they are locked in a steel cage in my brain and there is no earthly way they are going to escape and travel down my vocal cords and into the world. I do the next best thing and start nodding furiously. Then my brain tries to calmly explain that I am acting like a lunatic, oh my God, get it together you weirdo.

Then, somewhere in a world far behind me, I hear Jay calling out, *sotto voce*, like a redeeming angel: *"Aaaaallan and Poooollyyyyyy."*

"Oh!" I manage to shout. "Oh! How are Alan and Polly?" This comes out in a single breath. The man has no time to answer when I choose to provide some crucial information Stephen King is clearly not in possession of. "You know! From *Needful Things*."

He favors me with a smile (indulgent? pitying? worried?) and says, "They're doing just fine."

Just fine! Alan and Polly are doing just fine! Cool! Awesome! Off to the side, George Beahm snaps a picture of me. I still have it. My worry that I looked like a lunatic is well-founded and well-documented. Stephen King hands my books back to me, and it's only then that I realize he'd been signing and writing in them

Oct 12 - 16, 1978
World Fantasy Convention
Fort Worth, TX
The Stand

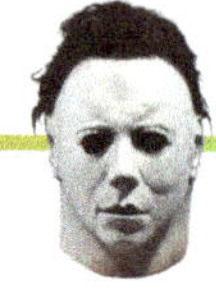

Nov 17, 1978
Open Space Bookstore
Bangor, Maine
The Stand

the whole time, like a professional person who is not deranged might do.

The line has to keep moving, and I'm shown the way to the back door, where I must again enter the realm of the actual world. I stumble out into Bangor at night. A small park awaits me. Streetlights whisper their lights down toward the sparse population below. The wind has picked up and I can barely feel it. Inside me is fire.

I open *Bag of Bones* and King's signature is there. I open *The Dark Half*, and the same signature illuminates the title page. I open *Misery*, and Stephen King has written

To Kevin / Best wishes from your #1 fan / Stephen King / 11/23/98

...breathing too hard. Breathing fast. Am I hyperventilating?

It's too much. It's too

It's

Black, and the sensation of falling, the sensation of *lightness*. I am only vaguely aware of my books tumbling out of my hands, of my knees buckling, of my whole body going down, *down*, and to this day I don't remember hitting the pavement.

I had only fainted once before, and that was when I was even younger and stupider and thought that riding my bike off a porch would impress my brother (it did not). Slowly, I inch my way out of the black, aware that my friends are hovering over me like in the last scene of *The Wizard of Oz*. In this scenario, I'm Dorothy, the tornado is my brain, and Oz is the twilight time of Bangor, Maine.

Bob crouches down, "Um. So, you fell."

Jay is howling. "Dude, you *fainted*."

They help me up. I'm still dizzy. Someone offers me my books and I take them with numb hands. Are my hands numb because I fainted or because I've prioritized trips to Bangor in mid-winter over gloves? Who can say?

George Beahm procures me some cocoa and I sip it, coming back to myself. I'm ridiculous and I know it. Part of me understands that right now, standing under these arc-sodium lights with my friends from the internet, that I'm allowed to be kind of ridiculous. As I've said, I was twenty-two, only four years out of high school. Maybe I sense that there is going to be a more grownup road for me in the future, one in which I still read and study the works of King, but at a little more of a scholarly remove. These may be the last days when a glimpse at a signature is enough to make me faint dead away, in a state I don't live in, around people I only barely know. That's probably good, though sometimes I miss those days when I could be so overwhelmed by happiness that my brain has no idea what to do with it. That's okay. I have my memories.

Well, except for those five minutes or so I was on the ground; those are completely gone. Yipe stripes. But it's been a good path forward.

Alan and Polly are doing just fine nowadays.

So am I.

Dec 2, 1978
Mr. Paperback, Maine Coast Mall
Ellsworth, Maine
The Stand

Dec 4, 1978
Betts Bookstore
Bangor, Maine
The Stand

Dec 9, 1978
University of Maine Orono
Orono, Maine
The Stand, Christmas Scholarship Fair

Why *The Monkey* Is One of the Best Stephen King Adaptations Ever

by ***Ariel Bosi***

Next year, it'll be 50 years since Brian De Palma's *Carrie*, the first Stephen King adaptation ever made, hit theaters, starting a journey that will probably outlast all of us—just like many of Stephen King's stories will. From that moment on, we have seen more than seventy adaptations, including movies, TV miniseries, and episodes in TV shows based on his works (and I'm not even counting derivative films such as sequels, unofficial adaptations, or dollar babies. If I did, we'd be looking at over 500 adaptations). We've had excellent films like *Stand by Me* and *The Shawshank Redemption*, great films like *The Mist*, good ones, poor ones, and some that were just plain bad. We've been scared by several: *1408* and *Salem's Lot* are two good examples. And I can't forget how the *IT* miniseries scared the shit out of me when I was 11 and saw it for the first time on TV. We've also felt hope and heartbreak more than once (*The Green Mile*, I'm looking at you). Every Stephen King adaptation has triggered a reaction in me. My anxiety peaked the first time I watched *Misery*—and during every rewatch since—and I can't help but laugh every time I see Steve in that white jacket saying, "C'mon over here, Sugar-buns. This machine just called me an asshole!" Over the years, I've experienced almost every emotion—except laughing to the point of tears. Until I watched *The Monkey*.

For the last twenty years, I've been so immersed in the Stephen King universe that I

lost something—especially when it comes to adaptations: the element of surprise. I learn about projects early on—who will be directing, what kind of films they usually make, who's starring and how they typically perform, and who's financing the adaptation and how

1970s

Jun 23, 1979
Tales from the White Hart Bookstore
Baltimore, Maryland
The Stand

Aug 23, 1979
Lauriat's, South Shore Plaza
Braintree, Massachusetts
The Dead Zone
I worked at this store 15 years later

Ariel and his new friend at the Abasto theater, in Buenos Aires, Argentina.

much creative freedom they allow. All this information gathering, which I love sharing with other Constant Readers, means that while I eagerly anticipate each new project, I more-or-less know what to expect: how the film will turn out and, most importantly, whether I'll like it or not. I knew I was going to enjoy *Doctor Sleep* a lot, just as I knew *Mercy* (the 2015 adaptation of *Gramma*) was going to suck. Surprises still happen now and then (*Chapelwaite* was a great one, while the 2019 version of *Pet Sematary* was a bad one), but I can count those on one hand.

The Monkey, however, was a major surprise. I knew it would be funny because Osgood Perkins said last year that he was adapting it as a dark comedy. I expected some smiles and maybe a laugh or two—the kind I had while watching *Creepshow* more than three decades ago—but I wasn't expecting the film it turned out to be. *The Monkey* is hilarious, dark, and sets the tone in its very first scene. Yes, you know it's about a monkey toy (OK! It's not a toy! I get it! 😊) that causes death every time it plays its instrument. You know Theo James will deliver a great performance (or two, actually), as will the rest of the cast (kudos to Christian Convery for two amazing performances as well). The ambiance, lighting, props, and soundtrack all align perfectly with the film's tone, enhancing the experience. You can imagine it being funny, but I never expected it to be this effective. The film has a flawless rhythm: it lets you laugh your ass off during the first third, then slows the pace to build darkness around the story and characters, and finally delivers a brilliant exit with a twisted biblical reference and one last amazing laugh.

This is a film that dared to break the mold, doing something never-before seen in a Stephen King adaptation—and that made all the difference. It surprised me. And in an era of so many formulaic stories that refuse to step outside the comfort zone, that makes it even more valuable.

Hollywood, please learn from Osgood Perkins… and take risks. It's a good path to take.

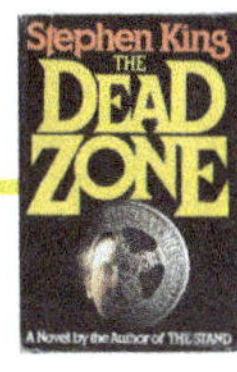

Aug 29, 1979
Tavern on the Green, DZ Publishing Party
New York, New York - *The Dead Zone*
Approximate date; newspaper article is a day after this, so I have guessed

Sept 8, 1979
Dark Carnival Bookstore
Berkeley, California
The Stand

Meeting Stephen King

by **Tyson Blue**

Although we've corresponded off and on over the years, I have met Stephen King in person six times, as near as I can recall. Once on his birthday, on the set of *Maximum Overdrive*; once at a press conference in Atlanta covering the movie's release; once at the American Booksellers' Association awards dinner; once at the "Reading Stephen King" conference at the University of Maine at Orono; once during his *Insomnia* motorcycle tour at Cornell; and once at Legal Sea Foods in Boston when we were both in town for a Red Sox game. All but the last have been written about in various places, and they've all been memorable in their own ways, ranging from a handshake and a few quick words to a short conversation.

Only two of these meetings have taken place while King was on tour to promote a book or movie; two were at commemorative events; and one was just a chance encounter at a restaurant.

That leaves the first, when *I* was the one on the road, for a visit to King "on the job" as director of his first, and so far only, feature film.

The *Maximum Overdrive* set, the Dixie Boy gas station, was a standing set built alongside the highway leading to Wilmington, North Carolina. I almost drove past it, because at a quick glance it looking like a real truck stop. it was only when I took in the bright movie lights and the crashed and burned trucks lying around that I realized that this was the place.

Parking my car, I made my way onto the set and soon found King, clad in jeans, a t-shirt

1970s

Sept 9, 1979
Change of Hobbit
San Francisco, California
The Dead Zone

Sept 18, 1979
Regency Bookstore
Omaha, Nebraska
The Dead Zone

and a fedora, seated in his director's chair at the center of a cluster of crew members. I introduced myself, shook hands, and stammered a few pleasantries. "We'll talk later," he said, and they went back to work.

I sat at a picnic table out of the way and talked with veteran actor Pat Hingle, who played the villainous Hendershot, and star Emilio Estevez. Hingle was very gracious and conversed with me easily, while Estevez, who had an exclusive interview deal with another reporter, simply looked at me like I had the proverbial lobsters growing out of my ears. Female lead Laura Harrington was nearby between takes, engaged in a high-kicking Rockettes-style rendition of "New York, New York."

After a while, shooting wrapped outside the building, and there was a pause while everything was moved inside for the next shot. King disappeared for a while, and when he came back, he signed several of my copies of his books, including *The Bachman Books*, which he signed as both King and Bachman, reminiscent of Walter Gibson, the creator of *The Shadow*, who signed books as both his pseudonym, Maxwell Grant, and himself. That makes these books a bit special, since they were signed by King and Bachman, and because they were signed on September 21, 1985 — King's 38th birthday. He was going to sign the rest of my books for me later in the evening, but was too tired to do so once shooting wrapped for the night in the wee small hours. He did eventually sign everything up through *The Tommyknockers* eventually — more than he has done for anyone else, he once told me.

Shortly after midnight, all the press people there sat down with King at a table in the Dixie Boy for a conference that lasted about an hour, beginning with everyone singing "Happy Birthday" to him. After snagging a pack of

cigarettes from the rack behind the counter, and joking about how he would be chided by the continuity people if he was caught, the interview began, dealing first with the movie, its soundtrack by AC/DC, the upcoming "five-book year", when he would release *IT, Misery, Eyes of the Dragon, The Drawing of the*

Oct 12 - 14, 1979
World Fantasy Convention
Providence, Rhode Island
The Dead Zone

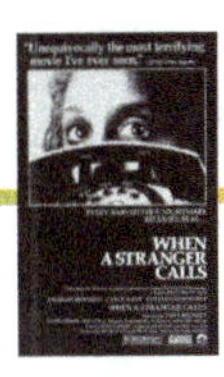

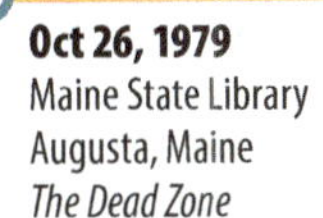

Oct 26, 1979
Maine State Library
Augusta, Maine
The Dead Zone

Three and *The Tommyknockers*, before taking some down-time to let the well fill back up. We also discussed the 1985 version of *The Twilight Zone* that was gearing up for release shortly, featuring an adaptation his short story "Gramma", featuring a teleplay by Harlan Ellison, for which he had high praise.

The interview transcript has been published in its entirety in the issue of *Castle Rock: The Stephen King Newsletter* dealing with the movie, and formed the basis of the article about the film I wrote for *Rod Serling's The Twilight Zone Magazine*. The latter piece was written on a borrowed typewriter in the film's production office and express mailed to the magazine, which was two weeks late for going to press, and was holding two pages open for me. Those two articles were the beginning of my professional writing career, and led to an incredible number of other jobs.

For those who are curious, the scenes that were being shot that night centered around the part in the film where the lights go out in the diner, reducing one of the waitresses to hysterics, and the sequence where Emilio Estevez and others head over to the truck stop's showers so they can make their way through the drainage system to the ditch where the dying Bible salesman lies, in an effort to rescue him.

My next encounter with King took place the following year in Atlanta, while he was touring to do press conferences to promote the film. In the meantime, I had become a Contributing Editor for *Castle Rock*, and was writing pieces for *The Twilight Zone* as well, and had spoken to King on the phone once. I arrived at the hotel where the conference was taking place, and waited with the other press folks for things to begin.

King arrived about thirty minutes late, explaining that they had stopped on the way to make a drug deal. Everybody laughed at what they thought was a joke, but knowing what we know now, I suspect he wasn't kidding. I started the conference off with a question about King's bet with the sports editor of the *Bangor Daily News* that King's beloved Red Sox would be in the race for the pennant by Flag Day, with the loser having to eat a chicken dinner — symbolic crow — in his underwear, on the front steps of the paper.

As it turned out, the Sox were not only in

1980s

Feb 1, 1980
New Gloucester High School
Gray, Maine
The Dead Zone

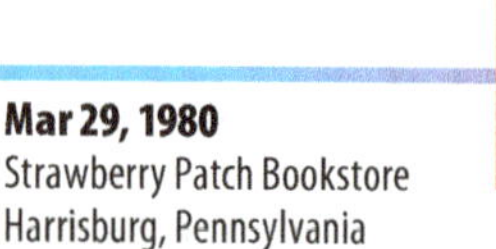

Mar 29, 1980
Strawberry Patch Bookstore
Harrisburg, Pennsylvania
The Dead Zone

the running, but were in first place, and the sports editor obligingly showed up in long johns adorned with Yankee pin-stripes, to chow down in front of King, resplendent in his tuxedo. "It was," he quipped, "the best day of my life!"

The rest of the presser dealt with the movie, some of the ups and downs of shooting, the music of AC/DC and its appearance in the film, as well as upcoming book news and whether or not he would direct again.

After it was over, I chatted briefly with him about a baseball-themed horror novel I had seen, and about his current novel — which happened to be *IT*, which I was reading in galleys at the time. Then we were both on our way.

The next time King and I encountered each other was at the Cornell stop on his motorcycle tour to promote his novel *Insomnia*, in the fall of 1994. The tour was marketed as though it was a tour by a rock band, complete with a t-shirt with cover art on the front and a list of tour stops on the back.

There was a press conference in a small, airless room on the Cornell campus, at which I asked him a question about the recently-deceased Robert Bloch, who had been a prime influence on him. After the conference, we chatted briefly and he posed for a picture with me before heading off to an independent bookstore before returning to the campus to speak to a gym full of eager fans.

All the other encounters were shorter: The next was in 1996 at the "Reading Stephen King" conference at UM Orono. I was the only non-academic person invited to speak. My topic was "Religious Imagery in *The Green Mile* and *Desperation*," which was attended by King's English professor, Burton Hatlen. I spoke briefly with King while waiting in line for the dinner preceding his evening keynote address, and introduced him to my sons, Justin and McKenneth, who had accompanied me to the event.

Stephen King grills... directs his actors.

My next meeting with King was at the American Book Awards dinner in New York City, where he received the group's medal for Outstanding Contribution to American Letters. I spoke with him briefly on the rope-line outside the event, and chatted with him and his wife, Tabitha, following his speech. I had noted that his skin looked pale and waxy, and was not surprised to learn that he had gone into the hospital with pneumonia the next day.

The last time I spoke with King was when my wife, Janice, and I were in Boston for a Red Sox-Yankees game, and stopped for lunch at Legal Sea Foods, one of our favorite eateries. As we checked in, I glanced over the maître d's shoulder and saw King, seated at a table with his family. I stopped and said hello, he said "Nice to see you," and that was about it.

I haven't encountered King since, but as the last incident bears out, you never know.

The cast of *Maximum Overdrive*

Aug 13, 1980
Betts Bookstore
Bangor, Maine
Firestarter

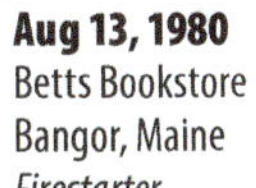

Aug 19, 1980
New York, New York
Firestarter

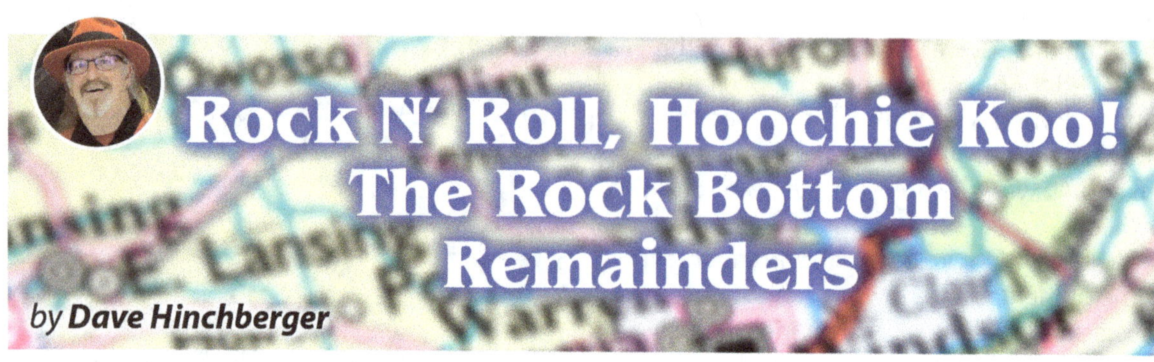

Rock N' Roll, Hoochie Koo! The Rock Bottom Remainders

by ***Dave Hinchberger***

The Roxy, Atlanta, May 27th, 1993

"The first rock and roll record that I ever owned, this is going to date me, but it was a 78, rpm, "Don't be Cruel", you know, with Nipper the dog in the middle (of the RCA Records label). I loved Elvis, but what I think really sort of flipped all my dials into the red zone was Jerry Lee Lewis. What I discovered was a kind of music that belongs to people like me, people that felt a little bit too smart, and maybe wore glasses or sort of geeky, sort of something like that"—Stephen King,

Stephen King did tour with an actual *rock band* back in 1993, the beginning of what would eventually become a thirty-year run of concerts and tours. A band of authors, The Rock Bottom Remainders were born in 1991 and took the stage May 25th, 1992 at their first live event at the American Booksellers Association. Anaheim, California. Many reading this Annual have either heard, or had the good fortune of seeing this rock band of writers "in person." I was fortunate to see The Rock Bottom Remainders on this, their inaugural tour.

On the back flap of the *IT* dust jacket the author text states: "He played in a rock band when he was in high school and, as the photograph on the back of the jacket shows, can still be persuaded to take the stage now and then, as long as it's not the Richie Tozier 'All-Dead' Rock Show." This photo he references, from the back cover of *IT*, was from a show at the University of Maine (4-12-86) where Stephen King took the stage with John Cafferty and the Beaver Brown Band (who gained fame as the sound for of the band in the film *Eddie and the Cruisers*). And to this day he still shows up at shows in Bangor to see visiting bands. Waiting in line like everyone else, and just as recent as September 2023 to see the Dropkick Murphys who began their tour at the Maine Savings Amphitheater in Bangor.

Stephen King was raised on Rock n' Roll, and he *loves* it.

Kathi Kamen Goldmark (founder of The Rock Bottom Remainders): "Stephen King was the only remainder I'd never met before... and I got his address from Barbara Carr and Dave Marsh. We just thought he'd be great and he (Dave) told me he played guitar. I wrote him a letter he wrote back and he said, 'as long as nobody took it too seriously, he'd love to do it'".

Stephen King: "I thought it over and decided that 3 chords and an attitude would still be a pretty good model in life. So, I said yeah, sign me up. It would be fun… and it has been."

When I first heard of this tour I wasn't exactly sure what to expect when they announced authors as a newly formed rock band were coming to Atlanta, featuring Stephen King! I was still working for Polygram Records back then, and selling Stephen King books in my

1980s

Aug 22, 1980
Change of Hobbit
Santa Monica, California
Firestarter

Aug 26, 1980
Kroch's & Brentano's
Chicago, Illinois
Firestarter

side mail-order bookstore, so this fused both of my worlds with this announcement. I was in heaven! Rock n' roll delivered by Stephen King, and this new band of wordsmiths.

Thirty years ago, Stephen King and The Rock Bottom Remainders stopped into Atlanta for a show, at the Coca-Cola Roxy Theater in Buckhead (now the Buckhead Theater). I informed a buddy at CNN, Jack Poorman, that there was to be a press conference at the Hard Rock Café in downtown Atlanta, taking place on the morning of the day of the show. He got a crew together and we met in the stage room (curtained off from the public when it wasn't in use) of the Hard Rock Cafe. I was there as Jack's guest. There were TV stations and local newspaper reporters lined up in a semi-circle in the audience area about midway from the stage at the back of this small venue.

Stephen King and Dave Hinchberger hold *The Overlook Connection Catalog* at the Hard Rock Cafe, Atlanta, May 27th, 1993

Then the authors came out onstage, one after another, all in a row: Stephen King, Dave Barry, Roy Blount, Jr., Kathi Kamen Goldmark, Barbara Kingsolver, Amy Tan, Ridley Pearson, Al Kooper et al., and took a seat on the stage. Seeing Stephen King up there was cool. It was like Paul McCartney (I'm a big Beatle fan) had just sauntered up there and sat down. Let's face it, Stephen King *is* a rock star among authors. They were led out by their tour manager, Bob Daitz. A man who, along with his curly scraggly hair, and beard, was securely in charge and introduced the band. Let me tell you a bit about this man: Bob Daitz is a part of rock n' roll royalty. He'd been the tour manager with the Ike & Tina Turner Revue in the 70's. For almost 50 years, Daitz had remained in the world of live-music. In the eighties, when Tina Turner was going solo, he had committed to being her tour manager and left a good gig as the first tour manager for Poison, who had just caught on fire with the rock world. He'd worked with Fleetwood Mac, Sammy Hagar, Van Halen, and so many more. He is the man who helped Kathi Kamen Goldmark, the founder of The Rock Bottom Remainders, get a lot of

Sept 20, 1980
Waldenbooks, Maine Mall
Portland, Maine
Firestarter (signing with Kirby McCauley, who just put out *Dark Forces*)

Sept 23, 1980
Caldor
Stamford, Connecticut
Firestarter

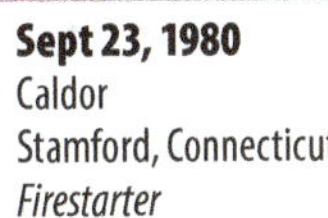
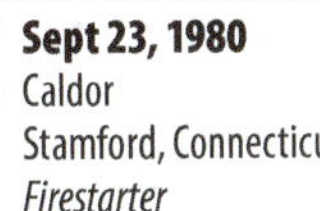

THE ROCK BOTTOM REMAINDERS

I was basically looking at Stephen King when I said this, and he immediately recognized me, at least by name, and offered up a smile. Steve had not only done a few things for our then *printed* catalog over the years, but he was also a customer for rarer items of his that he would give to family members. Plus, I always sent him the Overlook Connection Bookstore catalogs and we'd had other communications over the years.

After they took turns explaining how they came together with Kathi Kamen Goldmark being their escort

merchandise and instruments donated to help get this band of author's up and going for their literary charity endeavors. In my book, Bob is a champion.

Bob looked at the press and said: "If you have any questions by all means the band is ready for ya, ask away."

There was complete silence. Nothing, nada, you could hear the stage lights buzzing it was so quiet.

I had been looking around the room to see who would speak up first. It was obvious they didn't know what to make of these New York Times best-selling authors-turned-musicians sitting on stage in front of us. Dead silence. I was there as a guest, not a press person, so I didn't want to step on any toes, this was their job, but look… I had *plenty* of questions.

To hell with this, I'd waited. I stepped up, broke the silence, and just began asking questions.

"How did all of you author's come together as a band?" I asked. "Are many of you already musicians?"

Bob Daitz asked, "What's your name and who are you with?"

I said "My name's Dave Hinchberger and I'm with The Overlook Connection Press."

when they came to San Francisco to promote their latest book. She would take them around to bookstores, TV, and radio stations for interviews, and learned that several of the author's played instruments, sang in a band, etc. When Kathi thought of putting some of these author's together for a charity concert, voila'! More author's had heard about this endeavor and wanted in. Thus, The Rock Bottom Remainders were born… "with three chords and an attitude," that is.

Now with the *dam-of-silence* burst, others in the press began to ask questions and it took off from there. I think the whole conference was about 30 minutes.

When the press conference concluded I walked up to the front of the stage and Steve stood up and walked right over to me at the stage edge, with his hand outstretched, and we shook. He said, "Dave, you saved the day, thanks!" Of course, I was happy to be a part of all of this, and glad someone, me, from the "community" was there to help get this going. Let's face it, this was new territory this group had taken on and I understood why there was some confusion among the press that day. Glad it all came together.

1980s

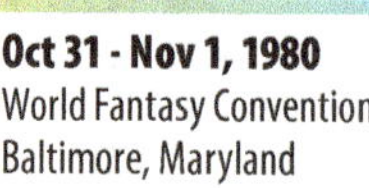

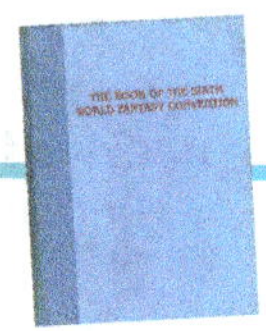

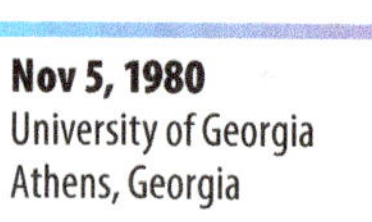

Naturally I brought a book along for Steve to sign. What is more appropriate than to bring a first printing of *The Shining*, my first King novel. This novel is also why I named a business that was just created to sell off my extra King finds so I could purchase *more* King works… The Overlook Connection Bookstore (and then I just kept going!). I had a photographer tag along with me that I would use for projects at Polygram Records events and he took the photo of Steve and I together, holding our latest catalog (I gave Steve that one).

The Roxy theater

I was working this day when the press conference took place. Thankfully, that was early, so I made it into work promoting the new Bon Jovi album, *Keep the Faith* (I had a great time working with that band over the years). After work we headed down to the Roxy theater in Buckhead, the north part of Atlanta. When we arrived, I stood in front of the theater, waiting for the doors to open when my old buddy, Ed Yarb, stepped up with his lovely wife. Ed gave me a big hug and thanked me for letting him know about this concert. The irony here is that Ed had lived in Atlanta for years, but had moved down to the Tampa area. They drove the whole way back just to see this special show. Now that's dedication! (You can read more about Ed's adventure in the Calendar section of this Annual).

The doors opened and we all went in and yeah, sure enough, they had a merchandising table and we headed straight for it. They had bumper stickers, a poster, and I believe t shirts, but I did not buy one. However, I did buy an 8x10 of the whole band... that was personally signed by everyone, including Stephen king! It didn't cost much and I was certainly surprised that this was available. But then again, this was their first tour, and they were trying to raise money for their charities and did everything they could to help.

These were the days where no cameras were allowed and certainly cell phones weren't available, so there isn't much photographic evidence to offer up from this show. But normally I would have taken a picture of the merchandising table, something I still do today that's part of the whole event of attending a show.

Now we're all in the audience, the lights have gone down and the crowd is going crazy as Roy Blount, Jr. steps up on the stage. He introduces the band, one by one, the band members taking their place on stage. When Stephen King was announced, they really we're hootin' and hollerin' for him. Stephen King came out with guitar in hand and stepped up to the mic. Roy then says to the crowd "Suspend your credibility… for the Rock Bottom Remainders!"

As the band began to play "Money (That's What I Want)" with Dave Barry on lead vocals, and he was quite good. Ridley Pearson's version of "Good Rockin' Tonight" was also a

Nov 8, 1980
B. Dalton Bookstore
Bangor, Maine
Firestarter

Nov 11, 1980
University of Iowa
Iowa City, Iowa
Firestarter – First public reading of a portion of *It*

Nov 22, 1980
University of Maine
Orono, Maine
Classified Employees Scholarship Fair

high point. The Remainderette's, and the band, sang "Bye, Bye, Love", in tune and in unison, and the audience sang with them. In fact the audience (who mostly consisted of ages similar to the band members on stage), sang throughout most of the concert. Dave Barry's rendition of "Gloria" would have given Van Morrison pause.. maybe wishful thinking on my part, but what fun! Great job, Dave! "These Boots Were Made for Walkin'" by Amy Tan was one sexy number, she sang and played this to the hilt, another fun performance. I'd look over at Al Kooper on different numbers, either on guitar or a stint on the keyboards, and was just thinking how did they get him? He played and recorded with so many bands, on so many albums. The Rolling Stones, Blood Sweat and Tears, The Who, B.B. King, Jimi Hendrix! As well as *Alice* Cooper, and Super Session with Stephen Stills (one of my faves). He produced the first two Lynyrd Skynyrd albums by god! Rock n' Roll royalty, and here he was with the band of writers. They were fortunate to have him, and I'm sure he had a blast with his newfound flock.

The Stephen King songs. Since I have a captive audience here, I know you want to hear about these. He sang and played rhythm and acoustic guitar (I think). He sang "Sea of Love" (with the rising hoots in the right places), "Stand by Me", well, this one is close to my heart and I'm sure as well as the rest of the King fans there, the song from the same film based on King's "The Body". Then, "Ladies and gentlemen… love, death, and the Senior Prom" as Stephen broke into "Teen Angel." I would venture to say this is the one I enjoyed the most. This song is a story of love, and loss, and its almost a spoken sing-song narrative tune. So here he is, telling us a story. I'll say that most of his songs were okay, he wavered now and then, but man I give him "A" for effort because he was into it. It takes of lot of hutzpah to do something that isn't normally what you do, especially in front of an audience of hundreds. The whole audience was in sync singing with him on most tunes. I had taken quick notes for some key songs in the show, but I was having such a grand time watching and singing along with the band I know I didn't scratch it all down, as evidenced by my crinkled notes (yeah, I still have 'em). How many times in your life do you get to sing classic songs along with your favorite author? Exactly. What a night!

Rare Rock Bottom Remainders Crew t-shirt. Signed by Stephen King, Amy Tan, Dave Barry, Tad Bartimus, and Roy Blount, Jr.

"I do know that I never had as much pure fun playing, before or after, as I did at the Roxy... When we came on stage… in Atlanta, we came on in a euphoric rush. The first tune at every show was the old Barrett Strong classic "Money," and when Al [Cooper] counted it off at the Roxy, he did it fast, driving us into an accelerated performance that never really let down. We stumbled off stage at the end of the show exhausted and sweat-soaked, but still feeling as

1980s

Dec 20, 1980
Pro Libris Bookshop
Bangor, Maine

March 28, 1981
B. Dalton Bookstore
Bangor, Maine
Danse Macabre

high as a handful of kites. The group consensus was that we had put on the best show of the tour." – Stephen King, *Mid-Life Confidential*

We'd heard at the press conference what hotel the band was staying at, (I don't remember the hotel now). Although the photographer and I had discussed possibly going to the hotel after the show, I hadn't really planned on doing that. Being in the music biz I knew from experience that bands like to take a break after the show and the backstage visits, so they can relax and catch their breath, so to speak. However, after the show we decided this was a once-in-a-lifetime moment… and drove to the hotel. We decided to check the hotel bar… where any band may go after a show… and sure enough, there they were! Roy Blount, Jr., Dave Barry, Ridley Pearson, and Stephen and Tabitha King. I hadn't realized she was on tour with them, but why not? This was a new experience for all of them, and their spouses (those that could come, I mean… they were traveling by bus, Aretha Franklin's tour bus that is) and life on the road isn't a walk in the park. Still, what a time for folks who are usually behind a computer keyboard. This was an opportunity to have a unique experience. You only get so many memorable moments in life, and what a time this must have been for them.

I met my photographer, Dave, at the hotel. Much to my surprise he'd taken the afternoon to have some 8x10 photos printed up that afternoon from the press conference, and he handed one to me of Steve and myself. It had already been some special kind of day. The press conference, talking to Steve and "saving the day," seeing the show, and now, here I was, holding a photo from that morning of Steve and I. I was gobsmacked. I spoke with Steve and had him sign the photo you see here. He was a bit surprised to see that the photo had been produced so quickly as well. I pointed to Dave and said, "he's the

man that made it happen."
Steve grinned at him and took the silver pen to sign the photo moment. His message was kind and I appreciated the sentiment, but in all truthfulness he's been the "hero" all along. Driving the bus that us Constant Readers continue to climb aboard.

What a day, and night, that was. I'll never forget it and glad to have finally have it published to share with all of you. That was an exciting time in my life in music, and seeing The Rock Bottom Remainders was the icing on that cake.

That was 1993. It's now 32 years later and we're still, all of us, on this ride that began when we read our first Stephen King story. How fortunate are we that we've had this writer in our lives all these decades, who's still working, every morning, doing what he enjoys. And if you're new to King's work, then you have a lot of fun and intrigue waiting on your bookshelves, or if you're like me, we're always waiting on his new novel, collection, or the surprise short story that pops-up here and there. The great thing is, Stephen King is just a page turn away.

"When I was a kid, you played music to get girls, and I played briefly with some guys that play rock and roll. Most of my performing was on the folk scene. You know, coffee house on the college campus, and that sort of thing. In the years since then it's been mostly just me but I just love to make music." – Stephen King

April, 1981
Mr. Paperback
Waterville, Maine
Danse Macabre

May 8, 1981
Kubla's Ninth Khanphony
Nashville, Tennessee - *Danse Macabre*
9th Kubla Khan Convention, run by the Middle Tennessee Science Fiction Society

"This is my first stadium show!"
— Stephen King

Tsongas Center at UMASS Lowell
First Annual Chancellor's Speaker Series: Stephen King.

I will never forget Friday, December 7, 2012. This was one of the best days of my life: I spent the day hanging out with Stephen King. The events you are about to read are true, but names were changed to protect the identity of my new best friend.

This story details Kim and Glen's most excellent adventure with Stephen King.

Kim and I have attended over 20 Stephen King events over the last 30 years, starting with his motorcycle tour promoting his novel *Insomnia* (1994). This was my first-time seeing Stephen King in person and my first autographed book from the Master of Horror. Twenty years later, my wife and I made it our mission to see Stephen King whenever/ wherever possible. I have had the incredible experience of getting 140 books autographed by Stephen King – in person. Over the years I have curated and collected over 640 signed

1980s

Aug 16, 1981
B. Dalton, Monroeville Mall
Monroeville, Pennsylvania
Cujo

Oct 30 - Nov 1, 1981
World Fantasy Convention
Berkely, CA
Cujo

books by Stephen King. I imagine that I am one of the few people in the world that has every US first edition/first printing of Stephen King's books in their collection. I include all 6 paperback copies of *The Green Mile*, "Umney's Last Case," all 4 US paperbacks of *The Bachman Books*, *Storm of the Century*, "My Pretty Pony" and *Blockade Billy* as part of this collection. However, my friend Rick recently pointed out that I am missing *The Dark Man* trade edition – if anyone wants to take pity on me, that is the book I need to complete my signed US trade signed collection.

How it all started:

When we saw that Stephen King was going to be at UMASS I contacted the university to purchase tickets. Having attended the event at George Mason University a year earlier and getting 4 books signed, we were ready for another adventure. Stephen King was chosen as the first author to speak at the First Annual Chancellor's Speaker Series at UMASS Lowell. We booked a hotel on the UMASS Campus and prepared for the trip. I called the University and inquired about VIP tickets for the event, I was lucky that day, because Marsha answered the phone (if anyone else answered our story would be over). She listed different sponsorship levels, which were all out of our price range. With a starting price of $1,000. Marsha stated that sales were slow, I informed her that if I win the lottery, I will buy up all the sponsorships, she laughed at my bad joke, and we ended our call. One week later, Marsha called me back and offered a private sponsorship for $150 each, I said sign me up! She pointed out that this ticket would not include a signed book or photo opportunity at the end of the night. I told her okay, disappointment in my voice, but I thanked her for everything she had done. We talked about our love for Stephen King for an hour, I informed her that we were staying at the campus hotel, and asked if she would like to meet up when we arrived. She inquired about our arrival time and said she was busy, but would seek us out, if she could get away.

Event #1: Stephen King Q&A with UMASS students

We checked into the UMASS hotel at 1:30, there was a note at the front desk from Marsha, she informed us that Stephen King would be speaking down the hall at the hotel to a group of English Majors at UMass. She put our name on the list. Had we been 30 minutes later we would have missed the event. The room held about 100 people, and I secured a front row seat. Andre Duboise, author of *House of Sand and Fog* (spoiler alert, this is important later) was the moderator and Stephen King did a talk about writing, etc. and then took questions from the students. After it ended, Stephen King went out the back door, everyone else out the front. My wife went back to our room to unpack, I walked around the lobby and ran into Stephen King and Andre Dubois. I introduced myself and asked Stephen if he would sign my copy of *The Long Walk*. He kindly agreed and it was an amazing day.

Dec 5, 1981
B. Dalton, Bangor Mall
Bangor, Maine
Cujo

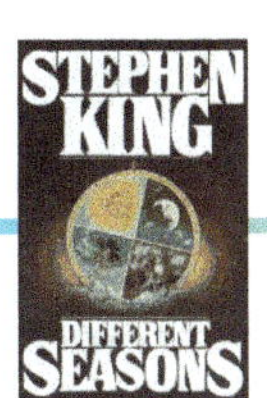

Mar 30, 1982
Palmyra High School, Lancaster, Pennsylvania
Different Seasons, Writing seminar at high school; unsure if books were signed

Event #2: Stephen King and I attend a reception with the English department faculty

I ran to our room to show my wife my newest signed King book, she walked out of the room and said that Marsha – from the University – had just called and asked us to meet in the lobby. Introductions were made and Marsha coyly asked if we wanted a glass of wine. Neither of us drank, but she offered us soft drinks and said to follow her. She led us to a breakout room where there was a reception – a faculty reception for Stephen King. Having just met Stepen and Andre in the lobby, I introduced my wife to Stephen and said hello to Andre (again). Stephen King was signing books for the faculty and guests, and inscribed copies of "New Lieutenants Rap" and *Startling Mysteries* for me and my wife. I would estimate around 30 people in the room. He was sitting at a table and signing/inscribing books and chatting to anyone and everyone. Simply amazing.

Glen Reitz and Stephen King at UMass at Lowell

Event #3: VIP reception with Andre Dubois' mother and mother-in-law

Time to attend our VIP event with Stephen King – We are the first to arrive for the reception, we find a table and put our belongings down and head to the bar. While we were getting our sodas, two ladies (in their sixties) sit at our table, we come back and introduce ourselves, they offer to find another table, but we insist that they stay. I told them about our amazing day, and they introduced themselves as Andre Dubois' mother and his mother-in-law. This was another amazing coincidence. When Steve and Andre walk into the reception (notice I am calling him Steve by now) they head to our table. Introductions were made and Stephen King signed 4 more books, one for each of us (Steve signed them all). The reception was larger than I expected but Stephen King was in great spirits and was signing anything and everything that people put in front of him! It was a dream come true!

Event #4: Over 5,000 at The Tsongas Center

After the reception, we took the escalator down to the auditorium. Over 5,000 people were in attendance. Steve said it was the largest crowd he had ever spoke in front of! Steve and Andre talked for an hour about stories, writing, movies, etc... They took questions from the audience and then King signed the chairs that they were sitting on. They auctioned off the chairs to benefit the English Department. I did not win the chair, but that was probably a good thing, I had no way to get it home.

As we headed back to the hotel after our event, I saw a lady that works at the hotel

1980s

July 23-25, 1982
Chase Park-Plaza Hotel
St. Louis, Missouri
Archon 6 SF/Fantasy Convention

Oct 9, 1982
B. Dalton, Bangor Mall
Bangor, Maine
Different Seasons

Stephen King and Andre Dubus III hold court with an audience of over 5,000 in the Tsongas Center.

carrying an overnight bag into the hotel lobby, quickly followed by Stephen and Andre. Exhausted, and with no books left to sign, my wife and I went to our room and dreamt about our amazing day. I dreamt that Stephen King slept in the hotel room next door and invited us to breakfast.

The whole event was covered in the UMASS quarterly magazine, my wife and I are in several pictures in the magazine, so I know this day was not a Fevre Dream, the magazine is framed in my King library, and an exciting reminder that it's just one of my many encounters with Stephen King.

Stephen King signs *11-22-63* at Umass at Lowell, Massachusetts

Nov 11 - 12, 1982
University of Oklahoma
Oklahoma City, Oklahoma

Nov 13, 1982
Brewer Cinema 4
Brewer, Maine
Creepshow

What a Long Strange Trip It's Been. Confessions of a Lifelong Constant Reader

by **Donna Girard**

I read my first Stephen King novel in 1976 at the age of 15. Growing up North of Boston as a kid I was a huge fan of all things horror never missing a *Saturday Creature Double Feature* (channel 56) or *Simon's Santorum* both of which aired classic, current, and campy horror movies in the early 1970's. There were also my most beloved TV shows, *The Twilight Zone*, *The Outer Limits* and *Night Gallery*. To put this in a frame of reference at the time there only 3 major networks, 2 other UHF channels and one public access channel. The TV would only run until midnight at which time it would play the National Anthem and display a TV test pattern until 6 am when regular programming kicked back in.

Yeah I'm that old. Currently I am 62 years and frankly I'm shocked to still be upright and taking the air. One thing about time the older you get the faster it goes. But I digress…

I have been a voracious reader since childhood a great lover of the classic *Grimm's Fairy Tales* and Folk Tales both foreign and domestic. As I got older I dabbled in Sci-fi and mystery reading such classic greats as Ray Bradbury, HG Wells, Edgar Allan Poe, and Alfred Hitchcock. I started picking up some of my mother's books, *The Exorcist* (William Peter Blatty), *Rosemary's Baby* (Ira Levin), and *The Other* (Thomas Tryon) and I was happy with that for a time. In 1976 the movie *Carrie* came out. I discovered the writer, Stephen King, had another novel out called *'Salem's Lot*. I fell in love.

Next I read *Night Shift*, *The Shining*, *The Dead Zone*, *Firestarter* and *Cujo*. I think I started writing him letters around 1978 after reading *The Stand*. Imagine my gushing embarrassment making the trip to Bangor years later and meeting Marsha Defilippo, King's personal assistant and finding out she was the one who had been reading my letters for years. At least I didn't get relegated to the "back room" which housed letters written by fans considered unstable and possibly dangerous in several large file cabinets. Somewhere in the 80's I made my first pilgrimage to Bangor, Maine. I packed my dog into the car with a paper map and a copy of It seeking out King's iconic house and the locations from his books: The Standpipe, The Barrens, The Library and the Paul Bunyan Statue. I knew he birthed the book in these places, walking and writing longhand on countless yellow legal pads. I was a disciple in mecca.

Around 1991 King came to Harvard University and did a reading from his new novel *Gerald's Game*. It wasn't a "signing" but he did sign my *The Eyes of The Dragon* book. They were hosting a reception and this was where I met him for the first time. He was literally larger than life I was dumbstruck.. and to this day after all this

1980s

March 31, 1983
University of New Hampshire
Dover, New Hampshire
Christine

April 22, 1983
Billerica Public Library
Billerica, Massachusetts
Christine

Donna Girard, Cheryl CJ Beaulieu and Dawn Whitten

time, he still always has the same effect on me. I remember his son Joe (who has gone on to become a great author of horror in his own right) was with him, a teen at the time, and he brought him a coke. I left there feeling like I had died and gone to heaven.

There was one thing that changed my Constant Reader status and dialed it up to 11: The Internet.

In the beginning… I fired up the old modem connection and found SKEMERs… Stephen King emailers. This was a newsletter type format. You sent in a post by email and it was compiled into a newsletter sent back to you via email. The world opened up. I found there were other people out there who were just as devoted to the man as I. At this point I had gone to a few signings in Maine at Betts Booskstore, and BookMarc's, but I was always alone not knowing anyone.

In 2003 in Pleasantville, a little town in upstate New York, there was a showing of the movie *Cujo* celebrating it's 20-year anniversary. Stephen King was in attendance. I arrived early and spotted him going into a restaurant to eat. I sat down at an outside table and waited for him to come out. When he did I waved first printing of *The Dark Tower: The Gunslinger* at him, gushed pleasantries and asked him to sign. He did. This was the event where I first encountered Cheryl "CJ" Clickstein, who knew more about Stephen King than anyone else I had ever met. We became fast friends.

SKEMERs decided to hold an actual meeting in Bangor… the first Skemercon. It was decided that there would be a *Carrie* prom. I showed up wearing a prom gown with a sash reading SKEMERS2004. We had a whirlwind weekend carpooling around Bangor visiting all the sites, playing King related Bingo and Trivia and attending a BBQ hosted by Stu and Penney Tinker of Betts Bookstore. I drove out to Bar Harbor/Arcadia for the first time and we all ate and drank and stayed up all night laughing and talking.

Time went on and things progressed. There was a King event in NYC and I started corresponding via email with a girl from Connecticut named Dawn (Kemp) Whitten.

Donna in front of the most famous home in Bangor, Maine.

Things fell through and we did not end up going together but somewhere in 2004 CJ and I picked Dawn up at a rest stop on Route

April 26, 1983
Forbidden Planet bookstore
New York City, New York
Christine

April 30, 1983
Mr. Paperback, Airport Mall
Bangor, Maine
Christine

From top left: Mt. Holyoke Campus Bookstore, South Hadley MA - (w/Richard Russo not pictured) - 2008; Ghost Brothers of Darkland County Afterparty, Four Seasons, Atlanta - 2012; Joe Hill Talk, Lovell Library, Maine - 2023; In front of Bookmarcs, Bangor - 2000; Benefit for Pine St. Inn, Harvard University, Boston, MA - 1991; Dark Tower VII signing with Michael Whelan, CT - 2004; Liseys Story signing (with John Irving not pictured) for Maple Street School, Vermont - 2005: with CJ, Mark Twain House, CT - 2013

95 (her family was terrified she would be kidnapped and murdered by strangers she had met on the internet..lol) and we attended our first signing together.

I remember that particular signing of *Dark Tower VII* for a bunch of reasons. We arrived the night before prepared to camp out in line because the tickets were limited and on a first come first serve basis. The bookstore saw the turnout and decided to issue us numbers and told us to come back the next day. We hadn't planned on a hotel room and ended up going home with a couple we had just met in line.. Don and Chelsea MacIsaac... crossing yet another state line into NY at a tremendous rate of speed.. (Don was a cop and drove like one) where about 8 of us crashed on the couches and floor. We returned the next day and had brought a gift for King… a Red Sox Jersey with the number 19 on the back. When King saw it he was so overjoyed he actually kissed me. Once again all thought went out of my head and I lost all my words.

Michael Whelan, a well-known fantasy artist, who done the illustrations for Dark Tower VII was also at the signing. So, we got our books signed by both King and Whelan, the Red Sox finally broke the curse and won the World

1980s

Nov 5, 1983
Books N Things
Oxford, Maine
Pet Sematary

Nov 19, 1983
Geronomo Springs Museum
Truth or Consequences, New Mexico
Pet Sematary

Stephen King and his guest, Rocky Wood, at the premiere of *Ghost Brothers of Darkland County*, Four Seasons Hotel, Atlanta, April 11, 2012

Series and the Hippiechick Ka-tet was born.

Around 2012 Stephen King's office started the Official Stephen King Message Board (SKMB) and most of the SKEMERs migrated there. Now we had Live access to chat rooms and also the ability to search and post on many different thread subjects. CJ was also running real-time trivia games and our circle expanded.

In the Summer of 2013, a group of girls from the SKMB came together in Maine. We rented a cottage on a lake and did a bunch of King related events in Maine including a Kingkon for a wider set of SKMB members, worming our way (bythepowerofIyn) into the interior of the Standpipe and visiting King's radio station WKIT. We had tickets for a book signing and cocktail party at the Mark Twain House and Museum and we drove to CT (which is about a 5-hour drive… one way lol). That night was purely magical.

Another notable trip was to Atlanta in 2012 to see the premiere of King's collaboration with John Mellencamp *Ghost Brothers of Darkland County*. This is where I met Dave and LeeAnn Hinchberger of the Overlook Connection (Bookstore of the Fantastic!) It was a great production followed by a private cast party at the Four Seasons Hotel. For once I was at an event I didn't have to sneak into… lol! I sat

Publisher Dave Hinchberger, and author Rocky Wood, with their book *Stephen King: Uncollected, Unpublished*, Atlanta, April 11, 2012

with yet another good friend I made in King… Rocky Wood. Rocky, a native of New Zealand, was the president (2 terms) of the Horror Writers Association, and the author of many books on King and his writings, Rocky worked for King as a researcher while he was writing *Doctor Sleep*. He was gracious enough to put me up at his home in Melbourne when I was in Australia. Rocky was rare man. He was brilliant, funny, kind and accomplished. He lost his life in 2014 to ALS a horrible disease. I miss him and think of him often.

Ironically, in 2020 I moved out of Massachusetts and into Maine less than 10 miles away from the King's summer home on Kezar Lake. This was not by design... I just kind of landed here.

In the end I have spent decades in the pursuit of Stephen King. Because of that journey I have made many great lifelong friends. I am forever in the debt of Stephen King for his stories and for the people and adventures they have led me to.

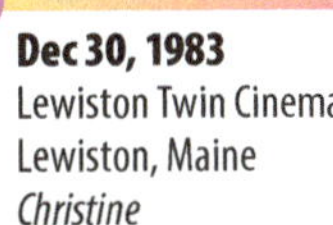

Dec 30, 1983
Lewiston Twin Cinema
Lewiston, Maine
Christine

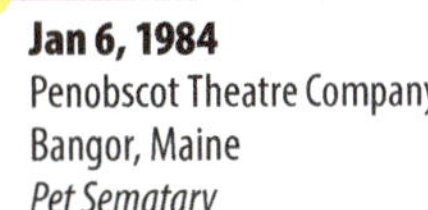

Jan 6, 1984
Penobscot Theatre Company
Bangor, Maine
Pet Sematary

Close Encounters of the Stephen King Kind

by ***Jim Argendeli***

An introduction is warranted about Jim's piece here. Stephen King was invited to write a monthly article, "The Pop of King," in the popular culture magazine, Entertainment Weekly. *He wrote this column from 2003 to 2011, movies, music, and definitely, books. In fact, he mentioned our new edition of* Off Season *(Overlook Connection Press) by Jack Ketchum in this column and we sold over 500 copies that month!*

I've known Jim for quite some time, going on two decades plus. In a recent visit to the Overlook Connection Bookstore, and over a nice Southern BBQ lunch, I brought up the interview that Jim made happen at CNN's Headline News with Robin Meade and Stephen King.

Yes, it's because of Jim Argendeli, and his persistence, that this interview took place during a visit in Atlanta during Steve's Under the Dome *book tour. I've always thought this was a great story that Jim experienced, on so many levels, as a fan, a reader, and a writer himself that I asked him to share it with us here at the Stephen King Annual. Take it away, Jim! – Dave*

So, the man behind the curtain, Diamond Dave Hinchberger, has asked me to write up the story of my close encounter of the Stephen King kind for his latest Stephen King Annual.

I am a horror book reader junkie. Stephen King was probably my first fix and I have never been off the juice in over thirty-five years. I also work at CNN/Headline News. In addition to my technical duties at Headline News, I was a freelance book reviewer for the CNN and HLN.com groups reviewing works by such amazing writers as Joe R. Lansdale, Simon Clark, Tim Lebbon, and even some Stephen King titles. I also did freelance writing for Turner Classic Movies.

In 2009, Stephen King released *Under the Dome*. I heard a rumor that King was going on a major book signing tour to promote the novel. I had read the occasional article that King had written for *Entertainment Weekly* "The Pop of King" giving his entertaining take on pop culture in the new century. In one of these articles, he mentioned watching Headline News in the morning calling out by name Robin Meade and the weather guru Bob Van Dillen. I believe my name was originally mentioned in the article as well but those fine editors at EW probably cut it out. Ha!

Anyhow, with the *EW* mention and an upcoming book tour, I mentioned to the higher salary types that it would behoove them to get Stephen King in for a live on-set interview. I supplied them with the date of his Atlanta bookstore appearance as well as contact information for his publisher and Mr. King's assistant, Marsha DeFilippo. At first, they were not interested but my persistence paid off.

Later, I was told that indeed Stephen King *was* going to be interviewed by Robin Meade live on-set. Shocked though I was at this accomplishment, the best was still ahead. Management asked me to provide Robin with questions and background information for her interview. I provided A LOT of background information and a list of about a dozen questions which would be the envy of

1980s

Jan 23, 1984
Brunswick Naval Air Force Base
Brunswick, Maine
Pet Sematary

Feb 2, 1984
Sears Roebuck
Manchester, New Hampshire
Campaigning with Gary Hart

BIG BROTHER
IS WATCHING

interviewers the world over and sure to win me an Emmy, a Pulitzer, an Edward R. Murrow award and, well, you get the picture.

My work was given to the producers and I thought that was it. Well, not quite. I had taken off the week that King's interview was slated (a vacation planned long ago) and I was asked if I would like to escort Mr. King around for the interview.

Even though I was staying in town, I politely declined and…

Who am I kidding? This Greek-Canadian jumped at the chance!

I arrived at work and was told to meet Stephen King and his driver at the security check-in for all non-employees. When Stephen King arrived, the company talent booker introduced me to him, then she left, leaving me alone with Stephen King! (ahem, and his driver).

Now don't think I took this lightly. I had met and become friends with several writers through the years by attending World Horror Conventions along with my wife Cindy (and here she didn't think I would mention her… brownie points for me) but I never thought I would have the opportunity to meet Stephen King, much less giving him a tour of Headline News. So, here I am, standing next to Mr. King after shaking his hand. He was wearing a worn-looking leather jacket, looking quite fit, and very engaging in his demeanor. It is at this point I should mention that in addition to the previously mentioned freelance writing work, that I had just sold my first short story to the book *The Anthology of Dark Wisdom* edited by William Jones (Elder Signs Press). The book includes writers such as Gene O'Neill, Tom Piccirilli and Peter Straub. I was honored to be included in the table of contents page and, in fact, my story "And on the Fourth Day…" closed out the anthology.

Robin Meade was Host of Morning Express on HLN for 21 years.

I had decided the previous night to grow a pair and offer a copy of the book to Mr. King. I mentioned that this was my first fiction sale and told him that I would really like to give him a copy. His reply "That would be great, but you will have to sign it to me." Huh…what the *@#!&*?. He saw the confused apoplectic look on my face and said "yeah, sign your story to me. In fact, make it out to Steve and Tabby."

So, there I am with Stephen King and he's waiting for *me* to sign my short story to *him and his wife*. Luckily, I had a pen with me (thanks again, Cindy!) and so I quickly thought what does an unknown like me write to a known *real writer* like him? I thought it through and this is what I came up with:

"To Steve and Tabby, I hope this helps with your career. Thanks for the inspiration.
Sincerely, Jim Argendeli"

Feb 27, 1984
Nashua, New Hampshire
Campaigning with Gary Hart
- specific hotel unnamed

March 23, 1984
Boca Raton Sheraton
Boca Raton, Florida
Skeleton Crew (pre-publication)
5th International Conference on the Fantastic in the Arts

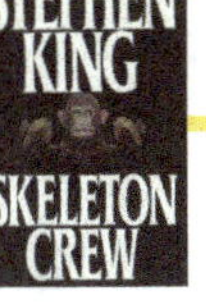

I gave him the book and when he saw what I had written he gave me a grin.

We went into the CNN complex and we're making our way to the makeup room to prepare for his interview. We talked about *Fangoria* magazine and he mentioned the upcoming novel *The Passage* by Justin Cronin telling me if I liked *'Salem's Lot* and *The Stand* I would probably like this one as well. He gave me a playful punch in the shoulder and then we were in the makeup room. There was not enough room for me to sit so I stood in front of Mr. King while he waited for his turn in the chair. He started thumbing through the book stating "ok, I know him, him….." He then came to my story and started reading it out loud. Again, what the *&!@#^?. Stephen King is reading the words of my short story out loud right in front of me. I assumed the role of a gawky statue. He read the first couple of sentences and said "good beginning." I just nodded and said sheepishly "Thanks."

Stephen King with Robin Meade on Morning Express 11-13-09

Stephen King at B&N Atlanta 11-13-09

Later, after his makeup was applied, he was being interviewed by Robin Meade, live on Headline News (with my questions!) I was holding *his* leather jacket. I just made like a human clothes hanger and waited in the wings during the interview.

At the conclusion of the interview, I walked with Stephen King (and his driver), to the limo, thanked him again, shook his hand and told him I would see him at his Barnes & Noble signing that evening. I thought about getting some older books signed that were in my car but changed my mind. What had happened was already pretty damn good! Let's face it, I had a few intimate moments with Stephen King, and this was far better than I could have imagined.

That night at his signing when it was my turn in line, he remembered who I was and said he liked my story. My only witness to this was my brother Bill who had met me at the bookstore.

Now, I do not know whether Mr. King read the story or even actually liked it but it was extremely gracious of him to say that and make this first-time published writer's day.

That night, me, Bill, Diamond Dave, and his wife LeeAnn, and writer Bev Vincent, who had flown in from Texas for this event, drank and talked at an Irish Pub about my unbelievably surreal day with Stephen King.

So, there you have it. I hope you enjoyed this long-winded tale of my meet and greet with the main man… Mr. Stephen King.

1980s

May 9, 1984
Bangor Civic Center
Bangor, Maine
Firestarter
Firestarter movie World Premiere

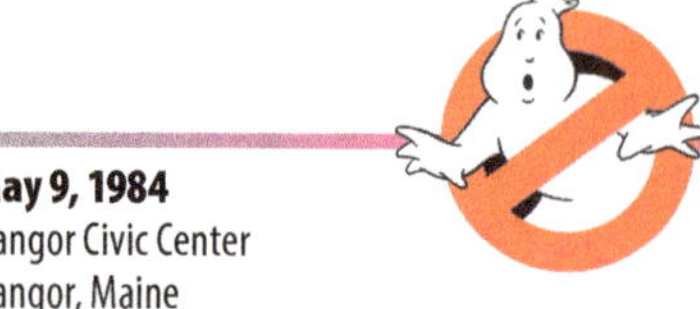

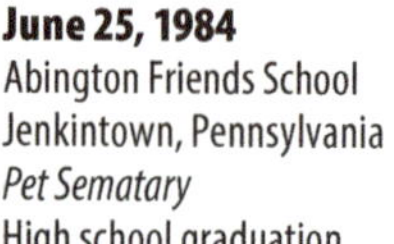

June 25, 1984
Abington Friends School
Jenkintown, Pennsylvania
Pet Sematary
High school graduation

SALON@615 PRESENTS

An evening with

STEPHEN KING

JUNE 11 2016

RYMAN AUDITORIUM

NASHVILLE, TN

Oct 28, 1984
Joe Bob Briggs World Drive-In Movie Festival
Dallas, Texas

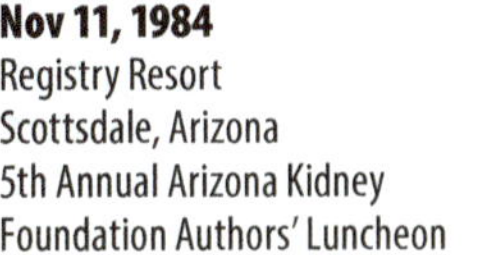

Nov 11, 1984
Registry Resort
Scottsdale, Arizona
5th Annual Arizona Kidney Foundation Authors' Luncheon

2009: The Dome Settles On Atlanta

by ***Dave Hinchberger***

Barnes & Noble bookstore, Buckhead, Atlanta, November 13, 2009

When it was announced that Stephen King would be coming to Atlanta to sign his new novel, *Under the Dome*. All you had to do was sign up at BarnesandNoble.com to attend. There were only five hundred available tickets.

This ticket would allow you entry into the event and allow you to get one signed copy of *Under the Dome* and meet Stephen King. It would be quick, but at least you'd attain a personally signed copy of the book, right in front of you, by the man himself. Considering how many readers he has, a rare moment indeed.

I had spoken to Marsha DeFilippo, Stephen King's assistant (now retired) in Bangor, Maine about the signing that year. They had a system where it's possible that he can sign all these books and just keep the line moving. That's a lot of books to sign, in basically, a 2-hour period. She told me, even though there were 500, Steve did allow for some overage signing. This wasn't guaranteed but he usually managed all who attended with a ticket to sign. It worked like this: you would exchange your reserved ticket for a wristband they placed on your arm that couldn't be removed until after the event. These wristbands are the same bands used if you were I'd for drinking alcohol at 21 and over clubs. Once removed they could not be reapplied or given to someone else. These wristbands we're in blue for the first group, and they were guaranteed a signed copy.

However, there was a second group that was allowed to stand in a different line, and those folks turned in their ticket to receive a yellow wristband. There are so many people that wanted to attend that if Steve still had the get up and go, he would continue to sign books for the yellow band attendees too.

And you know what? He signed each book for *anyone* who had a wristband. I was impressed.

LeeAnn and I went down to meet up with Bev Vincent, who had come in from Texas for the event. As you've read from the first article in this Annual, Bev will travel, to see *the* King. We just wanted to see Bev, and hang out, maybe grab some food, and catch up. We usually saw Bev at an annual convention, Necon, in Providence, Rhode Island (highly recommended for readers and writers). I had been attending for years, but now I was starting to skip a year here and there, due to family and other constraints that just wasn't allowing me to head up to New England. So, this was a great opportunity to see a friend.

You see, I have plenty of signed Stephen King books so we didn't get a ticket for this event. Sure, it would've been great to see Steve, but when it was originally announced, I wasn't even sure we were going to be in town due to prior commitments. Why take a ticket when another fan could see him?

As it turns out, we were in town, so we just thought we'd go down hang out with Bev,

1980s

Nov 5, 1985
Books N Things
Oxford, Maine
Pet Sematary

Dec 21, 1985
Betts Bookstore
Bangor, Maine
Skeleton Crew/Bachman Books

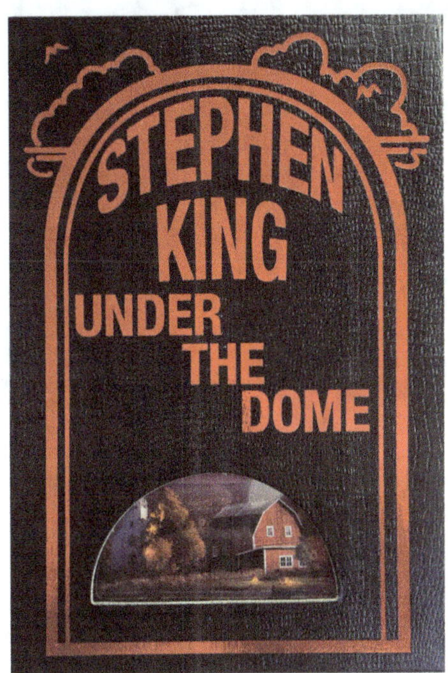

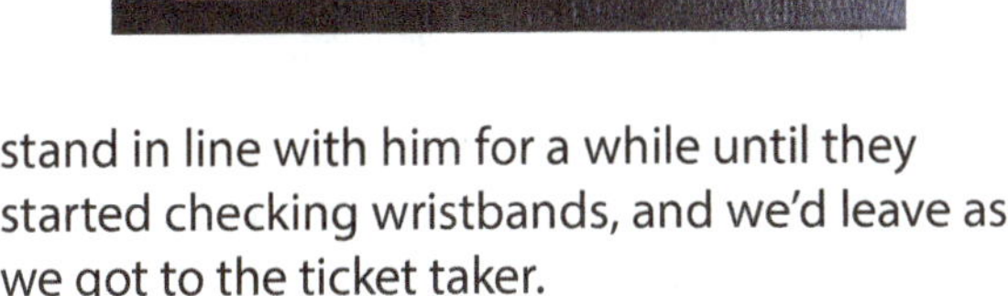

stand in line with him for a while until they started checking wristbands, and we'd leave as we got to the ticket taker.

Surprise, surprise, one of the folks in line with us said their wife couldn't make it to the event, so he had an extra wristband, so he gave it to LeeAnn. That was very kind of him and certainly an opportunity for her to see Steve.

While we were in the line outside, Jim Argendeli (see his article on his CNN/Headline News visit with Stephen King in this Annual), was inside when Stephen King entered. He said "The crowd applauded as King walked in. There was a sense of anticipation in the crowd that this may be their only chance to get a King autograph and meet the great one himself."

We got up to the person who would confirm the blue ticket and give you a wristband. I was about to step out of line when the woman looked at me and said, "just stick out your wrist"... I did, and she promptly put on the blue wristband never asking for the ticket. You know, the ticket I *didn't* have.

I was very surprised. I saw her looking at other people and getting their tickets. I don't know, I'm a tall, some would say, an imposing figure. I had on a sport coat and my usual black fedora and she obviously assumed *this guy* has a ticket... well, I was very pleased at this juncture of luck, and I was able to continue my visit with everyone. At this point, we had all been talking for hours in this line, so you tend to get comfortable and we exchanged other stories and personal thoughts of Stephen King's work, where they're from etc. As I'm sure you've read in some of this Annual people come from miles around, and even many states away, just to meet Stephen King. And this appearance was no exception.

Stephen King doesn't go to every big or medium city. He tries to spread out where and when he goes over the years, to get to as many locales as possible.

So here we are slowly moving forward in this long line of humanity, and we see a place ahead that is all curtained off in black cloth.

July 27, 1986
Max's Diner
San Francisco, California
Part of the *Maximum Overdrive* Press Tour

Aug 28, 1986
Winham Community Center
Windham, Maine
It

It's basically curtains on a framework of rods that hold this all together, almost to the ceiling, and on all sides where Stephen King is signing within. Only when you come up and around the bend of bookshelves, do you see Stephen King.

But we weren't there yet.

We were getting close. Now we were next to the curtained off area, and we could hear Steve talking to folks on the other side these curtains.

There had been a biker way out in front of us, with the back of his jacket emblazoned with his biker gang logo. We heard him on the other side of the curtained off area, talking to Steve.

The biker asked him "Are you still riding?"

Steve paused, "Yes, I'm still writing. That's why I'm here today signing these books".

My guess is Steve was indeed signing books, and not looking up when the biker asked. It was a simple misunderstanding, but we all got a little chuckle out of it. The biker said, " no, no I mean, do you still ride, as in your Harley?".

At this point Steve must have looked closer to the man and it was then their turn to have a nice laugh... Everybody within earshot of this exchange was laughing.

That biker has probably told that story hundreds of times in the 15 years since that signing. Those are the best, the unintended moments. And sure enough, as I'm sitting here writing this down telling you all about it as I'm sure other Constant Readers from that day have also been relating this comical moment.

We eventually made it around the bend of bookshelves, and we could see Steve ahead at the signing table. As we looked down the way, where behind the long table he stretched over and signed books, all we could see was *Under the Dome* books, everywhere! Bookshelves on the left and right, forming a column for us to go follow, filled from top to bottom with *Under the Dome* copies. All available to select and hand it to the handlers, who then will hand it to Stephen King, with the title page open for him to sign, designed to keep everyone moving. All he has to do is lay his hand down and sign the book, one right after the other. *Next!*

Under the Dome Collector's Set, Scribner 2009

As we're inching closer I picked out an *Under the Dome* (they had alternate colors for the title) for Steve to sign. LeeAnn had already picked out her copy... She was ready to meet the man. So, they asked us not to use any flash photography. No worries there I'm happy to comply. Except, as we got up there, I did want to get a picture of LeeAnn standing there in front of Steve as he signed her book. I had a new camera, and something had jammed. I had to restart the camera. This was a smart camera, but as it turned out, it wasn't very smart, *at all*. Camera now reset and as we got up close, I pointed it at LeeAnn and Steve and wouldn't you know it? The damn thing flashed!

Immediately, a handler was like, "Sir, sir, we asked you not to use the flash." I apologize, but then, as soon as that happened, I was standing in front of Stephen King. As my aunt would say, "I was mortified," mortified, because Steve knows who I am.

1980s

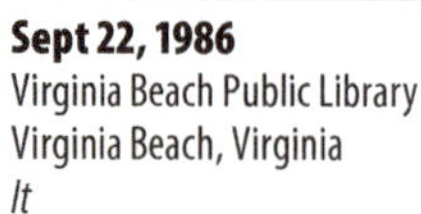

Sept 22, 1986
Virginia Beach Public Library
Virginia Beach, Virginia
It

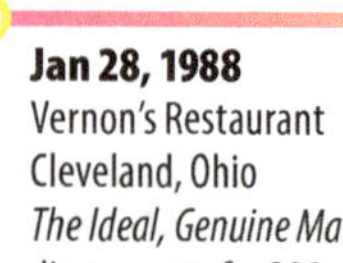

Jan 28, 1988
Vernon's Restaurant
Cleveland, Ohio
The Ideal, Genuine Man
dinner party for 200 guests w/Don Robertson

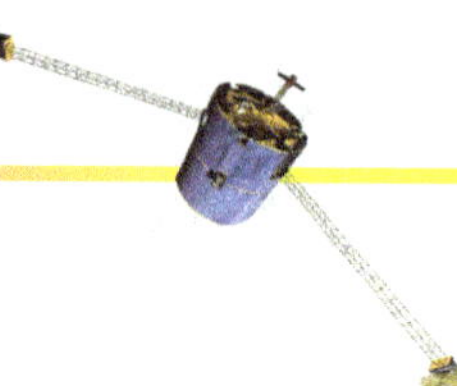

I stepped up, said "Hi Steve, it's Dave Hinchberger," he immediately stuck out his hand and we shook and said, "Hi Dave, how are ya?" I said something about I'm still running The Overlook Connection bookstore, thanks for everything. And it was that quick, they had to keep the line moving.

What was also interesting? It's that there were now, get this, *nine* Atlanta police officers, in full garb, standing against the wall, pulling after work security duty. They obviously didn't expect any trouble, but I tell ya I wasn't expecting that many officers. We had to pass them right after we met Steve. I believe LeeAnn was saying, "thank you for your service." This is something she normally acknowledges with service members. I just nodded in unison. I kept looking at all these black leather coats lined up, firearms in their holsters, their caps expertly affixed on top.

A group of us walked outside the front of the store and just talked for a bit, while Steve was still inside signing away. While we were standing there, the yellow wrist fans were now being let in. I was very happy for them. I then realized I hadn't paid for my book! It's natural for me to have a book in my hand most of the time, at work, at home. So, I didn't think anything about it when we walked outside as a group, talking away about the evening. So, I promptly went back inside, got in line, and paid for my book. This line was unique as almost everyone in it was holding a signed Stephen King *Under the Dome*. I noticed on one of the tables that they had the recent Bev Vincent Stephen King Illustrated Companion publication. I went ahead and bought a new stack of those, although I had some for the store already, B&N was the only place you could attain it, and… Bev could sign some since he was right outside. I don't know if you've ever seen it, but it's a fascinating book. An oversized collection with reproductions of original manuscript papers, letters, tickets, small posters, etc. You can remove these from the glassine envelopes attached within (it was later reprinted but not with the removable items). If you don't have it, I highly recommend you go get it. It's an informative and interesting book. Although this wasn't Stephen King's idea to put this together, but because Bev was asked to write it, Steve did help him with it and gave him a lot of information and photos. It's because of Bev we received a much finer exclusive edition.

Afterwards, a small group of us went to a local Irish pub, had a beer, and a bit of grub, and we waited to see if Steve would call Bev. Bev had mentioned that Steve said he might call him and they might go out for a little bit if he was able. Unfortunately, the call never came, but I have to say, I really enjoyed the group of us sitting around talking about the night, and just sharing a rare moment together.

Signed first printing of *Under the Dome*, signed at Barnes & Noble, Atlanta, 2009.

Jan 29, 1988
River Oaks Bookstore
Houston, Texas
The Ideal, Genuine Man w/ Don Robertson

The Elusive Photo

by **Ariel Bosi**

There's a big lie we Constant Readers tell ourselves from time to time: "It's just a one-time opportunity, and I gotta take advantage." I lost count of how many times I've said it, but I'm pretty sure the first time was twenty years ago when I saw a nice illustrated edition of a book I already had. "This will be my only duplicate," I said. Yeah… right. A couple of years later, I repeated the same mantra about books signed by Stephen King: "I only want to have one." Last time I checked, there are around 120 items signed by King in my collection.

In April 2009, I learned that Stephen King was going on tour to promote *Under the Dome*. This time, for me, it really was "once in a lifetime" because I live 5,521 miles away from Stephen, in Buenos Aires, Argentina.

I should introduce myself: My name is Ariel Bosi, I'm 44, and I've been a Stephen King Constant Reader for almost 30 years, ever since that very first moment when I read *The Green Mile: The Mouse on the Mile* I was 16 back then, and while it was not my first Stephen King read (it was the third, after *Thinner* (which I read when I was 13) and *Christine* one year later), "The Green Mile" was the one that ignited the fire. I finished it on the same day the sixth part was published and said, "Ok, I need to read everything this guy wrote," and, lucky me, King had written A LOT. Fast forward to 2003, the year I caught up with all his previous works and started collecting. I bought my first limited editions, filled my first two bookcases only with books by Stephen King, and wrote two articles per month about King's work for a web magazine. Two years later, I started receiving and reviewing his books prior to their publication. I was as happy as one Constant Reader could be, but like everyone else, I wanted more. So, in 2007, I decided it was time to travel to Bangor and visit those places that inspired Stephen King. It was a difficult and expensive mission, but far

from impossible. It took me nearly two years of savings to finally travel in 2008 and spend 22 days visiting ten states in the USA. Besides Maine, I visited Donald Grant's offices, stopped by Michael and Audrey Whelan's house (where I saw all his "Dark Tower" originals), spent some

1980s

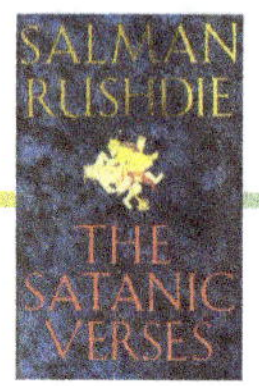

time in front of Lovecraft and Poe's graves in Providence and Baltimore, and I even did my own "Dark Tower" tour in NYC. Sixteen years have passed, and I still remember as if it were today the first time I set foot on that small place located on the corner of 46th Street and 2nd Avenue—a truly magic place for Tower Junkies like myself.

46th Street & 2nd Avenue. The Tower. The Rose. A Tower Junkie.

And then I visited Bangor, which was the cherry on top. I spent five or six hours there because my schedule only allowed me that time. First stop? Bangor's most famous house, the one located at 47 West Broadway. Yes, we've all seen pictures of that house a thousand times, but no picture is as cool as the one we Constant Readers take in front of those iron fences guarded by bats (actually, there are even cooler ones: those that have King himself there 😊).

There were no tours back then, but Betts Bookstore (still under Stu's management in 2008) gave me a map detailing several iconic places. I spent the next couple of hours visiting most of them, doing one thing at each: remaining silent, breathing, and fixing everything in my memory. My favorites? The Barrens, Mount Hope Cemetery, and King's house, of course. And while I was able to visit more (like the parking lot where *Bag of Bones* starts, for example), I missed several places due to lack of time, so I promised myself I would return.

It was an amazing trip, but I spent way more than I should have and kept paying installments until April 2009…when I learned that King was going on tour to promote *Under the Dome*. For me, it was crystal clear: IT WAS A ONCE-IN-A-LIFETIME OPPORTUNITY. I NEEDED to attend one of those events and, if possible, shake the hand of the writer I admired the most and have a picture with him to treasure for the rest of my life. So, in November 2009, I embarked on a trip I'll never, ever forget.

I traveled with a friend and, yes, I visited NY again, relaxed for a bit where the tower/rose is, visited the Whelan's again, and on November 10th, I finally saw Stephen King live for the first time in my life. It was outside the Good Morning America studios, on Broadway. I hoped to get my Spanish *IT* copy signed. Chances were good because there weren't many people with me (I counted 19, I swear it!), but when the show was about to end, King left the building and jumped into a car. I didn't care: after all those years, I finally saw King just a couple of feet away from me.

I visited Scribner's offices (I had a friend there), left some presents for Stephen, and in the afternoon, I headed to The Times Center where King's first event took place that night. That night I met a friend I had been talking with for a couple of years. His name? Mark Stutzman, the magnificent artist who did the cover artwork for *Cell, Lisey's Story, Duma Key, From a Buick 8*, and the favorite of many (including myself, of course!), *Everything's Eventual*.

It was a cool event. We were in the second row, really close to the stage. King spoke for an hour and a half, and we left the place two hours later with six signed copies of *Under the Dome*. Cool, isn't it? But the best was still to come. That night we slept only two hours, and at 3 AM, we took the car and drove to Dundalk, Baltimore. King was going to sign 400 books personally there on the 11th, and we didn't want to miss that chance. We got there by 6 AM, and there were fewer than 100 Constant Readers in line (my wristband was #88). During the next hours, I was interviewed by Fox News, visited Poe's grave, and by 5 PM we were back at Walmart and waiting for Stephen, who appeared on stage even before the arranged time, in a great mood, and even allowed questions from the audience.

Aug 16, 1989
Little League Eastern Region Complex
Bristol, Connecticut
During son Owen's Little League away game

And that's another moment I'll treasure forever. I raised my hand, King saw me, pointed at me, and I had my first verbal exchange with Stephen. I asked if there was going to be another Bachman book published.

"Well, he's dead. Bachman is dead, but sometimes someone finds a book.... there might be another one."

If you want to see a happy man, you can search for the video on YouTube and see my face.

Two minutes later, King started to sign, and it was FAST. Each person had only around ten seconds in front of him. I was thinking about what to say and asking my friend to take a good picture of me.

When I got in front of King, lucky me, I didn't remain frozen as I had feared:

Me: "Hi!"

SK: "Hi!"

Me (while he signs): "I came specially from Argentina for this event."

SK stops signing, looks at me: "Oh, yes! I heard about you! Thank you!"

He finished signing the book, I shook his hand, he said, "Enjoy!" and I left. It was the perfect moment. Simply perfect. Sadly, my pictures were far from perfect.

Fifteen years have passed, and I'm still looking for that lady in the purple dress behind me.

She took the picture I wanted.

The next day, I wrote to my friend at Scribner and got an answer about how King knew about me. They told him when he stopped by Scribner minutes after I left.

Our initial plan after the events was to travel to Bangor, but we decided on a different destination. That's why, on the evening of Friday the 13th(!), we took a flight to Denver, drove for an hour in the night, and around 2 AM we arrived at the Stanley Hotel or, as we Constant Readers know it, The Overlook Hotel. Of course, the first thing I did was find room 217 and take a picture in front of it. We spent two

Stephen King standing at the gate of his house in Bangor, Maine. 1982

nights there, and I visited every single corner of the hotel. There weren't many guests, it was snowing (in Buenos Aires, we only had snow once in 2007 after… 81 years!), so it was beyond any expectations I could have had. The only thing I regret was not booking earlier to stay in room 217. We left on the 15th, and I returned to Buenos Aires that night, carrying with me a total of five signed copies of Under the Dome (my friend got another four) and a memory of a lifetime. I made the most of that once-in-a-lifetime opportunity and couldn't be happier…

…but I still needed a good picture, so in January 2015, I traveled once again with my friend, this time to Bradenton, Florida, where "An Evening with Stephen King" was going to take place on the 29th. I did my own *Duma Key* Tour, visiting places in Sarasota, walking and driving through Casey Key (at one moment, King was just behind us driving!), but the event itself wasn't as expected, and things didn't go as planned. First, the conditions were changed (when I bought the tickets, it was announced as a signing, but it was later changed to allow the purchase of a previously signed book). I told someone from the organization that this change wasn't nice and that I had traveled from Argentina just for that event. They tried to make amends and took me to the VIP section, but the permissions took too long, and by the

1990s

Jan 30, 1990
Bellevue Hotel Ballroom
Philadelphia, Pennsylvania
Appearance at a baseball symposim, unsure if he signed

March 6, 1990
First Parrish Unitarian Universalist Church
Portland, Maine
"An Evening with Stephen King," unsure if he signed

time I got there, King had already left. Then they promised we would have a picture with Stephen the moment the event was over. The event was okay; we got out of the place, King arrived (he was six feet from me), the photographer was ready and… King said, "Thanks everyone," turned around and left.

In the end, it was a great trip, and I returned with five signed copies of *Revival*. It was the fourth time I saw King live and the second time I had him in front of me, but I still didn't have a good picture with him.

You could say it was Strike Two. For someone who by this time already had a family to take care of, it was probably enough, right?

Well, no. In 2019, I learned that Stephen King and Joe Hill were going to have an event together in Boston. I contacted my friend again (whose wife was six months pregnant), and we agreed on traveling for just two days, buying a lot of things for both families (I have two daughters who were six and three at that time). I studied the theater where Stephen and Joe were going to be, took my chances that King would probably enter the place from the back door, and stood there until he arrived.

No, I couldn't get a picture (he said, "Sorry folks, but if I stay, I'll never leave"), but I got a decent selfie, saw the event from the very first row, and returned home with a signed copy of *The Institute*. And while I wanted to sleep just two hours and travel to Bangor, in the end, I was happy just to visit Boston Common (where *Cell* starts), Poplar Street (yeah, I'm a nerd, and I wanted to have a picture next to the sign of the street where *The Regulators* takes place), and 38 hours after we arrived, we returned home, thinking it might have been our last trip to see Stephen King live.

By that time, I was already working for Stephen King's Spanish publisher, and both Warner Bros and Sony Entertainment invited me to the USA to attend the movie events for *Doctor Sleep* and *The Dark Tower*. I met and talked with Mike Flanagan, Idris Elba, and Ewan McGregor (among others), but… not King.

We all know what happened in 2020 and beyond. I know that in March, I received a phone call from a TV producer to work on a documentary about Stephen King that would be filmed in the USA. After presenting the project, the COVID-19 pandemic stopped the whole world.

I also know that the document I started working on in 2009 with all the King-related places I wanted to visit grew from two pages to 16 by the time I wrote this, and I still dream of traveling for two weeks to the eastern coast of the USA to visit Lisbon, Lovell, Bangor, and all those places where Stephen lived, imagined, and wrote those stories that amazed millions like myself.

While I can't save as much these days, Constant Readers always want more, and I'm still not giving up on meeting Stephen King again, shaking his hand, and (finally) having a decent picture with him. Because while I don't have idols, Stephen King is the person I admire the most from that far-away moment when I finished *Coffey on the Mile* and felt my heart was as helpless as ever before.

March 12, 1991
King's Office/Bangor International Airport
Bangor, Maine
Signed books at airport, brought Marine back to office

April 26, 1991
SK Film Festival
Syracuse, New York
Needful Things
Unsure if he signed!

You Talkin' To Me?

by **Stephan Behrndt**

My name is Stephan Behrndt and I live in the north of Germany. I've been a Stephen King fan since the late '70s when I discovered the Brian De Palma movie cover version of *Carrie* on a returns table. Since then, a 47-year passion for reading had developed, with over 180 books by and about Stephen King. Collecting every German first edition and other things related to King.

In 2013 I found out from my best friend, Udo Erhart, that Stephen King was coming to Germany for two readings. I managed to get tickets for both dates. That's not all, my friend also pointed out to me that HEYNE (King's German publisher) was giving away 3 Meet & Greets for Hamburg and Munich on Facebook. I registered on FB specifically for this purpose and, I couldn't believe it… I had won! So, Udo and I travelled 1,666 kilometers from Rotenburg/Wümme via Fürth to first went to the reading in Munich. Then from Munich via Fürth and Rotenburg/Wümme to the next reading in Hamburg.

Stephen King on stage in Germany to discuss *Doctor Sleep*, November 2013

I made a drawing of his son Owen especially for the meet and greet in Hamburg. I gave it to Stephen King as a token of my admiration. I had on a T-shirt with a print of *Taxi Driver* (my favorite movie). To which Mr. King was very positive and expressed his own enthusiasm for the film with a gesture, and asked me "Are you talkin' to me?". The meeting was, for many reasons, one of the most outstanding events in my life. In retrospect, the readings came to a wonderful conclusion. I sent Mr. King a print of a photo of the two of us at the M&G. Of course, I also mentioned my drawing of Owen again. Stephen King did something he doesn't do

1990s

June 4, 1991
American Bookseller Convention
New York, New York
Needful Things
Unsure if he signed!

Dec 4, 1991
Betts Bookstore
Bangor, Maine
Needful Things/Waste Lands

Stephan Behrndt with Stephen King and he was indeed, "talkin' to him", here in Germany promoting *Doctor Sleep* in November, 2013

much anymore, he sent it back to me, *signed*, with a quote from *Taxi Driver*, "Are you talkin' to me?". It couldn't have been better, and I'm still very, very grateful to him for that kind gesture.

A big thanks also goes to my friend Udo. Without him I would never have met the Master, and without him I wouldn´t have the wonderful photos of that moment.

I also drew Stephen King as well, as you can see here.

Here's hoping that maybe one day he'll be back in Germany, and I can shake Stephen King's hand, one more time.

Event held at "Circus Krone" in Munich, Germany

Feb 20, 1992
Robert Parish/Jeremy Kane Autographs
Bangor, Maine
'Salem's Lot/The Shining
Autographs for two individuals

Aug 12, 1992
US District Court
Bangor, Maine
Signed for jury pool after not being selected for jury duty

Stephan Behrndt holds up a Randall Flagg lithograph, signed by the artist, Bernie Wrightson. He had Stephen King sign it during this visit in Germany

Udo Erhart and Stephen King

Stephan Behrndt and Udo Erhart

Win a "MEET & GREET" with STEPHEN KING Unbelievable, but true: Six of you have the GREET opportunity to meet STEPHEN KING in person. We are giving away three places each for a "Meet & Greet" in Hamburg and Munich. What do you have to do? Write to us in the comments box why you should meet the "Master of Horror". We will be giving away the places among all fans of our page who have commented up to and including November 7, 2013. We're keeping our fingers crossed for you!!

– Original Facebook post by Heyne publisher, from 2013

1990s

May 20, 1993
WHJY Radio Station
Providence, Rhode Island
Stop on the Rock Bottom Remainders press tour

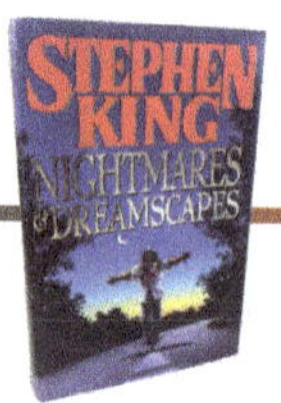

Dec 15, 1993
Bookmarc's
Bangor, Maine
Nighmares & Dreamscapes

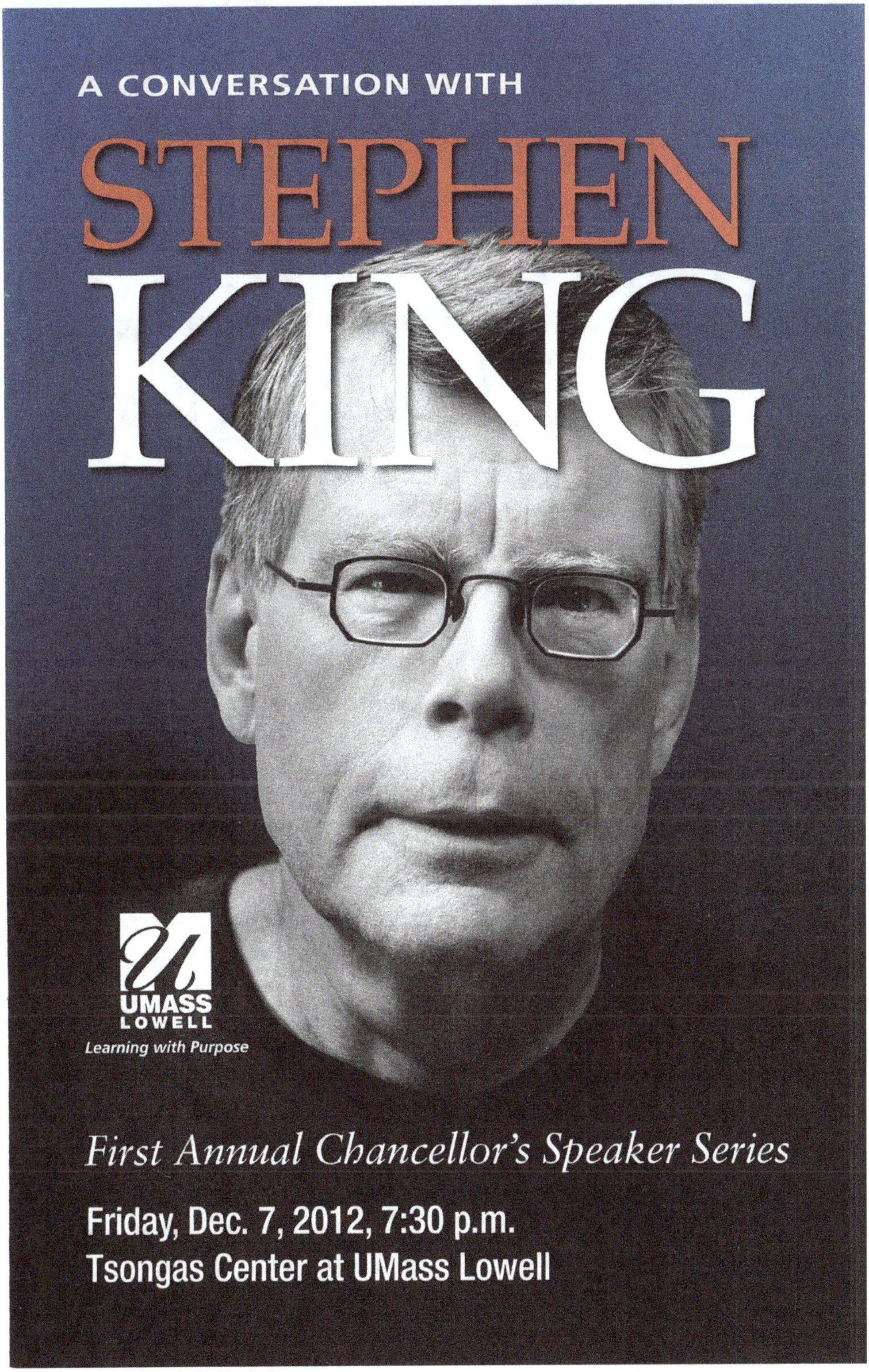

A CONVERSATION WITH
STEPHEN
KING
UMASS
LOWELL
Learning with Purpose
First Annual Chancellor's Speaker Series
Friday, Dec. 7, 2012, 7:30 p.m.
Tsongas Center at UMass Lowell

THE
STAND

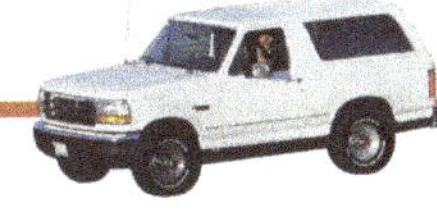

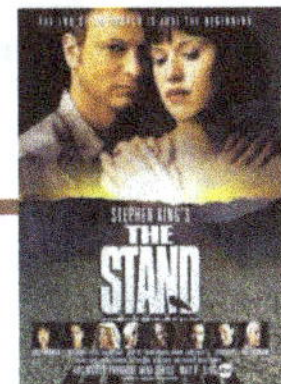

Oct 4, 1994
Northshire Bookstore
Manchester Center, Vermont
Insomnia

INSOMNIA
STEPHEN
KING

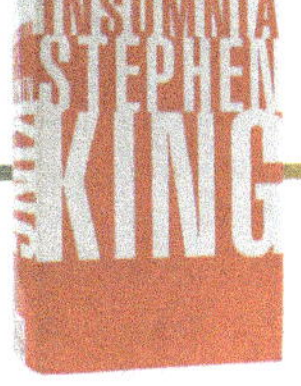

Oct 6, 1994
Cornell University Bookstore
Ithaca, New York
Insomnia

Stephen King Visits Germany, 2013

by **Robin Amstutz**

"That's him, isn't it!?"

We were all gathered outside the beautiful, Romanesque, First Baptist Church of Newton built in 1888 (outside Boston, Massachusetts) on Beacon Street in 2017. We're waiting for the doors to open for a visit with Stephen and Owen King on tour for their new novel, Sleeping Beauties. Marsha DeFilippo, Stephen King's assistant, noticed me in line and came over for a visit. It had been several years since we'd seen each other and we were chin-wagging our way in a lengthy conversation when we'd heard "you're the kind lady who comforted me in Germany!" We turned and there was this lovely young lady, holding her little dog, and looking straight at Marsha. This was our introduction to the effervescent Robin Amstutz, as she greeted Marsha and related her tale of first meeting her and Stephen King in Germany. Marsha remembered her instantly and we all were privy to a quick recounting of that meeting.

Upon hearing this story, I knew this was something that would be perfect for our Stephen King on Tour Annual… and here we are. As it turns out there was a lot more to the story and I'm proud to have Robin share it with you here.

– Dave Hinchberger

In late November of 2013, almost two months after the publication of *Doctor Sleep*, Stephen King travelled to Germany to visit with wounded soldiers at Landstuhl Regional Medical Center and headline a reading event at Ramstein Air Force Base. The theater where the event took place, the Hercules Theater, is small, with a capacity of approximately 500 people. Each Air Force unit stationed at Ramstein was given a small number of tickets to give to their active-duty members to attend the event, where everyone would receive a signed copy of *Doctor Sleep*. As the spouse of an active-duty army officer stationed almost an hour away in Baumholder, I was ineligible to receive a ticket to the event, but I knew in my heart that fate had sent my favorite author to Germany, and I was going to do everything possible to meet him.

USO Warrior Center, Ramstein Air Base, Germany. November 18th, 2013

The weekend of the event, my husband, Erik, suggested driving to Ramstein base to walk around the shopping area and food court to see if we could spot Stephen King. I didn't have high hopes, but I agreed. After walking around the bookstore, we ventured to the food court. Standing near the entrance and glancing around, I almost immediately spotted a tall man with gray hair covered by a baseball cap,

1990s

Oct 8, 1994
Little Professor Book Company
Columbus, Ohio
Insomnia

Oct 10, 1994
Joseph Beth Booksellers
Lexington, Kentucky
Insomnia

wearing a tee-shirt and jeans, and surrounded by a small entourage of around 5 people. I shakily turned to Erik, pointed, and whispered, “That’s him, isn’t it?” “Yep” he answered. I began to shake, and tears ran down my face while Erik sauntered up to their small group and said loudly, “Hello sir, Mr. King, my wife is a huge fan,” and asked if we could take a picture. He graciously agreed, and I marveled at meeting the Master of Horror at a food court on an Air Force base in Europe. As I cried, and trembled, and had a minor emotional breakdown, a small, gray-haired woman reassured me, and held and patted my hand. I later met this woman at another Stephen King event in Boston, Massachusetts and thanked her for the kindness she showed me that day. Her name is Marsha DeFilippo, she was Stephen King’s assistant for many years, and I will never forget her comforting me on the day I met my hero and sobbed hysterically in front of him.

After taking a photo quickly we spoke briefly with him and the group he was with about how we might be able to get tickets to the event, and we were told to come line up the next day first thing in the morning because if there were any extra seats, we would be allowed to attend. King then sauntered off toward Johnny Rockets to grab a burger. (When I met him again at a signing in Bridgeton, Maine, I mentioned our meeting in the food court in Ramstein and he excitedly recalled the delicious hamburger he ate that day.)

So, at 7am the next morning I bundled up and went to go sit out in the cold German weather and waited in line for approximately 8 hours in hopes of attending the event. And once again, I was blessed with amazing Stephen King luck and was given a ticket.

It was the first time I had ever heard him speaking at an event in person, and it was one of the best experiences of my life. King is so hilarious, entertaining, kind, and witty. Throughout the years, I’ve been lucky to see him in person many times, for many different events all over America, yet this one will always hold a special place in my heart. Along with receiving my first signed book that day which catapulted me into the wonderful world of Stephen King collecting, I met one of my heroes, and he was everything I had hoped

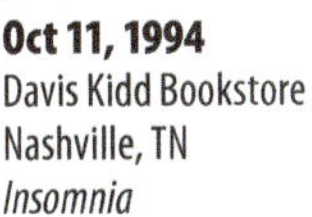
Oct 11, 1994
Davis Kidd Bookstore
Nashville, TN
Insomnia

Oct 14, 1994
Library Ltd
Clayton, MO
Insomnia

"This has been really extraordinary. He's very down to earth and real — just to listen to him talk, like everyday conversation. That's what I expected and that's what he gave, and I'm just thrilled to be a part of it."

Prolific author speaks to packed house during USO stop in Germany

King signs a copy of his new book, "Doctor Sleep," for Andrew Bolton and his mom, Laura, right, prior to his book reading Nov. 18. The Boltons won tickets to the event in an American Forces Network contest.

ephen King, American author of contemporary horror and suspense, spoke Nov. 18 at Ramstein Air Base, Germany, on his first USO tour.

King of horror comes to town

Displayed is the frame of Robin's moment with Stephen King. Below is her signed copy of *Doctor Sleep* and her ticket to this unique event.

he would be, and more. From taking the time to visit with wounded service members in the hospital, to showing an overexcited fan like me kindness and graciousness, to speaking at a free event and signing enough books for every attendee to receive, Stephen King is more than the Master of Horror, Constant Readers. He's a regular guy who loves a good hamburger too!

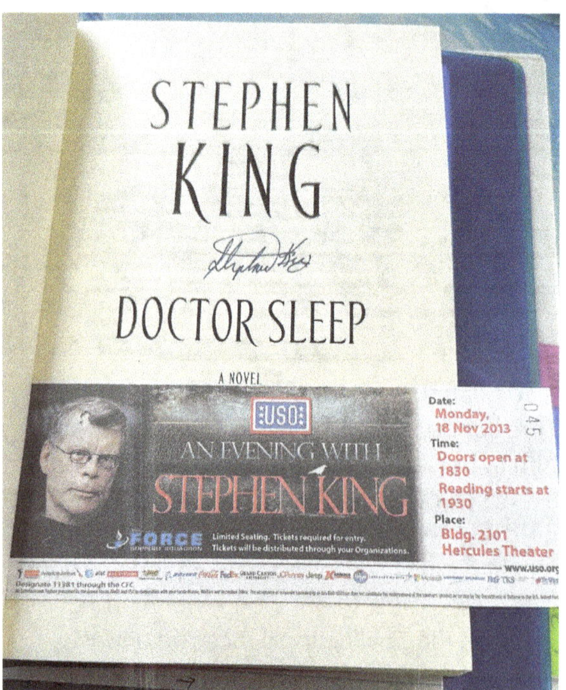

Author Stephen King reads from his then recently released book *Doctor Sleep*, a sequel to his 1977 horror novel *The Shining*, Nov. 18, 2013, Ramstein Air Base, Germany. King led a multi-stop USO tour around the Kaiserslautern Military Community area, which included visits to the U.S. Army Garrison substance abuse program, Landstuhl Regional Medical Center, USO Warrior Center and concluded with a public reading and open forum. (U.S. Air Force photo/ Airman 1st Class Jordan Castelan)

1990s

Oct 16, 1994
Varney's Bookstore
Manhattan, Kansas
Insomnia

Oct 18, 1994
McKinzie White Booksellers
Colorado Springs, Colorado
Insomnia

Stephen King Accepts The Mason Prize: 2011

by **Glen Reitz**

WHEN: September 23, 2011
WHERE: George Mason University
WHY: Stephen King is presented with the Mason Prize
SPECIAL EVENT SNEAK PEEK: The forthcoming *Doctor Sleep*
TICKETS: A Golden Ticket got you in front of Stephen King for a signed book!

"The best thing that ever happened to me, in terms of being famous, was at Nathan's hot dogs in New York. This was around the time of *The Dead Zone* when I had this beard, it was black. I ordered my hot dogs, drinks, and fries and I sit down and begin eating. I see there's a pass-thru into the kitchen and I see the cook back there looking at me, and pretty soon he's looking again. He then sees me looking at him. I'm thinking to myself (smiling) 'he knows who I am.' So finally, he came out and said 'aren't you Francis Ford Coppola?'
I said, 'yes,' and I signed him an autograph."

"The thing is people look at us, and they know us from somewhere. If you knew how many times people walked up to me and said 'aren't you Steven Spielberg?' And I always say… Yes!"
– Stephen King, George Mason University

GENADM GA 10274 $0.00 $0.00 PRO
"GOLDEN TICKET"
Entitles bearer to 1 signatur
Limit 2 people in signing-lin
House Right Lobby
GMU Concert Hall
Fri Sep 23, 2011 8:00PM
GMCGRN1223SEPL T604471 846kw12561 ML NO REFUNDS/EXCHANGES

tickets.com
SECTION GENADM
ROW GA
SEAT 10274
GMCGRN1223SEPL 604471 PROMOTER
03551101965178

On September 23, 2011, Stephen King spoke at George Mason University's Fall for the Book before a packed Center for the Arts audience. He read from his soon-to-be-published novel, *Doctor Sleep*, a sequel to *The Shining*. Stephen King was there to accept the Mason Prize for his extraordinary contributions to bringing literature to a wide audience of readers.

Stephen King accepts the Mason Prize

Since 1999, Fall for the Book, an independent nonprofit literary arts organization based at Mason, has hosted such award-winning authors as Diana Gabaldon, Mitch Albom, Amy Tan, John Lewis, and Angie Thomas, among others.

The festival promotes reading by sponsoring year-round events, including the festival held every October. Partners include the Fairfax County Public Library, the Fairfax Library Foundation, and the City of Fairfax. Now in its 25th year, *Fall for the Book* is Northern Virginia's oldest and largest festival of literature and the arts.

Stephen signs one for Glen, Look at that smile!

Oct 20, 1994
Ex Libris Bookstore
Sun Valley, Idaho
Insomnia

Oct 25, 1994
Bookshop Santa Cruz
Santa Cruz, California
Insomnia

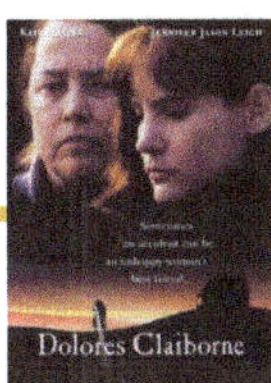

Lilja meets King in Hamburg

November 20th, 2013 began early when my friend Anders and I travelled by car, plane, and bus from Örebro, Sweden, to Hamburg, Germany, to meet Stephen King. This was to be my second meeting with Stephen King, the first having been at a publisher's party in London back in 2006. This time, King's German publisher Heyne had invited me to his reading in Hamburg but also to the informal reception that was being held before the reading.

We had strict orders to be at Congress Center Hamburg no later than 6.30 PM. If we were late, we could not be guaranteed to meet Stephen King. Anders, me, and everyone else invited came early. Nobody wanted to risk missing out. On arriving, everyone was given a bracelet to prove our right to attend, a ticket to the reading and a name tag to wear at the reception. Then we waited. At exactly 6.30 we were escorted backstage where we would meet King in less than half an hour. While we waited we were offered snacks and drinks. A few had some, but most of those present were much too nervous to eat anything.

Then the time came. Tension in the room was almost palpable. People nervously looked in the direction where King would enter or looked at each other with nervous smiles. Then he was suddenly there.

Stephen King knows how to handle his audiences. He calmly walked around to shake everyone's hand before heading for the table where he would sign our books. He was running a few minutes late and it was decided that he would just sign his name, not add any personal notes; that way, everyone present would be able to get a signed book.

Here, I must again stress how professionally King acts when meeting his readers. He not only signed quickly and efficiently, but also calmly and naturally shook everyone's hand again, took the time to exchange a few words and let all who wanted to take a photo. When my time came I handed him the copy of the German translation of *Doctor Sleep* I had decided to get signed. I had selected between that one and a copy of the Swedish translation of *The Dark Tower VII: The Dark Tower* which I had also brought but since *Doctor Sleep* was the book he was in Germany to promote, I thought it the preferable alternative. King signed it, and when I asked for a photo, he said, "of course".

1990s

May 9, 1995
Bangor Civic Center
Bangor, Maine
For the World Premiere of *The Langoliers*

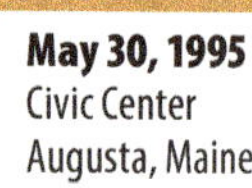

May 30, 1995
Civic Center
Augusta, Maine
Insomnia

Hans-Åke Lilja and Stephen King
Hamburg, Germany, November 20th, 2013

In advance, I had asked Anders to be ready to take a picture. But at the same moment he did so, the photographer hired by King's publisher also took one, and the result was that King looked at him while I looked at Anders. Luckily I realized this and asked King for a second photo, one where we both looked at the same camera, and he agreed to this. It turned out to be a great picture. Then I shook his hand, thanked him for all his books (this too, Anders managed to capture) and made place for the next person in line.

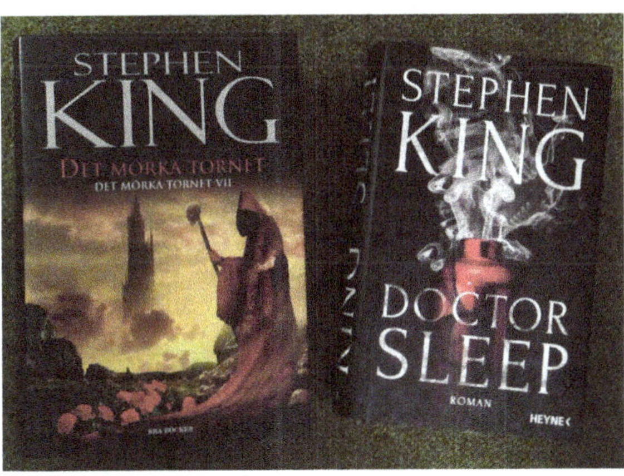

It went on in the same way until King said that he would soon have to leave and only had time to sign a very few books more. I realized that those now in line already had had one book signed and now were waiting to have another one. Since I, too, had brought a second book, I fetched my Swedish copy of *The Dark Tower* and placed it before King. He signed it, said, "Okay, that's it, thank you all", and left. The informal meeting was over. But it had been a more than memorable experience.

If you want to read more about this, the reading after or other facts about Stephen King you can do so in my books *Stephen King: Not Just Horror* and *Stephen King: Stories From Five Decades of Storytelling*.

Hans-Åke Lilja has been reading Stephen King for over 40 years. Since 1996, he has run the website Lilja's Library – The World of Stephen King and has published six books related to Stephen King that has been translated into 17 languages. Hans-Åke has met Stephen King three times, interviewed him twice and has lectured regularly about him since 2017.

Visit **liljas-library.com**

Sept 15, 1995
Bangor Auditorium
Bangor, Maine
Rose Madder

Stephen King Performs at Hank's Place

by **Dave Hinchberger**

The Ryman Auditorium, June 11th, 2016, 8 p.m.

My wife and I were travelling through North Carolina. We stopped by a Barnes & Noble. Why? It's a bookstore, that's why. This is what we do. It's late in the evening during the week so the store is almost empty. LeeAnn had to go to the other end of the store for something. Within minutes I hear this exclaim of excitement rise to the rafters. I knew it: She ran into a student. I mean we're literally off the beaten path, a couple of states away from home, but they find her. She taught thousands of students at middle school for over thirty years, it's happened many times in many places. She brought Graham over, a working adult now, to meet me. We spoke for a bit. He gave glowing reviews of her time teaching when he was there. I took a photo of them and we left the store but not before checking out at the cashier (I'm sure I found some books in the sale section…).

Stay tuned for the rest... of the story.

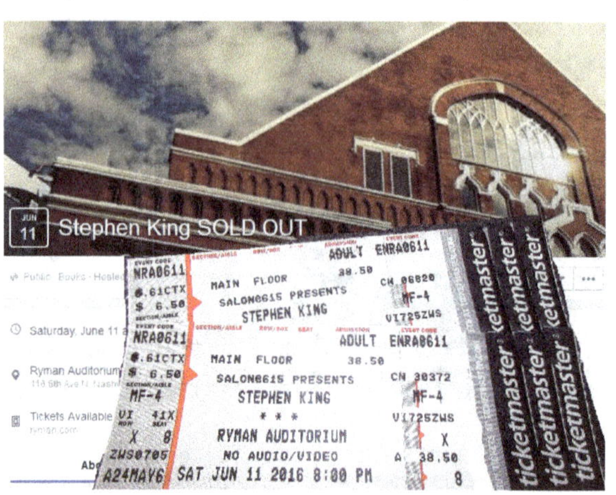

The next day she comes up to me and says "you know, Stephen King is going to be in Nashville this summer. I think we should go." She had me at 'King…in Nashville!' Only four hours from Atlanta and the fact that she was already on board with going, this trip was already happening. This tour was for the *End of Watch* release, no. 3 in the Bill Hodges killer thriller trilogy. With *Mr. Mercedes* (no. 1) previously winning the Edgar Award (Edgar Allen Poe, ya know) from the Mystery Writers of America, I was curious to see what he may have to say about the trilogy now with the final book release. But who are we kidding? His long career of over 60 novels (at that time), original screenplays, short fiction, and all those media adaptations! He could cover any area of his writing and the audience would be at attention, hanging on every sentence, every word.

A day in the life of a King reader trying to get tickets, planning the trip, and travel.

Now the adventure begins. First off we must get tickets! Tickets were about $35 (with fees) and every attendee would receive *End of Watch*. What a bargain! You get the new book and Stephen King in person! To top it off, some copies will be signed! These copies however were given away at random as you left, so there was no guarantee you'd receive one. Only 400 copies were pre-signed at each event on this tour. The Ryman Auditorium can seat 2,362 folks. That's basically a 1 in 5 chance for a signed copy. Here I am, getting ahead of myself. I don't even have tickets yet!

1990s

June 30, 1996
Greater Bookland Mall Plaza
South Portland, Maine
Desperation/Regulators

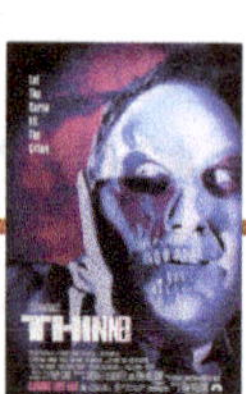

To maximize our opportunity for just acquiring tickets I got in touch with a good friend in Knoxville, Tennessee, Mike Jackson. Mike is often out of town running TV cameras for every Super Bowl, The Masters in Augusta, and sports and music events all around the world (he's won an Emmy for his work!), so he may not be in town. However, he was willing to try and get tickets and we'd figured that between the two of us we could nab at least a couple of pairs.

The morning, 10 am precisely, tickets went on sale, online. The maximum we could get was 8 seats. What the hell, I went for the max. I kept refreshing the website a minute before 10 am until the order button became live, hovering over the keyboard to push enter. There it was! I quickly hit enter… waiting, waiting, the spinning cursor of death kept rotating, and then…it came back with 8 seats! On hold, and I had six minutes to complete my purchase. It was row X.

My son, Ian, had a good question for those uninitiated: he said "Stephen King goes on tour? What does he do?" A valid question. When you hear the word "tour" and at an auditorium, you think bands, not writers. As this row X was staring me in the face I had a quick thought to retry with a lower number of seats and maybe get closer to the "man."

I knew better. I hit purchase, and it completed.My bank account less, but my heart full. Who was I kidding? I've been following this man, this writer, for decades since high school, and he certainly didn't get to where he was because of me and a few others. This man has an immense following! This following was hovering over their keyboards as well. Better to have 8 on X, than 4 of nothing.

I was curious though as this took only about 3 minutes, let's see what else there might be available. 4 tickets: not available. 2 tickets: not available. 1 ticket… there were four single tickets up in the nosebleeds of the Ryman. Basically, it was sold out. Immediately.

I called Stephen King's assistant, the wonderful Marsha Defilippo, to inquire about the tour and told her of my astonishment that the Ryman had sold out, quickly. She said that the Ryman sold out in less than five minutes. Almost 2,500 seats… GONE! I checked in with Mike Jackson to see how many seats he attained. Absolutely nothing. He said he couldn't get into the website. Well Mike, no worries, we got 'cha covered!

So now here I was with four extra tickets. As far as I was concerned these were the hottest tickets in Nashville, hell, the surrounding states, as this was the only appearance in the South. I knew what to do. Since the tickets were inexpensive, I mean let's face it, we were able to see Stephen King for basically the price of his latest book. It was an easy decision and the

What can I say Driving people out of their minds comes naturally

What can I say? Driving people out of their minds comes naturally to me. Just ask my wife HAHAHAHA.

May 22, 1997
Bookmarc's
Bangor, Maine
Six Stories
Didn't sign there, signed for lottery system later

only person I called was Bryan McAllister. You may not know Bryan, but you've been handling his work with every layout of the Stephen King Annuals, and any of our published books from our Overlook Connection Press for years. We've been working together, and friends, for over twenty years. Here was a perfect opportunity to come down from St. Louis (only 4 ½ hours) to Nashville. We would have some great Nashville food, see the sights, and listen to Stephen King in the grand ol' palace they call, The Ryman.

Plans were set. We had Mike Jackson and guest, Bryan and Laura, and LeeAnn and myself. That left us with two last tickets. I had a brilliant idea: Let's auction those off and give the proceeds to Stephen King's Haven Foundation. His charity helped author's and artists in need and gave a grant four times a year to fortunate recipients for almost two decades. Although the Haven shut down recently, it was truly a gift to those who were in dire straits. To do this I wanted to make sure we went about this the correct way and that

Email communication with Stephen King

from: **Dave Hinchberger** <overlookcn@aol.com>
to: **Stephen King** <SKing@hisEmail.com>
date: May 16th, 2016, 2:17 PM
subject: **Nashville Tickets up on eBay for the Haven Foundation - 100 damn percent of it :-)**

message: Yo, Steve!
I try to help the Haven Foundation where I can, especially when we have special projects at the stores.
I was able to donate a pair of tickets for your sold out Nashville / Ryman appearance and we put it up tonight on eBay. 100% of the proceeds will head over to the Haven Foundation when it's completed Sunday night, May 22nd.
I've discussed with Marsha and sent her the link, as well as with Parnassas Bookstore there in Nashville, and they have the Ryman on board with this too.
I wanted to share the link with you in case you want to pass it along to the Constant Readers.
Marsha mentioned that this last Haven meeting had one of the highest requests for need ever. I hope this auction will help.
Thank you, again, for all your support over the years. I'm glad, through you, I can offer some support in return to the community.
Hinchy hugs.
Dave
Dave Hinchberger

STEVE's RESPONSE:
Thanks, Dave. You're a good guy.
Steve

DAVE RESPONDS:
Oh... and.. how did you, Mr. "author," get the "Ryman" auditorium during the CMA Music Festival - the biggest country music event of the year?
I hope you bring yer geetar.
Hey, we'll see you from the Ryman cheap seats (but aren't they all? :-)
Have a great tour, Steve.
Dave
Dave Hinchberger

STEVE's RESPONSE:
"Your Cheatin' Heart." Key of G.
God, they better not ask me to play it.
I can't yodel like Hank.
Steve

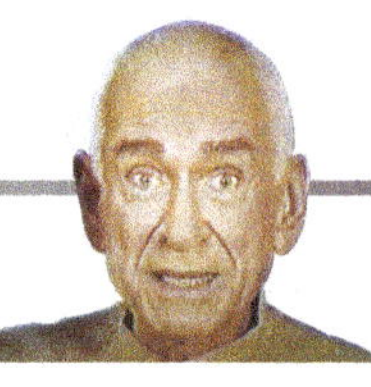

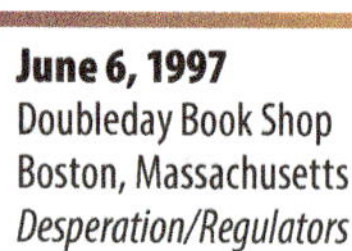

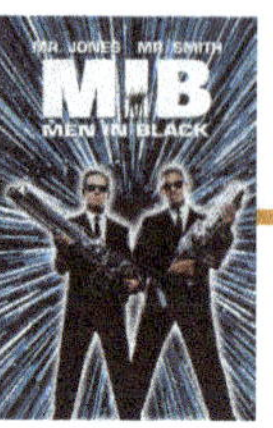

Tootsie's Orchid Lounge, Nashville, Tennessee

Emmy winner(!) Mike Jackson, and Dave Hinchberger

the parties involved knew we were auctioning this off for charity. I got in touch with Parnassas Bookstore, who was supporting the event, The Ryman folks, and spoke again with Marsha Defilippo, Stephen King's Senior Assistant. All was a go.

I also thought I'd get in touch with Steve and see if he would promote it via Twitter (remember this is 2016). Here's my conversation with him via e-mail:

During Stephen King's Ryman talk he mentioned that he had Hank Williams old dressing room. Yes, I hear that eerie music in the background too.

The auction went well. We sold the tickets for the auction end price of $405 to a lady in Georgia.

We're all set. Hotel, friends attending with us from all parts, auction tickets delivered, and check sent off to the Haven Foundation. Several months later it's the day of the show. We all meet up at our hotel and head into town to have a wonderful dinner with our group. Next stop: The Ryman.

As we arrive Nashville is hopping! You see it's Country Music week and they close off some of the streets so folks can listen to music, party about town, and the folks are out in droves. The famous Tootsies Orchid Lounge (since 1960) backs up to the Ryman Auditorium and players would get off stage and come out to sneak into the back of Tootsies for a quick drink or play on one of their three stages. When the Overlook Connection crew showed up to the Ryman, the Constant Readers were lined

Constant Readers lined up for Stephen King.

Oct 29, 1997
Dymoks
Sydney, Australia
Everything's Eventual
No signing

Bryan and Laura McAllister, Hatch Show Print shop, Nashville

up around the whole auditorium, amidst the hoopla of Country Music Week. I walked the whole building taking photos of the crowd and was amazed at this sight of King readers waiting patiently among the loud country music coming out of Tootsies, and all the other bars, right next to us. Oh, the dichotomy of it all. It was interesting to see *Carrie*, Stephen King Rules, and *Misery* shirts next to Carrie Underwood posters on the street.

We entered the venue and I told the gang we had to find where they are selling the Hatch Show posters created for the King event (it's the first image you see in this book). I knew we had to get there fast because they only made 200 posters for the event. 200 was a low number, as they don't know King fans. We discovered they were selling them upstairs. We got in the short line and as I was purchasing mine I said "how many are left?" "what you see here." About ten were on the table. Of course, I purchased a second copy. I think Bryan and Mike purchased a couple and they were… gone.

We met up with our auction winner at our wooden pew, row X. The Ryman was originally a church when built in 1892, thus pews for seating, and stained-glass windows give this grand hall a unique, even grandiose, feel. This lovely lady, all dressed in black, and surprise… was very pregnant. And alone! She said her husband couldn't make it and her mother had to bow out at the last minute. She drove all those hours, pregnant, just to see Stephen King, and of course paid quite a privilege to do so. We made sure to keep her close with our group and we helped her throughout the evening and made sure she received her book,

All photos outside and inside, the Ryman Auditorium

etc. She'll have this story to tell her offspring the rest of your life, "yes, you were there, at the Ryman, with Stephen King on stage."

The evening began with Parnassus Books co-owner, Ann Patchett, who introduced author Donna Tartt, who in turn introduced Stephen King. He entered the stage to a standing ovation with the widest smile on his face. He gave Donna Tartt a hug and then spoke directly to the crowd. "A standing 'O' in the Ryman," he said. "Well, it's all downhill from here. I'm going to talk about writing, but I'm in the Ryman so cut me some slack!"

1990s

May 1, 1998
University of Maine
Bangor, Maine
Reception for a scholarship fund provided by the Kings

Bryan McAllister on row X, Ryman Auditorium

He told the hilarious story when working on an idea he had for *Gerald's Game*, wherein he asked his 14-year-old son, Joe, to help him work it out by tying him to the bed. This is when his wife Tabby, and Joe's mom, came in and asked what was going on. The crowd roared at this as we could all picture the hilarious scenario. He talked about how he'd practically scared himself writing about the woman in room 217 in *The Shining*. He also told us he decided to release *'Salem's Lot* as his second novel, even though he knew it might label him as a horror writer. He mentioned that the original title was Second Coming but Tabby told him it sounded too much like a "sex novel" and that idea was nixed. He also took a moment to inform us that he is working on a novel with son Owen, a novel set around a women's prison in West Virginia, which we now know is *Sleeping Beauties*.

He talked about Jerry Lee Lewis and what he pulled from his biography. The first time Jerry Lee saw a piano he wrote, "I didn't know what it was but I knew I had to get at it." King said that "comes as close as possible to summarizing what that is, that something that speaks to a person. A guitar, a typewriter, a certain kind of story. For me it was finding a box of my father's paperbacks in the attic. My father left my mother when I was 2, and he left behind many things from his days in the Merchant Marines. What I liked was a box of pulp paperbacks and it contained a collection of H.P. Lovecraft stories called *The Thing From*

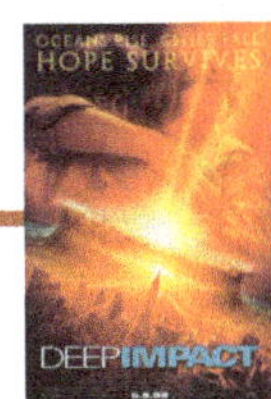

Aug 1, 1998
Borders Bookshop
London, England
Bag of Bones

The Auction Winner! and Dave Hinchberger

the Tomb, and I looked at that book and I just knew I had to get at it. Whatever it was awoke in me."

He explained how he thought he became "The King of Horror."

"There was a moment where these two books were sitting on my editor's desk. On one curb I was just Stephen King the adult novelist, and on the other I was Stephen King the horror writer. I said to Bill 'which one of these books do you think I should publish?' Bill said, 'Well, that depends on whether or not you want to be known as a precious novelist, that kind of writer, or go for the big casino and try to grab the brass ring because the vampire novel is a lot better, but he said you'll be known as a horror writer.'" Stephen King said "as long as they will pay me… and then I stopped, I looked down and there was a twenty-dollar bill laying there. I picked up the twenty and I told him let's publish the vampire novel! And that's how I became known as (said in a booming voice) *The King of Horror.*"

"What really happened is Boris Karloff died, then Rod Serling died, and then Alfred Hitchcock died, and then somebody up there said 'okay, that's it, you're the Great Pumpkin!'" The crowd then roared in laughter.

During a discussion to an audience member's question, King said: "Writing a novel is like crossing the Atlantic in a row boat. It's tough, and it's not a job for sissies. So, you can't give in, you can't weaken and I think that's pretty good advice for a lot of things."

An audience member asked "what was a good King novel to start with for a first-time reader?"

Stephen King replied: "for 10 or 11 year-olds, *The Girl Who Loved Tom Gordon* or *The Eyes of the Dragon*. What I really like is the outlaw kids who go out on their own, find their own kind of books, and read them under the covers."

Before closing out the night, King remarked, "Everything is happening in Nashville this weekend," he said. "The CMA Fest, Bonnaroo is close by…and look at this place, full of people who read books."

The Overlook Connection crew, Nashville

Dave and Bryan, good old friends in Nashville

1990s

Aug 22, 1998
Borders Bookshop, Oxford Street
London, England
Bag of Bones

Aug 22, 1998
WH Smith
London, England
Bag of Bones

Public Posts

Stephen King

10 hrs ·

Thanks to everyone who came out tonight to the Ryman in Nashville. We had a good time, didn't we?

261 Comments 61 Shares 

Like Comment Share

As we left the Ryman we all had to exit out of one set of doors as this is where they were distributing the books. My group was already ahead of me as I stepped back to let some group in front of me that was obviously together. When I got outside the doors there were two groups of people handing out books. The table to the left of me was closer so I took that path. I was handed a copy of *End of Watch* and to my right a lady screamed as she opened her book and saw it was signed. With my book in hand I took a quick peak at the title page… and damn… hot damn!… It was signed! I found my crew and told LeeAnn… she promptly traded her unsigned book… for mine…lol! My wife, such a cut-up that one.

Stephen King told a lot of familiar stories, some expanded, that I've heard over the years at these book events, and I was glad to hear them again, as well as many new tales. He knows how to engage his audience and this reflects how he's able to pull them in on stage, but especially, on the page.

We called it a night and turned in. The next morning we'd checked out of the hotel, and met in the lobby to head out. We were leaving the hotel and we passed the female cashier – went outside to give the valet our ticket and realized I needed a few bucks for his tip. I went back inside to the cashier stand and now there was a young gentleman there. "Can I help you?"

Graham and LeeAnn, Nashville

Lo and behold, it was LeeAnn's student, Graham. I said "Graham?" He looked at me and said "Mr. Hinchberger?" I said "yep, and your teacher is right outside, let me get her." I went out and told her "there's someone in here who'd like to see you." She looked at me quizzically but followed me back in. She went wide-eyed when she saw him.

Yes, there were screams and hugs again.

What are the odds?

If I hadn't needed change…

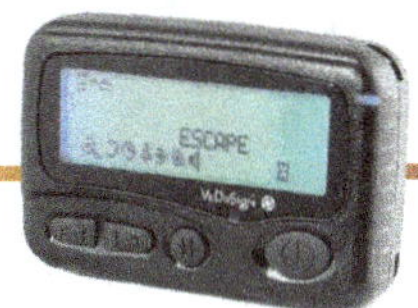

Aug 24, 1998
Dillons, The Bentall's Centre
Kingston Upon Thames, England
Bag of Bones

ROCK-KING AND ROLLING: An Interview with Ridley Pearson

by **Andrew J. Rausch**

Ridley Pearson is a bestselling novelist who has written more than sixty books and performs alongside Stephen King and other bestselling authors in the band known as the Rock Bottom Remainders. He's also the author, under a pseudonym, of the 2001 Stephen King TV Series, Rose Red, *tie-in novel,* The Diary of Ellen Rimbauer.

AR: How did you become a member of the Rock Bottom Remainders?

RP: I got lucky in my career. God only knows why, but I became a bestselling author. Part of that is that you go on these massive book tours. One book I did was six weeks, but most of them I did were three. Because there were premium bookstores across the country, every time you did a book tour, you went to a lot of the same cities. One of those cities was San Francisco. The publisher would hire a media escort in each city. In those days, the radio stations were like eight miles out of town and under a bush somewhere, and you just couldn't get there if you were on your own. They hired young women and young men in their thirties or forties to drive you to bookstores and drive you to public events. I think it stemmed from the days when the authors got so drunk that they needed someone to come to their hotel and drag them down to the event. But those days have since passed. You would spend the entire day with these escorts, and you'd do that [with them] once a year. After four or five years of this, you had spent eight hours in a car with that same media escort. You really got to know each other. One of these women was Kathy Goldmark in San Francisco. Kathy was a very good musician. She would invite authors, including me, to her gigs if we were interested. Not wanting to be a wallflower, I said, "Absolutely." So, a couple of different times on my tours, I would go and listen to Kathy and her crazy bands. I think a couple of times I might have even sat in. She's passed on now, but she was a really bright, really fun person to be around. And all of the authors loved her. She was a landmark on the tour circuit.

One year, in 1989, I think, the ABA (the American Book Association) was having one of its annual conventions. In those days, they went all around the country. This one was going to be in the LA area. Kathy Goldmark had this idea that she would put together

1990s

Aug 25, 1998
Waterstones
Leadenhall, England
Bag of Bones

Kathi
Kamen Goldmark

Kathi

an all-authors rock band, and we would be schooled up by Al Kooper from Super Session and Bob Dylan. In five days, we would try to put together two sets, or a set and a half, of cover songs from the '50s and '60s. We'd sing them and have a good time, and hopefully the crowd would have a good time because we'd be all book people, and we'd raise a bunch of money. We'd played at a place called Cowboy Boogie in LA, and we were absolutely awful. We were—and still are—the world's worst rock band. In those days, the authors were Barbara Kingsolver, Stephen King, Amy Tan, Robert Fulghum, Dave Barry, and me. But we went up there, and we played horribly. [laughs] We tried to do something like The Tubes, where we did a lot of silly skits on stage. We played songs like *These Boots Are Made for Walkin'*, and Amy Tan would dress up in Lycra and walk across the stage and whip our butts with some sort of riding crop. We did that first show, and it really went well. It was really funny, and the crowd went crazy. On the way off the stage, Stephen King was right in front of me. He turned his head back as we're walking off to thunderous applause, and he said, "Ridley, we're not done here!" He had gotten the "I want to be a rock star" bug.

AR: What is the chemistry of the band like, both as musicians and as people?

RP: That's why we've been playing for more than thirty years now. What we realized as a group was that we all adored each other. And no one was bigger than anyone else. Stephen wasn't the big dude, Amy wasn't— Look, I had had one tiny bestseller, but these were people I had been reading my whole life. "What am I doing in this band?!" I thought it was going to be a battle of egos, but nobody had any ego. I've been in a lot of bands, and that's very rare. The beauty of this band is that, for whatever reason, we gelled as friends. We realized how horrible we were, but we laughed it off. We had Dave Barry to keep us amused. Stephen King is one of the brightest, funniest guys you'll ever meet. He's goofy. He's brilliant. He knows every lyric to every song, as does Dave Barry, as does Mitch Albom. Mitch Albom can sit down and sing any song you name, and play it all the way through. He can also tell you who produced it and who was on the album. These guys love their music. I think because we've always been so terrible, it's just been nothing but having fun. If we'd ever been trying to be good, I think it would have been horrible. But we completely ruled that out after about two songs. And poor Al Kooper! He was just looking at what he had to work with, and swear words were flying—many of them at me, because I'm the bass player! It's like, "Can't you keep us in rhythm!" "No, I can't keep anybody anywhere!" We were all over the map!

Dave

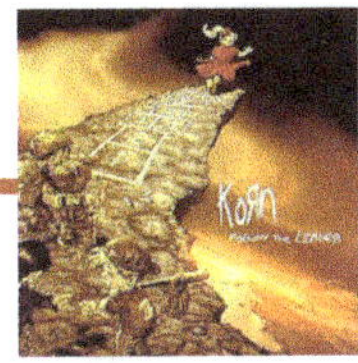

Aug 26, 1998
WH Smith, Heathrow Airport
London, England
Bag of Bones

Stephen wasn't wrong—we weren't done. After that, Stephen went to his publisher, which I think was Viking at the time. He went to Viking and said, "Hey, I've got this crazy idea. Here's who's in this band... And you're gonna pay me—" I can't remember how much it was, but it was quite a sum. "You're gonna pay the band this much money, and we're gonna rent a bus, and we're gonna raise money for non-profits down the east coast. And then we're all gonna write a book for you." And that's what happened. We rented Aretha Franklin's tour bus. At that point, all of us were still in the band. Others would fade out after the tour ended. We started in Providence, we played Boston, we played New York, Washington, DC, Atlanta, all the way down the east coast.

Ridley Pearson
plays: bass
Ridley

We had found this thing called America Scores, which still exists, and is about bringing literacy to under-served kids in urban communities by getting them into soccer. If you combine soccer and poetry, you've got America Scores. America Scores lured the kids in by giving them uniforms and shields and balls and shin guards if they would stay after school on Tuesdays and Thursdays to do poetry, rap for rap music, and generally some reading and writing. It advanced all the kids' scores, and it still does today. It's huge. But this was in the early days for America Scores, and they badly needed money. We raised several hundred thousand dollars, maybe half a million dollars for them with this tour just by us basically being absolute idiots at the state fair.

At the end of that tour, we still weren't done. We started playing once or twice, maybe three times a year, for the next twenty-eight years or so.

AR: Do you guys get together and rehearse? How does that work?

RP: The short answer is yes, and that's sort of the most fun we have. If we have a Saturday gig, most of us fly in on a Thursday night. We rehearse on a sound stage somewhere all Friday, and then Saturday we play our gig. So, we get all of this time together in a sound room, having a blast like idiots. Then we usually get most of the day to just hang out and go for walks and have meals together. Then we play that night and fly out the next day. That's usually how it works. It's always for non-profit—we've never made a dime on any of this. We've raised, I think, three-and-a-half million dollars for non-profits over the years.

AR: What are some of your favorite Rock Bottom Remainders memories?

RP: There's a lot of bandwidth on that, because some of the fun memories are on stage. And many, many of the fondest memories are just, you know, getting invited up to Stephen's massive presidential suite, and just hanging out and talking for hours. So, it covers the gambit. We've had really, silly, moments. Frank McCourt was in the band for about five years. We were invited to play at the Rock and Roll Hall of Fame for our second time. It was kind of a small gig. There were maybe two or three hundred people there. Frank had a few too many martinis. We played *Danny Boy*, and Frank couldn't remember the words. That was one of the great moments! Another time, we all played at the Sun Valley

1990s

Sept 25, 1998
University Temple United Methodist Church
Seattle, Washington
Bag of Bones

Writers Conference. We played at a little bar downtown. That was the first time that Frank played with us. He was a guest at the conference, and Dave invited him up on stage. We were going to play "Love Me Do," so we all learned the words. But Frank came on stage and played a different song. We're in the middle of the song, and Dave is shouting at Frank, "That's the wrong song, Frank!" We're all trying to find the right chords. Oh God! There are just a million memories like that. Mostly of idiot things we did that we had great fun and laughter doing.

Dave and I were the only two runners in the band early on. I would see him in the lobby when I went out to run, and he would see me and go, "Let's run together!" Then we would come back and have scrambled eggs at the hotel. The next day, we'd say, "Do you want to meet at 6:30 and run?" So, on that tour down the east coast, Dave and I ran every morning and had breakfast every morning. We became, really close friends, and have remained really good friends. He and I ended up writing together for ten years. We wrote middle school books that did very well. Those ten years were probably the most fun I've had in my career. There are those types of memories where my entire career or my life changed because I went running with Dave Barry one morning. Mitch Albom and I are very close friends. I went down the January before last to an orphanage he has in Haiti where he takes kids who don't even have names. He brings them into this incredible compound, where there is all this support personnel, and they're raised with love and tenderness and are educated through high school. I went down and taught English there, just for a very brief time. Mitch and I have become close over the past few years. You become close with everybody in different ways, and those are really the memories that you take home.

"Stephen King... turned his head back as we're walking off to thunderous applause, and he said, 'Ridley, we're not done here!' He had gotten the 'I want to be a rock star' bug."

We've played with Bruce Springsteen. We've played with Darlene Love. Warren Zevon was in the band for four years. Roger McGuinn is still in the band. He's played with us for seven years. There have been some amazing music moments. But, of course, it's the friendships and the connections that have lasted.

RP: Do you want to hear a couple of Stephen King stories, Andy?

AR: Of course.

Sept 29, 1998
Chicago Public Library
Chicago, Illinois
Bag of Bones

Stephen King

plays: rhythm guitar

RP: One thing I can tell you is that Stephen being Stephen, he won't do anything unless he does it well. He loves fooling around on guitar, but he'd never been on stage for guitar, and he'd never sung with a band. So, Dave Barry and I ended up working with him in the early days, in order to get him to play chords faster and keep up with the tempo. Steve being as brilliant as he is, he was a very fast learner. Steve would have these crowds in the palm of his hands. He's a ham, and he knows how to work a crowd. He wouldn't play with us all the time, but he played with us for that whole tour. After that, he would only play with us every other year. As you can imagine, some of Steve's fans are crazy. There are two Stephen King stories that I think will set the stage here.

One is, we pulled into an Alabama truck stop. It was four in the morning. We all poured off of Aretha Franklin's tour bus to take a pee. By the time we leave, we've probably been inside this place for ten to fifteen minutes, max. We come out to get back on the bus, and there are four people standing at the pumps with multiple Stephen King books in their hands! Here's the math, Andy... We got there, we got out, the guy who was gonna pump the gas must have recognized Stephen, so he calls his friend and says, "He's here, goddammit! He's here!" That guy calls his friend... Four of them get up, get dressed, locate their Stephen King books at four in the morning, and make it to the pumps in time to meet Stephen as he enters the bus! In fifteen minutes! It's insane! So, Stephen, knowing that we were probably going to get burned up if he didn't do it, stops and signs all of their books. They drive off, and we're like, "Steve, it's four in the morning!" And he just says, "I know." [laughs] You know, like this isn't unusual at all.

There's another night. I think we're in Nashville. We're playing in this shit-kicker bar. It's a dive. There are no doors on the stalls in the bathroom. The place is packed—because of Stephen, I'm sure. The audience is out of their minds for the band. Again, we suck, Andy, so it's weird when people like us. And these people loved us. We never play encores, because no one ever wants to hear more from us. [laughs] But we decided to play an encore. It was some rock song, something simple. Some idiot in the back probably lit a cigarette, and

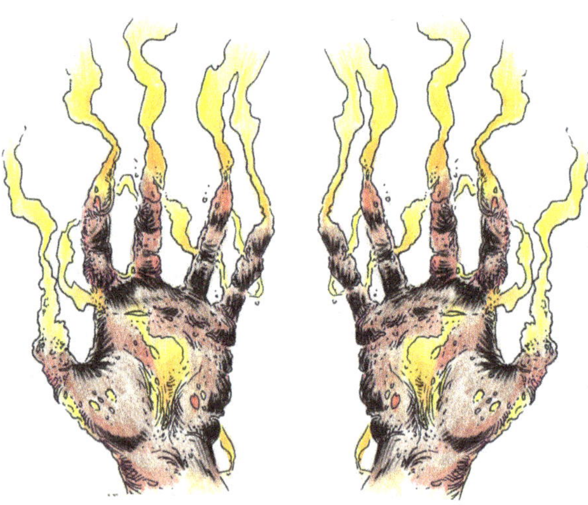

then somebody held up their cell phone. So, they had the Bob Dylan thing going for us; a thousand people are swaying back and forth with their iPhones and their matches and their lighters up.

We're on about a four-foot stage. It was a very high stage for a bar. I look down in front of Stephen, and there's a very attractive thirty-five-year-old blonde woman. Her chest is

1990s

Nov 23, 1998
Betts Bookstore
Bangor, Maine
Bag of Bones

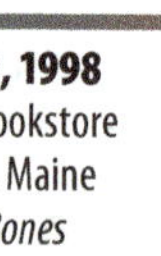

probably at Stephen's feet, and she's looking up. And all ten fingernails on fire! She's looking up at Stephen with this maniacal jaw-opening look that says, "I love you and I'm burning all my fingers off!" I went running over to Dave on stage and said, "Check it out! Check it out! Check it out!" He looks over and he sees this woman, and he just falls down on his knees in hysterics. I shout out at him, "I never want to be that famous!" I never have been, by the way. [laughs] It was a self-fulfilling prophecy!

Those are the kinds of moments you have with Stephen—a woman setting all ten fingernails on fire, standing there loving Stephen from a distance. I could go on and on with Stephen fan stories, but those two give you an idea of what you're dealing with. When we would arrive at any hotel, there would be fifty to seventy-five people there, all with stacks of books. He would say, "This is not a workday for me—I'm going to sign one of each of your books." And he would sign for the whole line. Sometimes the band would form a little line around him to get him into places. And all through it, he's sweet and he's kind. He's never upset about it.

He went on a rant on the bus one night at like two in the morning and just started reciting poetry. I don't know if he was making it up or if he was reciting it, but it went on for like fifteen minutes. I was just like, "Who is this man?" He's crazy in a brilliant crazy way! I love the man. He's bigger than life and always will be.

Learn more about America Scores at **americascores.org**

"This Taschen set on Stanley Kubrick's *The Shining* is the deepest dive into this film that I can imagine. I just finished reading the 900-page making-of volume, and going in detail through the incredible 'Scrapbook' of photos. It was like being there from initial concept through the entirety of shooting to the very end. If you love Kubrick's *The Shining* as much as I do (or filmmaking in general), this is a must have, and a testament to a great artist." **– Chet Williamson, author of *Ash Wednesday*, expanded version now available at Amazon.com**

Stanley Kubrick's *The Shining*. 1396 pages, in color, 2 volumes, slipcased.

Conceived and edited by Academy Award-winning director Lee Unkrich, dubbed by *The Hollywood Reporter* as "the world's foremost *Shining* aficionado," with text by best-selling author J.W. Rinzler and a foreword by Steven Spielberg. Includes hundreds of never-before-seen production photographs from the Stanley Kubrick Archive and the personal collections of cast and crew, rare documents and correspondence, conceptual art, an exclusive look at deleted scenes, and more. gathers hundreds of hours of exclusive new interviews with the cast and crew in an unprecedented look at the 1980 cult classic. Slip in through the back door of The Overlook Hotel to witness Kubrick's endless rounds of script rewrites, his revolutionary use of the Steadicam, the mechanics behind the infamous blood elevator, the mysterious mid-filming fire at Elstree Studios, and the countless takes needed to satisfy the meticulous force that was Kubrick.

Nov 30, 1998
Circle Cinemas
Brighton, Massachusetts
Bag of Bones

Dec 9, 1998
Bookmarc's
Bangor, Maine
Bag of Bones

The Rock Bottom Remainders Farewell: 2024

by ***Glen Reitz***

On November 23, 2024, at the Miami Book Fair – Miami Dade College the Rock Bottom Remainders performed, what could be their final performance! Their first concert was at the American Booksellers Association convention in Anaheim California in 1992. 32 years later the band is still Rocking! While members of the band have come and gone, many of the originals are still playing in the band to this day. Stephen King, Scott Turow, Amy Tan, Dave Barry, Sam Barry, Mitch Albom, and Roy Blount Jr. were all on stage. Also joined by Mary Karr, Ridley Pearson, and Alan Zweibel. Hundreds of fans started lining up early to see this historic band perform under the lights of Miami. Miami is a favorite city for the band to perform, the Rock Bottom Remainders have performed more than a dozen times in the city. Their last performance in Miami was in 2016. Greg Iles was not able to perform, and the concert was dedicated to him and the band stated how much he was missed.

All of their greatest hits were performed at the concert, including *Stand by Me, Rockaway Beach, Runaway,* and *Wild Thing*. The crowd went wild every time another song was played! If you've never seen a group of your favorite authors sing, dance, and perform, you don't know what you are missing. *Moby Dick* was a classic and you need to go to YouTube or CSPAN to see this group of authors singing such a classic song and having way more fun than they should be at their age.

Dave Barry is quoted as saying "If the band was on a road trip, and they all died in a bus crash, the headlines would read "Famous Author Stephen King and others died in crash", the audience got a huge laugh at this!

When prompted, sophisticated, smart, and classy author Amy Tan recounted a story of her dinner with President Barrack Obama, at dinner he said he heard that she was in a band, he asked her what her role in the band was... With no trepidation she said, "I play the dominatrix,

1990s

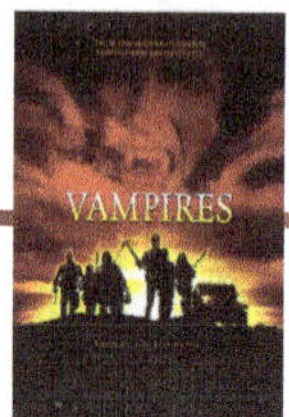

and at the end of my song, I spank all the male band members"

Their performance was a huge hit, well staged and a complete and spectacular success. When I ran into Scott Turow the next morning, I asked him "was this the last performance for the Rock Bottom Remainders? He stated that he thought that the last performance was their last". I was told by the planning committee at the fair that Stephen King could not wait to get back to the concert stage and perform with his friends. And that is exactly what they did!

If it is their last performance, it will be remembered as their greatest performance ever. If, and when, the band does decide to perform again (and I am still able to walk), I will be in the front row and center just like I was that last night!

Rock on Remainders!

Glen Reitz taking it all in with The Rockin' Remainders in Miami

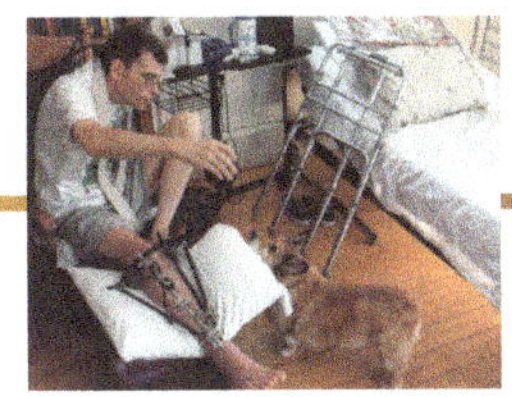

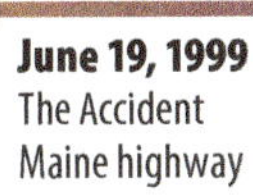

June 19, 1999
The Accident
Maine highway

The Stephen King Diaries

Reflections of a Fan, an Editor, a Constant Reader

by **Joseph Pittman**

AUTHOR'S NOTE: Most of these "diary" entries were first featured, in slightly different form, on the Facebook group page, 19th Edition.

The reason why began innocently enough, when I posted on my page a photograph of the cover for *You Like it Darker* and commented on my fear of alligators. Yup, I was afraid of a Stephen King cover. A friend of mine, realizing I was a fan of the author, recommended I join the group, which I did.

I mentioned to the members that I had worked with Stephen King during my publishing career and that I'd be happy to share some of my stories. What I initially thought of as a five-part series turned into more, as I realized how many memorable moments I'd had both as a fan and while working as an editor at New American Library/Signet Books.

Now, I'm happy to compile those, as well as some that are exclusive to this the *Stephen King 2025 Annual*, into one continuous tale into the many worlds of Stephen King, all experienced with my own, at times, insider eyes. I hope you enjoy the quest.

DIARY ONE: *A Boy on a Porch*

So, what rabbit hole did I fall through that allowed me to become part of publishing history, and to work with one of the most celebrated, prolific, and best-selling authors in the world? Even I couldn't have imagined the journey that was going to beset me, but I'm grateful for the opportunities provided for me, and thankful to the people who entrusted me in being even a part of a story only a little boy could dream.

I hope you enjoy this trip down Memory Lane.

Let's start with a bit about my background. I, myself, am a published author now, writing under my name and that of Adam Carpenter. Yup, I have a pseudonym, and you might meet him along the way. As to what I write, it's not horror. Mystery and suspense are my primary genres, though I have published some "feel-good" novels as well.

My recent books found me veering into the nonfiction arena, with *The Shadow Diaries*, co-written with my dog, and *The Broadway Diaries*, about my "second" life as a Broadway usher. Which is a long way of saying when I post one of these, it's because I too like to tell a story. Maybe this is The King Diaries. Shall we begin?

It's September 1981, and for my 17th birthday my friend Renee gave me a book. The gift was the paperback edition of *Firestarter* by Stephen King. It was a new release, the edition that was on shelves in either a black or white cover with the orange flame and eyes in the center. I was already an avid reader (Agatha Christie was my favorite), but I hadn't yet discovered King.

So, I blazed forward and began turning the pages. I'll admit, I wasn't pulled in. The pace was too slow for my young tastes back then. I actually set the book down halfway through it, and for months, didn't finish it.

2000s

Aug 2, 2000
Red Lobster
Butler, Pennsylvania

Months passed and soon it was the next summer, when I was working several odd jobs in a small town that could have doubled for Castle Rock, as I was about to find out. One job was at a used bookshop called Marijane's Book Exchange, three doors down from my house. She would also stock new titles, recently released paperbacks. What did I see that early July day? *Cujo*.

Intrigued by the cover, I was instantly hooked, and I needed more. And there was more. I began to read like a kid eating a blueberry pie at a county fair. That summer was wonderful and innocent, a boy discovering these amazing new books by an author whose command of story and character was unmatched in my, granted, limited experience. I read *The Dead Zone* next, then something transformative occurred.

At the local Waldenbooks, I came upon a dump display, all the books King had published so far. And there, waiting for my hard-earned cash, was "the ultimate in evil.," *The Stand*, all, 800-plus pages of glorious, epic horror. I read it in record time for me, one hundred pages a day at least. At night curled up at a family camp while a fire crackled nearby, or by day, away from the glaring sunshine while sitting on the shady side of my porch.

Before the summer ended, I would finish *Firestarter*. You know, it's still not gonna be one of my favorites. But other books would battle it out for that title, so many novels over the years....but we'll save talk of those for another time, different seasons.

I guess that's enough for my first entry. I thought a bit of context would help explain my lifelong journeys to Castle Rock, to Derry and beyond to worlds both horrific and fantastical. Shall we continue down that dark path again?

DIARY TWO: *Different Seasons Changing*

We're inching closer to when I interviewed at New American Library/Signet and began to assist in the publication of Mr. King's books. But there's more backstory, which I think helps establish what a thrill it was for me to be an editor at such a renowned house, and why that little boy found delight in chasing shadows.

I was headed off to college in 1982, just as I was reading Stephen King's newest release, *Different Seasons*. My first hardcover of his! That was exciting, because my personal library had grown from paperbacks. Just as I was growing up, *The Body* spoke to my own childhood adventures, all of which would help inspire my own serial-killer novel, *The Original Crime*. As I left for college that fall, I was presented with a copy of the first trade paperback edition of *Danse Macabre*. Given to me by Marijane, the lady who owned the used bookstore I worked at part-time. I still have it in my King collection, inscribed by her. The aforementioned novel, *The Original Crime*, is dedicated to her.

Marijane and I would have one more memorable King moment. In the trade publication *Publishers Weekly*, there was a full-page ad for an upcoming release of the book "Stephen King was afraid to publish," as the copy proclaimed. *Pet Sematary*, was its title, misspelled on purpose. (I still can't spell that word properly!) Seems that the publisher, Doubleday, was giving away advance reader's copies to the first 500 booksellers to write and request one.

I wrote the letter, she mailed it. And a few weeks later...we got our copy! All the way from the publisher's offices in New York City

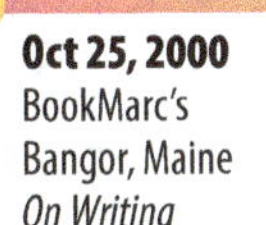

Oct 25, 2000
BookMarc's
Bangor, Maine
On Writing

to Manlius. Wow. That was amazing that our little bookstore had secured this rare edition. I devoured it like a rabid dog (cat, perhaps?). Back at school and knowing the hardcover was soon to be published, I walked into the offices of my college newspaper and asked if they were looking for a book reviewer.

My review of *Pet Sematary* was my first-ever published piece of writing, and I would go on to write a weekly book review for *The Stylus*, as well as ascend its editorial ranks each semester. My career had begun. (Fun fact: I also reviewed *Caretakers* by Tabitha King.)

And so, the road was paved, the seeds had been planted, and my own dark tower toward the world of Manhattan publishing was rising, building from fantasy to reality. What an apt pupil I was. Who knew the excitement awaiting me in New York City?

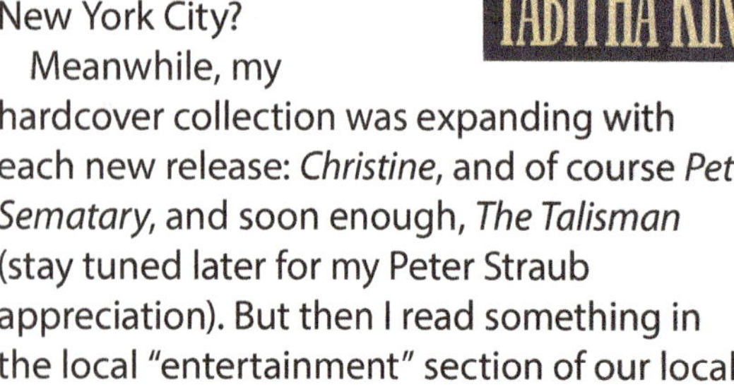

Meanwhile, my hardcover collection was expanding with each new release: *Christine*, and of course *Pet Sematary*, and soon enough, *The Talisman* (stay tuned later for my Peter Straub appreciation). But then I read something in the local "entertainment" section of our local newspaper: Stephen King was retiring.

Looking back, that might be the scariest notion of them all. Thankfully, *IT* was not true…

DIARY THREE: *The Putnam Pair*

I'm emerging again from the mist to tell another tale of my publishing experiences, sort of the beginning of my professional association with the works of Stephen King.

It's 1986 and college has ended. I've graduated with a Bachelor of Science in journalism. I'm already thinking of getting a job in publishing. I've done over 50 book reviews for the school newspaper, including *Cycle of the Werewolf* and *The Talisman*. I think I've done enough critical thinking to pursue a career as an editor.

But all those big jobs were in New York City, and I was back home in the Syracuse area. I got a job at an independent bookstore and among my duties was keeping the fiction and bestseller shelves stocked, as well as setting up the "dump" displays. I was in heaven. King was a huge seller then, and I kept his paperbacks well stocked on the shelves. I of course kept up my reading, finalizing my collection with the early books. Finally, though, a new book was coming: *Skeleton Crew*. But for the publishing enthusiast, something was wrong!

Maybe that retirement rumor was true: because this was just a short story collection, with a novella to start things off. Was that all that was left in the tank? And what really caused a scare in me was the fact the book was being published by a different house: Putnam.

Not knowing the vagaries of contracts and option clauses back then, I needed to find out why Viking had lost 2/3 of its imprint name. So, I began to plot my investigation. One day at the bookstore, I saw an ad in *Publishers Weekly* for an employment agency in NYC.

Two weeks later, there I was in New York. I met with the woman I'd previously spoken to on the phone, staying with my college best friend (and Straub fanatic) who had moved there a year ago. Once then, I also poured over the classified ads in the *Times* and found a listing for an editorial assistant, called the number and on Monday afternoon had an interview with a major New York house. That's how it was done back then.

But what house? Was it NAL, perhaps Viking/Penguin? Was Stephen King edging ever closer? I could almost feel the rush of anticipation, or

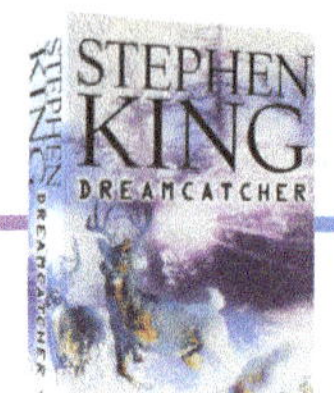

April 7, 2001
Dunn & Dunn Books
Naples, Florida
Dreamcatcher

worse, the fear of rejection. Turned out to be a mixed bag. The job was for children's books, and despite my hesitation, they offered me the job. The house? Putnam.

I gave notice at the bookstore and two weeks later moved to New York to start my career. But not before the mystery of *Skeleton Crew* deepened. The paperback had come out at this point, and it was published by…Signet, King's paperback publisher. What was going on?

Who was Stephen King's publisher? Because the confusion continued with the first book I read on the long subway ride to the office: the recently released epic, IT. A Viking publication. Huh. But during my time at Putnam, they published another King book, *The Tommyknockers.*

I was now a man on a mission, and at last, I was working from the inside. Roland would soon come calling to help me on my quest.

DIARY FOUR: *The King of Viking*

Ready for a plot twist? The story of working on Mr. King's books takes an interesting turn here, I hope.

I left Putnam behind after a year, having accepted a new position at Viking Penguin in the managing editorial department. Holy shit, after dabbling with two King books at Putnam, here I am at the real hardcover publisher! I have a small cubicle which I can decorate as I see fit.

So, I use dust jackets from some of Viking's forthcoming titles. Among them? *The Dark Half.* But I also have *Eyes of the Dragon* and *Misery* on display. One of the production editors noticed my love of King, and with a knowing wink said she worked on *Misery.* What did you do, I asked? It was her handwriting on the page proofs and in the finished book—she filled in all the missing "N" letters missing from Paul Sheldon's manuscript. Cool job!

Someone else on the staff saw my interest in King's books. His editor, and future agent, the late Chuck Verrill. One day he called my name as I was walking past his office and invited me in. Gulp, I thought, I'm in the inner sanctum of King's publisher…his editor. And it's legit, I work here.

Chuck took a book from his shelves, and, as he handed it to me, informed me that it was finally going to be available soon in bookstores. There it was, the cover almost rising to the sky. *The Dark Tower: The Gunslinger.* This was the first-ever trade edition of the limited-edition book (Donald Grant press), published by NAL, Signet's trade paperback imprint. A gift to me.

I'd first noticed the title "The Dark Tower" on the ad card for *Pet Sematary,* but had no idea what it was or how to get a copy. Amazon and Google hadn't yet been invented yet! But now I was holding a copy in my own hands, given to me by a man one degree of separation from the King. I read it, and of course was left waiting for more.

I would leave Viking after a year, seeking to advance my career. Bantam Books hired me, working as an editorial assistant to a senior editor who worked with big name authors like Jonathan Kellerman, Rita Mae Brown, Michael Palmer, and eventually, the great Robert Ludlum (another of my favorite authors). No more King in my daily life, but I took solace in my new address: 666 Fifth Avenue. But just as we all had to wait for future volumes about Roland, my quest was on hold, not only to be resumed but escalated a few years later.

During one storm of the century later, I would find myself back within Stephen King's orbit, as I was interviewing for an editorial position at New American Library. Otherwise known, to the reader in me, as Signet Books. I couldn't sleep the night before, anticipation

May 11, 2001
Private Home/SK's New Home
Casey Key, Florida

winning out. The time was four past midnight, and I had insomnia.

DIARY FIVE: *"Dolores! (Seinfeld, anyone?)"*

King thinks we like it darker? Well, yeah, mostly, when it's on the page. Not when you're in the middle of a nor'easter trying to get to the most important job interview of your life. Imagine, it's a December afternoon, the sky is as pitched as black, gray clouds swirling with powerful gusts of nature's fury on every corner. The rain is insistent, torrential. I'm in a taxicab, trying to weave through this storm and Manhattan traffic. Going from Upper East Side to SoHo. Should I cancel?

Not an option. I had to prove my mettle; this interview was for a full-fledged editor job at New American Library. Signet Books to the pulp novel fan! I was meeting with a woman named Elaine Koster, the president and publisher of NAL. For Constant Readers, you may know her name as Elaine Geiger, the shrewd editor who acquired the paperback rights to Carrie for a princely sum. The rest is history.

I finally arrived, with ten minutes to spare. Thanks to the cab my suit is dry and I'm not a subway-rumpled mess. I checked in and was soon brought to her office. We greet each other and she comments on the weather, thanks me for braving the elements. Not small talk, but impressed with my fortitude. All around me I see copies of copies of so many books I'd read—Ken Follett, Robin Cook, and of course, Stephen King. Hardcover, paperback. Lots of paperbacks.

One of those on display is *The Waste Lands*, and I remarked how I presently reading that. Volume III of the "The Dark Tower" had been released earlier that month and was currently sitting atop the Times bestseller list. She asked, "have I read much of his work?" I think "all" was my answer. But the job wasn't about his books, I was interviewing and would eventually get (no suspense there) a job acquiring and editing mysteries, thrillers, some glitz & glamour, and true crime. Close to the kingdom but looking over the walls.

And that's the type of book that I worked on for my first year. What happened next was happenstance, the kind of moment where you believe in the hand of fate. Our upcoming lead title was the paperback edition of *Dolores Claiborne*. Waiting outside Elaine's office, I noticed the cover mechanical in her in-box and so I asked her assistant if I could look at it. Sure.

This step is supposed to represent the final mechanical, circulating for every department head to approve. Elaine, as publisher, is the last stop before it goes to the printer. Except, hold the presses! There's kind of a major typo on the front cover. The title? *Dolores Clairborne*. Me being me, I spoke up.

Elaine later left a yellow Post-It note on my chair. "See me." With her tiny initials below. Not written but more than implied, was the word NOW. Was I in trouble for over-stepping my duties? With trepidation I knocked and entered. Have a seat, she indicated.

When I left a few minutes later, I was elated. Elaine said she was bringing me into her world of Stephen King, adding me to the distribution list for all things having to do with his hardcover reprints. Which meant, coming down the pike, *Rose Madder* and *Insomnia*, plus *Nightmares and Dreamscapes*, all in various stages of production.

I had one foot inside the kingdom. Soon, oh so soon, I'd have both feet in and hopefully be drawn in further. I'd happily walk a mile with those feet, even a green one, especially a green mile.

2000s

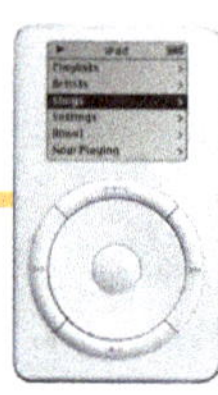

Feb 2, 2002
Town Hall
New York, New York
Black House
Wavedancer Foundation Benefit

DIARY SIX: *"A Book With Any Cover Would Still Sell the Same"*

Let's talk book covers. As we, as Constant Readers (and observers) all know, King's books have had many cover iterations over the decades.

In publishing, we call covers "packaging." It's our way of establishing a brand, giving an author a particular look. In the early days, King's books had their own individual identity. I have the first paperback edition of *Carrie* with the double step-back cover of flames, and I had the cover of *Night Shift* with the cutouts.

But eventually an author as popular as King gets "a look." First, it's in the type design, which many of the Viking hardcovers had. Think of how King's name appeared on many of the hardcovers in the 80s and early 90s—*It*, *Misery*, *Gerald's Game* to name a few. All from Viking. That's branding.

But now here I am, working at NAL/Signet, getting my first taste of being part of the Stephen King team. My job entailed a lot of prep work for each book that I'm involved in, from acquisition, to editing, and then formulating a publishing plan. Not just for King, I had a full list of authors that included suspense authors like Michael Prescott, Canadian horror writer Michael Slade, and Bentley Little (more on him in another entry; great story).

But back to King. I'm still operating behind the scenes, writing title information sheets for the paperback editions of *Nightmares and Dreamscapes*, and *Rose Madder*, cover briefs too, all filled with vital information used by sales and marketing. My boss, Elaine, of course had to approve them all. What editor's initials appeared on these forms? EK. During our monthly launch meetings, she would present King's books, with me sitting on the sidelines. All guts, no glory.

But that was about to change. I got a wake-up call in the name of *Insomnia*. See, the Viking hardcover had just been released using a dual-colored red-and-white dust jacket. Our paperback edition would be released 10 months later. Thoughts had already been voiced: the NAL paperback edition needed to look different, more "mass market" and marketable.

Something was brewing that would keep me up at night. In addition to a fresh new cover look for *Insomnia*, NAL was embarking on an ambitious project: the first-ever repackaging of the entire King backlist. Another meeting in Elaine's office, where I was asked to provide new cover copy for each book. This was the biggest moment of my career.

Despite the fact we had an entire copywriting department, Elaine had taken a liking to my copywriting skills—not just the words but thinking about the layout of the back cover, as well. The idea was for each title to follow the same format. Cover design, a copy/headline unique to that to book, new descriptive copy, updated facing quote pages. A new, uniform author photo would grace the entire back cover.

This was a huge undertaking for all involved, a major push from NAL to boost the sales of the new book and the monthly orders for the backlist titles. For me, this was a dream job, and so I poured through each of the previous editions, grabbing great lines to use in the copy, or to write clever (I hope) copy lines. Not

July 28, 2002
Charlotte Hobbs Library Gazebo
Lovell, Maine
Kicking off Old Home Days

Sept 24, 2002
Barnes and Noble - Union Square
New York, New York
From a Buick 8

only would Elaine approve my work, each draft was being sent to Stephen King, also.

Some of my favorites, clearly taken from parts of the book:

"Death is a Mystery. Burial is a Secret."

"How Do You Kill Something That Was Never Born?"

"Just Another Lovers' Triangle, Right?"

Guess my work passed muster, as my uniform approach was signed off on by both parties. If you have any of the paperbacks with this cover design, then you have read my work. We're talking *Carrie*, through *Insomnia*, 26 titles in all, including the existing "Dark Tower" titles.

Two awesome events happened as a result of my cover brainstorming on behalf of King's backlist. From this date forward, any Stephen King title listed on the production schedule that circulated to everyone in house would indicate EK/JP as the book's editor. That 16-year old boy reading *The Stand* on the porch, consider his mind blown.

The second awesome event? Oh, that's another story for another diary. But how about a little tease? Let's call that tale "How I Met Stephen King." No more dead zones for me, I was now a needful thing.

DIARY SEVEN: *The Green Mile Trilogy, Part One*

The serial thriller begins…

I debated whether to save this entry for last, but it kept nagging at me. Tell it, tell it, tell it. So, okay, relax, I'll tell it.

Here's the behind-the-scenes look at one of the most monumental and impactful stories in the annals of modern publishing history. Hyperbole? Kinda, not really. It was a concept not tried since someone wrote a Dickens of a story more than a century ago, and there was no measuring stick as to how this bold idea would be received.

Haha. Never underestimate the brilliant mind of Stephen King, and to their credit, the people whom he surrounded himself with. So, grab a cup of Coffey, sit down in your favorite old sparky, and I'll tell you how I came to be involved in, you guessed right: *The Green Mile*.

Like that other now-famous green tale where so much happened before Dorothy dropped in, much wicked planning had gone into the plans to publish King's new book. The thing of it was--the book wasn't yet written. Not all of it.

I was in my office in early 1996 when I'm summoned to my boss's office. Elaine had me take a seat and began to outline this audacious idea of a serialized novel and how she wanted my full involvement. With that, she handed me a copy of a rather thin manuscript, especially considering Stephen King had written it. Read it tonight, tell no one.

And that night I read *The Two Dead Girls*, "part one of what would become the six-part serial novel, *The Green Mile*. Holy crap. I had in my hands one of only a few copies of this manuscript in existence. Tell no one, indeed!

That next morning the entire plan was revealed to the staff, with Elaine and, at her side, me, spreading the incredible news. I was suddenly part of a new team, now invited to all the high-level meetings with sales, publicity, marketing, as well as King's representatives. (Read the fascinating introduction to the Scribner hardcover edition written by the late Ralph Vicinanza.)

Time for our first launch meeting to feature *The Green Mile* at the top of the leader list. As per usual, Elaine was scheduled to present *The Green Mile* herself, but that morning she asked me to join her at the head of the conference table. All eyes fell on us as Elaine explained to the whole company that I was to be the contact person for any in-house questions,

2000s

Sept 25, 2002
Jacob Burns Film Center
Pleasantville, New York
From a Buick 8

and then I would filter them through to her for appropriate guidance.

To say that this was a feather in my career cap was another understatement. The idea, we said to the rapt room, was that Signet would publish the book in six volumes, short "chapbooks" starting in March and ending in August. One each month for six months. Price: $2.99 each.

There was a lot of skepticism from several executives. Bookstores buyers would object to having to take display cases and floor space away from our competitors. Would consumers shell out a total of $18 for what was considered a mass market paperback?

But those were other people's problems. Executives had to make those decisions.

I had my own duties to attend to, and it would be much more creative than balancing budgets. Because not only were my initials listed on all in-house paperwork for this project (it read EK/JP), but another new task also found its way to me.

Elaine said, as before with the backlist project, I would be writing the cover copy for each of those books. Gulp (or was that six gulps?). Now that was a lot of pressure, high-profile at the highest level. But I loved writing cover descriptions; I do it today for my own books! The catch? Only one person had approval on those words I would write.

Golly, I wonder who.

Alas, the answer will have to wait, as this wouldn't be a true tale about *The Green Mile* if it ended after one part. Guess, constant readers, you'll have to wait for the next chapter to come forth from Pittman's Hands.

DIARY EIGHT: *The Green Mile Trilogy, Part Two*

The serial thriller continues…

Actually, the first line of copy I wrote for the serialized novel, *The Green Mile*, was "The serial thriller begins….". It's there on the front cover of part one. Not the most original copy line ever written, but it said all that was required.

The Two Dead Girls was published on March 28, 1996, and our little $2.99 book shot to #1 on the *New York Times* bestseller list immediately. The buzzy excitement was palpable in the Signet offices. I was thrilled, because I had the first #1 of my editorial career.

But there was much work to be done. Month by month, King would submit the next part, and of course that set off the never-ending carousel of our publishing into faster rotation. The drill was the same: read it overnight, discuss cover concepts, present at launch meetings. I did all that—and then there was the copy.

Yup, *The Mouse on the Mile* was on schedule for an April publication. We had decided the front cover line starting with the second volume would be "the serial thriller continues," all the way until the final book, which fittingly read, "the serial thriller concludes."

Nothing had concluded on my end. Holed up in my office, I crafted not just the words used on the back covers, but came up with an entire "look." That same uniform approach where the length and style of each book matched what I'd used previously, worked perfectly with this series. One paragraph described the plot of the particular volume, another paragraph summarized the series concept–the latter text used for all six books.

Like I was working in an old-style newsroom, the fresh kid with his first article, I'd run my finished copy down the hall and drop it into Elaine's in-box. Then the copy would go through a series of approvals, including agents, King's Viking editor down the hall, and of course, to the author himself. My approach and

LinkedIn

Sept 29, 2002
Borders Books
Ann Arbor, Michigan
From a Buick 8

writing were all given the green mile…I mean, the green light.

So, part two was published, and again, became an immediate #1 smash bestseller. And we noticed a funny phenomenon. Not only was part one still on the list, but its ranking also grew higher. Hmm, something big was brewing. We'd captured the zeitgeist. Readers wanted more.

And more was coming, each and every month. Going to work—ha, if that 16-year-old boy still living inside me could call it that—was fun, exciting; opportunity was knock, knock, knocking at the door. Nope, no tommyknockers here. I was gaining a name for myself in the world of New York City's big publishing world.

Then came volume three, *Coffee's Hands*, then part four, *The Bad Death of Eduard Delacroix*, (I checked the proper spelling on Eduard more times than I could count—Eduard, not Edward), and then *Night Journey*, part five. Same release, same success, #1 from the moment each volume was published. And all of them still riding high on the Times bestseller list—simultaneously.

Of course, it wasn't just *The Green Mile* story that had its twists and turns. A monkey's paw of a wrench was about to be thrown into our well-oiled machine. Along with maybe a bit of industry backlash.

Wait, what's this? A cliffhanger…

DIARY NINE: *The Green Mile Trilogy, Part Three*

The serial thriller concludes…

By this point in our story, the publication of each volume of *The Green Mile* is a huge, unqualified success. The first five titles have dominated the Times bestseller list. Taking up five of the allotted fifteen slots on the printed list. You can imagine how angry the other mass market publishers like Bantam, Ballantine, and Pocket were reacting. Little room for their big authors to make the list. Many bookstores discounted books based on what books cracked that Top 15, which of course drove up sales.

Industry backlash had begun, with the primary concern being: was each volume its own "book" or should they be considered one entity, one novel? An interesting dilemma, but not one solved by the time August arrived, and with it, the release date of part six, *Coffey on the Mile*.

The other publishers would have to wait, since there was another issue facing us in-house at NAL/Signet. The manuscript for the final volume had been delivered, and it was longer than the previous five. Which meant we had to reconfigure the costs. Not that I was witness to much of these discussions, but the basic problem was the profit and loss statement didn't work with the usual price of $2.99. We'd have to raise the price by a dollar.

Like I said, lots of discussions happened behind closed doors, way above my pay grade. Would we look like we were price gauging the consumer? Demanding more money from them after already investing so much money on the first five volumes? But the decision was made, and we stuck to it: *Coffey on the Mile* would be priced at $3.99.

Booksellers might have objected, but consumers didn't. *Coffey on the Mile* debuted at #1 on bestseller lists across the country. And I like to think that it's a testament to just how GOOD the story was; it delivered on every page, every cliffhanger. Readers needed to know how it all ended. Our hope was that the past six months, as crazy and frenetic and stressful

2000s

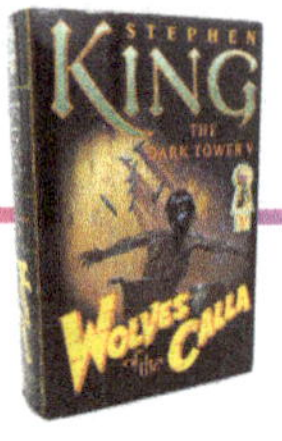

Oct 30, 2003
Jacob Burns Film Center
Pleasantville, New York
Dark Tower V: Wolves of the Calla

as it was, they were all needful things to endure in achieving our goal.

A rare and unmatched publishing event, *The Green Mile* was both a cautionary tale in fiction and reality. Mimicry is the sincerest form of flattery goes that old saying. News came of other authors writing their own serial novels, notably fellow-horror writer John Saul with his *The Blackstone Chronicles*, and less successfully, Jackie Collins' four-part glitzy tale, *L.A. Connections*. By then, a new rule had been instituted by the *Times*: all multi-volume serials would be considered one book.

The publication success of *The Green Mile* would go unmatched. It would produce an Oscar-nominated movie starring Tom Hanks, and a year later, NAL would publish, even though I'd heard it wouldn't happen, a first-ever all-in-one trade paperback edition. A few years later, Scribner, King's new publisher, would release a hardcover edition.

One last item remained, a crowning achievement for an already king-sized venture: *The Green Mile* would go on to receive Best Novel at that year's Bram Stoker Awards, presented by the Horror Writers Association at their annual dinner. While King wasn't present, I was there along with my boss, Elaine. I even found a photo from that night in my files.

And so, at last, we come to the end of this journey. I'm exhausted all over again just thinking of those crazy six months, but also thankful for the experience. I appreciate you all for indulging me while I spread this story out over three diary entries. Being a part of *The Green Mile* remains the most rewarding and unpredictable time of my career; I also thank Mr. Jingles for help in stirring up these bite-sized memories!

There's more to come: My dark half has something to say about pseudonyms.

DIARY TEN: *By Any Other Name*

It's Joseph, I'm back with another diary, and this time I've brought along a friend of mine. His name is Adam. See, I'd like to discuss, in stark terms, the concept of the pseudonym.

I'll explain about Adam a bit later. Right now, my old friend Claudia Inez would like me to, at last, talk about her husband, a guy by the name of Richard Bachman. No rage, please, while we take this long walk on a stretch of pavement that requires roadwork. It made the running man thinner. Had enough?

I would first encounter the name Richard Bachman when *Thinner* was published in an NAL Books hardcover, back in 1985. I bought it for the same reason most people did: because there were rumors abounding that it was actually written by Stephen King. Did NAL publish him as well? Sneaky guy!

The truth was out, only to discover it wasn't King's first book to be published under that name. There were four earlier books, paperback originals released by Signet. Sneaky publisher!

My friend Marijane up in Manlius still owned the used bookstore, and on a visit to the store I scoured the shelves for any sign of Richard Bachman titles. As luck would have it, I found two of them, and I still own them today. I'd looked for and never would find the other two, not at the then cover-price of $2.50.

But wait, NAL had a golden opportunity here; this was long before I graced the hallways of this publisher. They could reintroduce the four books as having been written by Stephen King, and that's just what they did. A 4-in-1 volume known forever as *The Bachman Books* arrived on bookshelves, published

Sept 20, 2004
Just Books, Too
Greenwich, Connecticut
The Dark Tower 7

Oct 23, 2004
Fenway Park
Boston, Massachusetts
"We Mainers Believe" Banner

simultaneously in hardcover and trade paperback editions. A bonus came with it in the form of an introduction by King—"Why I Was Bachman."

So thankfully I don't have to explain why here. He already took care of that. Nice guy!

Okay, now we jump ahead a few years. *The Bachman Books* omnibus was eventually released in mass market paperback, and *Thinner*, too, though that cover stated "Stephen King writing as Richard Bachman." All that readers were lacking were individual mass market paperback editions of the originals under the King writing as Bachman byline. We'd have to wait a bit, and even then, they came with a caveat.

Bachman grew quiet after that period, and rumor had it that he had passed away. At some point, though, found in an old trunk was a manuscript. Maybe Claudia was going through some of her husband's things and stumbled upon it. It was decided that Richard Bachman's last-known novel would see the light, to be shared with the reading public. It was called *The Regulators*, a book that had some odd similarities to the new novel Stephen King had just delivered. Sneaky Bachman!

A plea of desperation came from the sales department, suggesting that both King's and Bachman's publishers' team up and publish them at the same time. And thus began a tale of two books that would forever be linked, by covers, by characters, by a singular person given two voices. We'll discuss what happened, appropriately, in the next of this two-part diary.

Looks like I'll be on vacation, so perhaps I'll let my friend Adam Carpenter write that next one. He'll explain the double joy of having a pseudonym. Sneaky writer!

DIARY ELEVEN: *By Any Other, Other, Name*

Joseph is away, so allow me to introduce myself. I'm Adam. Wait, who, you ask? I'm Adam Carpenter, and I happen to be Joseph's

pseudonym. I'm the author of many books, but best-known (by some) for the eight books (and two novellas) in The Jimmy McSwain Files, a gay private detective series. Joseph has asked me to finish his piece about Richard Bachman.

It's kinda fun being a figment of an author's imagination. You can write what you want without "hurting" the host's reputation. Gives you freedom to say things somewhat differently. But it can also come with its share of handicaps.

In the case of Stephen King, as I've heard it, conventional publishing in the late 70s and early 80s dictated a "one book per year" mantra, otherwise you might scare your audience by flooding the market. I thought Stephen King was all about scaring his audience. Well, with such thinking, Richard Bachman was born. Five books until King and Bachman were outed.

So now we jump to that rediscovered manuscript mentioned in the previous diary. That of *The Regulators*. Dutton, the hardcover imprint of New American Library, would release the book at the same time Viking would publish the hardcover of *Desperation*. A new King, and a reintroduction of Bachman. I was part of the team.

The plan first came to me in the fall of 1996. My boss brought me into her office, as she liked to do, and told me what was

2000s

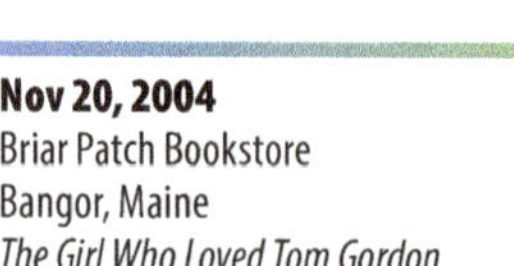

Nov 20, 2004
Briar Patch Bookstore
Bangor, Maine
The Girl Who Loved Tom Gordon

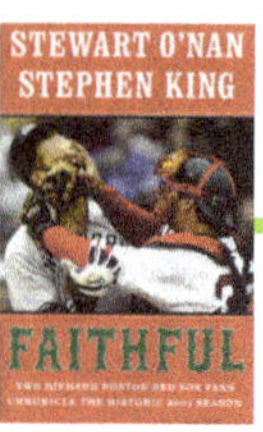

going on, and that I would be overseeing the production schedule for *The Regulators*, while King's Viking editor would handle the same duties for *Desperation*. Her office was down the hall, so coordinating our efforts was seamless.

I left Elaine's office with the manuscripts for each book. Time to get reading. Of course, the inner kid in me was thrilled to be given such early access to a writer who had influenced me so strongly. I think I let this feeling cloud my professional judgment. See, somewhere along the way I made a serious gaffe.

The incident happened at a marketing meeting, and we were trying to figure out how to ensure the general public knew of the connection between the two books. I blurted out something about how, as a fan, I'd buy both books. Empty faces stared back at me. After the meeting I was called back into the boss's office and given a lecture. No fanboys were welcome here. It's still hard to relive that moment, easier to write it as Adam. My head back on straight, I forged ahead. Both books were published and became bestsellers, though the King outsold Bachman title. Even with the cool cover art that, put together, completed the cool illustration, the dual identity was confusing to some consumers. If the same person wrote both books, why two names?

Then it came time to plan for the paperbacks. Signet would release them both, so the duties toward publication fell under my purview. Still on the copy assignment, I devised an idea where the back cover for each would closely match the other, in tone, style, and design. Clever review quotes pointed out the connection even more clearly than could the hardcover artwork. At the same time, the four-volume edition of *The Bachman Books* was reissued with a NEW intro by King—"The Importance of Being Bachman." Another way to help explain pseudonyms.

Anyway, both paperbacks of *Desperation* and *The Regulators* were bestsellers when they were released, with a bit more recognition then for Richard Bachman. But paperback was always more his style anyway, it's where he got his start, on the spinning racks in truck stops and drug stores. In the end, the publishing of these two titles was fun and challenging, momentarily humiliating, and ultimately a successful publishing "experiment," akin, almost, to that of *The Green Mile*.

My final experience with Richard Bachman came a couple years later, when the powers that be (no doubt with King's permission) decided to release three of the four original Bachman titles at last under the "Stephen King writing as Richard Bachman" banner in mass market paperback. The titles were added to the schedule, and the editor listed on the production schedule for these three publications—yup, the initials JP. (I'll explain that development later.) We would release *The Long Walk*, *Roadwork*, and *The Running Man*, in April, June, and August respectively of 1999. The covers and descriptive copy would follow the same pattern as all the other King reissues I'd worked on several years ago.

It's funny, I began writing this entry as Adam, but quickly fell back into Joseph's style. They are my memories, after all. But I think that only illustrates my point of how another voice, another name, can change you and free you and open your creativity to new levels. It keeps us all on our toes.

Short commercial here, if you don't mind. I'm presently writing a novel in which Adam's Jimmy McSwain detective co-stars with my own Todd Gleason con-man character. The two of them representing two opposing sides of the same coin. Perhaps somewhere along the way we've both been inspired by the genius work of two other one-person authors. Did I say that right? Did we?

June 24, 2005
Maple Street School
Manchester, Vermont
Lisey's Story

DIARY TWELVE: *Ghostly, Shadowy, Floating*

No discussion of Stephen King is complete without mentioning his influence on, and vice versa, a writer by the name of Peter Straub. I've got a few stories about Straub that interconnect with my job working with Stephen King, and some that don't.

But Straub deserves his own entry here, so please bear with me.

It was at college, and, as an avid reader and newfound collector of hardcovers, that I found this deal I couldn't resist—6 books for $1. The advertisement was right there in the middle of that week's *TV Guide*. Of course, I'm talking about those famed book clubs, The Literary Guild and Doubleday Book Club. I joined and received my six books. No King titles, alas, as his books were exclusive then to the Book-of-the-Month Club, a rival book club. But they did have this other horror author whom I'd yet to read. His latest novel was the Featured Selection of the Month. *Floating Dragon* by Peter Straub.

I read it, and I'll admit it was a tough read for my developing mind. Much more cerebral, less in-your-face than, say, *Cujo*. But I loved his writing and wanted to find more of his books. *Ghost Story* came next, which I still consider my favorite of his. For some reason, I never got around to reading *Shadowland* back then, though I did read several of the earlier books. And then went a long stretch when I didn't read Straub, mostly because Straub hadn't published in a while. With one exception.

The Talisman, the brilliant, epic collaboration between Stephen King and Peter Straub, which I read over Christmas the year it came out. I remembered devouring the fantastical story of Jack Sawyer and Wolf, trying to depict which author wrote which parts, and failing at that. I had to reread just to enjoy it for what it was. Don't be an editor all the time!

It's now 1992 and I'm working as an Editorial Assistant at Bantam Books. The mystery editor there had a project tailor-made for a young editor such as me. The plan was to reissue all the classic "Nero Wolfe" mysteries by Rex Stout, with modern covers as an attempt to reintroduce this great crime writer to a new audience. The whole project was dumped in my lap, but eager to learn and make a name for myself in the crime fiction world, I came up with the idea of having a different author write an introduction to one of the Nero Wolfe books; their choice which one. I wrote to several bestselling authors, and everyone agreed—they were big fans. I got Koontz, DeMille, Robert B. Parker. And Peter Straub, among many others.

I'll admit to a bit of trickery in my query letter. I signed it as "Assistant Editor" instead of with my unimpressive title of "Editorial Assistant." I promoted myself to sound more legitimate in the eyes of these BOLD-FACED authors. And of course, I got busted. But the tactic worked, because I got the new title, scoring big points for being so aggressive in going after such big names.

Sorry, couldn't resist telling that story. So, yes, Straub agreed, but it turned out that by the time he'd committed to it, my last day at Bantam arrived (that's another tale for another time) but I had to get his contract signed. I did what any shameless almost-an-editor does: I called him and completed the deal. He couldn't have been lovelier.

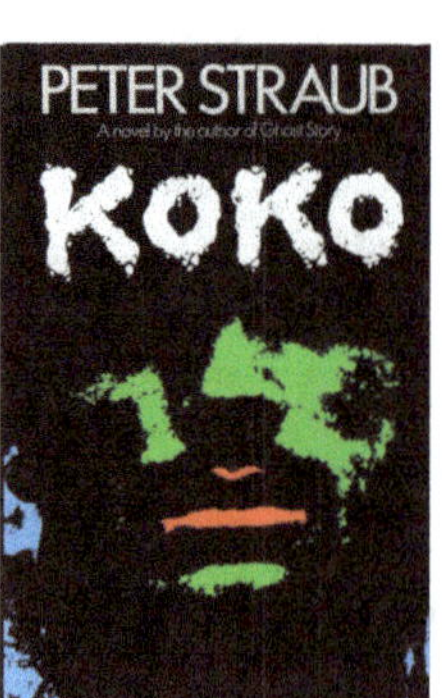

During my time at Bantam, Straub had returned to print with his first book in over six years. *Koko* and soon after that came, *Mystery* (my second favorite), both published by Dutton, the hardcover division of NAL. A few months after I left Bantam is when I joined New American Library and who had a new book coming out?

2000s

Sept 24, 2005
Barnes & Noble
New York, New York
Lisey's Story
New Yorker Festival

YouTube

Peter Straub, with *The Throat*, while Signet released the paperbacks of those other two books in the so-called "Blue Rose" trilogy.

There we all were, happy under one publishing roof. King, Straub and...Pittman? At the 1996 Bram Stoker Awards, I would finally get to meet Straub, as we were sitting at the same table. It was the year *The Green Mile* won for Best Novel. (And in a stroke of good luck, Owl Goingback, another author I was editing, won Best First Novel for *Crota*.)

My final Peter Straub story comes in 2010. I was working at a Broadway show as an usher (which I'd done for years) called *The Norman Conquests*, by British playwright Alyn Ayckbourn; the show was actually three separate plays, and on Saturdays the cast would perform all for a day-long marathon. Who comes to the aisle I'm working? Peter Straub. And what book do I oddly have hiding in my Playbill bin? At last, I was reading *Shadowland*.

I re-introduced myself, showed him the book and he, with a laugh, signed it right there.

Class act, Mr. Straub.

DIARY THIRTEEN: *Little Known Bentley*

It's a revelation if you get the joke in that title. That line was a hint, too, of who we're discussing now. A writer named Bentley Little.

I'll tie-in him to Stephen King soon.

I'm at work, it's just a typical late afternoon of my boss coming to my office with a thick pile of paper in her hands. What manuscript awaited me for my nighttime reading? Whenever she did this, she'd want a report on it by the next morning. An author I'd never heard of, Bentley Little, and his horror novel, *University*. By now at Signet, I'd become the "horror" editor, as I worked with people like Douglas Borton/Brian Harper/Michael Prescott, Owl Goingback, and Michael Slade.

I enjoyed *University*. Bentley Little had a unique, fresh, no-nonsense writing style, and the plot certainly wasn't lacking in horrific moments. I recommended we acquire and publish the book, and that's when I learned this submission came with a bit of bad blood. Great. Signet had, published Bentley's first novel, *The Mailman* a few years ago, and though it got nice reviews the sales weren't as hoped. A second novel was published, but under a pseudonym.

Signet was getting a second (third?) chance here. I had a good rapport with the agent, and maybe a fresh editorial eye, an enthusiastic one, would help get the sales department to ignore the previous sales record. Oh, and one other important detail was shared with me: Stephen King was a fan of Bentley Little's work. (See, I told you I'd work him at some point.) We agreed on a two-book deal.

King provided a new quote for *University*, but it turned out to be usable for all of them we'd publish: "Absolutely the best...a master of the macabre!" And we were off and running.

I'd end up working with Bentley on maybe ten of his books, among them, *The Store*, *The Town*, *The House*, *The Ignored* (my personal favorite), and *The Town*. While his titles seemed unimaginative, fear not or be fearful, he more than made up for originality for what happened on the pages. What wild, fun, unique and creative stories. King was right. A master.

Two instances come to mind when thinking about King and Little. An odd oxymoron of names, huh? The first involves, unfortunately, the car accident. I remember being on vacation (in Alaska, as if I couldn't be further away and still be in the States) when I received a call

Feb 1, 2006
Florida State University
Tallahassee, Florida
Cell

from my boss. There was a little tidbit in the news article, a small detail about the accident. Seemed King had, while walking along the side of the road, a paperback book with him. It was a Bentley Little title; which one, I now can't recall. Based on the year, I'd guess *The Town*. Anyway, lurid as it was, bookstores were clamoring for copies. "Who is Bentley Little?" was the question of the day, and the company needed my input…all the way from a whale-watching boat-ride off Seward, AK. We had to reprint; Bentley Little got a nice sales increase. People are curious creatures.

Which leads me to a fun story—I saved the best for nearly the last. Bentley had turned in his latest novel; I'm guessing this was 1999. A book called *The Walking*. I thought it was his best work to date. He'd raised the bar on his own intuitive talent. I convinced my boss, Signet's new publisher, that we had to finally give this author a major push. *The Walking* was elevated to our lead position for January of 2000, but it came with a caveat. Could we secure a new quote from King to justify our faith in this author?

I sent the galley proof to King's office, hoping for the best.

One morning my phone rang, my assistant picks it up and says, "Joe Pittman's office." A slight pause, and then she was standing in my doorway, rather than using the intercom. "Uh, Joe, Steve King is on the line?" My heart beating, I picked up the receiver and with a savviness that belied the truth, said, "Hi, Steve." Niceties were exchanged, and then he asked me if Signet was really going to give Bentley a big push. I said, "that's the plan." Good, got a piece of paper and a pen? Even better, I had my computer. I cradled the phone, and then King proceeded to dictate the quote to me right over the phone. Niceties completed, the call ended. By the time I looked up, half of the editorial department was jumbled up against my office door.

That was a good day. Because I'd done as my publisher asked: I got the quote.

Class Act, Mr. King. Uh, Steve.

DIARY FOURTEEN: *The Dark Tower Rises Again*

Argument: Like many of Stephen King fans, sometimes we readers felt like Roland of Gilead ourselves, setting out on our own quests, because we too were searching for the next, ongoing installment in the *The Dark Tower* series. The publication history of this series is complicated, between limited editions, trade paperbacks, mass markets, hardcovers, small presses and major houses, this twenty-plus journey was filled with starts and stops and finally, a finale.

I had my own experience with *The Dark Tower*, both personally and professionally.

In an earlier entry, I detailed how I got my hands on a pre-publication copy of *The Gunslinger* while working at Viking/Penguin. After that, a friend gave me as a birthday present the Donald E. Grant hardcover of *The Drawing of the Three*, and then I would buy the NAL trade paperback. Did-a-chick, Dum-a-chum, anyone? I think it's my favorite of the series. When interviewing for the job at NAL, I was by chance reading *The Waste Lands*, and was able to produce the mass market edition from out of my bag to impress the lady that was interviewing me.

Good timing!

Now we come to *Wizard and Glass*, the long-awaited fourth volume in the series. This came during the waning days of my working on King's books, which I'll get to in a moment. For now, I was given a copy of the manuscript, and sure, I'd read King's unpublished works before, but this time was different. Elaine asked for my

2000s

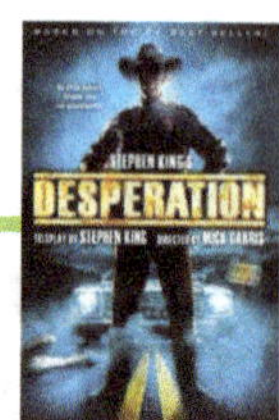

editorial input on the novel. Gulp. Stephen King was asking for my opinion. Well, yes, and well, sort of no. My comments weren't the only set of notes being presented to King, but I know he read mine because he thanked me for my specific and thoughtful comments.

I was fascinated by the connection King was making between *The Dark Tower* and the devastated world in *The Stand*. It's always fun when an author begins to meld his different worlds into one big universe. I've been guilty, happily, of doing that with many of my books; perhaps King was more than a reading experience for me, but an educational tool on how to be not only a writer, but an author. Thinking of the fans and anticipating their reaction when a familiar friend popped up unexpectedly.

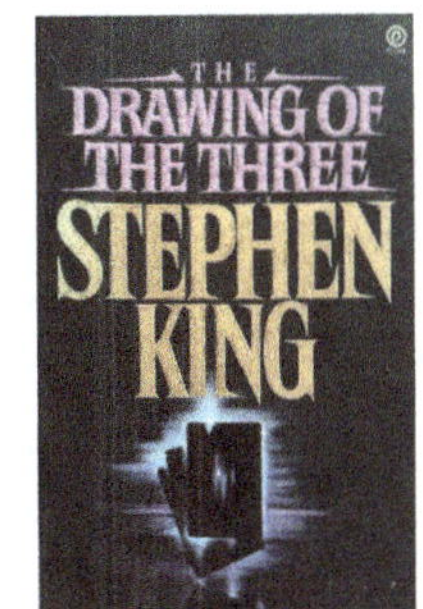

Even when that "friend" is Randall Flagg.

Publication for *Wizard and Glass* was planned for November of 1997, and along with its "First Time in Print" status, we were also going to repackage the first three volumes with covers to match the new title. Those were the beautiful, colorful covers with artwork by John Jude Palencar (except for #1, which used the original *Gunslinger* art from Michael Whelan). Each book also featured the full-color illustrations from the previous editions; different artists contributed to them. *Wizard and Glass* would have never-before-seen illustrations.

Then, as the books made their way through the production process, it was my job to once again write the back cover copy for them, and, like the reissue program and *The Green Mile* covers, I was tasked with coming up with a uniform style. A paragraph describing the book, one to sum up the series concept, and of course, a copy line.

If you have those editions in your collections, that's my writing on the back covers, with the final tagline, "Join the quest for the elusive Dark Tower."

Again, nothing fancy was required. Just a quick, easy-to-digest hook to entice readers.

Wizard and Glass would be the last of *The Dark Tower* series to be published by NAL/Signet, and it would make the last original title of Stephen King's books that I was involved with. The fifth through the seventh, as well as the stand-alone entry, *The Wind Through the Keyhole*, would be published by Scribner. (More on that twist of fate in the concluding diary.)

A new millennium was approaching. I could feel a shift in the night.

DIARY FIFTEEN: *Taking My Bag of Bones*

It's just after sunset as I write this, the final entry in my diaries. It's been an amazing trip down memory lane for me, and I hope, for you, constant readers, it's been a fulfilling journey. August is here, again, which makes me realize it's been 43 years since Stephen King entered my life. His stories have thrilled me, entertained me, scared me of course but mostly kept me smiling. With the publication of each new book, I find myself returning to that innocent age, that same porch, that same crackling fire where wonderment and fear somehow became the norm.

I remember a lot since then.

I remember reading *Carrie* while at college, on a Sunday light at my library work-study job. With that cool, double step-back cover with the flames. I still have it.

I remember finally reading *Salem's Lot*, on an airplane headed to a business trip.

I remember scaring the hell out of the girls in my dorm, knowing they were watching the movie of *The Shining*. Skulking down the hall, I rapped on their closed door, then hid behind a corner when they answered. They waited, went back to the movie, but left the door open. Still, I

Oct 24, 2006
Peter Jay Sharpe Theater
New York, New York
Lisey's Story

knocked once more. This time I pounced while they approached, yelling "Redrum" repeatedly, and they all screamed. College fun.

Speaking of *The Shining*, I remember being invited to a private day-long screening of the TV mini-series for that book, with Stephen King in attendance. It wasn't the final cut, since the CGI hadn't been added yet. Still, there was enough of a creep factor involved knowing I was in the audience with the mind that created this unforgettable tale.

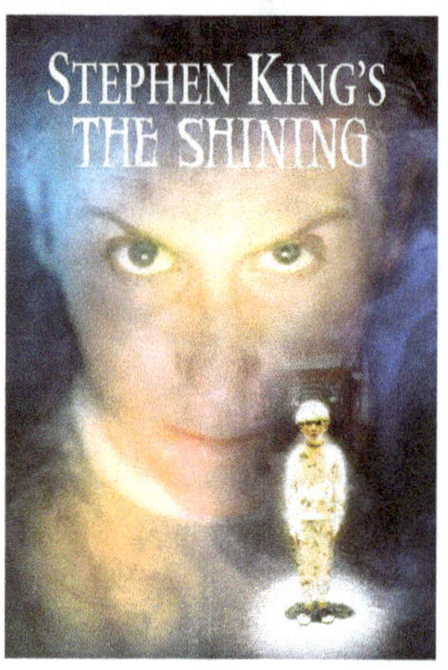

Elaine saying to King, "You remember Joe."

He did indeed, shook my hand and welcomed me.

I remember the bittersweet parts. When Putnam and Penguin merged companies and far too many staff changes occurred, including the departure of my #1 champion, Elaine Koster, president, and publisher of NAL. I knew nothing would be the same after that. The company was in negotiations with King on his next contract, all while I was busy reading the manuscript of what was intended to be the first book of that contract: *Bag of Bones*.

That would become the first book published by Scribner.

It was the end of an era at Signet Books, and a shift in my mood at the company. There were still a lot of books to acquire and edit, but management had changed and the demands were different, and I lost a couple of my other "big-name" authors to rival publishers. The magic of those days of "The Green Mile" had gone, dissipated, a waft of air leaving our Soho office for the congestion of midtown and the Simon & Schuster building.

What had once been a division named Dutton/Signet, a companion to Viking/Penguin, the new team from Putnam made some adjustments to the editorial vision of those names. Dutton and its trade paperback imprint, Plume, would have its own set of editors, and the more "commercially minded" editors (read: paperbacks, as if that was a judgment) would concentrate, be assigned, to the newly reinstalled name of NAL, New American Library, and all its imprints: Signet, Onyx, Roc, and a couple lesser known names. Hell, I was proud to be a Signet editor—now a senior editor. Paperbacks are in my blood, and if it bleeds, you know it's real.

Two years later, in August of 2000 (there's that month again), I gave notice at NAL—my choice, as I was ready to move on to new adventures myself. I'd gotten my first book contract, and who was the agent who sold that book? Elaine Koster.

Tilting at Windmills was the novel, and again, there was Elaine once again at the forefront of my publishing career, albeit in a new capacity.

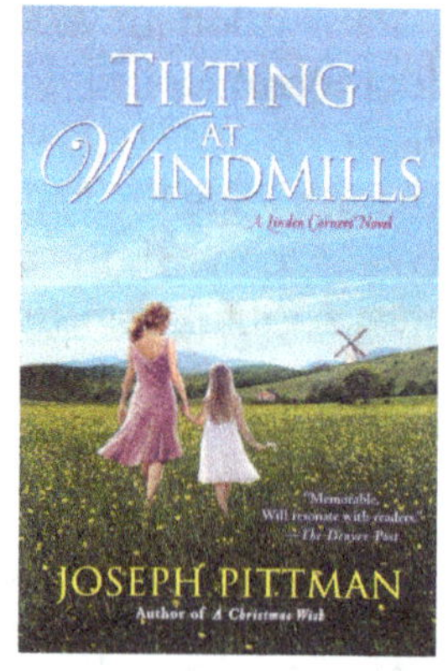

Once again, irony reared its clever head: my book was acquired by Pocket Books, which is a division of Simon & Schuster. Yup, I was going uptown, too!

I continue to read Stephen King, adding to my collection with each hardcover release. I finished reading *You Like It Darker* while writing these diaries. Funny, when I received the book in the mail, I already knew to fear that cover.

2000s

Oct 30, 2006
City Arts & Lectures-Herbst Theater
San Francisco, California
Lisey's Story

Nov 1, 2006
S. Mark Taper Foundation Auditorium
Seattle, Washington
Lisey's Story
Traded bought books for signed books

I just don't like alligators. But admitting such a thing led me to the 19th Edition Facebook group, to these diaries, where I served up a behind-the-scenes glimpse of what I was lucky enough to experience, and to still cherish. I've learned a lot about publishing. Books come, they go, they go out of print, they get reissued and given new covers and new life. Books are constant, no matter the author, no matter the genre. But when it's someone as influential, as unique and special as Stephen King, you realize that a book, any book, is a friend forever.

Alas, that time is fast approaching when I must bring these diaries to a close, and along the way thank you all for indulging me. It's now four past midnight as I type these final words, clouds are swirling, and a thunderstorm looms in the dark sky. A fitting ending, allowing me to fade into the mist. As Stephen King himself says, Everything's Eventual.

Joseph Pittman at home, in front of the many Stephen King titles he worked on at King's New York publishing houses.

Nov 2, 2006
Arlene Schnitzer Concert Hall
Portland, Oregon
Lisey's Story
Presigned books

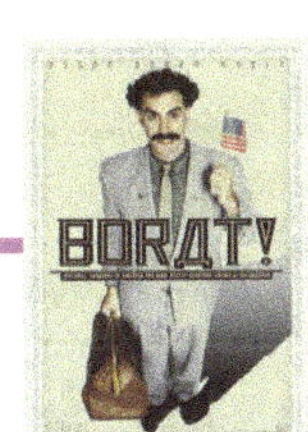

Nov 3, 2006
Fine Arts Theater
Los Angeles, California
Lisey's Story

EXTREME KING

Diana Petroff

Noah Mitchell

FIRESTARTER

2000s

Nov 7, 2006
Border's Books
London, England
Lisey's Story

Nov 8, 2006
Middle Temple Hall
London, England
Lisey's Story
Lisey Gala Event - Invite Only

1980 was a banner year for Stephen King.

Two fan-favorite stories were published that year: "The Mist" and *Firestarter.* "The Mist" is a novella that King wrote for his agent, Kirby McCauley, who was editing an anthology. What began as a short story ended up as a 100-page novella and was published in *Dark Forces*. It was subsequently collected in *Skeleton Crew* in 1985, and went on to become a box office sensation in Frank Darabont's film adaptation in 2007.

However, your Extreme King columnists are not here today to discuss "The Mist," but to share with our fellow Constant Readers a look at the making of King's first signed limited edition: Firestarter, which was released by Phantasia Press prior to the trade edition from Viking.

Included this year are contributions from Alex Berman, Phantasia's publisher, Michael Whelan, the dust jacket artist, and Bob Jackson, world-renowned collector and the custodian of the original *Firestarter* painting.

We thank all of them for their time and energy in helping us to have a look behind the curtain. – Diana Petroff & Noah Mitchell

FROM ALEX BERMAN, FOUNDING PARTNER OF PHANTASIA PRESS:

By 1979, Phantasia had published mostly reprints of some classic Science Fiction and

fantasy. That was what other specialty publishers in the genre had been doing. In particular Donald Grant, had been producing beautiful books by classic authors like Robert E. Howard.

By that time, there were other small presses also publishing older material. Most of it was difficult to find in either pulp magazines or paperbacks and was indeed worthy of a deluxe treatment.

I felt that, rather than follow the herd, Phantasia Press would try something different. As collectors, we sought out FIRST EDITIONS, whether they were hardcovers or paperbacks. Of course, the major authors of the time were always the most collectible and many first editions were quite expensive, even then.

So, having a collector's perspective, I began looking at future titles which were to be published by the majors. Of course, I was mostly interested in the most popular authors of the day.

I had been scheduled to go to New York on SFWA business (I was their first attorney) and scheduled appointments with the subsidiary rights directors of a handful of publishers. I already knew which titles and authors I would ask about. I really had no idea how my proposal, to publish signed/limited/deluxe editions of highly-anticipated books, would be received.

I was, of course, familiar with the Limited Editions Club, the Folio Society, and others. But they were not particularly interested in Science Fiction (except maybe Ray Bradbury.)

I recall that my first two meetings were with Holt, Rhinehart, Winston and Viking Press. I was pleasantly surprised when the sub rights people were receptive to my proposals. They had been used to selling paperback and foreign rights. This was new to them, and provided another source of income. I also stressed that the authors would be thrilled to see their works in beautiful editions.

My first meeting with Holt resulted in agreements to publish Jack Williamson's *Humanoid Touch* and Larry Niven's *Ringworld Engineers*. I was thrilled. Both were sequels to extremely popular novels.... But, I knew that to be really desirable to collectors, our editions had to be published before the trade editions.

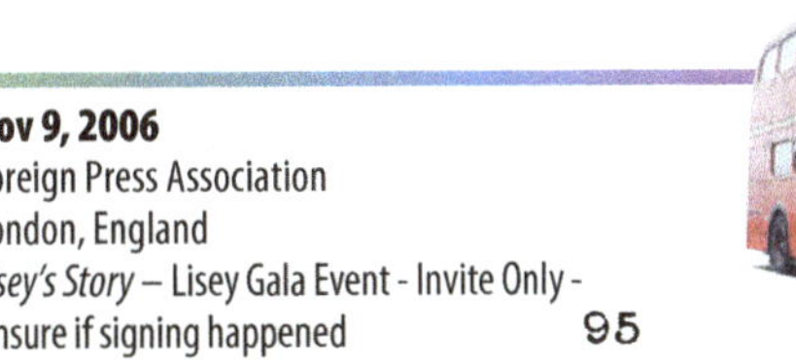

Nov 9, 2006
Foreign Press Association
London, England
Lisey's Story – Lisey Gala Event - Invite Only - Unsure if signing happened

Thus, our titles would be the true first editions. Surprisingly, the publishers were ok with Phantasia Press publishing first.

So, the contracts, which I prepared, stipulated that our editions had to be published first...After making deals with Holt for the Williamson and Niven, I received a letter from the Viking Press sub rights director, with a list of forthcoming titles.

I was a little reluctant to make more deals, since we were already committed to publishing five or six titles. But one author on the list caught my eye: Stephen King. I was a fan of his books at that time, having read everything he had published. But it was mostly horror with science fiction aspects. Also, he was a fairly new author without a track record as being "collectible."

I asked for an advance copy of *Firestarter*. It was a photocopy of a typescript with hand corrections throughout. Sadly, I no longer have it. Or just can't find it. Anyway, when I read it, there was enough of a Science Fiction element to be a proper Phantasia Press title.

The deal had to be approved by Stephen King first, but his agent , Kirby McCauley, contacted me quite promptly and advised that Mr. King would be thrilled to have a signed limited deluxe edition of one of his books....Again, Viking had no problem allowing our edition to be published first. And they agreed to print a statement on their copyright page indicating that our limited edition was the true first edition. How many copies to print? As the time for production got closer, we realized that SK was in fact becoming a collectible author, in addition to being a number one best-seller.

So, we took a chance and decided on an edition of 725 numbered copies. We announced the book, once it was at the printer, to those collectors on our mailing list. And orders were mailed to us. No internet in 1980. And we would not accept verbal orders. So, the checks began to arrive. By the time those on our mailing list made their purchases, we had sold around 400 copies.

Our next step was to offer copies to book dealers and specialty bookstores at a discount (20% off for 5 or more copies). The books were priced at $35, which at that time was expensive for a hardcover book. I believe we sold another 200 or so copies to the dealers. The remaining copies we schlepped to conventions.

Finally, at the 1980 WorldCon in Boston, I believe we sold the remaining copies. We sold quite a few at that convention. Finally, we sold out. Phew.

We had only done one of our books in a lettered state by that time (*Ringworld Engineers*) and had decided to be selective on the books which would have a lettered edition--bound in genuine leather.

We felt that *Firestarter* warranted the lettered treatment, but what design? We had always considered that leather-bound editions were the best choice. I had recalled that one of the most valuable books published in the early 1950s, and much sought after, was a small signed edition of *Fahrenheit 451* from Ballentine. They were, however, bound in a raw asbestos material which could be used in binding. This was, of course, before the significant danger of asbestos inhalation was known to the public. Through the years the binding began to flake and turn to dust. This was the most serious risk from asbestos: to breathe in this dust. The technical term was "friable."

I had a copy myself and had to keep it in a plastic baggie. Not very attractive on the shelf. I mentioned this book to our bookbinder, Jon Buller, stating that it was too bad that all forms of asbestos were too dangerous to use with our edition. Coincidentally, Jon had just read of a new aluminum-coated asbestos material. Since the asbestos was basically trapped behind the aluminum, this material would be completely safe. Jon checked further and found that this material was available in the thickness which could be used on a book. Thus, the asbestos edition was born.

These books cost around $80 each to produce.

2000s

Nov 10, 2006
Tesco's at Lakeside Thurrock, England
Lisey's Story

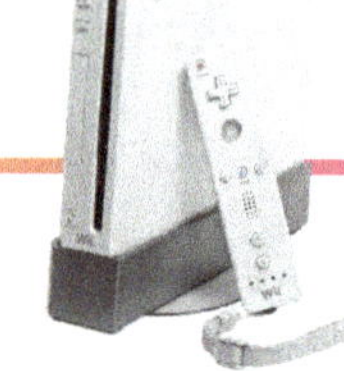

With a copy going to Stephen King and a few copies for me and Sid, we had to set a price of $100. Probably the most expensive science fiction book at that time.

As a result of the cost and the fact that many collectors were put off by the use of asbestos, I had a difficult time selling the 19 or 20 copies which were made available. Ultimately, I traded two of my copies for other books and now own only one copy ("A," of course.) Eventually, we did sell all the copies, without a discount. It didn't take long for the price to skyrocket, as Stephen King became a very collectible author.

We didn't make any money on the two states of our limited edition of *Firestarter*, but the chance to work with Stephen King and to produce a seminal collectible edition was well worth it.

The Signature Pages: Four Dates - The story of the infamous "dating" of *Firestarter*

Of the 49 books Phantasia published, only Stephen King decided, on his own, to date each page he signed. It took him four days to sign 725 copies. I'm sure he never considered the ramifications of dating the books. I didn't even discover the different dates until several days later, when I began receiving letters and phone calls (this is before the internet) asking for pre-ordered copies to be exchanged for earlier dates. I was confused since I had only looked at a few of the lower numbered copies, which were all dated July 5th, 1980......What a mess...... Mr. King had inadvertently created 4 additional states of Firestarter in addition to the Asbestos lettered edition.

Most copies (but not all) had been pre-ordered and shipped out the same day we picked them up from the printer (we had to make sure our edition was released before the Viking trade edition.) The copies were allocated based on the date of the order....So those who purchased the book earlier received the lower numbers and the earliest date.....It was impossible to exchange books with later dates, since by that time they had all been sent out.....Of course, the most avid collectors wanted the earliest date, or a copy with each date. This created some complaints, but I had no idea until it was too late. I doubt if Stephen King realized the problem he created, since this was his first limited, signed book. In 1979, when I made the deal with his agent, he was not yet a known COLLECTIBLE author, although his books were already best-sellers.

According to Berman, King numbered and lettered each copy of the book himself when he signed the tipsheets. King had no influence in his choice of artist, Michael Whelan. Berman selected Whelan personally, and *Firestarter* was Whelan's first King jacket. King was so pleased with the cover painting that he insisted Whelan do the "Dark Tower" series for Donald Grant.

This first edition of *Firestarter* by Stephen King is limited to seven hundred twenty-five copies, all of which have been signed and numbered by the author.

This is copy 7

Stephen King
July 5, 1980.

Numbered copies were signed July 5 to July 8, 1980

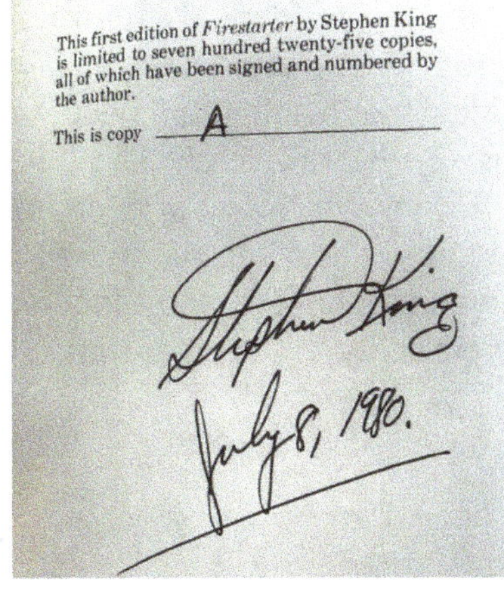

This first edition of *Firestarter* by Stephen King is limited to seven hundred twenty-five copies, all of which have been signed and numbered by the author.

This is copy A

Stephen King
July 8, 1980.

All the lettered copies were signed on July 8, 1980

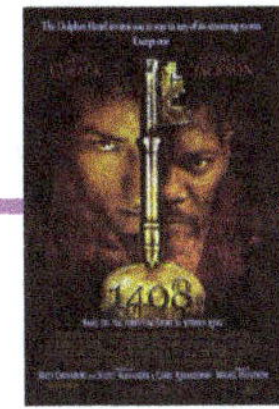

Aug 14, 2007
Dymocks
Alice Springs, Australia
Lisey's Story

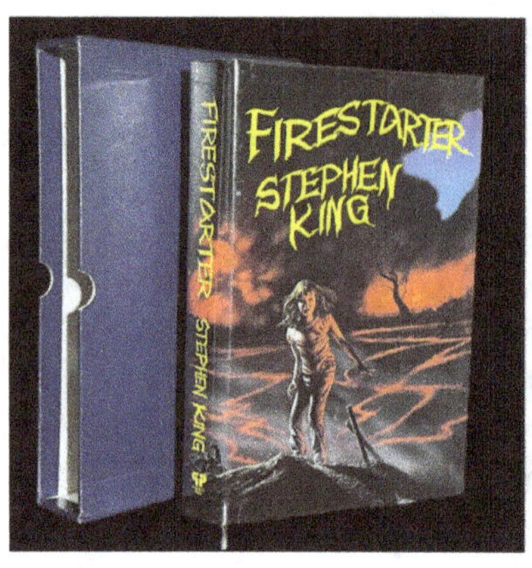

About Alex Berman:

A pioneer of the modern small press movement, Alex Berman was one of the first to start producing editions that were both signed, limited editions and true first editions for top-tier science fiction authors of his time.

From 1978 to 1989 Phantasia Press published 49 novels. Many of its offerings were true first editions; others, the first hardcover editions of works previously published in paperback. In 2023, Phantasia Press returned to the publishing world, with their fiftieth release, *Mickey7*, and Alex has resumed his position at the helm of the press that he started more than forty years ago.

He states: "I am an attorney by trade and [prior to establishing Phantasia], I met Jack Williamson, whom I had read and admired for a long time. We started up a friendship. He was then the president of a fairly new organization, the Science Fiction Writers of America. He asked me to help them become established as a 501(c)3 and to officially become their attorney, which also opened up a lot of new doors. George R.R. Martin was the treasurer at the time, I believe, and a lot of great authors were active in the organization."

The First Edition Designation:

Viking published the first TRADE edition of *Firestarter* in the US, but the Phantasia Press limited edition was issued several months earlier, making it the true first edition. Here are the original proofs or "mock-ups" that Viking used for their first printing. What is missing is the numbering indicating the printing number. Phantasia had to send it back to Viking so they could correct the spelling of "Phantasia." Fortunately, this was accomplished in time.

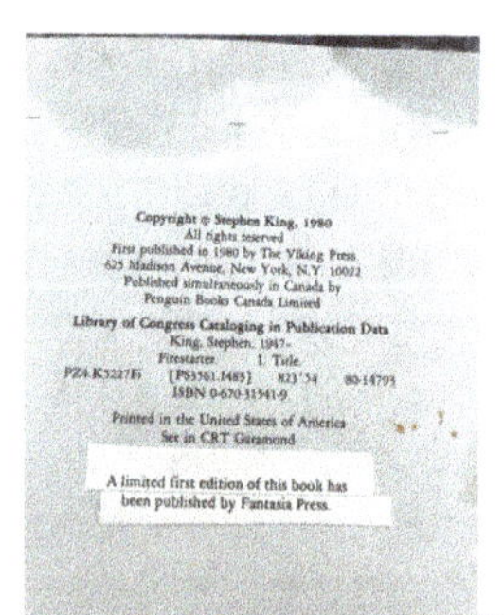

Copyright © Stephen King, 1980
All rights reserved
First published in 1980 by The Viking Press
625 Madison Avenue, New York, N.Y. 10022
Published simultaneously in Canada by
Penguin Books Canada Limited

Library of Congress Cataloging in Publication Data
King, Stephen, 1947-
Firestarter. I. Title.
PZ4.K5227Fi [PS3561.I483] 823'.54 80-14793
ISBN 0-670-31541-9

Printed in the United States of America
Set in CRT Garamond

A limited first edition of this book has
been published by Fantasia Press.

Copyright © Stephen King, 1980
All rights reserved
First published in 1980 by The Viking Press
625 Madison Avenue, New York, N.Y. 10022
Published simultaneously in Canada by
Penguin Books Canada Limited

Library of Congress Cataloging in Publication Data
King, Stephen, 1947-
Firestarter. I. Title.
PZ4.K5227Fi [PS3561.I483] 823'.54 80-14793
ISBN 0-670-31541-9

Printed in the United States of America
Set in CRT Garamond

A limited first edition of this book has
been published by Phantasia Press.

The Viking US first trade edition

April 4, 2008
Folger Theatre
Washington D.C.

Original advertising flyer, Product invoice and packing slip from the printer:

I just ran across a copy of Phantasia's original flyer for *Firestarter* Notice the projected publication date for *Firestarter*: Late July, 1980.

The Viking publication date was September 29, 1980....

In addition, here is the original packing slip from the printer. Plus, a recently discovered original order.

FIRESTARTER
by Stephen King

As announced earlier, Stephen King's new novel, FIRESTARTER, will be published by Phantasia Press in a limited FIRST EDITION, by special arrangement with the Viking Press.

This edition is limited to 725 copies, all of which will be numbered and signed by the author and slip-cased. The full-color wrap-around dust jacket will be by renowned fantasy artist Michael Whelan.

This deluxe edition is now at the printer and will be ready in late July, 1980.

All books will be shipped immediately upon publication. Since these limited editions normally sell out by the time of publication we request that payment accompany all orders. A 20% discount will be given for orders of 5 or more copies. Please add $1.00 if insurance or U.P.S. delivery is desired. Enclose a SASE if confirmation of order or inquiry is sought. If you would like to be assured of receiving a copy, we would suggest that you place your order promptly, as the edition is more than half sold out.

FIRESTARTER by Stephen King
Special signed & numbered 1st edition .... price $35.00

PHANTASIA PRESS

EDWARDS BROTHERS — PACKING SLIP

Phantasia Press

Firestarter

40 Cartons

STEPHEN KING's RESPONSE TO RECEIVING THE LETTERED *FIRESTARTER*:

This is a portion of a letter from Stephen King, after he received a copy of the asbestos *Firestarter*:

Dear Alex,

Thank you very much for the aluminum-coated, asbestos-bound version of FIRESTARTER. It was a truely wonderful surprise, and instead of shelving it with the other books, I've stuck it on top of the breakfront (I think that's what you call those pieces of furniture you put dishes in) in the dining room so people have to look at it. I was even tempted to stick it in the oven and turn the dial to 452^{0} F. just to see what would happen, but it's too nice a book to risk in any way. So...thanks again for your kindness and your thoughtfulness.

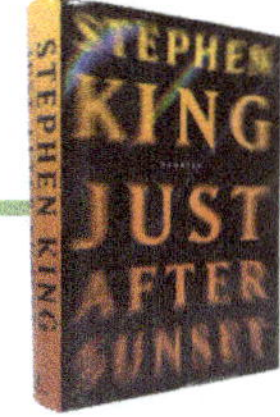

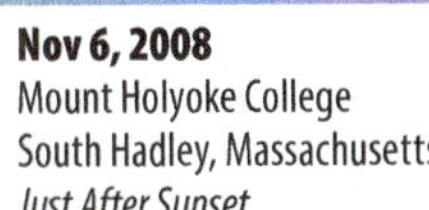

Nov 6, 2008
Mount Holyoke College
South Hadley, Massachusetts
Just After Sunset

INTERVIEW WITH MICHAEL WHELAN, ARTIST OF THE *FIRESTARTER* PAINTING:

First and foremost, thank you, Michael, for taking time out of your busy schedule to talk with us at Extreme King about the creation of the iconic cover painting for *Firestarter*'s limited edition from Phantasia Press.

EK: Firestarter was your first Stephen King title to illustrate. How did you get involved? What was it about the story that intrigued you?

MW: It was a long time ago. I'm a little fuzzy on the sequence of events, because it happened so long ago. I knew King was a popular writer, and I'd heard that the protagonist was a little girl, so it seemed like an attractive assignment to me– being the new father of a little girl myself. I hadn't read much of King's writing at that point. Reading the story, I was extremely pleased with it and eager to do an illustration for *Firestarter*. It was terrific, still one of my top five favorite King novels to date.

Your cover scene for *Firestarter* is a virtual wasteland with Charlie in the foreground. I love this image and it encapsulates what she can do in this story. What was the impetus, the seed, to create this particular image?

Well, the scene in the book where Charlie destroys The Shop installation, obviously. Ordinarily I avoid featuring scenes from the climax of a book but King's writing was so evocative that I felt "Yes, this has to be it!" I decided to use the black clouds of smoke as a device to conceal much of the background so one couldn't tell exactly where or when in the story the scene takes place.

Did you have other images in mind before you created the final cover art?

Probably, though to be honest I don't remember thinking of anything other than what I painted for the cover. That scene was imprinted in my brain—I just had to recreate it in paint. There wasn't any second guessing on that one!

After producing artwork for so many areas of fiction, film, and music such as H.P. Lovecraft, Isaac Asimov, Arthur C. Clarke, Meat Loaf, and The Jacksons how does this work stack up against working on Stephen King novels *Firestarter*, and later *The Dark Tower: The Gunslinger* and *The Dark Tower*?

Well, they're all different experiences so it's difficult to compare them in any meaningful way. Each company has its own personalities and way they like to do things, and people they want to appeal to, so things can be quite varied even among the editors in one publishing company, for example.

With book covers, usually I'll read the story and as the movie of the book plays in my head I'll stop and make note of passages that seem particularly compelling or descriptive. At the end of the book, I'll go back through my notes and sketches and try to winnow them down to the selections that seem best. Then preliminary

2000s

concepts are shown to an art director, one is chosen, and it's off to the races.

With other media (such as music album covers), there's a lot of back-and-forth; everyone from the musicians, their various agents and lawyers, the art department people at the label, the label's marketing team, etc., all have something to say about the content. As you can imagine, it's not much fun compared to doing book covers, where I'm almost always granted a much greater degree of freedom. When I was young and fantasizing about being an illustrator, all I wanted to do was book and magazine covers in the F/SF genre, and that has changed little in the past 50 years now. I love devoting most of my time to my gallery work, but my first love was always in the realm of publishing.

Each assignment is different. I let my impression of the source material determine what materials I'll use to create the image for it. I can't explain how that works, as it is a subjective instinct that I try to avoid analyzing. Generally, I'd rather just go with the flow and hope my instincts about it are correct.

Fantasy presents such an infinite realm of possibilities, how can one approach serve all the variables one might encounter? My attitude is to let the book or music speak to me and hope that an appropriate response will yield the best result.

I suppose the primary difference is in the amount of "input" I get from the authors. Most of the music albums I've done were virtually dictated to me by the artists, so I felt I had little control or independence in the resulting image.

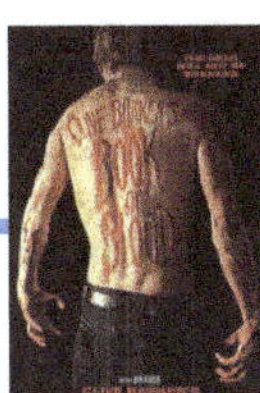

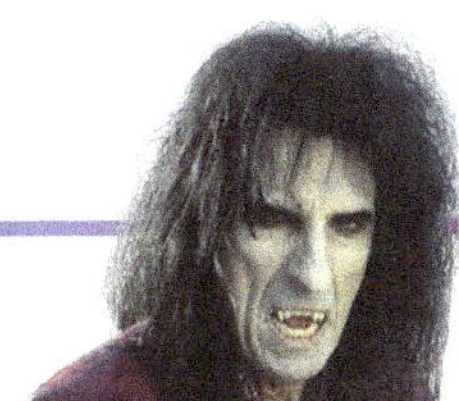

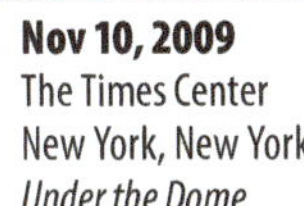

Nov 10, 2009
The Times Center
New York, New York
Under the Dome

Nov 11, 2009
Walmart
Dundalk, Maryland
Under the Dome

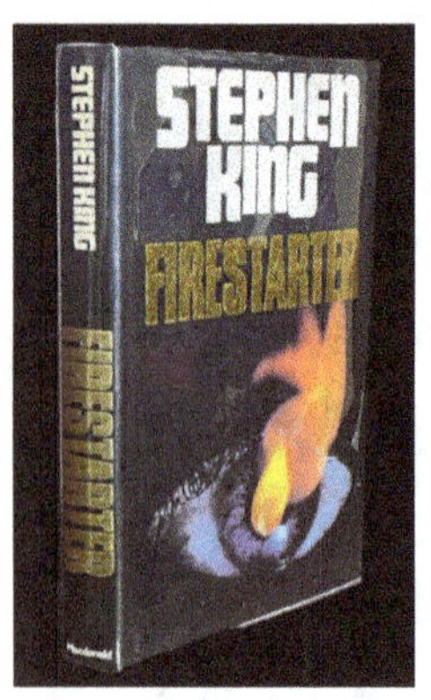

Firestarter was first published in the UK in September 1980 by Macdonald. The initial print run is estimated to be approximately 2,000 copies, a small fraction of the 100,000 copies published in the US.

UK First Edition

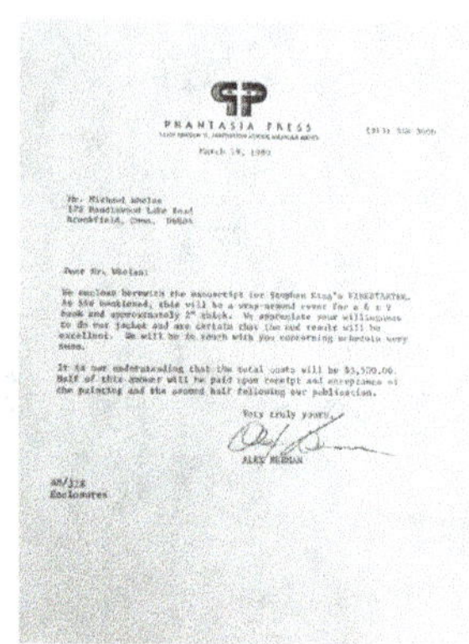

PHANTASIA PRESS

Dear Mr. Whelan:

Very truly yours,

ALEX BERMAN

Enclosures

My work for publishers is different; I'm allowed much more free rein to do what I feel is best. Not always, though! But getting back to *FIRESTARTER*, I was encouraged to do whatever I thought would work best, and they gave me total freedom. That's one of the most attractive aspects motivating me to accept the assignment in the first place.

This was your first time working with Phantasia Press and Stephen King. How much input did they have in the work?

I was encouraged to do whatever I thought would work best, and they gave me the freedom to do what I thought would work the best. That's one of the most attractive aspects motivating me to accept the assignment in the first place.

Let's talk about the creative process. When you accept a commission for a novel, what goes through your mind as you read the work?

Visualizing the story and discerning the main themes of the book.

Do you start with sketches and work with the publisher through the stages of its creation?

For book covers, usually I'll read the story and as the movie of the book plays in my head I'll stop and make note of passages that seem particularly compelling or descriptive. At the end of the book I'll go back through my notes and sketches and try to winnow them down to the selections that seem best. Concepts are done, in whatever media feels right to me at the time. One is selected and I then begin work on the final image.

A little about the specifics of the painting itself, what is the medium and the size of this piece? How long was the production period?

I don't remember. Acrylics on masonite, I believe. It was 44 years ago!

Did you choose the cover text design?

No. I want nothing to do with the type design. I leave that up to the publisher.

You recently remarqued 120 original dust jackets with 3 variants. They are extremely popular, and many collectors have had them framed and are proudly displaying them in their homes. Each style is unique in color inks used and number of sketches; what was the idea behind the 3 different styles?

The idea was to have fun with it! There were different images because I would have been bored with the project otherwise. I was thinking "What would I want to have on my own copy of the dust jacket?"

Tell us about how it felt returning to *Firestarter* after 40 years and working with Phantasia Press.

I still love the book, which I still regard as one of King's best…and I wish I had kept the painting for myself. It remains one of my faves. I'm very glad so many people liked it.

2000s

Nov 13, 2009
Barnes & Noble
Atlanta, Georgia
Under the Dome

Nov 16, 2009
Van Wezel Performing Arts Theater
Sarasota, Florida
Under the Dome

About the Artist Michael Whelan:

Michael Whelan is one of the world's premier painters of imaginative realism.

For more than 40 years he has created book and album covers for authors and musicians like Isaac Asimov, Stephen King, Ray Bradbury, Brandon Sanderson, the Jacksons, and Meat Loaf. His clients have included every major U.S. book publisher, the National Geographic Society, CBS Records, and the Franklin Mint.

Whelan became known for his dedication to bringing an author's words to life and his covers dominated the science fiction and fantasy field throughout the 1980's and 90's. He was largely responsible for the realistic style of genre covers of that era, and his stunning color and composition have influenced many artists to this day. He continues to do cover art for bestselling authors.

As the most honored artist in Science Fiction, Michael has won 15 Hugo Awards, 3 World Fantasy Awards, and 13 Chesleys from the Association of Science Fiction and Fantasy Artists. *Locus Magazine* named him Best Professional Artist 31 times, and the Spectrum Annual of the Best in Contemporary Fantastic Art named him a Grand Master in 2004. Other awards include a Gold Medal from the Society of Illustrators, a Vargas Award, a Grumbacher Gold Medal, and the Solstice Award from the Science Fiction Writers of America.

In 2009, he was inducted into the Science Fiction Hall of Fame in Seattle, the first living artist to be named to the distinguished list that features such luminaries as H.G. Wells, Steven Spielberg, Rod Serling, and Ursula K. Le Guin.

FROM THE CURRENT OWNER OF THE ORIGINAL *FIRESTARTER* PAINITNG, BOB JACKSON:

By the time I started collecting Stephen King books, around 1982, I was already behind. There was no internet back then and I was feeding my growing compulsion by reading the classified ads in *AB Bookman's Weekly* and *The Comics Buyer' Guide* and by haunting used books stores in the Seattle Tacoma area. I had lucked into my first Stephen King specialty press book (The Gunslinger) at Golden Age Collectibles in Pike Place Market in Seattle and immediately fell in love with the full color illustrations by Michael Whelan.

Through my reading I discovered that a specialty press (Phantasia Press) had earlier published a signed and limited edition of *Firestarter* and I further found that a bookstore in Los Angeles called The Book Sail had some copies. As I was about to travel through the area, I called and reserved a copy for the then high price of $175. When I got the book and took it out of the slipcase, I saw for the first time the dust jacket and the wonderful artwork by "that same guy that did *The Gunslinger* illustrations!" I was thrilled with my purchase.

Fast forward to an evening in 1999 when I again found myself in The Book Sail with three other collectors and the owner, John McLaughlin, for an evening by appointment

Nov 18, 2009
Fitzgerald Theater
St. Paul, Minnesota
Under the Dome

Nov 19, 2009
Canon Theatre
Toronto, Ontario
Under the Dome
Appeared with Cronenberg; no autographs

only store opening. In a dark corner of the store, I saw Michael Whelan's original painting for the *Firestarter* dust jacket. It was just laying against a wall in the dark collecting dust with some other less interesting artwork. I didn't feel that I could afford something like that at the time and was actually interested in some other items that were for sale so I didn't inquire too much about it but I remember thinking that I would treat that painting much better if I owned it.

Fast forward again to 2014. John McLaughlin had sadly passed away and a lot of his store inventory was being auctioned at Heritage Auctions. I was looking through the catalog and there it was again.....Whelan's *Firestarter*.... the painting I had adored for ages. The opening bid was high but not too high and I was shocked when the painting only got one bid. It has been hanging in my house ever since. I look at it every day and realize I'm very lucky to be able to do so.

About Bob Jackson:

My collecting started innocently enough as I'm sure many others did. I fell in love with Stephen King's writing by reading paperback books. At some point I decided I wanted to get "hardback" editions of all those stories I had grown to love. This naturally led to the discovery of first editions and limited editions. One thing led to another and I soon found myself searching for and buying magazines and journals that had the first appearances of King's short stories and nonfiction articles. Things were easier and, in my opinion, more enjoyable in the earlier pre-internet years of my collecting. At that time, I was one of just a small handful of serious collectors who had established relationships with most of the well-known sellers. Business was done with little more than a phone call when a prime collectible became available and snail mail catalogs were the main staple. Manuscripts, letters, and original artwork came next when my collection of the books seemed completed. Things have changed quite a bit since I started collecting but the thing that hasn't changed is my passion for continuing to add prime items to my collection. On the days when a King book with 100 signed copies goes on sale and tens of thousands of King collectors worldwide cause the website to crash you can be sure I am right there with you and just as frustrated as you probably are. Over the years I have seen many collectors come and go. For many it seems they lose interest after a year or two of heavy collecting. I have often wondered why my interest in collecting Stephen King's writing has lasted over 40 years. I can't explain why, but I consider it a blessing that I found something that has given me such great pleasure and introduced me to so many like-minded collectors and sellers that I now call my friends.

2000s

Dec 1, 2009
The Music Hall
Portsmounth, New Hampshire
Under the Dome

Dec 2, 2009
Northshire Book Store
Manchester, Vermont
Under the Dome

Sleeping Beauties

by **Hank Wagner**

Sleeping Beauties, by Stephen King and Owen King, Scribner, 2017

Sleeping Beauties, Issues 1 through 10, IDW, June 2020 through March 2022, adapted by Rio Youers, Alison Sampson, Triona Farrell, Christa Miesner, edited by Elizabeth Brei

Sleeping Beauties Vol. 1 and Vol. 2, IDW, 2021 and 2022

Sleeping Beauties, Deluxe HC, IDW, 2024

So, let's talk first about *Sleeping Beauties*, the novel. Therein, Stephen and Owen King collaborate to tell the story of the coming of the Aurora virus, a sleeping sickness that strikes every woman on the planet. Besides putting them into a deep sleep, the sickness also causes them to be enveloped in a dense, cocoon like web. But, don't try waking them by cutting into the cocoon, as what emerges is not a beautiful butterfly, or moth, but rather a murderous female, hellbent on eliminating whoever or whatever has woken her from her slumber.

Hardly the plot line of a fairy tale (actually, though…), where true love's kiss awakens a sleeping damsel, and her suitor is capable of turning that damsel from a commoner into a princess, or even a queen, and everyone, to coin a phrase, lives happily ever after. No, what's playing out here was dictated eons ago, when the world was young: even though they don't know it, every man on earth is being judged by an entity as old as time, who has left the ultimate decision to the women in their lives. What's at stake? Literally everything, as the women have an option to move on from their men, and inhabit a brave new world where they control their own destinies, and survive by their own talent and wit.

This drama plays out in the small town of Dooling, focusing on the marriage of Lila and Clint Norcross; Lila is Dooling's Chief of Police, and Clint is a psychologist who works at the women's prison located just outside of town. While the novel sports a large supporting cast, these two are the focal point, designated by the literal powers that be to represent their town; their town, in turn, is a stand in for the entire planet.

The powers that be take the form of one Evie Black, whose origins are never explained, only hinted at. Is she literally Eve? Lilith? Mother Nature? Mother Earth? Gaea? We're never told, explicitly. She's an enigma, a polarizing entity with great power, whose visit to Earth, and Dooling in particular, instigate a crisis. She's the heart and soul of this book, a character for the ages.

And, the ultimate decision? I'll let you read the novel for that. But I'd say that it truly could have gone either way, a tribute to the authors. I'm sure the audience's expectations were equally divided; that the decision went the way it did could be considered obvious from one perspective, and outrageous from another, equally legitimate perspective.

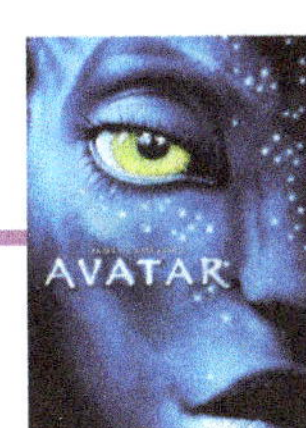

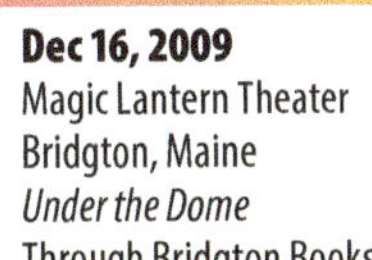

Dec 16, 2009
Magic Lantern Theater
Bridgton, Maine
Under the Dome
Through Bridgton Books

Sleeping Beauties is the product of two minds, a collaboration between Stephen King and his youngest child, Owen King. The blended voice felt close to vintage Stephen King, a plus; I felt I could see a difference only when it came to more modern references and slang, which I assume came from Owen. To this constant reader (I've been reading SK since 1978, my first year in college), it felt like it borrowed heavily from the elder King's prior works, chiefly *The Stand*, *Needful Things*, and *Under the Dome*, in that it dealt with an overwhelming global pandemic (in 2017, no less, several years before Covid), and the effects of said crisis on a small, all too American town. I don't know that I can say the root cause of the crisis was supernatural, as primal forces are at work, forces that might have been responsible for creating the world in the first place. The book's chief distinction is that it has much to say about the male/female dynamic, delving deeply into the mysteries, romance, and underlying tensions of those relationships.

As in any King novel, the characters (several of whom seem to enjoy a one-to-one correspondence with characters from *The Stand*) are what drive the action of the novel; ordinary folks, facing outsized dilemmas, doing the best they can under the circumstances. There are SO many characters, in fact, that the authors include a three-page list of players, divided between the citizens of Dooling and the denizens of the Dooling Correctional Facility for Women. Chief protagonists Lila and Clint Norcross are especially compelling and relatable; you'd like to get to know them even better than you do during the course of the novel. As I said, Evie Black is an enigmatic antagonist, charming, knowing, otherworldly, appearing to be about thirty or so. She is a Deus Ex Machina in the flesh, more like Q of *Star Trek* fame than a "capital G" God. She is both the problem and solution, judge and jury.

I believe IDW originally intended to publish the comic book adaptation as a monthly book, to unfurl over a two-year period, but eventually settled on making it a ten-issue offering. That's a lot to pack into roughly 220 pages of storytelling, but adaptor Rio Youers did an admirable job in paring the book down to its essentials, preserving critical character beats, and trimming nonessential asides and back story. Doing so, he honors the work of the Messrs. King, even as he moderately improves on it. Alison Sampson's art is simply stellar; once I accepted her visualization of Evie (I think it likely that every reader has their own unique idea of what she looks like), it was full speed ahead for me. I think readers will especially enjoy her rendering of the more fantastic elements of the novel, especially her depiction of Evie's home base. Triona Tree Farrell's Colors and Christa Miesner's Design and Lettering combine to

Feb 20, 2010
Cultural Center of Charlotte County
Port Charlotte, Florida
Under the Dome
Free talk with signed books for sale at event

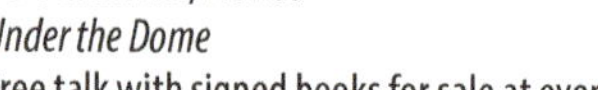

enhance the storytelling and the illustrations, with one notable exception, detailed below. I also enjoyed seeing the variant cover art being presented at the back of each issue, with each interpretation heightening the overall positive experience.

The original issuance in single issue form was marred by a spotty production schedule, probably due to Covid. The first four issues appeared monthly, starting in June 2020. Issues five and six appeared bimonthly. Seven months went by before issues six and seven, with the final three being published bimonthly. The original publication also featured jarring, nontraditional word balloons; instead of black letters on a white background, they sported white letters on a black background. Many found this juxtaposition disconcerting and hard to adjust to, this reader included.

The odd publication schedule became moot once the books were published in trade paperback format, initially in a two-volume set, each containing five issues. This problem was further ameliorated with the recent publication of a single volume Deluxe hardcover. The most recent publication also addressed the odd word balloon configuration of the original issues, opting for a more traditional black letters on a white background format, making it considerably less irritating to traditional comic book aficionados.

The Deluxe *Sleeping Beauties* also contains art, character studies, and breakdowns, plus commentary from Simpson, and also from Christa Miesner. I always enjoy creator commentary—having insight into "how the sausage is made" is always fascinating. That said, I would have loved to see a spread detailing the progression from original script to final pages, to see what alchemy took place between writer and artist.

Overall, I'd give the source novel a solid B; it's a good, strong read, worth your time and attention. I give the most recent comic adaptation a B+, as I found it to be a respectful and canny presentation and condensation of the original story. As a man, my intuition tells me that no one is going to fall asleep while reading this thrilling interpretation.

Dec 2, 2010
RiverRun Bookstore
Portsmouth, New Hampshire
Full Dark No Stars

I Nodded Off, During The *Insomnia* Tour

by ***Dave Hinchberger***

Stephen king took a tour of ten bookstores across the country… on his Harley-Davidson (his Hog). He not only used it to promote his new book, *Insomnia*, but to have instores only at independent bookstores. Stephen King does not like to fly. So, he decided to ride his Harley across the US to attend all the signings.

He had Bob Daitz, the tour manager for the 1993 Rock Bottom Remainders tour, follow him in a van along the way. Steve got to know him well on that RBR tour, and here was a sure way to stay safe for his 4,300-mile ride. Stephen King has had many ideas for promoting his books. This was such a cool idea he getting to ride his "hog" and parking, loudly, in front of every store.

Yeah, it doesn't get much cooler than that. He wore the requisite black leather jacket to boot!

With the announcement of the tour, I got in touch with the closest bookstore appearance to me, Davis-Kidd Booksellers, and I was able to order four tickets, which arrived promptly in the mail the next week. These were physically large tickets. I had never seen tickets this size.

So, me and my fellow passengers got together at my house, as I was driving all of us. It's four hours to Nashville, so it's a day long affair. And we got together early to prepare. As it turns out, I'm glad we didn't get on the road… there's a story, folks.

Early morning of the instore, I was on the internet, reading some posts ... back then, the internet was very basic. It was just scrolling through text, and emails (no images, no video) and I was part of a few Stephen king groups where you could check in and read what was going on with fellow King fans. I noticed they mentioned something about an instore, how the crowd had waited outside, and that King had pulled up to the store in his loud Harley. He was very nice, signed books. They were all so happy... they even had a special reading for a select group of winners, as he read by candlelight (see the story on this reading in the calendar section)… and… they mentioned… Nashville.

Wait... *what*?

I was in kind of an unbelievable panic... What store are they talking about? I saw Nashville mentioned, but that's tonight! I must have misunderstood. I went and pulled out the tickets...

And there it was... in black and white. The instore had been last night!

Sept 23, 2011
GMU Concert Hall
Fairfax, Virginia
Open signing

Nov 7, 2011
Columbia Point
Boston, Massachusetts
11/22/63

Nov 10, 2011
The Majestic Theatre
Dallas, Texas
11/22/63

Somehow, somehow… I had written the date down wrong on my calendar. I was in disbelief. I don't do things like that. I have schedules and people to meet, kids to take events too. I was bummed, it was an unfortunate thing, but now that thing included three other people in this adventure.

ADMIT ONE
INSOMNIA
TOUR
STEPHEN
KING
IN NASHVILLE
WAR MEMORIAL
AUDITORIUM
TUESDAY, OCTOBER 11
8:00 PM-Doors Open At 7:00
Davis-Kidd
Booksellers
4007 Hillsboro Road · 385-2645

When all the fellas showed up, I spilled the beans and told them about my screw up. I was probably the biggest Stephen king fan there, but I could see they were disappointed. I promptly took them to a restaurant and told them "they could order anything they wanted". We had a couple of beers and laughing it all off. They

were gracious and understanding. Those are the moments, with good friends, you never forget.

So yeah, I fell asleep somewhere, somehow. I was off by a day.

I gave everybody their ticket, and as I was a bookstore, I also gave them a copy of *Insomnia*. It was the least I could do.

But now… now I know what happened. Now…for the rest of the story. It's 30 years after that instore and I discovered what happened while researching for this piece. When I originally discovered the dates for this tour, it was listed from an official publicity list. It has Nashville down as October 12th. The ticket showed the correct date … but it was the 11th.

I had already noted this in my calendar and didn't think another thing about it. So there, at least I know what happened, mystery is solved, and as I learned back then, *always* look at your ticket details.

So, as you can see in this article, there's a copy of the ticket. I finally got to use it somewhere! If you order the limited set of this annual, I had it reproduced as one of twelve tickets from Stephen King's appearances through the decades.

Nov 11, 2011
A Real Bookstore
Fairview, Texas
11/22/63

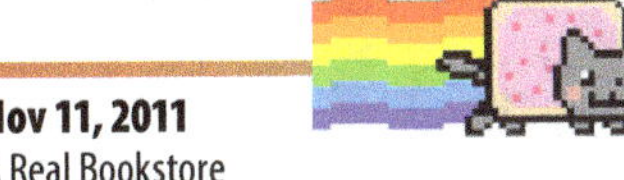

Nov 12, 2011
Octavia Books
New Orleans, Louisiana
11/22/63

Mike Flanagan Shows Us the Way Back to *The Dark Tower*

by ***L.L. Soares***

Mike Flanagan is a busy guy. Not only did he recently wrap up the film adaptation of Stephen King's *The Life of Chuck*, he also has the rights to King's "The Dark Tower" series, which he plans to turn into a continuing series, and maybe a movie as well. Lately, he's become the go-to guy for King adaptations.

Stephen King and Mike Flanigan 2019 Interview

Oh, and he was recently tapped to write and direct the next movie in *The Exorcist* franchise, as well. Where does he find the time?

I had seen some of his earlier films, *Absentia* (2011), *Oculus* (2013), and *Before I Wake* (2016), but didn't realize at the time that Flanagan had directed them all. The one that first left a big impression on me was *Hush* (2016), with his real-life partner, Kate Siegel, starring as a deaf and mute woman staying in a house in the middle of nowhere, who is terrorized by a creepy dude in a mask (John Gallagher, Jr.). The thing is, Siegel's character Maddie isn't a victim. She fights back with all she has, despite her disabilities. And it was this determination, and the way the movie built up its suspense and dread, that stayed with me.

The first time he adapted a King story was 2017's *Gerald's Game*, based on a book that was considered difficult to film, and yet Flanagan was able to pull it off brilliantly. Anyone reading a book called *The Stephen King Annual* is going to know all about this one already, but it revolves around a couple that is trying to spice up their love life. They rent a cabin in the woods, make sure that no one is going to bother them, and then get into some BDSM hi-jinks. But the wife, Jessie, played by the always reliable Carla Gugino, has misgivings when she is handcuffed to the bed, with real police handcuffs (she had thought he would get "velvet or fluffy ones"). She changes her mind, but her husband, Gerald (Bruce Greenwood), gets angry and refuses to release her. Then, while they're arguing about it, Gerald has a heart attack and keels over.

Without access to her phone (she can't reach it), or any way to get out of her predicament, Jessie slowly begins to lose her mind, realizing that chances are good she is going to die here, in this isolated place, in the most embarrassing of circumstances. In the book, her situation

2010s

Nov 14, 2011
Barnes & Noble
Sarasota, Florida
11/22/63

Dec 14, 2011
Walmart
Alpharetta, Georgia
11/22/63

Feb 19, 2012
Savannah Book Festival Trustees Theatre
Savannah, Georgia
11/22/63

was made even more vulnerable by the fact that she was only wearing a pair of panties and the handcuffs. In the movie, she gets to be slightly more modest, wearing a thin slip. Her mental state is represented by Greenwood as Gerald, who continues to talk to her, accuse her, and torment her even though he is dead. There are also at least two other versions of herself to add to the chorus of misery (a good Jessie, and a bad one, of course). And she has flashbacks to an incident in her childhood that was kind of a precursor to this disturbing – and probably final – incident of her life. If nothing else, she comes to face many personal realizations over the course of her ordeal – even though she may not have time enough to learn from them.

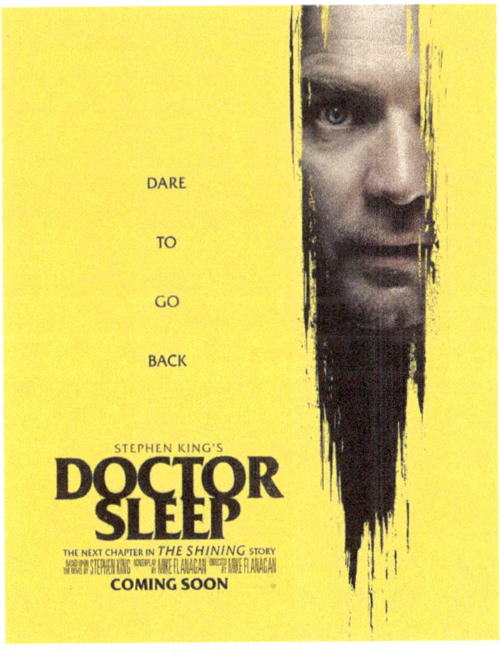

Doctor Sleep teaser movie poster

Oh yeah, and along with all of the mental shenanigans, there's also a feral dog that's in the mix. When they first get to the cabin, Jessie feels sorry for it, and gives it some Kobe steak (Gerald, of course, is angry that she "wasted" such expensive meat on a stray). This is the perfect example of Jessie's humanity and how

The mask from Mike Flanigan's horror film, *Hush*. BluRay cover

it can make her vulnerable – the dog comes back, still hungry, and somehow gets access to the cabin. It finds Jessie and Gerald and realizes that he looks very tasty. Then it looks at Jessie and starts licking its chops, realizing that its menu will soon get another daily special. *So much for her previous act of kindness!* In a funny inside joke, the "phantom" Gerald calls the dog "Cujo," which made me laugh. And there is also a mysterious figure called the Moonlight Man (Carel Struycken, the giant from David Lynch's excellent series *Twin Peaks*), who may or may not be another figment of Jessie's desperate imagination.

Gerald's Game works so well because of Gugino's central performance. Women in our society are the most common targets of abuse and violence, and Jessie's past holds secrets that she has difficulty facing. But the fact that she is handcuffed and spread eagle on a bed, like some sexual sacrifice, adds more weight to her vulnerability. It's the ultimate nightmare of helplessness.

Flanagan likes to work with actors he likes over and over, and this isn't a bad thing. Both Gugino and Greenwood turn up again and again in later Flanagan works and continue to give top-notch performances every time. He can rely on them to not only hit the ball every

April 11, 2012
Alliance Theatre
Atlanta, Georgia
Ghost Brothers of Darkland County Premiere

Dec 7, 2012
Tsongas Center at UMASS
Lowell, Massachusetts
Open Signing

time, but to knock it out of the park. In flashbacks, Henry Thomas (yes, the kid from *E.T.*) plays Jessie's father and Kate Siegel pops up again as Jessie's mother. More regulars of Mike Flanagan's very own "repertory company."

Flanagan had made some strong films before this, but *Gerald's Game* is the one that really put him on the map. An excellent film, it's also an excellent King adaptation.

A collage of Mike Flanigan TV series

He went on to create some wonderful miniseries as part of a contract for Netflix, including his "Haunting" trilogy (so far) about ominous, haunted houses (from classic literature) – *The Haunting of Hill House* (a prequel to Shirley's Jackson's superb novel – arguably the best haunted house book ever - which he made in 2018), *The Haunting of Blye Manor* (2020, based on Henry James's "The Turn of the Screw"), and *The Fall of the House of Usher* (Poe, of course, from 2023). He also made the vampires-take-over-a-small-town series *Midnight Mass* (2021, which is my favorite miniseries by him so far) and *The Midnight Club* (2022), about kids in a hospice center telling each other stories to distract themselves from impending death.

By the way, just about anything Flanagan makes is worth checking out.

In between his excellent collection of Netflix series, Flanagan took the time to direct a feature film version of King's *Doctor Sleep* (2019), his second King adaptation, and it's just as good as *Gerald's Game*. *Doctor Sleep* is not only a sequel to King's book *The Shining*, however, it is also a sequel to Stanley Kubrick's film version of *The Shining* (1980).

This is no secret. As soon as the opening credits for *Doctor Sleep* begin, after a prologue that introduces us to villain Rose the Hat, we see the pattern from the carpet of the Overlook Hotel, and the theme from Kubrick's *The Shining* (composed by Wendy Carlos and Rachel Elkind and performed here by the Newton Brothers) begins playing. The movie carries over key optics throughout, first through flashbacks, (featuring different actors than the original – instead of simply showing scenes from Kubrick's film) and later, at the hotel itself, when it becomes a key part of the story. This is especially interesting since King has expressed his disappointment with Kubrick's version. But that movie has become so iconic on its own, a horror film that only seems to become more beloved by fans as time goes on, and I'm sure it had some influence on Flanagan as a filmmaker as well.

Not only is *Doctor Sleep* a strong sequel to *The Shining*, story-wise and book-wise, it's also a pretty damn good movie on its own. Flanagan may not be in Kubrick's league, but he delivers a worthwhile continuation of the story of Danny Torrence.

There are several things that carry over from *The Shining* – from Danny Torrence, now an adult played by Ewan McGregor, struggling with alcoholism and self-loathing, trying to stop himself turning into his father, constantly on the move until he arrives in New Hampshire; to Dick Hallorann (Danny's mentor of sorts, played by Scatman Crothers in *The Shining* and here played by Carl Lumbly). Once we return

July 18, 2013
The Bushnell Center for the Performing Arts
Hartford, Connecticut
Joyland

to the Overlook, there are also familiar faces, including the evil "woman in the tub" in Room 237, the Grady Twins (played here by Sadie and Kk Heim), Delbert Grady himself (played now by Michael Monks), and Lloyd the Bartender (or… is it Danny's dad?).

Longtime Flanagan fans will also notice several faces from his regular repertory company here, including Bruce Greenwood as Dr. John, who runs the local AA meetings that Danny and his friend Billy Freeman (Cliff Curtis) go to; Carel Struycken (who had previously been the Moonlight Man in *Gerald's Game*) as Grampa Flick, the oldest of the bad guys; Henry Thomas (who plays that mysterious bartender who says his name is Lloyd but who is made up to look a bit like Jack Nicholson in *The Shining*); and Carl Lumbly, who was also in Flanagan's *The Fall of the House of Usher.*

The new characters are riveting, too, starting with Abra Stone (Kyliegh Curran), a young girl who appears to be following in Danny's footsteps as a powerful bearer of "the shining." And the villains of the piece, a group called The True Knot, led by Rose the Hat (Rebecca Ferguson, also in *The Girl on the Train*, 2015, and the last three *Mission Impossible* movies). The members of The True Knot are people with "the shining" who are using their powers for evil – or at least their own desires – and who travel around the country, looking for souls to eat. For, in this story, the powers of the shining and human souls are inexplicably linked (the shining even makes souls taste better!). The True Knot loves souls so much, Rose even has a whole fridge full of cannisters of life essences (which they call *steam!*), that they task out for "special occasions" or when the group needs a boost of energy.

With names like Barry the Chunk, Diesel Doug, Snakebite Annie, and Crow Daddy, this is a colorful bunch of characters, all taking orders from the queen bee of the group, Rose the Hat. They are formidable enemies for Danny

and Abra to confront – and they don't have a lot of choice in the matter, once they are "discovered" by the bad guys – but even the members of The True Knot are minor league compared to the Overlook Hotel, which is more than people or ghosts, but is a sentient, evil, haunted *thing*, hungrier for souls than Rose will ever be.

Cue the elevators awash in waves of blood!

I also liked a lot of the effects in this movie – which mostly take place in the world of human minds, and, as such, are limited only by the boundaries of the imagination (and the effects budget). Our main characters can travel and communicate with their minds, and that allows for a lot of creativity during the "mind travel" sequences especially. There's a great

July 18, 2013
The Mortensen Hall
Mark Twain House

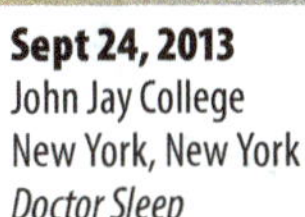

Sept 24, 2013
John Jay College
New York, New York
Doctor Sleep

Sept 25, 2013
Chautauqua Auditirium
Boulder, Colorado
Doctor Sleep

scene where Rose, trying to find Abra, uses her "second sight" to do so, lifting up into space (which is clearly also the *astral plane*), at one point gazing at the entire world from a place of freedom and power. As she "returns to earth," locating our heroine with pin-point accuracy, it is awe-inspiring, the sense of transcendence from the flesh, and the almost God-like grasp of her power. But once she enters Abra's mind, it's not so fluid and free, Abra creates traps for her, making her realize that she might not be as powerful as she once believed.

Which makes me realize that both King adaptations Flanagan has released so far deal a lot with the mind, and internal dialogue, what we used to call "inner space." And that he's damn good at representing it on film.

Doctor Sleep was considered a flop at the box office, but I thought it was unfairly maligned. It is a solid, compelling sequel, well-written and well-cast. Watching it a second time for this article, I liked it even more, and couldn't understand why it hadn't been as big a hit as the recent *It* movies.

With these two adaptations, Flanagan has shown himself to be a gifted translator of King's work, and I'm sure the *Life of Chuck* will just add to the oeuvre.

Not one to shy away from big challenges, like his three haunted house series for Netflix, Flanagan has taken a gamble by acquiring the rights to "The Dark Tower" series, which he plans to turn into a series, and maybe movies as well. I remember when Nikolaj Arcel's version of *The Dark Tower* (2017) was about to be released, I thought Idris Elba as Roland and Matthew McConaughey as Walter sounded like excellent casting, but the movie itself was a letdown. Flanagan not only has to turn in a satisfying version of the saga, he has to make us forget that misstep, which shouldn't be too difficult (I hope).

Then again, if he's able to put the Exorcist franchise back on track (where does he find the time for all these projects?), he might just be able to pull anything off. Maybe all the big plans for *The Dark Tower* will finally come to fruition and blow our minds.

Show us the way forward, Mr. Flanagan! The Tower awaits!

Mike Flanigan, Stephen King, Kate Siegel at the Toronto International Film Festival, 2024.

Postscript: And, in the spirit of this year's Stephen King Annual's *focus on* King on Tour, *I did meet Stephen King just once, in 2007, to get a book signed. It was a special event at Harvard University. I believe it was free, but I have no clue how we got tickets. The event was to celebrate the release of that year's* The Best American Short Stories, *which King had been chosen to edit. I remember King was there with his wife Tabitha and, I believe, his sons, and that it was a very proud moment for him, a major moment of mainstream literary acceptance for the guy who "writes horror stories." It was cool to be there and share that special moment with him.*

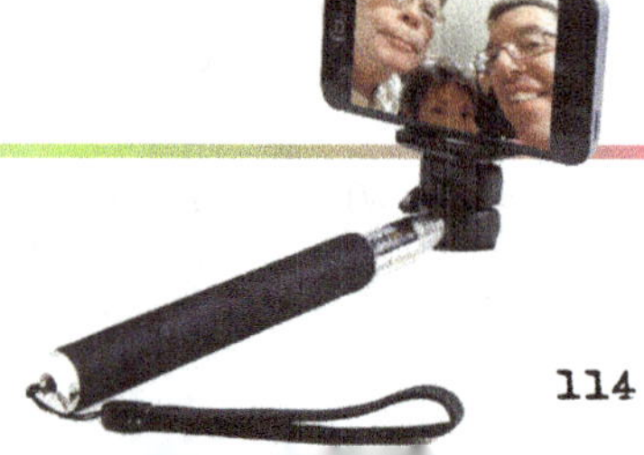

Sept 27, 2013
Memorial Church
Cambridge, Massachusetts
Doctor Sleep
Via the Harvard Book Store

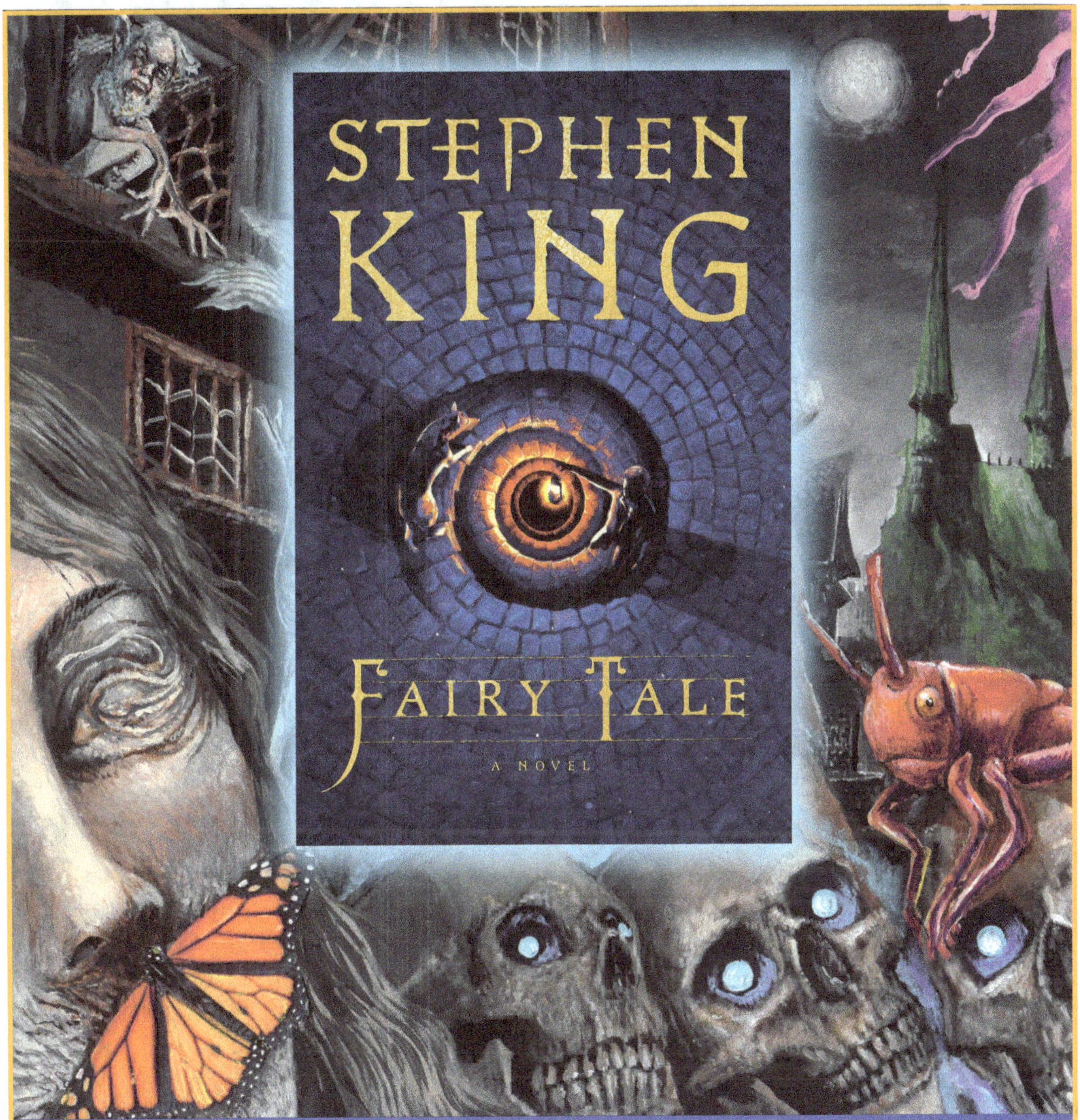

STEPHEN KING

FAIRY TALE

A NOVEL

FAIRY TALE - *Original Cover Art by Glenn Chadbourne!*

This original art featured here is an original dust jacket, signed by artist Glenn Chadbourne, that you can place on your copy of Fairy Tale. You can also frame this signed artist cover of this exclusive release from Overlook Connection Press.

Discover all the New Stephen King Covers in this exclusive series under the **Glenn Chadbourne** category on any web page at: **StephenKingCatalog.com**

Oct 24, 2013
Fleck Dance Theatre
Toronto, Ontario
Doctor Sleep
34th International Festival of Authors

Candy Crush SAGA

Nov 13, 2013
MK2 Bibliothéque
Paris, France
Doctor Sleep

Nov 16, 2013
Grand Rex
Paris, France
Doctor Sleep

Signing Bonus

by **Kevin Quigley**

I call it *pure research.*

I know writing about it is somewhere in the future. I know at some point, I'm going to have to turn my facts and figures into something cohesive, something worth reading. Maybe even something narrative. But this is the first phase, the first dive into whatever topic I'm about to be very well-versed in. *Pure research.* To quote Taylor Swift, it's a hell of a drug.

Stephen King is to blame for a lot of this. I've been reading King since I was nine and someone smuggled a copy of *Cycle of the Werewolf* into sleepaway camp. Later on, that same kid stayed over my place and brought *Creepshow.* I was hooked. By the time I was twelve, I was tackling *Night Shift* and *Rage* and *Pet Sematary* and It. And then something strange happened the year I turned fifteen. King scholar Stephen Spignesi released two books: *The Stephen King Quiz Book* and *The Shape Under the Sheet: The Complete Stephen King Encyclopedia*, and both invited me to not only treat the books as reading for pleasure (which they always should be first), but also as texts from which facts and trivia could be gleaned.

George Beahm's *The Stephen King Companion* came out around the same time, and gave me a primer into the real world of King's books – how they were published, how they were consumed, how they were marketed and banned and made into movies. King himself gave some insight into those things with his essays and forewords and afterwords. And these books about Stephen King alerted me to *other* books on King. The Starmont House/ Borgo Press stuff by Michael Collings and Tyson Blue. *The Art of Darkness*, by Douglas Winter.

A plethora of information, and I consumed all of it. I re-read the novels and paid closer attention to the minutiae, finding more to love about each book in the nooks and crannies. I went to the library and found massive volumes reprinting essays, critiques, and reviews of King's work (one of the things my young mind discovered is how very much 80s and 90s mainstream critics *hated* Stephen King, to the point where it often felt personal. The late-90s reevaluation couldn't come fast enough).

I wrote essays about King throughout high school (my English teacher senior year took me aside after class and said, "It's not that your essays aren't good. It's just that you need more than one subject." Apparently, "monographer" wasn't part of the curriculum that year). As I grew older, I started writing books about King, tackling niche subjects like the world of King audiobooks and comic-book writing and King and technology. Then I fastened on a concept that would drive me for years: Stephen King on the bestseller lists. The impetus that drove what would eventually become *Chart*

2010s

Nov 18, 2013
Ramstein Air Base
Ramstein, Germany
Doctor Sleep

Nov 19, 2013
Zirkus Krone
Münich, Germany
Doctor Sleep
No signing - Krimfestival / Crime Festical

Nov 20, 2013
CCH
Hamburg, Germany
Doctor Sleep

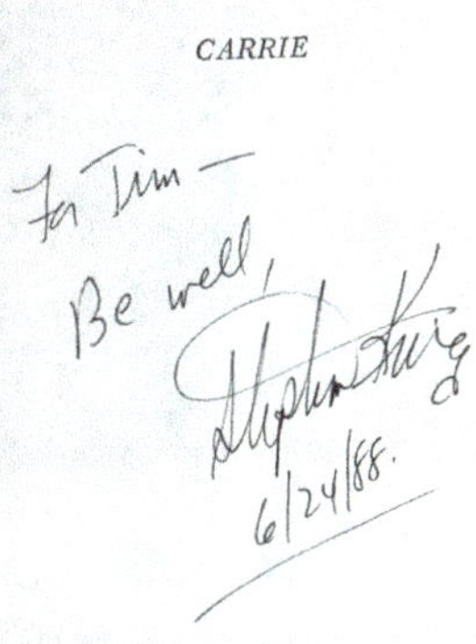

of Darkness (never let a good pun lie fallow) was that drive to research, to get into the facts and figures, the nitty-gritty of King history. Pure research, research for its own sake, before it becomes of use. I studied. I spent long hours at the library. I looked through *microfiche*. Headaches and insomnia and too much Red Bull, all in the name of getting the facts straight, getting the numbers right. But it's more than that. Because research, pure research, is about two stories intertwining. The first is the one that keeps whispering at the back of my brain, the one that demands to shape these facts and figures into something narrative, something cohesive, something worth reading. That one is the story I'm writing. The other one, the second helix? That's the story I'm *living*.

There was a point in *Chart of Darkness* when I stumbled across the publication schedule for *Christine*. It was nuts. Height of King popularity. John Carpenter had read the manuscript and started working on the movie immediately. Viking, King's publisher at the time, had to crush production of the book so hard. The hardcover had to come out and, within months, the paperback and movie tie-in paperback had to come out, because the film was set to hit the silver screen and there was a lot of cross-promotion. I loved writing about that, because it was a great weird little story from the days when Stephen King was the hottest brand on the planet, and both the publishing world and the movie industry were willing to go into maximum overdrive to utilize their stake in it.

But for a little while? That story was just for me. When I uncovered it, I stood up at the Boston Public Library, wide-eyed with my heart pounding. Didn't everyone in here reading old copies of *Outside* and blithely leafing through Hemingway understand how *unusual* this was? How *cool* a nugget of information it was? And how, despite all of this finagling and rigmarole, the book still only hit #2!? Isn't that weird?

That's research. Hard work. Dedication. Gumption. And, occasionally, you get a bonus: these moments of discovery so thrilling that I want to scream it all from the top of a mountain.

So, when Dave Hinchberger said, "Hey, would you be interested in doing a research project about Stephen King book signings?" I didn't tell him I was too busy. I didn't mention that I was already deep in research and writing another book on another topic that was taking all my energy and concentration. I further didn't say that I was working a full-time day job plus doing graphic design on the side and still trying to write fiction while also dealing with this other massive book project.

What I said was, "Neat, I'll start with pre-existing research on the topic and I'll build out from there. I'll create a spreadsheet with dates and venues, then I'll go back and search newspapers and announcements from 1973 on

March 16, 2014
Bookstore 1
Sarasota, Florida
Doctor Sleep

and clip out anything advertising Stephen King appearing places. I'll scour message boards and announcements and then cross-reference those with event pictures and editorials. I'll put everything in a series of digital file folders that confirm my research and exist as their own kind of thrilling ephemera."

You hire a researcher, you get an overachieving Type A who thrives on facts. Dave said, "okay."

A day later, I texted, "Why is King randomly in North Carolina to sign autographs at a screening of *Carrie* in 1977?" And then I texted again, "Campaigning with Gary Hart! High School Graduation! *Firestarter* World Premiere in Bangor!" And then I texted again, "Every article in the 80s talks about what kind of beer he's drinking! Whoa!" I couldn't stop. Here was an area of Stephen King history I hadn't considered as a viable topic of study, and now it was an avalanche of fascinating anecdotes about the ebbs and flows and excitements of Stephen King signing books. I had no idea it could be like this.

And there it was again. The thrill of discovery. The exaltation of facts colliding and fusing before a narrative comes along to make them fun and accessible. The unmitigated joy of pure research.

Within a few weeks, I got my "*Christine* crashes production" moment. Early research into King book signings is a little patchy, but a lot of local papers covered King's tiny *'Salem's Lot* tour. During one of his early signings that apparently didn't go very well, King said, "I'd like to leave one of these autograph sessions with my writing hand so swollen I wouldn't be able to use it for days."

For a long time, I gaped at that quote. It was so ironically prescient that I could barely believe it existed, but there it was in black and white, staring up at me from a dead newspaper published the year I was born. Somewhere down the line, I'll write some narrative nonfiction in which that quote becomes the oxymoronic epigraph, the thesis statement from which my whole story springs. I can only hope I can convey in words what seeing that quote made me feel.

In that moment, it was just me, and a picture of a very young Stephen King signing his second published novel, and a story about how badly he wanted to be the mega-popular writer he would eventually become. In that moment, it was just me and pure research, a thing that, as a bonus, becomes its own reward if you love it enough. And oh, do I love it.

Editor's Note: I would like to personally thank Kevin for all his efforts to compile (as much as possible) Stephen King's signings for the last forty plus years. It was an immense task that he eagerly accepted and his research truly shines in what I was trying to accomplish here. Well done, Kev!
– Dave

If you know of a signing that was not included in this Annual, please contact us at ServiceOverlook@gmail.com to add to this record of Stephen King on Tour.

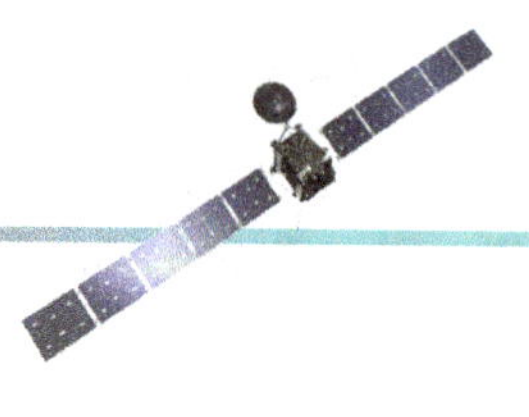

I KNOW WHAT YOU NEED: Exclusive interview with director Julia Marchese

by **Anthony Northrup**

To say Julia Marchese is a superfan of cinema would be an understatement. She's held more than several jobs, and performed just about every task imaginable in the film industry, and she's not slowing down. Julia took her talent and vision and brought them to the big screen with Stephen King's *I Know What You Need*. Before we dig into our conversation with Julia and her part in the Stephen King universe, let's get to know a little bit about her first.

Julia Marchese was born on March 18th, 1979. Originally from Las Vegas, Nevada, Julia attended the Las Vegas Academy. She furthered her education at the University of California, Irvine, where she studied drama and film. She has appeared in several independent films including *Deathcember, Golden Earrings*, and Joe Dante's *Burying The Ex*. She worked at the famous New Beverly Cinema Theater in 2006, and left in 2014. Also, in 2014 she made her first documentary feature film, *Out of Print*. This is a film about the history of the New Beverly Cinema, and 35mm cinema. The film won the Programmers Award for Best Documentary film at the Sidewalk Film Festival in 2014. In 2020, Julia got the rights to film *I Know What You Need*, a Stephen King Dollar Baby film, based on King's short story. The movie was filmed on location at the University of Maine and in surrounding areas, where the story originally takes place. Julia is a writer, director, producer, actress, and a complete fangirl of not just cinema, and pop culture, but has proven to be a 'Constant Reader' and has landed her place in the Stephen King universe. She currently lives in Los Angeles, California.

An Interview with Stephen King Dollar Baby filmmaker, Julia Marchese

Anthony Northrup - What was it like for you growing up in Las Vegas, Nevada? When did you discover the works of Stephen King (books and film)?

Julia Marchese - I'm glad I grew up somewhere kind of weird. And living someplace so hot, you stay inside and read and watch movies a lot, so that helped shape me for sure. I read *It*, *Carrie*, and *Pet Sematary* all back-to-back when I was eleven, riding the bus to and from school. I became obsessed, and even had friends that all went by Loser Club names (I'm an Eddie Kaspbrak girl myself). I had been kind of a scaredy cat kid, but I jumped straight from

Nov 11, 2014
Barnes & Noble, Union Square
New York, New York
Revival

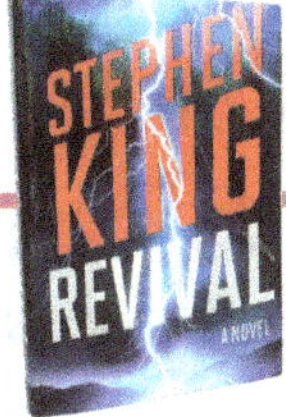

Nov 12, 2014
GW Lisner Auditorium
Washington, D.C.
Revival

Nov 13, 2014
Unity Temple on the Plaza, Sanctuary
Kansas City, Missouri
Revival

Laura Ingalls Wilder to Stephen King, with no *Goosebumps* kind of bridge, and my love for the film version of *Pet Sematary* was really where my love of horror started! That was the first horror film that I loved and watched over and over. I dressed up like a post-Micmac-burial-ground Gage for Halloween when I was twelve, much to the horror of my cheerleader and princess costumed friends. Something about Stephen King grabbed me even as a child, and I still love him as much as I did when I first started reading him. Nay, more! Going back in time and telling the eleven-year-old version of me hunched over my tattered copy of *IT* that in the future I would get to adapt my favorite short story by him? Mind blown!

AN - While at university, you studied film and drama. What did you enjoy most about those subjects?

JM - I was in a community theater group growing up in Las Vegas called The Rainbow Company. It was an ensemble company, ages 10-18, and if you were accepted, you became part of this ensemble. If you weren't selected to act in the half dozen plays they put on each season, you would be assigned a backstage role. Stage manager, lighting board operator, set builder, costumes. It was done with great respect and it taught me how important it is that everyone works together and pulls their weight - that making art is fun but can also be exhausting and needs a team to make it happen. It taught me basic professionalism as well - show up on time, be kind to your fellow actors, learn your lines, be respectful. These were values the company instilled in me when I was ten, and when I moved to LA at 22, I met a ton of people in the industry that had never learned these lessons, so, I am very grateful for learning them so early. I also went to a performing arts high school to study drama, so I got to focus a lot on my interests as a kid.

My degree at UCI was film and drama, and it was study of film, so I watched so many movies that really opened my eyes to cinema. I love watching and talking about films so much, so I was a very enthusiastic student. And I think everything kind of comes out of that genuine passion I have for film - so many job offers and opportunities have come my way because I just love movies and speak about them with knowledge and excitement. My Film study homework never felt like work to me because I loved doing it and was super interested in the subject matter.

And it's similar to my podcasts *Horror Movie Survival Guide* - I am watching movies for these podcasts with an absolutely academic

Nov 14, 2014
Eugene M. Hughes Metropolitan Complex
Wichita, Kansas
Revival

Nov 15, 2014
BookPeople
Austin, Texas
Revival

Nov 17, 2014
Books-A-Million
South Portland, Maine
Revival

Director, Screenwriter, Julia Marchese

eye, searching for details and themes and metaphors, taking copious amounts of notes and cross-referencing articles.

I love doing it because delving into films and learning the stories behind them is always so fascinating. Every film has a hidden story behind it in the actual making of the film that the audience never sees.

AN - You are known for having a huge love for films, especially the horror film genre. What is it, specifically, that you love so much about that genre?

What scares you? And, what film growing up scared you the most, and why?

JM - The first horror film I watched was *A Nightmare on Elm Street 2* when I was about 6 or 7 and it gave me awful Freddy Krueger nightmares for months. I can actually remember physically shivering with fear in my bed. But once I discovered *Pet Sematary*, both the book and the film, somehow those floodgates opened and I was able to watch anything. The original *A Nightmare on Elm Street* is my very favorite horror film now, and I've watched the sequel as an adult with no issues. (The idea of a pool being on fire is still fucked up though.)

I think I love horror so much because it is a thrill, but a safe one. I liken it to being on a roller coaster - you know for the next short span of time you will be doing something that gives the illusion of danger, but actually is safe and at the end you can exit the ride and you can go about your day.

Also, when my best friend Marion and I were in college, we ended up watching every horror film in the horror section of the local video store our senior year, because we realized that the more horror films we watched, the better chance we had at becoming the final girl. We kept a notebook of our reviews, and that's where my podcast *Horror Movie Survival Guide* started in 2017, revisiting that notebook. Now I do the show with my friend Teri and I am teaching her the ways of survival through horror as well! Maybe someday YOU will be pursued by a mad man in a mask while camping and perhaps

if you analyze and study enough horror films, you will know how to beat the killer and survive! So, it has practical reasons as well! And the horror community is really the kindest community there is. That helps too.

AN - How did you first discover the Stephen King Dollar Baby Program, and how you came to create *I Know What You Need*. What specifically drew you to this story?

JM – "I Know What You Need" is my very favorite short story of King's. Hands down.

He describes Edward in the first paragraph of the story and I fell in love with the character immediately. Unkempt hair, mismatched socks,

Jan 29, 2015
Bradenton Performing Arts Center
Bradenton, Florida
Revival

Jul 12, 2015
Bridgton Books Magic Lantern Theater
Bridgton, Maine
Finders Keepers

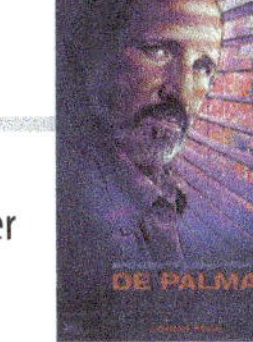

Fogler Library, University of Maine

and all – that kind of outsider misfit type who doesn't fit in, who is hiding something, but is intriguing and charming as well. So, I went along with Elizabeth reading the story for the first time and rooting for them, really interested in Edward, but knowing that this is Stephen King and that it's all going to end badly.

Fogler Library at the University of Maine

The thing I find so fascinating about this story is how insular and small it is. Edward has powers that are used in other Stephen King books to stop catastrophes and bring down The Shop or The True Knot, amongst other grandiose, explosive psychic power play in the King multiverse/ Edward just wants to use his powers to make "one girl" fall in love with him. That's all he wants.

Although he is clearly a sociopathic monster, there's also this strange romanticism to his character. The story also explores the difference between love and obsession, what a fine line that is. If someone is obsessed with you and you like them back, it's hunky dory but if someone is obsessed with you and you don't like them back, it becomes creepy. The actions are the same, but the feeling behind it is different. Elizabeth is a frustrating character because she lets other people push her around for most of the story, but I think ultimately this story brings her power that she needed, and I like that about it too. And the relationship between Elizabeth and her roommate is also so fascinating. Can you tell I am in love with this story?

Also, honestly, bring me a strawberry double dip ice cream cone and I will follow you anywhere.

Cast / Crew of *I Know What You Need*, Fogler Library

AN - Where was the movie filmed and how long was the shoot from start to finish?

JM - I was *thrilled* to be able to shoot this film in July 2021 on location on the University of Maine campus, where the story takes place!

That means that the places he mentions in the story - the library and the dorms - are the actual ones he references in the story. We stayed in and shot in Gannett Hall, where King lived when he attended the school (I got to sleep in the dorm room he stayed in – how cool is that?!) I think filming the story on campus and in Maine made such a difference to the feel of the film. I *always* want Stephen King films to be set in Maine, if at all possible. Everyone I

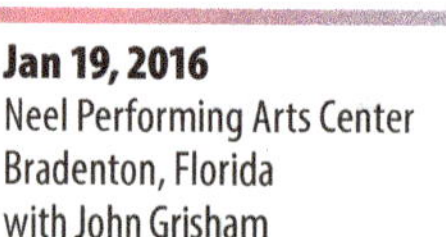

Jan 19, 2016
Neel Performing Arts Center
Bradenton, Florida
with John Grisham

met there was so incredibly nice. People really went out of their way to help the production, especially the staff at the University who I can't thank enough. The shoot was six days and the whole cast and crew stayed together in the dorms and ate on campus in the dining hall. That meant that everyone had a roommate, and our Alice & Elizabeth got to really be roomies for the week. It was super fun to have everyone working on the film all camped out together for the week.

AN - The story takes place in the early 1970's, how much fun was it for you to recreate that era? Where did you find some of the clothes and decor for that era?

JM - You bet your fur I set this film in 1976! It's is the year that the story was first published in *Cosmopolitan* Magazine (keep your eyes peeled in the film for that very issue of *Cosmo*!). First off, I love the 70's colors and look so much, it's Very Julia. Also, with this story, if you set it in modern day, it falls apart. One Google Edward's name and the story doesn't work.

Thomas Hill Standpipe, Bangor, Maine

I was very happy to be able to style the film to meet the period. The aesthetic of the film is after school special meets Brian De Palma. I didn't want this to be a dark, creepy King adaptation until the big reveal at the end. I wanted it to be pretty, bright, and sunny and give off an air of innocence - it is, after all, a love story. It's just a Stephen King love story. So, it will be a different kind of take on the story, but it is also very faithful to the original text, and I took much of the dialogue word for word.

My whole crew was so wonderful at making my very specific vision come to life. Everyone really did their homework on period specific camera angles, lighting, hair, makeup, costume, set dressing. I worked very closely with every department to be sure the film in my head was the one that ended up on screen.

We were also so thrilled to be able to use an incredible vintage 70's VW bus for the film, loaned to us by a fantastic local gentleman named Gus (who even put period specific license plates on the car for us!) Directing from the back of that groovy bus with my crew crammed in the back and the actors in the front seat driving past the Standpipe in Bangor is a memory I will never forget.

I want this film to feel as much like it came from 1976 as possible.

June 7, 2016
Loew's Jersey City
Jersey City, New Jersey
End of Watch

June 8, 2016
Sewickley Academy's Rea Auditorium
Sewickley, Pennsylvania
End of Watch

AN - Were there many challenges while filming? If so, what were they?

JM - It's funny, I panicked during pre-production for *months*, worrying about every single thing that could go wrong on this shoot, and nothing ever did. There were 22 of us all together, almost none of the cast or crew had met each other before. And everyone is sharing rooms with others, mainly strangers. That could go all sorts of pear shaped, but my incredible cast and crew all got along together so well, worked so hard to make this film what I wanted, and really went above and beyond. Everyone felt that we made something truly magical, it felt like it all clicked. I was in a zone of absolute concentration all week, no panic at all. Even after a long shoot day I never felt tired, and just wanted to continue, I was having so much fun.

AN - One of the props in the film is...ice cream. Who provided this and how good was it?

JM - *Lots* of strawberry ice cream indeed! It came from a local ice cream shop in Orono called Spencer's and they were very generous to donate the ice cream to the film.

When I walked up to ask if they would be willing to donate, I started by saying "I'm making an adaptation of a Stephen King story, "I Know What You Need" and the owner yelled "Ice Cream!" and I said "Yes! Have you read the story?" and she said "No, I was joking" and I said "But it really is ice cream! That really is what she needs!" She very sweetly donated a bucket of ice cream to us.

AN - There are a lot of Stephen King "easter eggs" in the film. Can you share with us some of those treats to look for?

JM - I snuck in *so many*. Nozz-a-la Colas are drunk many times in the film (so what version of Maine are they actually in?).

Edward is described as wearing a fatigue jacket in the story, so he does here, but I added a peace sign to the back of it as well – my nod to Stokely from *Hearts in Atlantis* – and he has some telling buttons on that jacket as well. You'll hear lots of names of people and places you might recognize as well. I went super hard on the details for this. There's a doctor's form you see for a split second in this film that is completely filled out with King references, from the names of the doctors, to the medications prescribed, everything is a reference. You'll never see it, but I know it was there. And that gives me constant reader joy.

AN - Let's talk about your two lead actors, Caroline Goldenberg, and William Champion. What were their auditions like, and what was it specifically they brought to the table that won them their roles?

JM - I am so very proud of all of the actors in this film - Caroline Goldenberg, William Champion, Colin Fin and Giovanna Drummond. There are only four characters in this whole story, so everyone has to be on top of their game. Auditioning was a lengthy process, but I was able to see lots of folks from all over the east coast, where we were casting from. Caroline sparked with Giovanna & Will too, as soon as I saw them on screen together I knew it was them, but it's hard because so many of the actors I saw were so good. As an actor, you're always told that when you didn't get the role, it had nothing to do with your level of talent, it was just what the filmmaker is picturing in their head for the role. And these characters could have gone in all sorts of different directions, but this is *my* interpretation of these characters and all of the actors brought them to life so beautifully.

Caroline is stunning, that's what hits you first off, but she also brings an innocence to this character that's necessary for the story to work. We need to believe that Elizabeth is a naive girl, to fall into the trap that Edward sets up for her without questioning it.

I knew Edward was going to be a *very*

June 9, 2016
Victoria Theatre
Dayton, Ohio
End of Watch

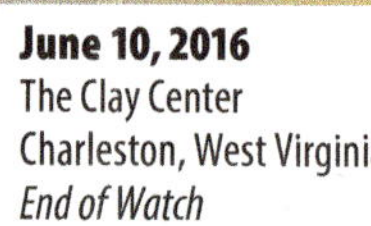

June 10, 2016
The Clay Center
Charleston, West Virginia
End of Watch

June 11, 2016
Ryman Auditorium
Nashville, Tennessee
End of Watch

hard role to cast. The character goes from weirdo geek to romantic lead to absolute psycho and he has to be convincing in all three of these personas – Will absolutely crushed it. He's charming enough to disarm you, and powerful enough to scare you too.

William Champion, director Julia Marchese, and Caroline Goldenberg

AN - What has been your proudest moment of *I Know What You Need*? Of course, I must ask the question… will your film be playing at any film fests?

JM - I can't tell you how happy all of this has made me. Getting to be a tiny part of the Stephen King universe – and knowing that at the end of this project that he himself will see the film? The mind boggles.

I think my proudest moment was the last day of filming, where we were filming in the Fogler Library on the University of Maine campus. I had been picturing this scene in my head for years by that point (I was supposed to film in summer of 2020, but, well, *things* got in the way and I had to postpone until summer 2021.) This particular scene, Elizabeth meeting Edward for the first time and him bringing her ice cream, which is my favorite scene. And it was actually happening – here were the extras dressed in period garb, the crew milling around being busy with their various jobs, *my* Elizabeth and Edward meeting for the first time, and me behind the monitor calling action. It was a true moment of happiness and I never wanted that day to end. I felt like the luckiest girl in the world.

AN - Lastly, What's next for Julia Marchese?

JM - I have my hands in a thousand pies as always. I host two podcasts, *JodoWOWsky*, all about the incredible artist and filmmaker, Alejandro Jodorowsky, and *Horror Movie Survival Guide*, which takes a deep dive into a different horror film each week and discusses how to survive the film. Both podcasts can be heard anywhere you listen to podcasts. I am also about to begin hosting a show for George A. Romero Foundation called *Horror X*, which will feature interviews with fantasmagorical women in horror.

I'm looking forward to lots more cinema related goodness in my future, whether it's talking about films, programming them or making them. I love cinema, and I love Stephen King. Hopefully I will get to adapt more of his works! I'm excited to take *I Know What You Need* to the festival circuit and see what people think. As faithful as it is, it's still Julia Marchese's vision of *I Know What You Need* so getting a response on that is going to be so exciting, especially from constant readers like you! I'm well chuffed to have had the opportunity to make this film and I am very, very grateful. Onward to see what the Wheel of Ka has in store for me!

Long days and pleasant nights, gunslingers.

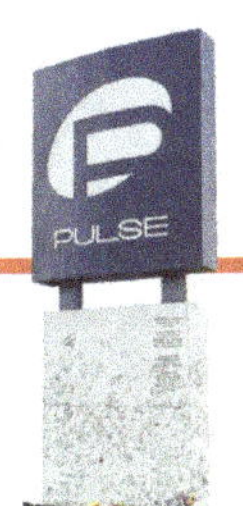

June 12, 2016
Iroquois Amphitheater
Louisville, Kentucky
End of Watch

June 13, 2016
Englert Theatre
Iowa City, Iowa
End of Watch

In Person with Stephen King

by **Bob Ireland**

First, let me tell you that I have been obsessed with reading all things King since reading *The Stand* in 1979 while attending college. I consumed it during a weekend and was hooked. Who was this Stephen King?

I was engaged at the time and my then girlfriend (now wife of 43 years) surprised me with a new hardcover first edition of *Firestarter*, a rarity for me then as I only could afford paperbacks while in college. I devoured it within a couple of days and my collecting bug took form. I needed every King book in hardcover, first printings if possible. As my collection grew and I discovered more and more King stories in old magazines and anthologies, my desires refocused. I needed to meet Stephen King, perhaps ask him a question or two and get a book signed.

My first opportunity came in November of 1998. *The Rock Bottom Remainders* were performing at The Bayou (a long since torn down bar in Georgetown, Washington DC.) The Bayou is a rather small place and I'm sure the occupancy rate was surpassed ten-fold. A spot at the front of the old wooden dance floor near the stage gave me the opportunity to see Stephen King up close, as well as Dave Barry, Ridley Pearson, Amy Tan, et al. It was a hoot when King was lead singer on "Werewolves of London," backed up by their wringer musician, Warren Zevon (I met Zevon on Kauai in 1978 but that's a tale for another time.) the man who wrote the song. I didn't get to speak to King, nor snag an autograph this time, but did grab a concert poster off the wall.

I had tickets to a *Bag of Bones* book signing, six days later, in Bangor, Maine. I flew to Boston where I grabbed a rental and then picked up my good friend Kevin Quigley (who I've known since the SKEMERS conference, in Bangor) We spent a few days hanging around Bangor checking out the sites like King's home, the Standpipe, the sewer-drain from IT and the Field of Screams, to name but a few. We spent quite a bit of time at Betts Bookstore having met Stu and Penney the year before.

We could have two books signed, if they were purchased at Betts. No need to have *Bag of Bones* signed, I chose *The Stand, Complete and Uncut*, and *Legends* which not only had A King story, "The Little Sisters of Eluria," but also "Debt of Bones," written by Terry Goodkind, who was also in attendance.

The line outside the store grew for an hour or more before the official signing time, but me and Kevin and a couple other friends sat on a park bench around the corner and across the street from the rear entrance to the store. We were hoping to get a glimpse of King before the signing. About fifteen minutes before the signing, Stephen King walked right behind us as he headed across the street. We called out his name and he waved at us.

Now stoked for the signing, we got in line at our respective spots and waited. When the line started moving you could feel the excitement in the air. The store was overflowing with people with the line snaking through the rows and rows of bookshelves. At one turn I met Terry Goodkind and got him to personalize my Legends. That was cool and had me hyped for meeting Stephen King. I kept thinking about what I would ask Stephen King and before I knew it… I was standing in front of Stephen King with my two books.

2010s

June 14, 2016
Kaneko
Omaha, Nebraska
End of Watch

June 15, 2016
Cain's Ballroom
Tulsa, Oklahoma
End of Watch

Vine

June 16, 2016
Kiva Auditorium
Albuquerque, New Mexico
End of Watch

Bob Ireland meets Stephen King, Betts Books, Bangor, Maine 1998

I told him that I had seen the *Remainders* the week prior at The Bayou and that Warren Zevon was awesome. I said that it was one of the best concerts I'd ever attended. He laughed and said *"then I guess you haven't seen many concerts! Oh, and yes Warren was on fire!"* I also mentioned that I'd met Zevon 20 years prior in Kauai and that we drank beers together into the night. King said "Warren doesn't drink anymore, nor do I and that's a good thing!" I moved towards the rear door and was allowed to stand and watch my friend Kevin get his books signed, taking a few more pics. We then departed, our dream moment having passed, and stood around a bit where… Kevin fainted! (see Kevin's story in this Annual). He hyperventilated proving he is the ultimate Stephen King fan-boy!

Over the years I went to several other readings, signing events and another *Remainders* performance in 2000 at DC Nation, *The Three Kings* event at Folger Theatre in DC, George Mason's *Fall for the Book* and the *Revival* talk at Lisner auditorium in DC. I got signed books at each of these events. One other event was my favorite of all time. I had VIP tickets for the *Remainders* at DC Nation. My wife was going to attend with me but backed out when I told her the VIP tickets were $200. She said it just wasn't her thing, but fortunately, humored my addiction and chance for VIP tickets.

Most memorable thing about the reception was meeting King and asking questions. King, dressed in what I call lounge wear, sat on a stool surrounded by fans, all aching for a chance at a question and a picture. I got both, but the best part was this: there was a fan on his cell phone with his significant other trying to convince her that he was standing in front of Stephen King. His call was loud and at one point Stephen King interrupted him and asked what was going on. The guy told him that his girlfriend didn't believe he was with Stephen King. King asked for the phone and said "Hello, this is Stephen King." The woman on the other end of the line said something along the lines of "quit bullshitting me, I know he's pulling a fast one." King said "Oh Well, your loss" and handed the phone back. He told the guy that he tried but she still thought he had put a friend up to it. We all laughed. After the reception I had a terrific time watching the performance and their special wringer, Robert McGuinn of *The Byrds* fame.

I did get my long sought after *Gunslinger* signed in 2012 at the George Mason *Fall for the Book* program, and I got both Stephen and Tabatha to sign my *Mid-Life Confidential* at *The Three Kings* appearance in '08. Although my collecting has slowed down, I still have several books special to me. My gift editions of *Insomnia* and *Desperation* I mailed to King early on in my collecting to get signed (a program no longer available), and got them back personalized to me! Waiting now for *Never Flinch*, *The Talisman 3* (or whatever title it becomes), and everything else from the man, Stephen King.

Rock Bottom Remainders at the Bayou, Georgetown, Washington DC.

June 17, 2016
Juan Diego Catholic High School
Salt Lake City, Utah
End of Watch

June 18, 2016
Barnes & Noble
Reno, Nevada
End of Watch

Taking a Stand in Vegas: KingCon 2024 Report and Photos

KingCon 2024

More than a year ago I came across this group on Facebook promoting a KingCon in Las Vegas. Once tickets went on sale it ballooned into several hundreds of people attending! The organizers did not forget the face of their fathers, but instead went all out for those dedicated constant readers making this a weekend that won't soon be forgotten.

We had renowned celebrities and publishers from the world of King. There were panels, surprise giveaways, artists, signings, Dollar Baby films and more. It was wild!

Mick Garris, the Master of Horror himself, was there to celebrate the 20th anniversary of Stephen King's *Riding the Bullet*. You may also know him as a director of several other King adaptations, including *The Stand* and *The Shining* miniseries. He was a kind, warm, and funny man who made himself available to all.

Robert Kurtzman, famed special effects artist who has worked on a number of King films – including *The Green Mile* and *Gerald's Game* (YES, that scene!!) – also attended. He demonstrated some of his skills on Kris Webster, the convention organizer, and did an outstanding talk about special effects artistry.

Actor Thomas Jane (*1922*, *The Mist*, *Dreamcatcher*) made a brief appearance as well. He recorded a podcast with The Kingcast in front of a room full of KingCon attendees.

Publisher's Paul Suntup (Suntup Press) and Alex Berman (Phantasia Press), were there too. Suntup unveiled a new limited *Duma Key* and together they did an excellent panel about small press publishing. The vendor room was a great highlight of the convention with meet-and-greets with everyone mentioned plus fantastic, renowned artists like Rob Wood, François Vaillancourt, Glenn Chadbourne, and more!

One top to all of this, we screened twenty-five Dollar Baby films and had Q&As with many of the filmmakers. There was even a panel about the Dollar Babies and the impact it's made.

Kristin Bird, Mickie Robertson and Megan Robertson

"Truly an amazing experience, a true KA. I was completely blown away to not only get to meet some of my favorite authors, artists, and book brokers, but to have real conversations with them and spend quality time with all of them. One of the best basic human experiences I've ever had in my life!" – Mickie Robertson

Sept 24, 2016
National Book Festival Library of Congress
Washington D.C
End of Watch – Pre-signed and unsigned copies were given out randomly. Pre-signed copies were available.

Marissa Hollenback as Rose the Hat
Photo: Marissa Hollenback

When I was 16, my mother gave me a book she had started reading and said, "This one is something you would probably like more than me." The book was *The Stand*, and I've been anxiously waiting for each-and-every Stephen King book to come out for the last 46 years.

My first time seeing a Coffin Box was at a book show. I was married and had a baby boy at home, so there was no way I could justify the $500 asking price.

My now 33-year-old son and I are currently reading through the Stephen King library together. For him, mostly first time reads, while I am enjoying revisiting old friends. We are currently about 80% of the way through the uncut version of *The Stand*. (We chose to read that instead of the cut version) I am so excited

We ended the weekend with a giant *The Shining* themed party/costume contest where the committee randomly selected attendees to get exclusive prizes including a rare, limited Coffin Edition of *The Stand* signed by the author and illustrator.

This convention was something special. Everyone there felt it. It will go down in history as legendary in the world of Stephen King.

No details yet - but it's coming again! Join their Facebook group for updates!

- Paul Inman

Paul Inman is the director of a Stephen King Dollar Baby film, *That Feeling You Can Only Say What It Is in French*, and he was a co-coordinator of the Dollar Baby segments of KingCon 2024. He also had the honor of interviewing director Mick Garris (who's filmed more Stephen King adaptations than any other director) who brought us *The Stand*, *The Shining*, *Bag of Bones*, and *Desperation*.

Michael Cicero (son) and Michael Cicero (father)

"We had a great time at the first annual KingCon in beautiful Las Vegas. The event was so well put together and we cannot wait to attend the next one. Of course, having it in the best city in the United States was the icing on the cake!" - Michael Cicero

Nov 7, 2016
Collins Center for the Arts
Orono, Maine
Hearts in Suspension

March 15, 2017
Bookstore 1
Sarasota, Florida
End of Watch

François Vaillancourt and Paul Inman

to having him meet my old friends and share their experiences.

When KingCon was announced, I knew I had to attend. When they said we could dress up as our favorite characters, and as KingCon was in Vegas, and I had to go as Randall Flagg.

My son has his family with 3 daughters at home and, like me with the Coffin Box when he was little, he just couldn't justify making the trip.

While at KingCon 2024, I met the incredibly nice Mick Garris, who directed the original miniseries of *The Stand*. He graciously signed the pocket of my Randall Flagg jean jacket. I also got to meet the equally nice Francois Vaillancourt, who has done the artwork for the newest limited edition of *The Stand*, due from CD Publications soon.

Mick Garris and Ben Higgins

The main giveaway at KingCon 2024 was *The Stand*: Coffin Box. When the drawing for it came, it was my number that was called. I didn't even know how to react. As I'm writing this, it's about 24 hours later, the book is still in its box in my library, and I still don't know how to react. I can't thank the KA-TET that organized KingCon 2024 enough. They may think they know, but they really don't know how much it means to me to own this book.

I like to think that my Mom was looking down on me last night, smiling at this point in the epic journey she started me off on all those years ago.

Here is a pic of me with Kristopher Webster and my wonderful wife, Kathy, holding the 2nd copy of *The Stand*: Coffin Box I've ever seen. The only one I've ever touched. The one I will soon display proudly in my library.

– David Thwaites

Stephen King artist, Glenn Chadbourne, at KingCon

Kristopher Webster, and David and Kathy Thwaites

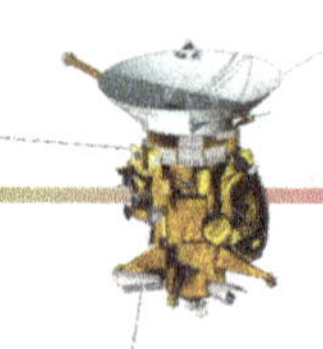

KingCon 2024
Las Vegas!

Sept 26, 2017
Books Are Magic
New York, New York
Sleeping Beauties

Sept 27, 2017
Oblong Books & Music
Annandale-on-Hudson, New York
Sleeping Beauties

Sept 28, 2017
Newtonville Books
Newton Centre, Massachusetts
Sleeping Beauties

Sept 29, 2017
Anderson's Bookshop
Naperville, IL
Sleeping Beauties

In memory of Ray Garton

Unless you lived through it, you cannot imagine the excitement and anticipation for Stephen King fans as they awaited the newest monthly issue of *Castle Rock: The Stephen King Newsletter.*

A monthly newsletter for a horror writer? Unprecedented! And the publication was also a clarion call to the world that Stephen King was to be taken seriously as a writer.

Ever see a Stuart Woods college course, for example? Don't get me wrong: I love all kinds of writers. The late Stuart Woods even approved me to write an official *Companion* to his books, but his publisher put the kibosh on it. My point is, much of King is literature, and in fact, I taught a Stephen King course at the University of New Haven. It was a full 3-credit Literature course. (It "sold out," so to speak, as soon as it was announced in the course catalog.)

Here is a look back at some highlights from *Castle Rock*, which was published from January 1985 through December 1989, for a total of 56 individual issues. Each issue was a banquet of King *stuff* ... interviews, articles, puzzles, excerpts, photos, reviews, and more.

These days, many authors have online newsletters. Enter an email address and you'll get a monthly (or more frequent) newsletter. Sometimes the writers' publishers produce them; many are fan-based.

To create a *printed* monthly newspaper in the mid-80s, and mail it to all subscribers was a huge commitment and undeniably a labor of love. It was an affirmation of the existence of a burgeoning Stephen King community. (And it's stronger than ever in 2025.)

After a "LDPN, nice to meet ya" debut issue, *Castle Rock* hit the ground in overdrive with Issues 2-5 which serialized King's novella *Dolan's Cadillac*. Unpublished King? This got the newsletter off to a roaring start. (Stephanie Leonard, editor of the newsletter and Tabitha King's sister, launched it with an Old English font for the first issue. It was lovely, but on newsprint, it was a little difficult to read. She switched to a straight serif font for Issue 2 and onward.)

2010s

FORTNITE

Sept 30, 2017
Boswell Book Co.
Milwaukee, Wisconsin
Sleeping Beauties

Oct 1, 2017
Left Bank Books
St. Louis, Missouri
Sleeping Beauties

Here are 25+ notable highlights from the run of *Castle Rock: The Stephen King Newsletter*:

- An article about how Stephen Brown discovered that Stephen King was Richard Bachman
- One of the first looks at collecting Stephen King limited editions by George Beahm
- Stephen King's short story "The Cat From Hell"
- A long essay by Stephen King about limited editions
- A piece by Peter Straub talking about *The Talisman*
- Our friend Tyson Blue's essay from *The Unseen King* about *The Plant*
- Tyson's review of Douglas Winter's *Stephen King: The Art of Darkness*
- A *Maximum Overdrive* issue
- J.N. Williamson's discussion of Stephen King's astrological chart. (I included his chart in my *Stephen King Encyclopedia*. It's amazing how accurate it is with hindsight.)
- Stephen King's discussion of film ratings called "The Dreaded X"
- A Dean Koontz interview
- A discussion of the differences between the book and film (Kubrick) versions of *The Shining*
- An essay by Stephen King called "Why I Wrote *The Eyes of the Dragon*"
- Excerpts from the "Dark Tower" books in progress
- An essay by Tabitha King about *Misery*
- A Michael Collings review of *The Tommyknockers*
- Details about the limited edition of *My Pretty Pony*, and a look at Owen King as GI Joe in *Creepshow*
- An interview with Clive Barker
- Details about the stainless steel limited edition of *My Pretty Pony*
- An essay by Barry Hoffman, publisher of *Gauntlet*, called "King's Kids ... Less Than Meets the Eye."
- A look at "King's Blurbs" by Stanley Wiater
- My first contribution to *Castle Rock*: "From Richard to Stephen to Richard: How Richard Matheson Influenced the Work of Both Stephen King and Richard Christian Matheson."
- "The Good and Bad of Film Adaptation" by our friend James Cole, one of the very first Dollar Baby filmmakers. He talked about his adaptation of "The Last Rung on the Ladder."
- Another piece by me called "Spignesi Updates King Encyclopedia"
- A 2-part interview with Rick Hautala
- An essay by Stephen King called "The Ultimate Catalogue," about mail-order catalogues
- A brilliant essay by Michael Collings called "Acorns to Oaks: Explorations of Theme, Image, and Character in the Early Works of Stephen King"
- An interview with Joe Lansdale
- A concordance to Stephen King's first published short story, "I Was a Teenage Grave Robber" from my *Stephen King Encyclopedia*. This was in the final issue of *Castle Rock*, December 1989.

Oct 2, 2017
Shakespeare & Co.
Missoula, Montana
Sleeping Beauties

Oct 3, 2017
Powell's Books
Portland, Oregon
Sleeping Beauties

Oct 5, 2017
Koerner Hall, TELUS Centre for Performance
Toronto, Ontario
Sleeping Beauties

The Shape Under the Sheet: The Complete Stephen King Encyclopedia Limited Edition (Overlook Connection Press)

The Plant, New King Cover Series painting by Glenn Chadbourne

Christopher Spruce, who took over as Editor after Stephanie Leonard left the publication, wrote a piece explaining the demise of the newsletter, particularly noting King's feelings. Here is an excerpt:

Then there is Stephen himself. I'm not sure he has ever been entirely comfortable with the idea of a newsletter devoted to "Stephen King." After all, he is yet a tried-and-true Yankee possessed of that sometime endearing quality of self-effacement who just might be a little embarrassed by the fuss. At the same time, he understands his faithful fans need both a source of information about him and an outlet for their comments about their favorite writer.

CASTLE ROCK
The Stephen King Newsletter
IT: A Journey into the Dark Sid
CASTLE ROCK
The Stephen King Newsletter
IT: Stephen King's Comprehensive Masterpiece
IT
Stephen King Comments on *It*

Today, Facebook "Stephen King" groups serve as that outlet. But scrolling *Castle Rock* Facebook posts about King and his work will never compare to the day the newest issue showed up in our mailbox.

I'll conclude with a quote from Uncle Stevie. It kind of sums things up ... in many, many ways:

Tough old world, baby.
If you're not bolted together tightly,
you're gonna shake, rattle, and roll
before you turn thirty.

Stephen Spignesi is the author of six books about Stephen King's work including *The Complete Stephen King Encyclopedia* (limited edition published and edited by Dave Hinchberger and The Overlook Connection Press team), *The Lost Work of Stephen King*, and his latest, *Stephen King, American Master.* He lives in New Haven, Connecticut.

2010s

Oct 6, 2017
Barnes & Noble
Sarasota, Florida
Sleeping Beauties

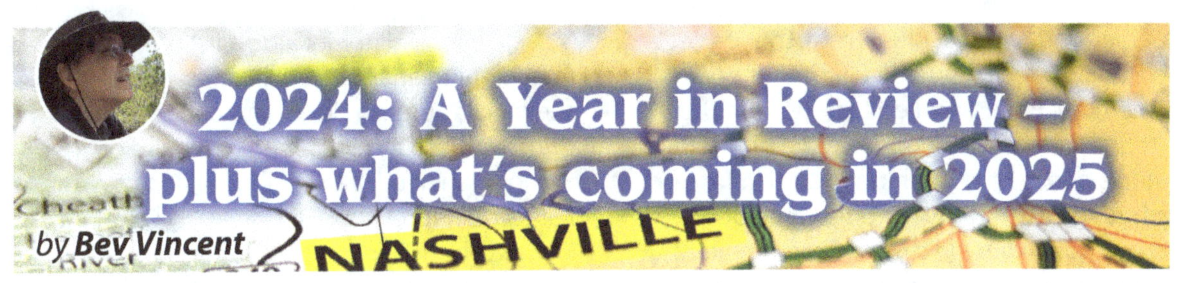

2024: A Year in Review – plus what's coming in 2025

by Bev Vincent

2024

The major King release in 2024 was *You Like It Darker*, a collection containing the seven short stories published since *The Bazaar of Bad Dreams*[2] and five new tales ranging in length from a novelette to a full-fledged novel. The book's title was inspired by the Leonard Cohen song "You Want it Darker." The new works are "Two Talented Bastids," "Danny Coughlin's Bad Dream,"

"Rattlesnakes," a sequel of sorts to *Cujo*, "The Dreamers," and "The Answer Man."

Although the shorter stories were all previously published, many had appeared in relatively obscure venues (although *Flight or Fright*, the anthology I co-edited with King, hopefully isn't all that obscure!), so it's possible that for some people the collection contained all-new-to-them works.

The only other new short story published last year was "The Extra Hour" in issue 79 of Cemetery Dance magazine. The same issue also includes an interview I conducted with King.

Another fun interview appearing in 2024 was not new. In 1984, Michael Small interviewed Peter Straub and Stephen King after the publication of *The Talisman*. He published an account of that interview in *People* magazine, but the raw audio has never been heard before and it is very entertaining and enlightening.

[1] After the book came out, King admitted that he'd forgotten to include one short story: "The Music Room," from the anthology In Sunlight or in Shadow: Stories Inspired by the Paintings of Edward Hopper edited by Lawrence Block. That story will appear in the paperback edition of You Like it Darker, he says.

Michael invited me to take part in his podcast, *I Couldn't Throw it Out*, to cast some light on the collaboration and to help him decide whether to keep the 30-minute audio recording (which is played in its entirety on the podcast). Listening to the two friends and co-authors bounce of each other was delightful. They *really* didn't want to answer questions about who wrote what.

In addition to the *Cemetery Dance* interview, I had two King-related publications last year. The first was *Stephen King: His Life, Work, and Influences* (Young Readers' Edition), which came out in September. This is an adaptation of the 2022 book *Stephen King: A Complete Exploration of his Work, Life, and Influences*, curated for a younger audience. The premise for the book is that young readers often begin their voyage into adult literature via King's works, so this is an introduction to the author for them. It includes a foreword by Sarah-Jane Smith, who led a successful year-long literacy campaign to bring King to Sussex Regional High School in New Brunswick, Canada in 2012.

The 2022 book, by the way, is now available in these languages: Croatian, Italian, Czech, Spanish, Hungarian, Japanese, German, Polish, Korean, and Serbian. I jokingly refer to the new edition as another translation—into teen!

May 10, 2019
Hilton
Minneapolis, Minnesota

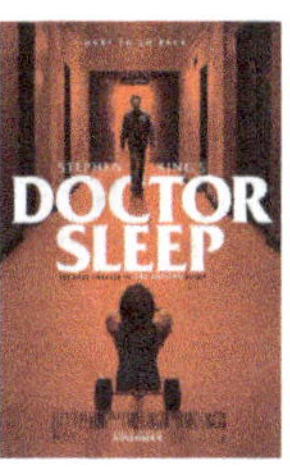

Speaking of translations, my other project was a 60-page chapbook I wrote for Brian Freeman's Patreon called *Lost (or Found) In Translation* that explores how the titles of King's books have been translated in foreign language editions. As with the previous chapbook, *What's in a Name?* the booklet features ten full-page illustrations by François Vaillancourt, and is accompanied by a packet of postcards with his faux-translated covers. To research this essay, I created a massive grid of King titles vs approximately fifty languages, resulting in a spreadsheet that, when printed, was nearly eight feet wide!

King surprised everyone by showing up at the Toronto International Film Festival in September for the world premiere of *The Life of Chuck*, adapted for the big screen by Mike Flanagan. In July, he made his second appearance on the *Talking Scared* podcast, revealing some information about things he might be working on, about which I'll have more to say below.

Last year, I did not include a list of forthcoming adaptations, because it didn't seem like there would be any, and I was almost right. Much to everyone's surprise and delight, the long-shelved feature film version of *'Salem's Lot* came out on Max (HBO) in early October. The two-hour film is a moderately faithful adaptation of the novel, although it does take several liberties, including a harrowing finale that takes place in a drive-in movie lot. They wisely decided to keep the novel's 1970s setting (how could you keep the events quiet in this social media era)?

2025

During a 2023 appearance on *Talking Scared*, King discussed a novel in progress then-titled *We Think Not* that was to feature Holly Gibney but only as part of a larger cast of characters, with Jerome Robinson playing a major part in proceedings. It appears that his original idea, inspired by the kidnapping of Lady Gaga's dogs, didn't pan out. In a couple of subsequent interviews, he alluded to the fact that the book was giving him trouble. Apparently he abandoned that plot and decided to write about Holly being hired as a bodyguard for a woman who's a flashpoint in US politics. "Throw in a stalker and stir," he said of the book, which is now titled *Never Flinch*, being released May 27th, 2025.

King has occasionally mentioned the possibility of writing a follow-up to *The Talisman* and *Black House*. He has a long letter from Peter Straub detailing a story idea inspired by Charles Starkweather, who has long been someone with whom King is also fascinated. As of his latest comment, he'd only reread *The Talisman* thus far, taking copious notes, and has yet to tackle *Black House*. That means he hasn't started working on the book, so it could easily be years before that happens, if it does at all.

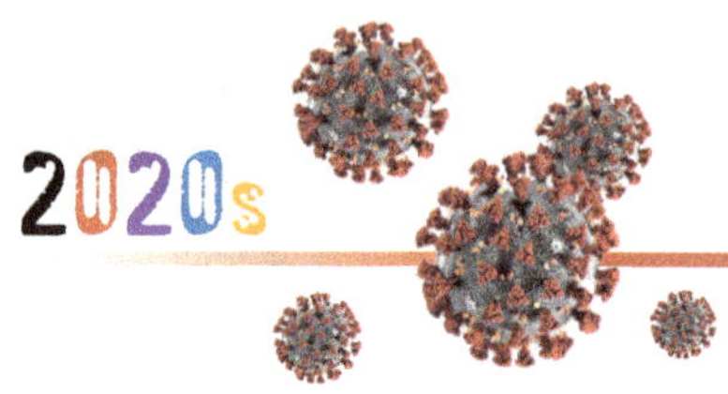

May 1, 2020
Bookstore1
Sarasota, Florida
If It Bleeds

King has written an introduction for *The End of the World as We Know it: New Tales of Stephen King's The Stand*, an authorized anthology of stories set in the world of The Stand, edited by Christopher Golden and Brian Keene. Contributors include Josh Malerman, Paul Tremblay, Richard Chizmar, S. A. Cosby, Tananarive Due, Alma Katsu, Caroline Kepnes, Michael Koryta, Scott Ian, Joe R. Lansdale, Maurice Broaddus and Wayne Brady, Bryan Smith, Somer Canon, Hailey Piper, Jonathan Janz, and me. In total there will be 34 stories by 36 authors. The book is scheduled for a August 19th, 2025 release from Gallery (Simon & Schuster).

Unlike this time last year, there is actually enough activity to merit a bulleted list of adaptations we *will* see in 2025.

- Osgood Perkins' adaptation of "The Monkey" will hit theaters on February 21, 2025. Theo James stars with Tatiana Maslany, Elijah Wood, Christian Convery, Colin O'Brien, Rohan Campbell, and Sarah Levy.
- Production began in Winnipeg last July on a feature film version of *The Long Walk*. The film will feature Judy Greer and Mark Hamill, as well as Cooper Hoffman, David Jonsson, Garrett Wareing, Tut Nyuot, Charlie Plummer, Ben Wang, Jordan Gonzalez, Joshua Odjick, and Roman Griffin Davis. The director is Francis Lawrence from a script by JT Mollner.
- *The Life of Chuck* won the People's Choice Award at TIFF, which is often considered a harbinger for the Best Picture Oscar. It stars Chiwetel Ejiofor, Karen Gillan, Tom Hiddleston, Mark Hamill, Heather Langenkamp, Carl Lumbly, Kate Siegel, Molly C. Quinn, and Jacob Tremblay. After the festival, Neon picked up distribution of the film, which announced it will be released in theaters May 30th, 2025.

- The *It* prequel series *Welcome to Derry* wrapped after a 237-day shoot, so stay tuned for that one on Max. It stars Madeleine Stowe, Stephen Rider, Taylour Paige, Jovan Adepo, Chris Chalk, and James Remar, with Bill Skarsgård.
- An eight-episode adaptation of *The Institute* started filming in Nova Scotia last September. Ben Barnes and Mary-Louise Parker star in the series, produced by Jack Bender and written by Benjamin Cavell. It will air on MGM+. Other cast members include Jason Diaz, Simone Miller, and Tyler Murree.
- *The Running Man* remake was slated to start production at Paramount last November, starring Glen Powell with Katy O'Brian as one of the contestants. Directed by Edgar Wright, it was given a November 7, 2025 release date.

With that impressive slate of pretty-much-guaranteed adaptations for 2025, there's no point in listing the projects that are *still* in development hell!

Stephen King and Peter Straub interview at **throwitoutpodcast.com**

Sep 5, 2023
Outside Chatwal Hotel
New York, New York

The Rock Bottom Remainders

5.25.92

Anaheim, California
The Cowboy Boogie
Al Kooper
In conjunction with the American Booksellers Association

5.20.93

Providence, Rhode Island
Shooters Waterfront Cafe
Al Kooper
Three Chords and an Attitude

5.21.93

Northampton, Massachusetts
Pearl Street
Al Kooper
Reception at Hotel Northampton - signings?

5.22.93

Cambridge, Massachusetts
Nightstage
Al Kooper

5.24.93

Washington D.C.
The Bayou
Al Kooper

5.25.95

Philadelphia, Pennsylvania
Katmandu
Al Kooper
VIP Dinner earlier in the night at Society for Professional Journalists First Amendment Center - signings?

5.27.93

Atlanta, Georgia
The Roxy
Al Kooper

5.28.93

Nashville, Tennessee
328 Performance Hall
Al Kooper

5.30.93

Miami, Florida
The Paragon
Al Kooper

12.4.93

Miami, Florida
Cameo Theater
Al Kooper
In conjunction with the Miami Book Fair ("a fraction of the RBR")

5.29.94

Los Angeles, California
Hollywood Palladium
Bruce Springsteen
Springsteen played on one song - "Gloria" / American Bookseller Association

9.1.95

Cleveland, Ohio
Rock & Roll Hall of Fame
Nils Lofgren
Gala the night before big ceremony to benefit the Hall

11.16.96

Miami, Florida
Bayside Marketplace
as "The Artists Formerly Known as the Rock Bottom Remainders" / Miami Book Fair

8.2.97

Hailey, Idaho
The Mint
Benefit for Ketchum's Comminity Library / Sun Valley Writers' Conference

11.22.97

Miami, Florida
Bayside Marketplace
Warren Zevon / Gloria Gaynor
Miami Book Fair

12.5.97

Orono, Maine
Alfond Arena
The Wallflowers
SK solo, guesting on the encore

5.8.98

Bangor, Maine
Bangor Auditorium
Warren Zevon

11.19.98

Georgetown
Washington, DC
The Bayou
Warren Zevon

11.21.98

Miami, Florida
Bayside Marketplace
Warren Zevon / Darlene Love
As "Artist Formerly Known as the Rock Bottom Remainders"

11.20.99

Miami, Florida
Bayside Marketplace
Warren Zevon

11.14.00

Englewood, Colorado
Gothic Theater
Roger McGuinn
Rock for Kicks
To benefit America SCORES / King's first show after accident

11.16.00

Boston, Massachusetts
The Roxy
Roger McGuinn / John Harkes (NE Revolution)
To benefit America SCORES

11.17.00

Washington D.C.
Platinum Club
Roger McGuinn
To benefit America SCORES

10.29.01

New York, New York
Halloween Tour 2001
Not a concert; a press conference announcing the tour

10.30.01

New York, New York
The World
Judy Collins
Steve Miller was going to play but dropped out due to family emergency

10.31.01

Chicago, Illinois
Park West
Steve Miller was going to play but dropped out due to family emergency

11.2.01

Englewood, Colorado
Gothic Theater
Steve Miller was going to play but dropped out due to family emergency

5.4.02

New York, New York
Webster Hall
Neil Gaiman (kazoo)
10th Anniversary Show
Book Expo

11.22.02

Coconut Grove, Florida
Scotty's Landing

11.23.02

Miami, Florida
Bayside Marketplace
Miami Book Fair

4.23.03

Seattle, Washington
Experience Music Project
Roger McGuinn

4.24.03

San Francisco, California
Great American Music Hall
Roger McGuinn

4.25.03

Los Angeles, California
UCLA
Steve Martin (banjo)
Los Angeles Book Festival / Interview with Steve Martin / performance with Martin

Rock On Remainders!

4.26.03

Los Angeles, California
UCLA
Roger McGuinn
Los Angeles Book Festival

10.26.04

St. Louis, Missouri
The Pageant
Roger McGuinn
WannaPalooza
To benefit America SCORES / no King

10.28.04

Chicago, Illinois
House of Blues
Roger McGuinn
To benefit America SCORES / no King

10.29.04

Cleveland, Ohio
Rock & Roll Hall of Fame
Roger McGuinn
To benefit America SCORES / no King

10.30.04

Pontiac, Michigan
Clutch Cargoes
Roger McGuinn
To benefit America SCORES / no King

4.17.05

Louisville, Kentucky
Freedom Hall, Kentucky Exposition Center
John Mellencamp
SK solo, with Mellencamp for *GHOSTS OF DARKLAND COUNTY* and guested on a few songs

11.19.05

Miami, Florida
Miami Dade College
Miami Book Fair / No King

4.26.06

Los Angeles, California
Late Late Show with Craig Ferguson
Craig Ferguson (drums)
Episode 274 of show / No King / This is air date, likely recorded earlier

4.26.06

Fort Worth, Texas
Gypsy Tea Room
To benefit America SCORES / no King

4.27.06

Denver, Colorado
Paramount

4.29.06

Los Angeles, California
Royce Hall
Los Angeles Times Festival of Books / to benefit 826LA / No King

11.18.06

Miami, Florida
Miami Dade College
Miami Book Fair / No King

5.31.07

New York, New York
Good Morning America
King Returns!

6.1.07

New York, New York
Webster Hall
Leslie Gore
15th anniversary "Still Younger Than Keith" Tour (of one show)
To benefit 826NYC / King returns!

11.10.07

Miami, Florida
Miami Dade College
Preceded by a fundraiser for Miami Scores / No King

11.15.08

Miami, Florida
Miami Dade College
No King

8.1.09

Ketchum, Idaho
Sun Valley Golf Course
YMCA's Annual Golf Classic & Dinner Social / no King

4.20.10

Washington D.C.
Harman Center for the Arts
Wordstock
"Besides the Music" - not a show, a conversation with the authors

4.21.10

Washington D.C.
The 9:30 Club
Roger McGuinn
Supporting Colin Powell's America's Promise / No King

4.22.10

Philadelphia, Pennsylvania
Electric Factory
Philadelphia Free Library / No King

4.23.10

New York, New York
Nokia Theater
Room to Read / No King

4.24.10

Boston
Massachusetts
The Royale
Jump Start / No King

6.22.12

Los Angeles, California
El Ray Theater
Past Our Bedtime Tour ("Final" Concerts)

6.23.12

Anaheim, California
Anaheim Convention Center
ALA Association Conference

8.6.12

Los Angeles, California
Late Late Show with Craig Ferguson
Episode 1563 of show, recorded earlier

11.24.13

Miami, Florida
Miami Dade College
Roger McGuinn
Miami Book Fair / No King / may have presented as "Artist formerly Known As The Rock Bottom Remainders"

3.13.14

Tucson, Arizona
Tucson Festival of Books
"First Reunion Tour"
No King

3.13.15

Tucson, Arizona
Tucson Festival of Books
No King

11.21.15

Miami, Florida
Adrienne Arsht Center
Miami Book Fair / No King

3.10.18

Tucson, Arizona
Tucson Festival of Books
No King

5.10.19

Minneapolis, Minnesota
First Avenue
Wordplay Book Festival / with King

11.29.19

Miami, Florida
The Porch
Miami Book Fair / No King

6.18.22

Nantucket, Massachusetts
Chicken Box
Nantucket Book Festival / no King

11.23.24

Miami, Florida
Chapman Conference Center
WITH King

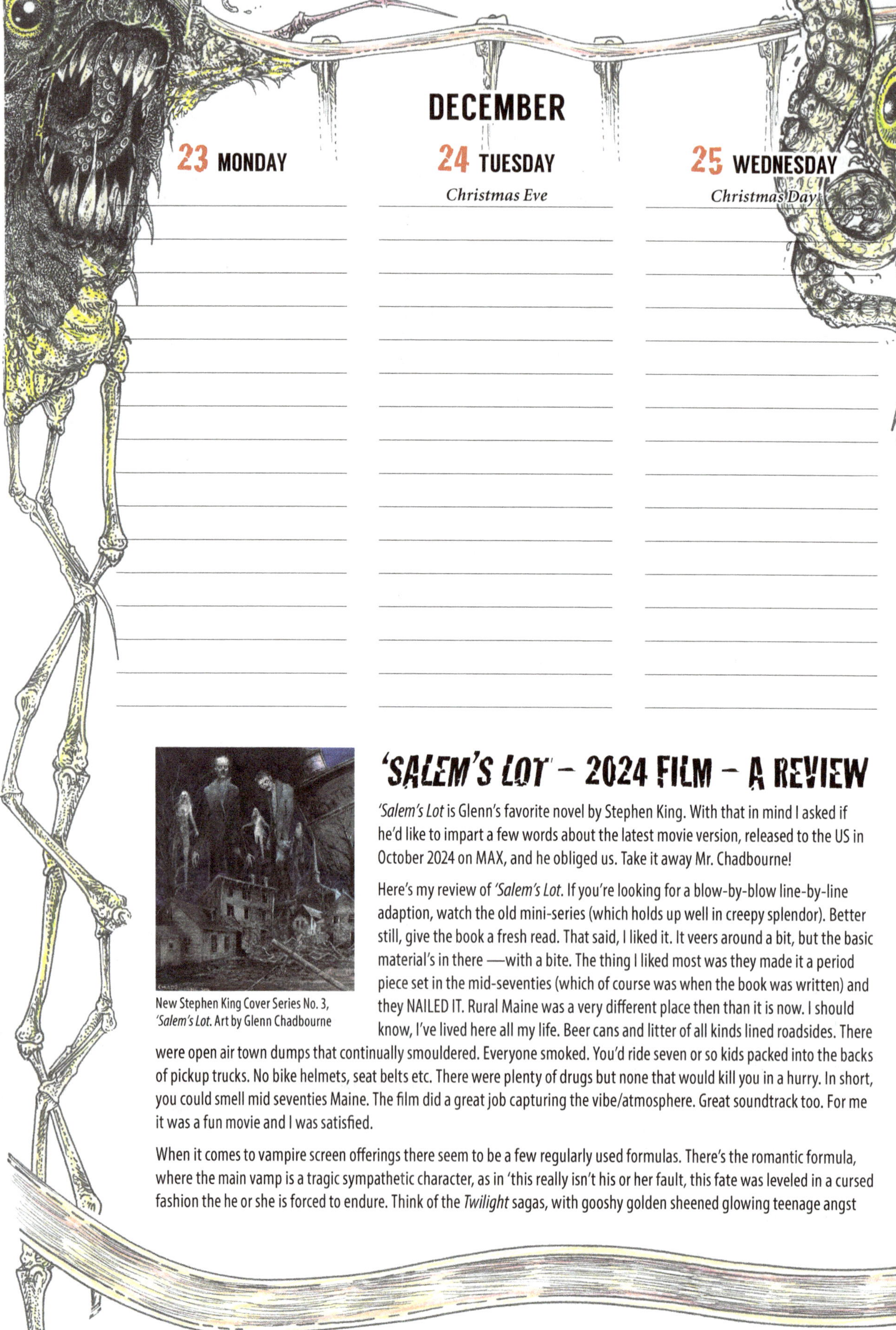

DECEMBER

23 MONDAY

24 TUESDAY

Christmas Eve

25 WEDNESDAY

Christmas Day

New Stephen King Cover Series No. 3, *'Salem's Lot*. Art by Glenn Chadbourne

'SALEM'S LOT – 2024 FILM – A REVIEW

'Salem's Lot is Glenn's favorite novel by Stephen King. With that in mind I asked if he'd like to impart a few words about the latest movie version, released to the US in October 2024 on MAX, and he obliged us. Take it away Mr. Chadbourne!

Here's my review of *'Salem's Lot*. If you're looking for a blow-by-blow line-by-line adaption, watch the old mini-series (which holds up well in creepy splendor). Better still, give the book a fresh read. That said, I liked it. It veers around a bit, but the basic material's in there —with a bite. The thing I liked most was they made it a period piece set in the mid-seventies (which of course was when the book was written) and they NAILED IT. Rural Maine was a very different place then than it is now. I should know, I've lived here all my life. Beer cans and litter of all kinds lined roadsides. There were open air town dumps that continually smouldered. Everyone smoked. You'd ride seven or so kids packed into the backs of pickup trucks. No bike helmets, seat belts etc. There were plenty of drugs but none that would kill you in a hurry. In short, you could smell mid seventies Maine. The film did a great job capturing the vibe/atmosphere. Great soundtrack too. For me it was a fun movie and I was satisfied.

When it comes to vampire screen offerings there seem to be a few regularly used formulas. There's the romantic formula, where the main vamp is a tragic sympathetic character, as in 'this really isn't his or her fault, this fate was leveled in a cursed fashion the he or she is forced to endure. Think of the *Twilight* sagas, with gooshy golden sheened glowing teenage angst

DECEMBER

26 THURSDAY

Hanukkah (1st day)
Kwanzaa

27 FRIDAY

28 SATURDAY

29 SUNDAY

New Year's Eve

love triangles. These are great if you're a brooding goth kid picnicking in boneyards. Actually, Gary Oldman's role as Drac' came across as a sympathetic character in the film's end. Drac' of course has as many interpretations as the many actors who've played him through the years. I'm a Christopher Lee man m'self. Then you have the dour, broody, Anne Rice versions in gothic splendor, richly outfitted with inner searching self-loathing complex characters. These too would find goth kids happily picnicking in the boneyard. Of these, both the old Brad Pitt/Tom Cruise film version as well as the recent series are pretty swell, in my humble op'. There are inventive versions of vamp culture that pop up every so often. The original *Fright Night* is a fun ride with a fresh feel for its time that I really enjoyed. *Near Dark* is a masterpiece in my view, with nasty outlaw vamps cruising around and sucking up the southwest states. Like *'Salem's Lot* Maine in the mid-seventies you could smell this outfit coming. If you want downright brutal scary as fuck vampires I'd have to hand that title to the *30 Days of Night* flick. That breathed fresh fear into the genre. Playing the mood in a pitch perfect key I'd hand it to the cable version of *Chapelwaite*, which delivers (I think) the perfect vibe of slow creeping dread brilliantly. It's played straight, and the vamps in that universe are believable and hideous. This is among the greatest film adaptations of SK's work (again in my humble op'). There are many other lesser-known films/tv series, etc., but these are the ones that pop into my noggin. I'd put the new Lot version more in the 'fun' category. As I said, I liked it, but if you're a purist, watch Tobe Hooper's *'Salem's Lot* mini-series from the 70's. In defense of the new film, they only had a couple hours to play with, and you can't jam all the intricate goings-on of the story sandwiched into that. In the end, vamps have always been with us and always will be. They suck, and we like to watch them do it.

– Glenn Chadbourne, October 2024

'Salem's Lot New King cover
available at
StephenKingCatalog.com

DECEMBER

30 MONDAY

31 TUESDAY

New Year's Eve

1 WEDNESDAY

New Year's Day

CHRISTINE. . . SAVES!

"...and suddenly there were arms around her, crushing, and a pair of hard hands were clasped together in a knot just below her breasts, in the hollow of her solar plexus. And suddenly one thumb popped up, the thumb of a hitchhiker signaling for a ride, only the thumb drove painfully into her breastbone. At the same time the grip of the. arms tightened brutally. She felt caught (Ohhhhhhh you're breaking my RIBS) in a gigantic bearhug. Her whole diaphragm seemed to heave, and something flew out of her mouth with the force of a projectile. It landed in the snow: a wet chunk of bun and meat." – Stephen King, *Christine*

Scribner trade paperback, 2024

My story regarding the King of horror is slightly different to the meet and greets or tour sightings, in fact for all I know he was three thousand miles away, furiously working on his next book when his work helped to save my life.

I was seven years old, that day in 1992 in fact as it was on my birthday that I almost died.

I was in the back of my parent's car heading to Thorpe Park (a UK theme park) to celebrate my birthday, happily sucking on a boiled sweet which suddenly slipped down my throat and became lodged. I remember frantically waving for my parents attention, only able to make guttural noises, when my mum noticed and screamed for my dad to pull over.

JANUARY

2 THURSDAY

3 FRIDAY

4 SATURDAY

5 SUNDAY

There we were, on the side of the motorway...I was yanked from the car and slammed on the back to no avail. My Dad hung me upside down and smacked my back harder but still the sweet was lodged.

I was becoming light headed and starved for air, the passing cars becoming a distant whisper when all of a sudden my lower chest was compressed and a gush of air dislodged the sweet, which went flying like a missile into the bushes

I greedily gulped in fresh air (as fresh as motorway air can be anyway) and from that moment forward never ate one of those sweets again.

"I remember it like it was yesterday; I'd not long since read *Christine* and after I felt Sean tapping my shoulder in the car I turned and realised he was choking, just like Leigh in the book. I remembered how the Heimlich manoeuvre was described so vividly and, after attempts to dislodge the sweet with hits to the back over his Dad's knee failed...I recalled exactly how the hitchhiker saved Leigh and I told his Dad to bring Sean to me. I got my arms around him, balled my fists together and squeezed hard just beneath the ribs...needless to say, it worked!"

– Rachael Chard, Sean's mum.

Whilst it was my Mum (who gets vast majority of credit for saving my life that day) that applied the Heimlich manoeuvre, it was the description of the manoeuvre from *Christine*, which she had recently been reading, that taught her the procedure, During the scene where the hitchhiker saves Leigh Cabot's life and therefore, my life was saved that day in part thanks to Stephen King! Thanks Steve!!

– Sean Chard, Constant Reader since 1995, England

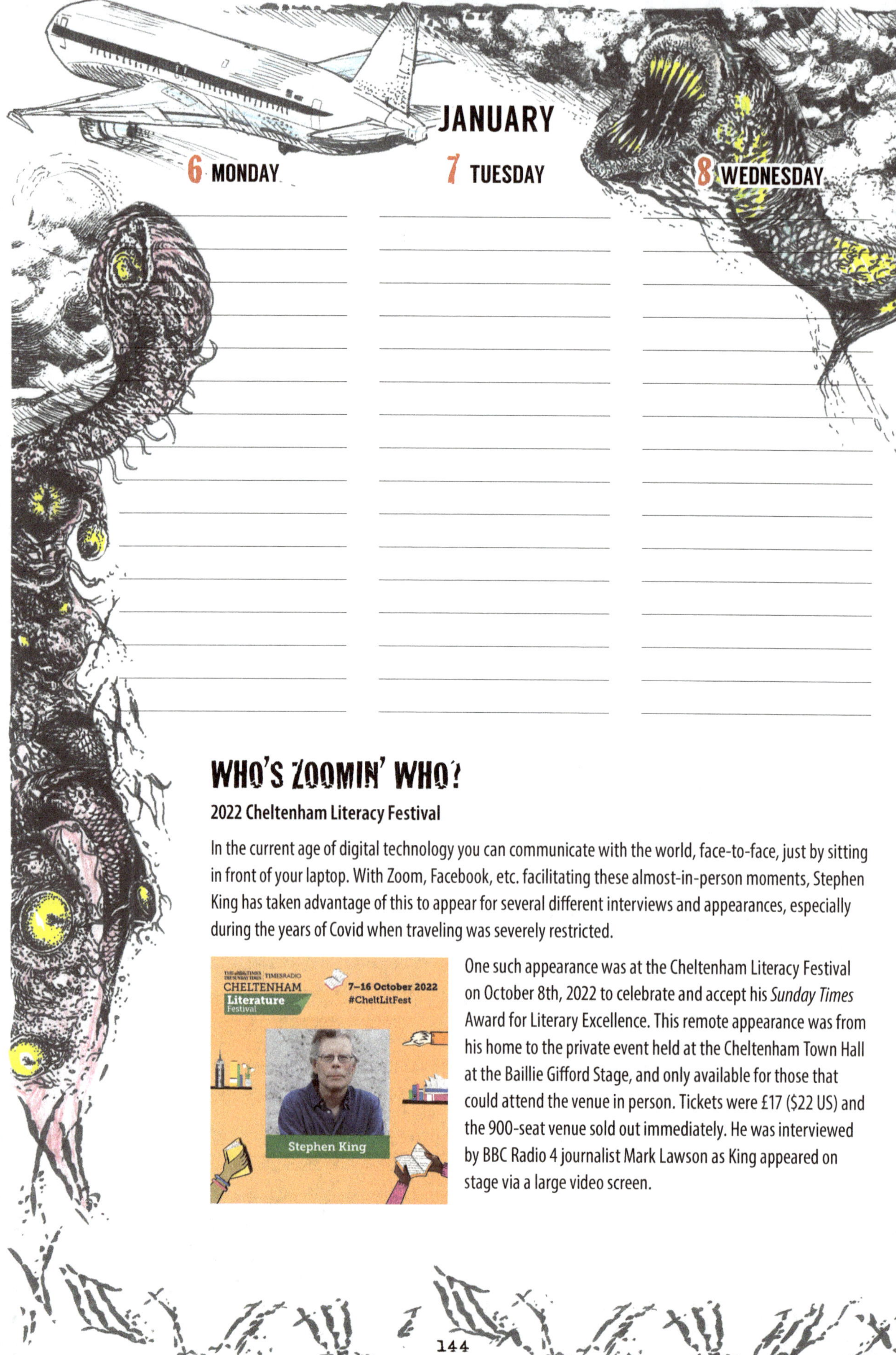

JANUARY

6 MONDAY

7 TUESDAY

8 WEDNESDAY

WHO'S ZOOMIN' WHO?

2022 Cheltenham Literacy Festival

In the current age of digital technology you can communicate with the world, face-to-face, just by sitting in front of your laptop. With Zoom, Facebook, etc. facilitating these almost-in-person moments, Stephen King has taken advantage of this to appear for several different interviews and appearances, especially during the years of Covid when traveling was severely restricted.

One such appearance was at the Cheltenham Literacy Festival on October 8th, 2022 to celebrate and accept his *Sunday Times* Award for Literary Excellence. This remote appearance was from his home to the private event held at the Cheltenham Town Hall at the Baillie Gifford Stage, and only available for those that could attend the venue in person. Tickets were £17 ($22 US) and the 900-seat venue sold out immediately. He was interviewed by BBC Radio 4 journalist Mark Lawson as King appeared on stage via a large video screen.

JANUARY

9 THURSDAY

10 FRIDAY

11 SATURDAY

12 SUNDAY

James Mortimer attended this event and had this to say about attending:

"I virtually met Stephen King (along with a sold-out audience) when he won a *Sunday Times* literacy award at the 2022 Cheltenham Literacy Festival in the UK. Even though he appeared on zoom he had the audience captivated. He discussed his new book, *Fairy Tale*, and told some really, funny tales.

Cheltenham Town Hall at the Baillie Gifford Stage

He did take questions from the audience. The host, Mark Lawson, asked King some pre-prepared questions and King would answer them and crack jokes in real time through the video link. After that the audience could post questions on an online site, which the host read out to ask King. King took quite a few questions from the audience which was fun to experience!

One question had an audience member asking why he hates dogs as they always end up dead in his books! Of course, he mentioned Mollie, "the thing of evil", to remind us he doesn't really hate dogs but uses them to create an emotional hold on the reader.

It was such an honour to be in an audience that where he got to communicate and chat with us digitally. and I am so glad I got the opportunity! Hopefully sometime soon he will come to the UK and I will be privileged enough to meet him."

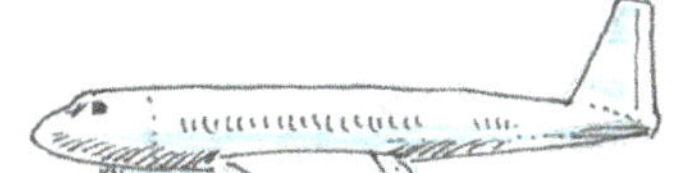

JANUARY

13 MONDAY

14 TUESDAY

15 WEDNESDAY

ENCOUNTERS

My first encounter with Stephen King was way, way, way back in the early '80s when he was set to appear at a middle school library in Truth or Consequences, New Mexico. He was hosting a screening of *Cujo* and signing books to raise funds for the library, where one of his friends worked. Living in El Paso, I eagerly hopped on my motorcycle and rode the 90-minute trek over Trans Mountain Road to meet my favorite author. I even still have the ticket!

The event was fantastic. After the screening, King took to the podium in the school gymnasium, sharing insights about the movie and reminding us with a chuckle, "No matter what the movie says... we all know the kid really dies..." He also touched on Kubrick's *The Shining*, but I'll spare you his colorful commentary on that for the sake of any family-friendly readers.

Post-event, They set up King at the Geronimo Springs Museum for the signing. The line was huge, far exceeding the crowd at the speaking event. After a couple of hours, I found myself near the front door, chatting with folks in line. Suddenly, a tall, lanky gentleman strode past—it was Stephen King himself. He addressed the entire crowd, apologizing for having to close down the line in order to make it to the airport for a late-night flight. Luckily, I was close enough to the door to allow him to usher me in with a few others. I got a photo of him signing someone else's book and had my copy of *Pet Sematary* signed. It was a fantastic night, and I became an even bigger fan, impressed by his personal touch in addressing the crowd directly, and not sending out an assistant to make the announcement.

JANUARY

16 THURSDAY

17 FRIDAY

18 SATURDAY

19 SUNDAY

№ 980

The Friends of the Truth or Consequences Library
invite you to hear

STEPHEN KING

Saturday, November 19, 1983, at 7:00 p.m.
Truth or Consequences Middle School, 4th & Grape

Donation: $2.00
Friends of the Library
Senior Citizens
Students

Donation: $4.00
Non-members

Reception to follow at Geronimo Springs Museum
where an assortment of Mr. King's books will
be on sale, including his newest:
"Pet Sematary"

Photo and ticket, Truth or Consequences New Mexico from Michael Edwards collection, 1983

JANUARY

20 MONDAY

Inauguration Day

Martin Luther King Jr. Day

21 TUESDAY

22 WEDNESDAY

STEPHEN KING DRIVE-IN

Fast forward to 1984: I had moved to Dallas and heard Stephen King would be attending the Joe Bob Briggs Drive-In Movie Festival at the Inwood Theater. No way was I missing that. I went, armed with the framed photo I'd taken of him the previous year, which I had blown up to movie poster size of 20x30. Along with the photo, I brought my original Land of Enchantment first edition of *Cycle of the Werewolf.* This was pre-iPhone, so no selfies, but I snapped quite a few photos from the event. Again, I was impressed as rather than showing up in a limo or with a driver, King drove up in a small rental car… parked and walked up to greet fans wearing a *Christine* t-shirt.

When I had the chance to talk to him, he loved the huge photo and signed it, "For Mike, Beast Wishes, Big Steve King" and then dated it. The autograph has faded over the years, but thankfully it's still visible. When I handed him my *Cycle of the Werewolf* book, he happily signed it, and Tabitha King, who was hanging out with him at the table, asked if she could sign it too. Of course, I said yes! So, she added her signature to it.

It was an amazing weekend, the best part being the opportunity for a few fans to have breakfast with Stephen King at the small restaurant that was attached to the Inwood Theater. Here's the catch: all you had to do was stay awake all night through an "Iron Man Marathon" of bloody movies and we hung out for a bit the following morning. All in all, it was an incredible experience for a Stephen King fan, but admittedly I still hold out hope for an opportunity to meet him just one more time!!

JANUARY

23 THURSDAY

24 FRIDAY

25 SATURDAY

26 SUNDAY

On a side note, just a couple of years before his passing, I showed the *Cycle of the Werewolf* book to Berni Wrightson, who signed both it and my first edition *Creepshow book*. Wrightson was truly a class act.

– Michael Edwards
Anderson Farms / Terror in the Corn
terrorinthecorn.com

Stephen King signing for fans
1984 Inwood Theater Dallas

John Bloom (aka Joe Bob Briggs) and Stephen King

Photos: 1984 Michael Edwards

1984 - Joe Bob Briggs Drive In Movie Festival

JANUARY

27 MONDAY

28 TUESDAY

29 WEDNESDAY

Lunar New Year

SIX-PACK TO GO

In 1981, the seventh World Fantasy Convention was held at the Claremont Hotel in Berkeley, California. Among the guests was Stephen King, who took part in several panels and was a World Fantasy Award nominee for Best Novel, for *The Mist*. He didn't win (that one went to Gene Wolfe, who won in that category again in 2007, the year I was a judge), but *Dark Forces*, Kirby McCauley's anthology *Dark Forces*, in which *The Mist* had appeared, did win for Best Anthology or Collection. So King shared in that reflected glory, at least.

King was already a literary celebrity, of course, and typically drew a crowd wherever he was in the hotel. At one point I was sitting in the hotel bar (then, as now, the place for socializing at WFC) when King entered. Knowing he couldn't sit at the bar and have a drink without crowds gathering, he bought a six-pack of bottled beer from the bartender and started back toward his room.

WFC 1981 Cover art
1981 by Edina and Orvy Junds

But the crowd had already arrived, and it surrounded him as he left the bar, barking compliments and questions in about equal measure.

King conversed with them for ten or fifteen minutes, as his cold beer warmed. After a while, I left the bar to visit the adjacent men's room, and while I washed my hands, King came in—followed by a fan. "Mr. King!" the fan said. "I just have one question!" "I just have to take a piss," King growled.

Presumably he did so. I was out of the restroom by then, and so was the chastised fan.

A couple minutes later, I was on my way to the staircase to meet someone, and King came out of the restroom, headed for the same staircase. But again, he was waylaid; this time by a mature, nicely dressed woman. I don't know if he knew her, but he paused when she said, "Mr. King, may I introduce you to someone?"

JANUARY

30 THURSDAY

31 FRIDAY

1 SATURDAY

2 SUNDAY

Groundhog Day

I didn't hear his response, but by now I was curious. The only other person in the immediate vicinity was a young woman sitting by herself on a settee with a red-tipped, white cane leaning beside her. I stayed put.

The woman led King straight to her. "Christine," she said, "This is Mr. King. Mr. King, this is Christine. She's been wanting to meet you."

I watched the smile spread across King's face. If you've seen it, you know the one I'm talking about: genuine enthusiasm combined with a hint of mischievousness.

"Christine?" said he, shaking her proffered hand. "I have to tell you about the book I'm working on."

With that, he sat beside her and started describing his work-in-progress.

Twenty or thirty minutes later, I passed by again. Stephen King and Christine were still sitting there, deep in conversation, his by now room-temperature six-pack forgotten at his feet.

Whenever someone asks me what Stephen King is like, I tell that story. It sums him up nicely, I believe.

– Jeffrey J. Mariotte

WFC 1981 Back cover art 1981 by Alfredo P. Alcala

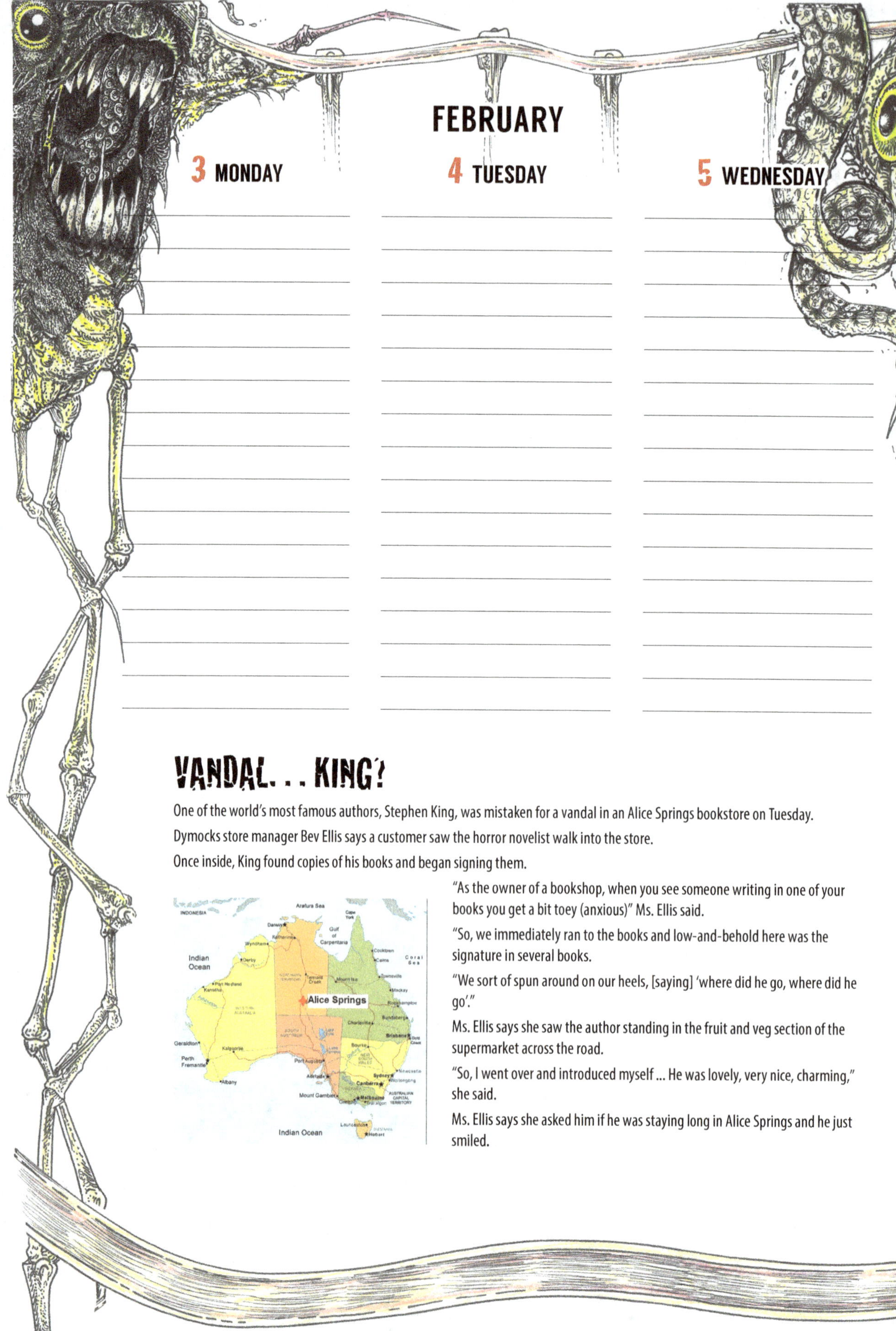

FEBRUARY

3 MONDAY

4 TUESDAY

5 WEDNESDAY

VANDAL. . . KING?

One of the world's most famous authors, Stephen King, was mistaken for a vandal in an Alice Springs bookstore on Tuesday.

Dymocks store manager Bev Ellis says a customer saw the horror novelist walk into the store.

Once inside, King found copies of his books and began signing them.

"As the owner of a bookshop, when you see someone writing in one of your books you get a bit toey (anxious)" Ms. Ellis said.

"So, we immediately ran to the books and low-and-behold here was the signature in several books.

"We sort of spun around on our heels, [saying] 'where did he go, where did he go'."

Ms. Ellis says she saw the author standing in the fruit and veg section of the supermarket across the road.

"So, I went over and introduced myself ... He was lovely, very nice, charming," she said.

Ms. Ellis says she asked him if he was staying long in Alice Springs and he just smiled.

FEBRUARY

6 THURSDAY

7 FRIDAY

8 SATURDAY

Lunar New Year

9 SUNDAY

Ms. Ellis also said she assumed the author was on a holiday and had come into the shop to check to see that *Lisey's Story*, his most recent book, had been stocked.

"[Then I said], well if we knew you were coming we would have baked a cake."

"He introduced me to his friends and we had a talk and then I said 'Well I'll leave you to the tomatoes.'"

Asked if it was the first time an author had simply come in a started signing, Ms. Ellis replied: "They don't normally just open the books and go for it."

But she said the high-profile writer was polite and well spoken.

King signed six books in total.

The customer that mistook the author for a vandal bought one. Ms. Ellis plans to give the remaining five copies to community groups who can auction them off to raise funds.

King's rep in Sydney confirmed that they did not know the author was currently in Australia. August, 2007.

The bookstore, Dymocks Alice Springs, owned by Bev Ellis and her husband since 1993, closed its doors in 2013 after a twenty-year run in the business.

Lisey's Story, Scribner 2006

This story created from combined news reports at abc.net.au and www.brisbanetimes.com.au

FEBRUARY

10 MONDAY

11 TUESDAY

12 WEDNESDAY

HITTING ROCK BOTTOM WRITING

In the "First Foreword" to Stephen King's *On Writing* he discusses how The Rock Bottom Remainders was to be a one-time event: "The group was intended as a one-shot deal—we would play two shows at the American Booksellers Convention, get a few laughs, recapture our misspent youth for three or four hours, then go our separate ways." And then he mentions how it obviously didn't happen that way as "the group never quite broke up." So then as the group continued to play and in 1993 went on tour across the country they found themselves in Miami Beach eating Chinese food before a show. Stephen King and Amy Tan were having a discussion, about the one question that was never asked during the Q-and-A following almost every writer's talk. He said Amy Tan was thinking it over when she finally said "No one ever asks about the language." Something obviously clicked because King said he owed "an immense dept of gratitude" for her response. He had been thinking of writing a book about writing but didn't trust his own "motivations," thinking since he'd sold so many books he might have something "worthwhile to say about

On Writing, Scribner 2020

FEBRUARY

13 THURSDAY

14 FRIDAY

Valentine's Day

15 SATURDAY

16 SUNDAY

writing." But just because he sold a lot of books he'd thought he'd better have a better reason than just being "successful." His reference to Colonel Sanders selling a lot of Fried Chicken doesn't mean folks want to hear how he made it. That's pure Stephen King right there.

Amy Tan's response, that nobody asks about the language gave Stephen King the go ahead to begin the book *On Writing*. He said "that no one ever asks (them) about the language." They ask "the DeLillos and the Updikes… but they don't ask popular novelists. Yes many of us proles also care about the language…" He dedicated the book to Amy Tan because she "told me in a very simple and direct way that it was okay to write it." *On Writing* was born while the Rock Bottom Remainders were on tour. Inspiration hits when it hits… over a meal before a show.

Photo: Shane Leonard

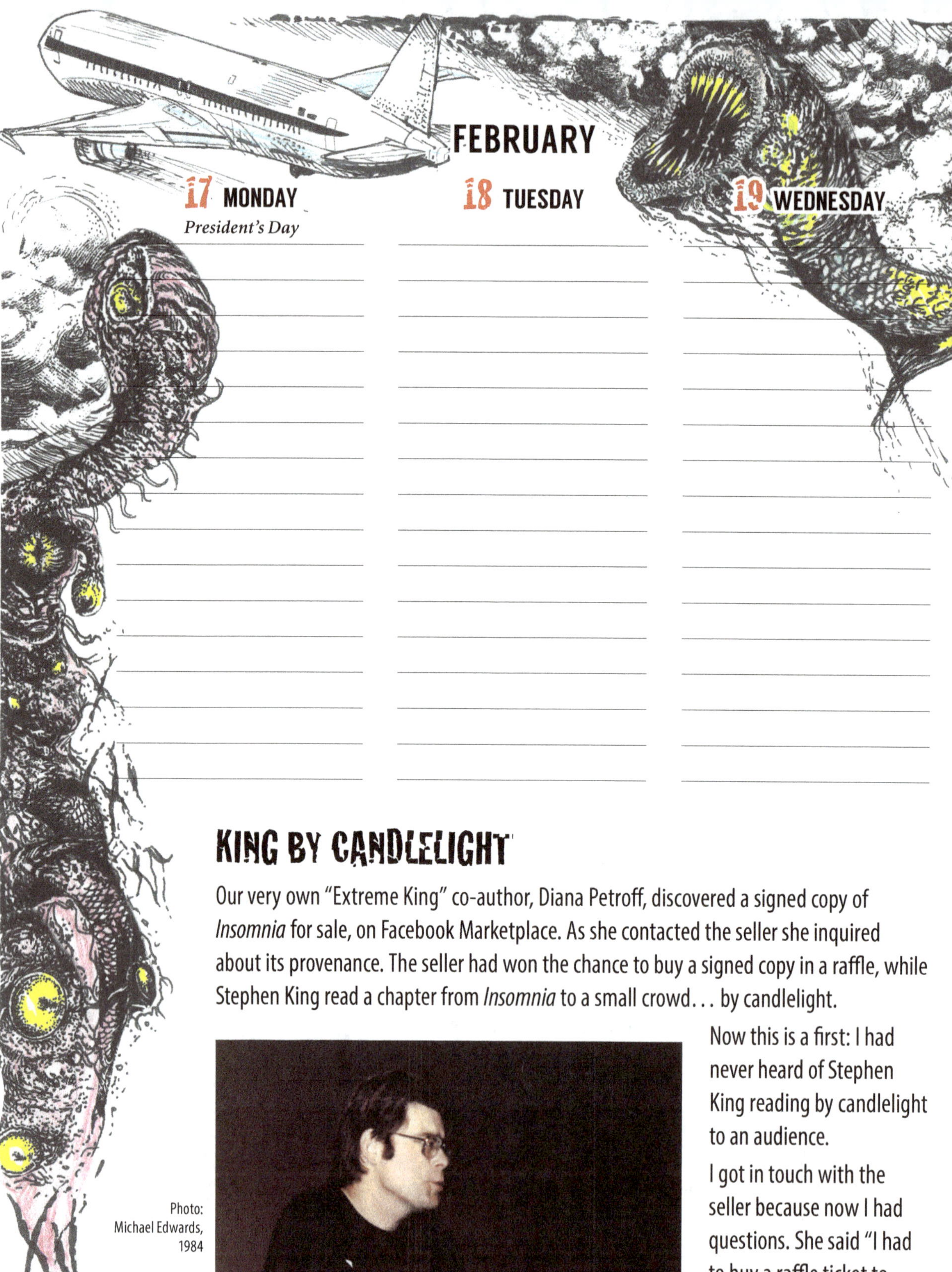

FEBRUARY

17 MONDAY

President's Day

18 TUESDAY

19 WEDNESDAY

KING BY CANDLELIGHT

Our very own "Extreme King" co-author, Diana Petroff, discovered a signed copy of *Insomnia* for sale, on Facebook Marketplace. As she contacted the seller she inquired about its provenance. The seller had won the chance to buy a signed copy in a raffle, while Stephen King read a chapter from *Insomnia* to a small crowd… by candlelight.

Photo: Michael Edwards, 1984

Now this is a first: I had never heard of Stephen King reading by candlelight to an audience.

I got in touch with the seller because now I had questions. She said "I had to buy a raffle ticket to win the chance to buy the book. That night, he read from *Insomnia* for those of

FEBRUARY

20 THURSDAY

21 FRIDAY

22 SATURDAY

23 SUNDAY

us that won, in a room in Legislative Plaza in Nashville. It was soooo creepy. he had one big blood red candle for light. There were about thirty people in the audience. I was in the front row so I didn't see exactly how many came in behind us, you know with just candlelight... one candle. It was called the War Memorial Auditorium. He had a tall black candleholder with a large red pillar candle. He read from a podium and I think he had a light over the book so he could read. It was from *Insomnia* but I have no idea which part. We all knew what was going to happen, and being scared was a crazy thought....after all, it's just a book. He told us a story to purposely make us afraid to walk back to our cars. I can't remember what it was though!

[Editor's Note: Stephen King had often used this tale to get his audience stirred up before an event... Look for "Sooner or Later" in this year's Calendar section.]

FEBRUARY

24 MONDAY

25 TUESDAY

26 WEDNESDAY

FILM REVIEW: I KNOW WHAT YOU NEED

Stephen King's short story, "I Know What You Need" was originally published in the September issue of Cosmopolitan magazine. It was later collected in King's 1978 *Night Shift*, his first short story collection. The story is about young college student, Elizabeth Rogan, who is cramming for a final exam when she meets fellow student, Ed Hamner, Jr. Ed is an outcast and a bit...different from the other students as he has a bit of paranormal ability to just "know things". He offers Elizabeth a strawberry ice cream as he knows this is on her mind, and she wants to take a break from studying. After he informs her he knows the answers to the final she's studying for; she later realizes he was helpful. Their relationship grows over several months and they become a couple, but something is wrong here...very wrong! Ed has a certain power over Elizabeth, one that would make her fall in love with him and become his.

Poster Art by Mike Baird

MARCH

27 THURSDAY

28 FRIDAY

1 SATURDAY

First Night of Ramadan

2 SUNDAY

With the help of her roommate, and some investigating of her own, Elizabeth's roommate informs her just who, and what Ed really is.

I know What You Need, 2023 Julia Marchese

This Dollar Baby film was amazingly adapted. It captures the look and feel of the 1970's, and transports the viewer right into that time period. I was intrigued by all the props, clothes, and set designs Julia and her crew found to help lend to the feel of the era. I enjoyed the locations throughout Maine, and the university as well. The two lead actors, William Champion and Caroline Goldenberg, gave excellent performances. I felt William came across as a Brady Hartsfield type from Stephen King's *Mr. Mercedes* trilogy, and Harold Lauder from King's *The Stand*.

Caroline played the young college student convincingly. This was a very closely adapted Dollar Baby film to King's original text. With the 1970's pop culture props, as well as the atmosphere, it makes this one of the great Dollar Baby films produced.

– Anthony Northrup

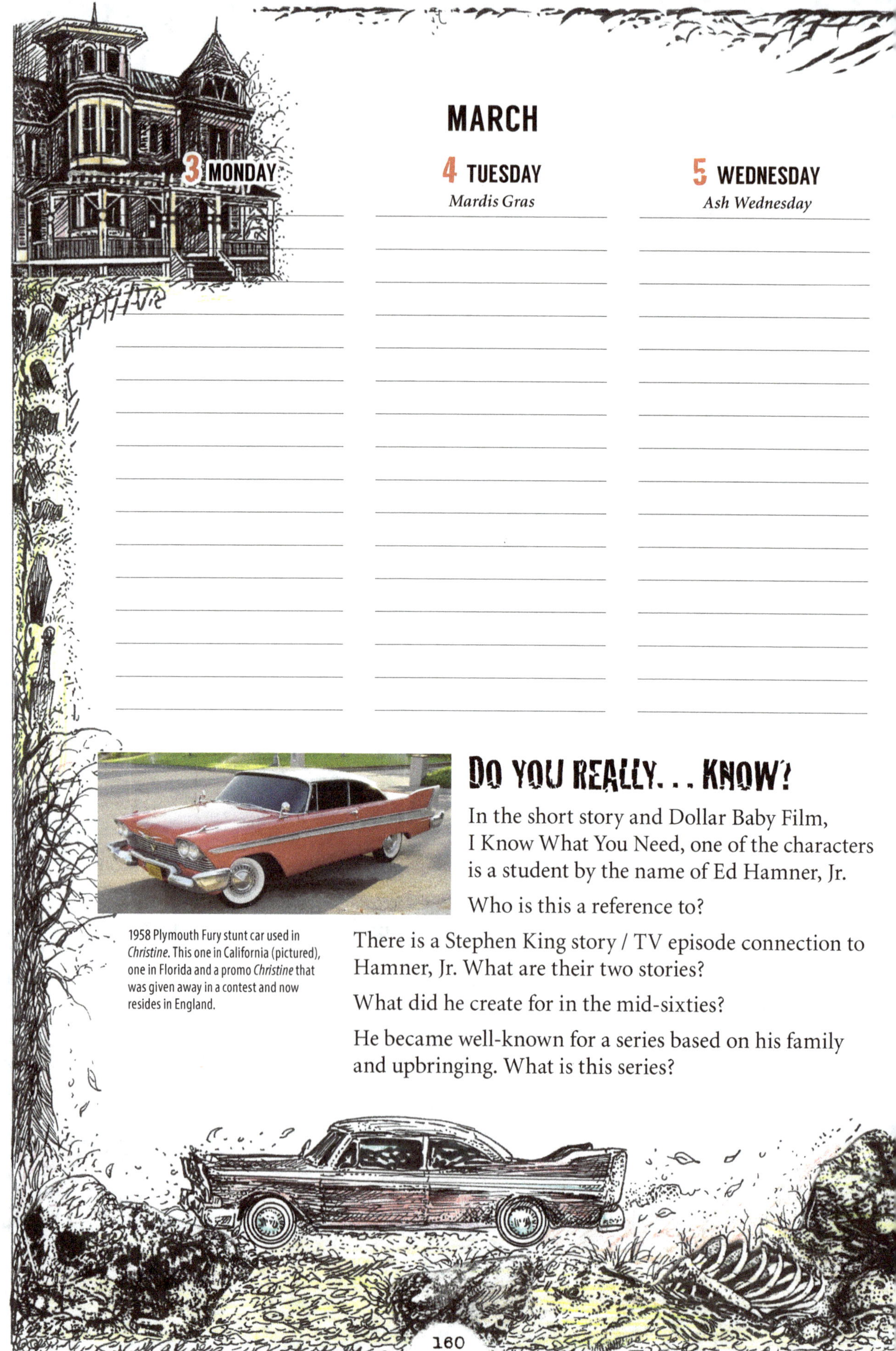

MARCH

3 MONDAY

4 TUESDAY
Mardis Gras

5 WEDNESDAY
Ash Wednesday

1958 Plymouth Fury stunt car used in *Christine*. This one in California (pictured), one in Florida and a promo *Christine* that was given away in a contest and now resides in England.

DO YOU REALLY. . . KNOW?

In the short story and Dollar Baby Film, I Know What You Need, one of the characters is a student by the name of Ed Hamner, Jr.

Who is this a reference to?

There is a Stephen King story / TV episode connection to Hamner, Jr. What are their two stories?

What did he create for in the mid-sixties?

He became well-known for a series based on his family and upbringing. What is this series?

MARCH

6 THURSDAY

7 FRIDAY

8 SATURDAY

9 SUNDAY

Daylight Saving begins

Answers:

A1: Earl Hamner, Jr., a writer in television. Featured in the original short story his full name in that is Edward Jackson Hamner, Jr. The fact that Stephen King added the "Jr." was a dead giveaway that this was a nod to Earl Hamner, Jr.

A2: Earl Hamner, Jr. wrote a *Twilight Zone* episode, "You Drive" (Season 5, Ep. 15), which features a man and his car that was involved in a hit and run. It seems his car has a mind of its own, a car with a conscience. This was used similarly two decades later in 1983 by Stephen King, in the evil *Christine*, albeit with its own unique way to solve issues it has with others. Oliver Pope in this episode is haunted by his car and forced in the end to do right.

A3: Earl Hamner, Jr. wrote many *Twilight Zone* episodes, eight total. One of his most famous is "The Hunt," along with many supernatural themed episodes like "A Piano in the House" and "Jess-Belle."

A4: *The Waltons*. This show, along with the movie, *Spencer's Mountain* (starring Henry Fonda and Maureen O'Hara), was inspired by his childhood. Hamner introduced each show with a voice-over narration for most episodes. He also created *Falcon Crest*, another long running TV series. I'll be honest with you readers, I'm just happy to include Mr. Hamner here. He brought a lot of fun and enlightening entertainment to me and my family growing up. He left us in 2016 but he has quite a legacy of story telling in his wake. Look up his work sometime.

MARCH

10 MONDAY

11 TUESDAY

12 WEDNESDAY

Simpsons episode "Please Homer, Don't Hammer 'Em" S. 18 Ep 3, featuring The Rock Bottom Remainders.

ROCK N' WRITE, ALL NIGHT LONG

The Rock Bottom Remainder's personnel list

From 1993 this is the original lineup of the authors, artists, and co-conspirators that began this unique musical trek.

DAVE BARRY, lead guitar, vocals

TAD BARTIMUS, Remainderette

LORRAINE BATTLE, wardrobe, shop till you drop

ROY BLOUNT, JR., Critics Chorus and master of ceremonies

BOB DAITZ, tour manager, scapegoat, non-navigator, Sammy you should see me now

BOB DANNIC, universal crew, driver

MICHAEL DORRIS, percussion (Anaheim and Bottom Line only)

CAROLE EITINGON, concessions, merchandising, life of the party

JIM ENGLAND, guitar technician, mysterious man from Maine

ROBERT FULGHUM, mandocello, vocals

KATHI KAMEN GOLDMARK, Remainderette and Founding Mom

MATT GROENING, Critics Chorus

HOOVER (CHRIS RANKIN), production manager, sound engineer, good shorts

JOSH KELLY, drums, best attitude in the biz (and the bus)

STEPHEN KING, rhythm guitar, vocals

MARCH

13 THURSDAY

14 FRIDAY

15 SATURDAY

16 SUNDAY

TABITHA KING, tour photographer, shop till you drop

BARBARA KINGSOLVER, keyboards, vocals

AL KOOPER, musical director, guitar, keyboards, vocals, video expert

GREIL MARCUS, Critics Chorus

DAVE MARSH, Critics Chorus, Teen Angel

MOUSE (DANNY DELALUZ), keyboard/drum technician, lead flashlight

RIDLEY PEARSON, bass guitar, vocals, Designated Worrier

JERRY PETERSON, saxophone, "Check it out!"

JOEL SELVIN, Critics Chorus, lead scream

AMY TAN, Remainderette, Rhythm Dominatrix

JIMMY VIVINO, keyboards, vocals

DAVE WORTERS, bus driver, tour guide

The Rock Bottom Remainders
VHS 1993
BMG Video

Drayton's Scout vehicle
The Mist film, 2007

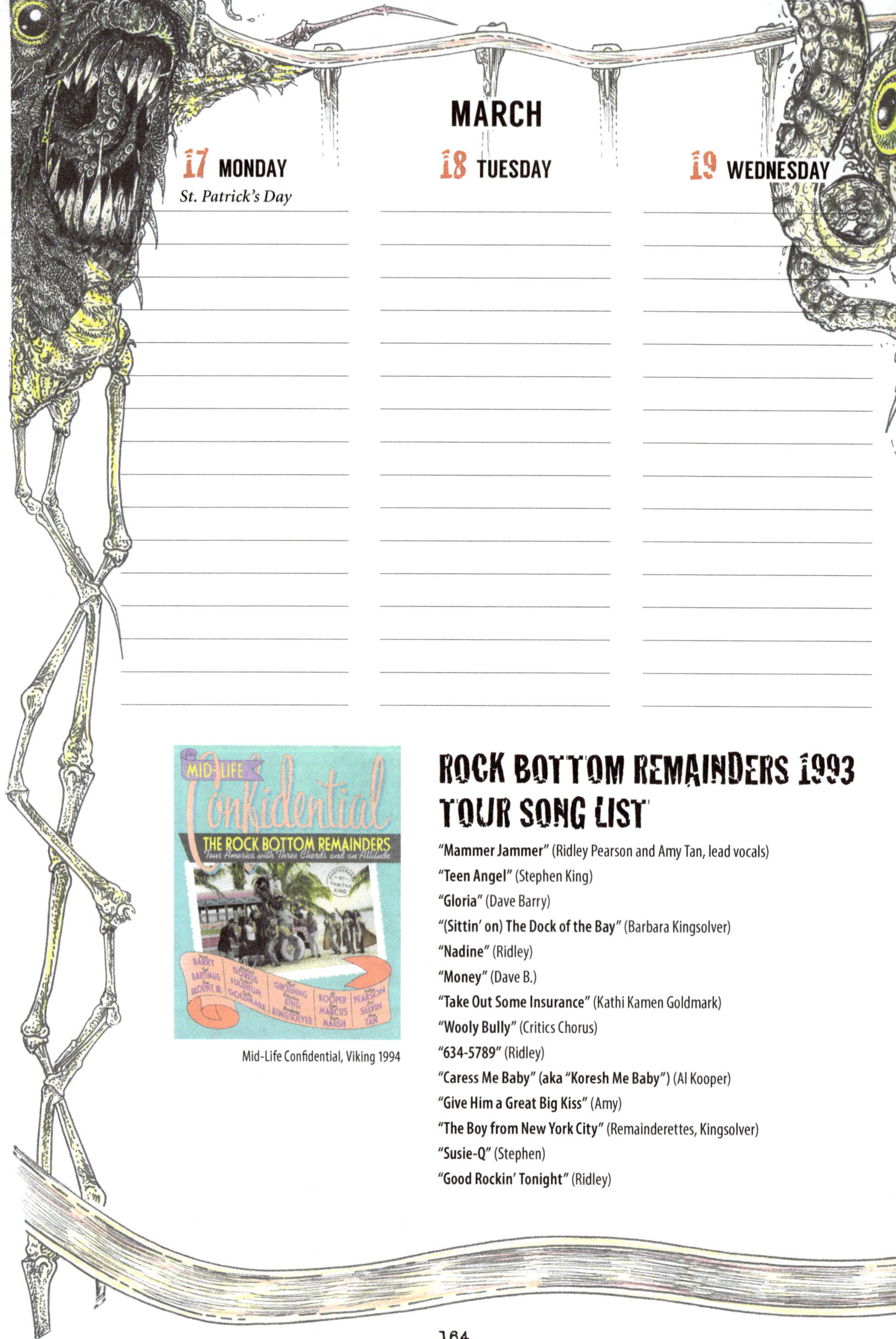

MARCH

17 MONDAY

St. Patrick's Day

18 TUESDAY

19 WEDNESDAY

Mid-Life Confidential, Viking 1994

ROCK BOTTOM REMAINDERS 1993 TOUR SONG LIST

"Mammer Jammer" (Ridley Pearson and Amy Tan, lead vocals)

"Teen Angel" (Stephen King)

"Gloria" (Dave Barry)

"(Sittin' on) The Dock of the Bay" (Barbara Kingsolver)

"Nadine" (Ridley)

"Money" (Dave B.)

"Take Out Some Insurance" (Kathi Kamen Goldmark)

"Wooly Bully" (Critics Chorus)

"634-5789" (Ridley)

"Caress Me Baby" (aka "Koresh Me Baby") (Al Kooper)

"Give Him a Great Big Kiss" (Amy)

"The Boy from New York City" (Remainderettes, Kingsolver)

"Susie-Q" (Stephen)

"Good Rockin' Tonight" (Ridley)

MARCH

20 THURSDAY

21 FRIDAY

22 SATURDAY

23 SUNDAY

"Stand by Me" (Stephen)
"Louie Louie" (Critics Chorus; Joel Selvin, scream solo)
"You Can't Sit Down" (Kathi)
"The Last Time" (Dave B.)
"Who Do You Love" (Stephen)
"Land of 1,000 Dances" (Dave B.)
"Last Kiss" (Stephen)
"Leader of the Pack" (Amy)
"Double Shot (Of My Baby's Love)" (Critics Chorus)
"He Will Break Your Heart" (Dave B., Kathi)
"My Guy" (Tad Bartimus)
"Chain of Fools" (Tad)
"These Boots Are Made for Walkin" (Amy)
"Endless Sleep" (Stephen)
"Midnight Hour" (Ridley)
"Short Shorts" (Critics Chorus; Remainderettes)
Source: *Mid-Life Confidential* 1994 Viking hardcover.

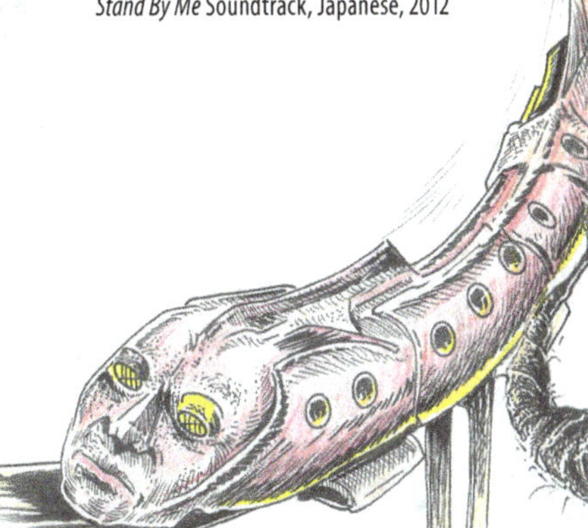

Stand By Me Soundtrack, Japanese, 2012

MARCH

24 MONDAY | **25 TUESDAY** | **26 WEDNESDAY**

I SAW SUE KISSING STEPHEN KING

The story of these photos actually starts 13 years earlier. On 9/22/1998 the novel *Bag Of Bones* dropped. On 9/29/1998 thousands of fans gathered at the the Harold Washington Library in downtown Chicago for Stephen King's stop on a tightly scheduled tour. The decision was made to put him at a table on the ground floor, to sit at the table "take book - look up and smile - sign Book - hand book to a gentleman that would hand the book back to the fan." Then gently guide said fan out of the way. This routine was so mechanical, so sterile. And I felt so bad for Mr. King.

Photo: Sue Marcus

When my turn came, I needed to shake things up a little. Before he could look up at me, I positioned a small gift I had brought for him (pertaining to Chicago) right on the unsigned book. He looked at the gift, then looked me as I explained what it was while we discussed it for a moment. Then, something I said, made his body guards jump! The four of us had a fun moment in conversation. This whole interaction with the men took much longer than the others before me... some staff in charge of "The Machine" were a little bent out of shape because of this.

He signed my book then as I walked away, I felt fantastic with our interactions. I had slowed him down just a bit and produced a small breather for him. But then a nagging thought crept in... it would have been perfection if I had only touched him. Doing that small gesture, would have been a little bit more personal (and memorable for me).

MARCH

21 THURSDAY

28 FRIDAY

29 SATURDAY

30 SUNDAY

11/31/2011. The Rock Bottom Remainder's had a Chicago concert on their schedule. There was also an option to attend a Meet & Greet Event at another location before their show. I brought only one book with me for possible signatures & photos: *Mid-Life Confidential* (FYI the book was written by the original band members, formed by Kathy Goldmark. With each member writing a chapter about their own experiences). The Remainders arrive, and as you can imagine, Stepen King was singled out and swarmed by the fans! He was very thin and pale from the van accident in 1999 (where King has stated he keeps weight off to keep the pressure off his leg, thus his look). A huge line was formed in front of him, with people waiting to get their books signed, and I mean, books bought before the event. It didn't matter that they were later printings, in hardcover or even paperback. People with books piled high in their arms. Really disturbing to me. There was another room where the rest of the band members hung out so that's where I went. I was busy greeting all of them. These authors are all great as far as I'm concerned. After I was done I sat at a table and visited with Amy Tan, her husband Lou, & Tabitha King. She hogged my book re-reading her chapter. When finished she looked up and said, "Huh, no wonder my books aren't selling". I would excuse myself to go check on the King line in the next room here and there. FINALLY, the line was small enough to join it.

Photo: Sue Marcus

I asked a friend, as I handed him my camera, "Take as many photos as if your life depended on it." And he did just that. MY TURN! Finally, to sit with The Master. So, as we talked, he signed his chapter in my Remainder book. Our subject being about his Chicago book signing in 1998. And almost, as an after-thought, I pointed my finger at him, and said: "You know what? All those years ago in Chicago, as I walked away from the signing line, I had such a sad thought. I Just WANTED to TOUCH your hand."
With that being said, he held and lifted my pointed finger hand... AND KISSED it!

My heart just melted. I will never be able to forget this evening, or that sweet kiss.

– Sue Marcus

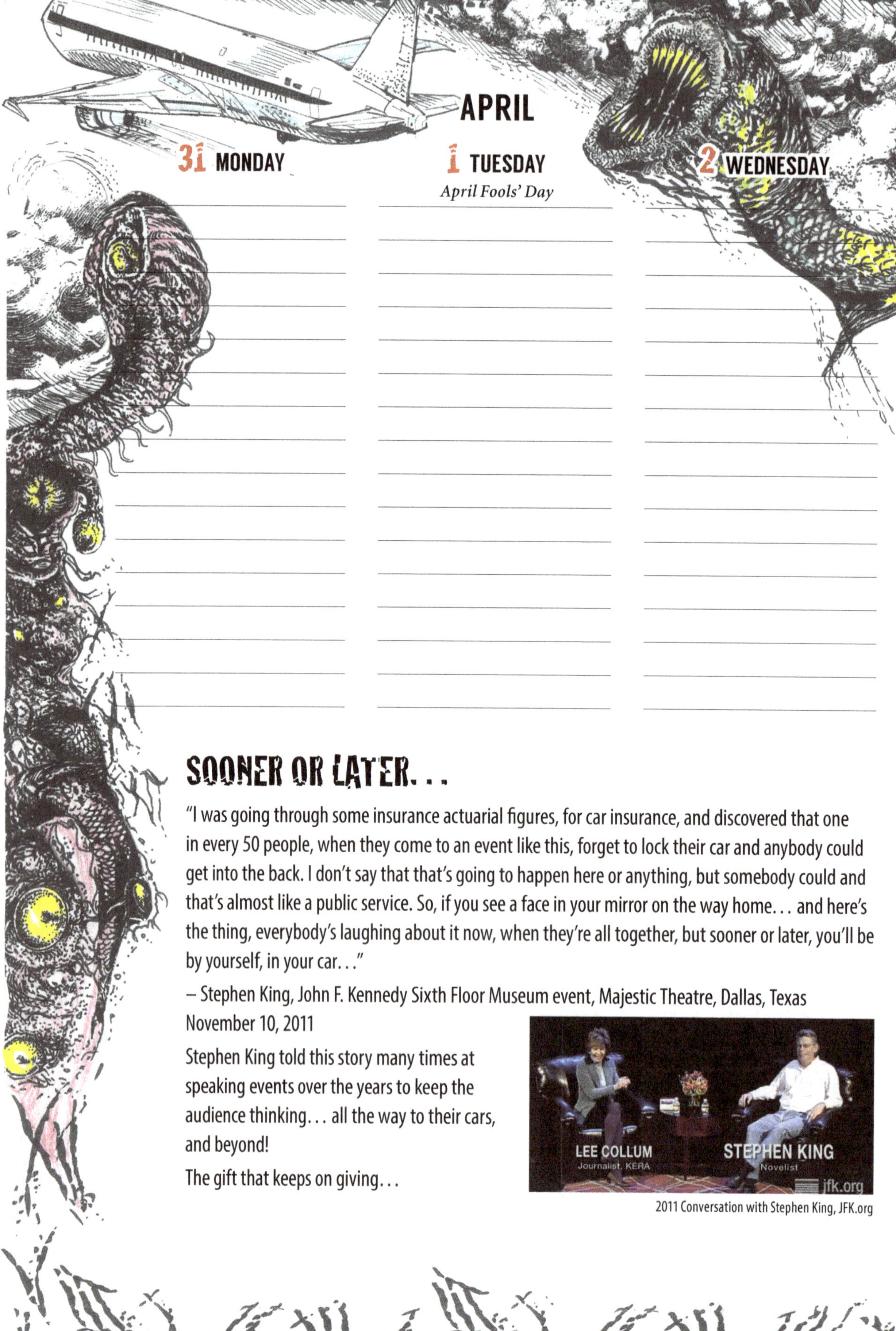

APRIL

31 MONDAY

1 TUESDAY

April Fools' Day

2 WEDNESDAY

SOONER OR LATER...

"I was going through some insurance actuarial figures, for car insurance, and discovered that one in every 50 people, when they come to an event like this, forget to lock their car and anybody could get into the back. I don't say that that's going to happen here or anything, but somebody could and that's almost like a public service. So, if you see a face in your mirror on the way home... and here's the thing, everybody's laughing about it now, when they're all together, but sooner or later, you'll be by yourself, in your car..."

– Stephen King, John F. Kennedy Sixth Floor Museum event, Majestic Theatre, Dallas, Texas November 10, 2011

Stephen King told this story many times at speaking events over the years to keep the audience thinking... all the way to their cars, and beyond!

The gift that keeps on giving...

2011 Conversation with Stephen King, JFK.org

APRIL

3 THURSDAY

4 FRIDAY

5 SATURDAY

6 SUNDAY

On November 22, 1963, President John F. Kennedy was assassinated in downtown Dallas.

If you had the chance to change history, would you?

Stephen King's novel *11/22/63* addresses this very scenario as the book's main character travels back in time on a mission to prevent the assassination of President Kennedy.

Stephen King's novel, *11-22-63*, was released on November 8th, 2011. It only seemed fitting that Stephen King was front and center at a fundraiser at the Majestic Theatre in Dallas on Thursday, November 10, 2011, benefiting The Sixth Floor Museum at Dealey Plaza. There was an exclusive reception that featured the author at 5:45 p.m. A conversation was facilitated by Dallas columnist and broadcaster Lee Cullum at 7 PM for an hour-long discussion in front of a sold-out audience.

2012 Scribner press, US

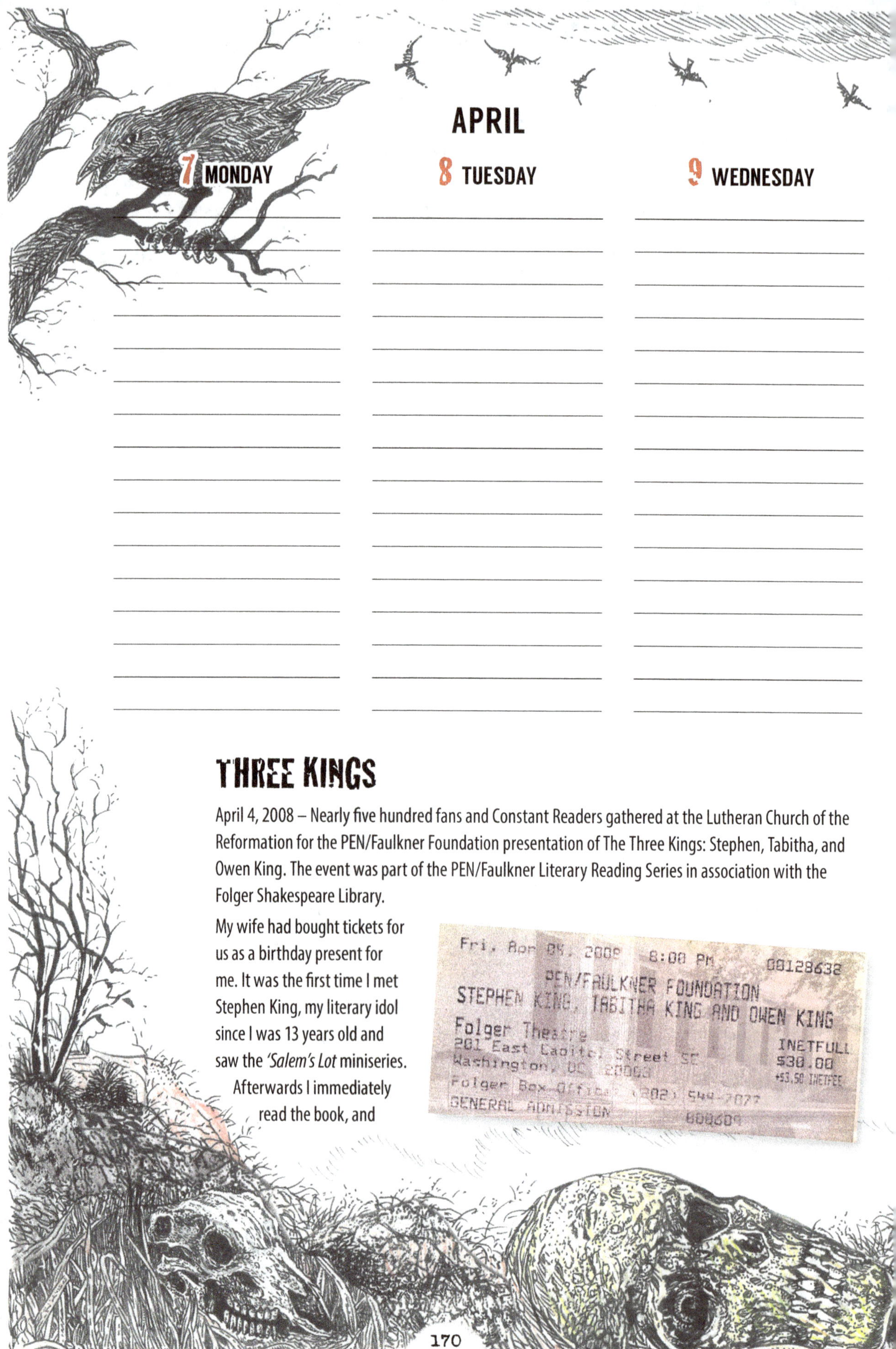

APRIL

7 MONDAY

8 TUESDAY

9 WEDNESDAY

THREE KINGS

April 4, 2008 – Nearly five hundred fans and Constant Readers gathered at the Lutheran Church of the Reformation for the PEN/Faulkner Foundation presentation of The Three Kings: Stephen, Tabitha, and Owen King. The event was part of the PEN/Faulkner Literary Reading Series in association with the Folger Shakespeare Library.

My wife had bought tickets for us as a birthday present for me. It was the first time I met Stephen King, my literary idol since I was 13 years old and saw the *'Salem's Lot* miniseries. Afterwards I immediately read the book, and

APRIL

10 THURSDAY

11 FRIDAY

12 SATURDAY

Passover

13 SUNDAY

Palm Sunday

eventually read the rest of Stephen King's published work. And on top of that, it was an opportunity to meet his wife and youngest son, marvelous authors in their own rights.

The reading portion of the event took place in the Lutheran church as the Folger Library did not have room for the crowd. The night opened with Tabitha King reading from a novel in progress. Owen followed, reading his short story "Nothing is in Bad Taste," a beautifully written tale of a souring relationship. I've wanted to read the story several times since then, but it has yet to be collected. Finally, Stephen read the opening chapter of his yet-to-be-published novel, *Under the Dome*. The fate of that woodchuck haunted everybody.

Following the reading, the crowd moved across the street to the Folger Shakespeare Library, where each writer agreed to sign one book for each fan. I brought along *Creepshow* and *Cycle of the Werewolf*. Not having anything in my library by Tabby or Owen, I had them sign the program.

An exciting, wonderful, and very memorable night.

– T. L. Emery

PEN/FAULKNER

PEN/Faulkner presents

The Three Kings

Stephen, Tabitha and Owen King

Introduction by Mary Kay Zuravleff

Friday, April 4, 2008
8:00 PM
Folger Shakespeare Library
Washington, D.C.

The Three Kings Program Booklet
PEN/Faulkner event
April 4th, 2008

APRIL

14 MONDAY

15 TUESDAY

Tax Day

16 WEDNESDAY

HOPE SPRINGS ETERNAL

I have been a Stephen King fan from the beginning. I read *Carrie* and was hooked and always tried to get the next book as soon as available. I moved to the Canadian Forces Base (CFB) in Lahr/Schwartzwald, Germany in 1975 and wondered how I would get my Stephen King books. Fortunately, there was an American Book Store on the Base and I would run in and order new books as soon as I learned about them. With the Book Store and a Doubleday Book Club membership (not my favorite but at least it was books), I survived the four years in Germany!

B. Dalton, Bangor, Maine, 1982

I returned to Canada in 1979 and we were posted to CFB Gagetown, Oromocto, New Brunswick. I was so excited when I observed how close we were to Bangor, Maine! I worked at the Base and each Canadian Thanksgiving about 14 of my female colleagues and I would plan a trip to Bangor for a "Girls Trip" and some early Christmas shopping. I always hoped to run into Stephen King but it never happened, that is... until 1982. Our daughters were allowed to come when they were 14 years old and so my daughter, Lezlie, was on this trip. We left on Friday, October 8th and went straight to the Bangor Mall to do some early shopping. I was so excited when I saw the sign at B. Dalton Bookseller that Stephen King

APRIL

17 **THURSDAY**

18 **FRIDAY**

Good Friday

19 **SATURDAY**

20 **SUNDAY**

Easter

would be there, in person, on Saturday and I knew where I would be. That evening we met my colleagues for a late dinner and that was all I could talk about–they were less enthused as they were not avid fans!

On that Saturday we were at the Bangor Mall early and I was about the fifth person in line for the book signing. Stephen was so charming to everyone ahead of me and then finally it was my turn. Stephen asked my name and signed my copy of *Different Seasons*. I then asked Stephen if I could take his photo and he said of course he didn't mind. My daughter was waiting with the camera and took his photo. Stephen then asked if the photo was for me and when I said yes he said "well get in the photo too" – I was thrilled and that is how I have the treasured photo of Stephen King and me.

Photos: Fran MacBride 1982

When I say treasured, I truly mean that. I kept the photos in my jewellery box for many years, I knew that in the event of a fire the first thing I would grab was my jewellery box! Eventually, as technology improved, I scanned the photos in 2014 as they bring back such great memories.

In closing, prior to COVID I wintered in Fort Myers, Florida. I remain a constant fan and I knew that Stephen and Tabitha King had a home in Sarasota and hoped to possibly see him on my visits there, but it was not to be. And, my daughter warned me that lurking around could be considered stalking!

Who knows perhaps I will see him again one day, some 40+ years after my first experience.

– Fran MacBride, 2024, Canada

HEARTS IN SUSPENSION:

STEPHEN KING REMEMBERS A LOST ATLANTIS

This publication marks the 50th anniversary of Stephen King's entrance into the University of Maine at Orono in the fall of 1966. The accelerating war in Vietnam and great social upheaval at home exerted a profound impact on students of the period and deeply influenced King's development as a writer and as a man.

Features in *Hearts In Suspension*:

- Stephen King's original story of this experience in his novella "Hearts in Atlantis" is published here.
- In his accompanying essay, "Five to One, One in Five," written expressly for this volume, King sheds his fictional persona and takes on the challenge of a nonfiction return to his undergraduate experience.
- Twelve fellow students and friends from King's college days contribute personal narratives recalling their own experience of those years.
- This book also includes four installments of King's never-before-reprinted student newspaper column, "King's Garbage Truck." These lively examples of King's damn-the-torpedoes style, entertaining and shrewd in their youthful perceptions, more than hint at a talent about to take its place in the American literary landscape.
- A gallery of period photographs and documents augments this volume.

Hearts In Suspension is a unique and one-of-a-kind Stephen King publication.

First printing hardcover available at **StephenKingCatalog.com**

APRIL

21 MONDAY

22 TUESDAY

Earth Day

23 WEDNESDAY

DO YOU REMEMBER ROCK N' ROLL RADIO?

Musician and producer Al Kooper joined up with The Rock Bottom Remainders, not only to help on keyboards and play guitar, but he was their musician mentor and helped shore up the authors-turned-musicians to become a band.

Al Kooper is a very famous musician. He has written, performed, and produced many bands, albums, and toured with artists. Can you name 3 or more artists that he has any association with?

Al Kooper played French horn, organ, and piano on what famous song by the Rolling Stones?

Al Kooper discovered, signed, and then produced albums, by what famous southern band?

How did Al Kooper end up joining The Rock Bottom Remainders in their early days?

mid-life CONFIDENTIAL
The Rock Bottom Remainders Tour America with Three Chords and an Attitude
STARRING
Dave Barry, Tad Bartimus, Roy Blount, Jr., Michael Dorris, Robert Fulghum, Kathi Goldmark, Matt Groening, Stephen King, Tabitha King, Barbara Kingsolver, Al Kooper, Greil Marcus, Dave Marsh, Ridley Pearson, Joel Selvin, Amy Tan

Hodder & Stoughton
1994, UK Edition

APRIL

24 THURSDAY

25 FRIDAY

26 SATURDAY

27 SUNDAY

Answers:

A1: Kooper has played on hundreds of records, including ones by the Rolling Stones, B.B. King, the Who, the Jimi Hendrix Experience, Alice Cooper, Stephen Stills, Mike Bloomfield, and Cream. He lived next to Jimi Hendrix and they played together often. He also created the band Blood, Sweat, and Tears, but left after the first album.

A2: "You Can't Always Get What You Want." It was named as the 100th greatest song of all time by *Rolling Stone* magazine in its 2004 list of the "500 Greatest Songs of All Time."

A3: Lynyrd Skynyrd. Kooper produced their first three albums.

A4: After his release of *Backstage Passes* (his autobiography) this qualified him as a member of the Rock Bottom Remainders. Look up Al Kooper, this is a small fraction of how he's impacted the music universe.

Al Kooper and Stephen King Performing with the Rock Bottom Remainders

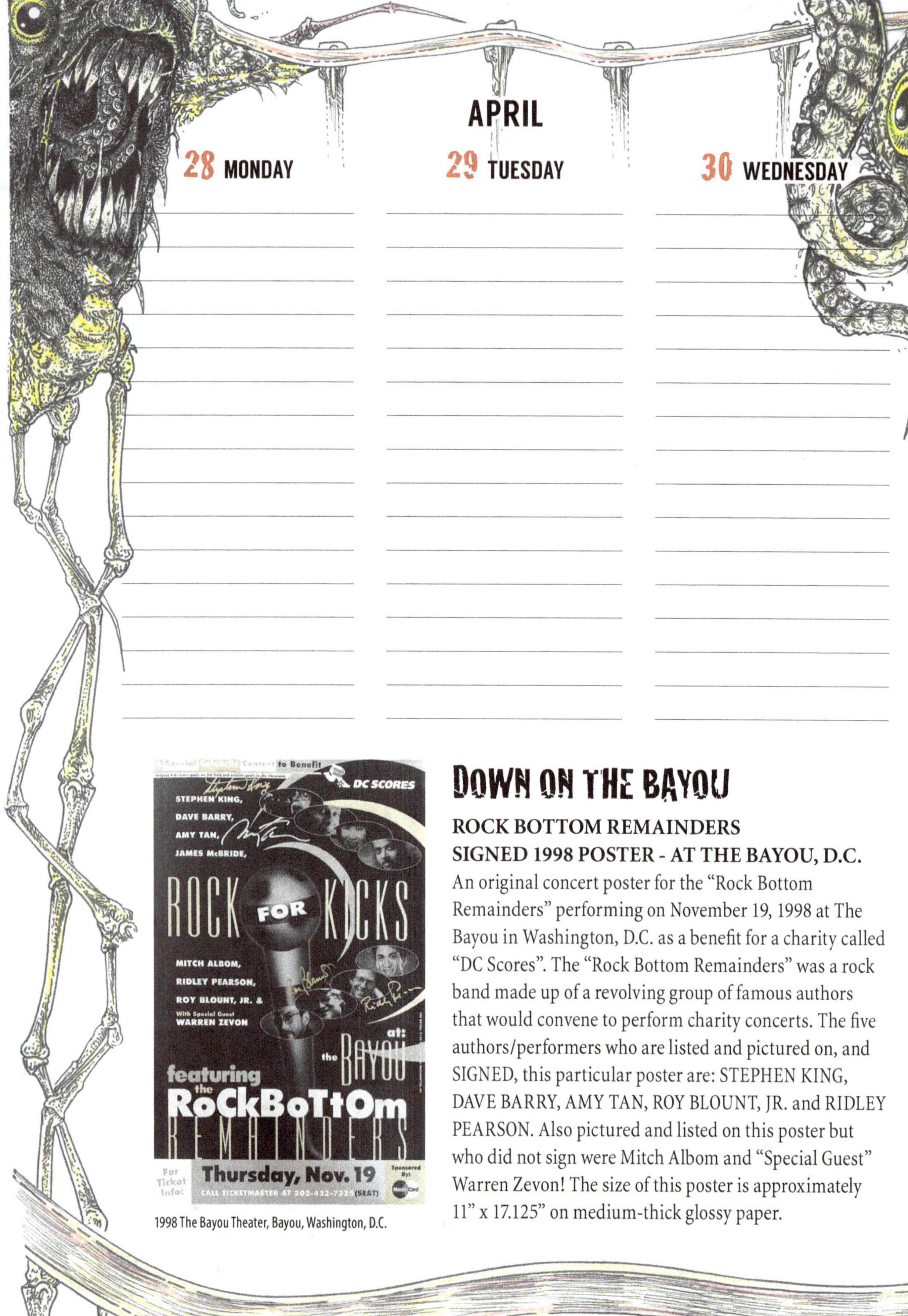

APRIL

28 MONDAY

29 TUESDAY

30 WEDNESDAY

1998 The Bayou Theater, Bayou, Washington, D.C.

DOWN ON THE BAYOU

ROCK BOTTOM REMAINDERS SIGNED 1998 POSTER - AT THE BAYOU, D.C.

An original concert poster for the "Rock Bottom Remainders" performing on November 19, 1998 at The Bayou in Washington, D.C. as a benefit for a charity called "DC Scores". The "Rock Bottom Remainders" was a rock band made up of a revolving group of famous authors that would convene to perform charity concerts. The five authors/performers who are listed and pictured on, and SIGNED, this particular poster are: STEPHEN KING, DAVE BARRY, AMY TAN, ROY BLOUNT, JR. and RIDLEY PEARSON. Also pictured and listed on this poster but who did not sign were Mitch Albom and "Special Guest" Warren Zevon! The size of this poster is approximately 11" x 17.125" on medium-thick glossy paper.

MAY

1 THURSDAY

2 FRIDAY

3 SATURDAY

Kentucky Derby Day

4 SUNDAY

Cinco de Mayo

Can you guess which authors have autographed this copy of *Mid-Life Confidential*?

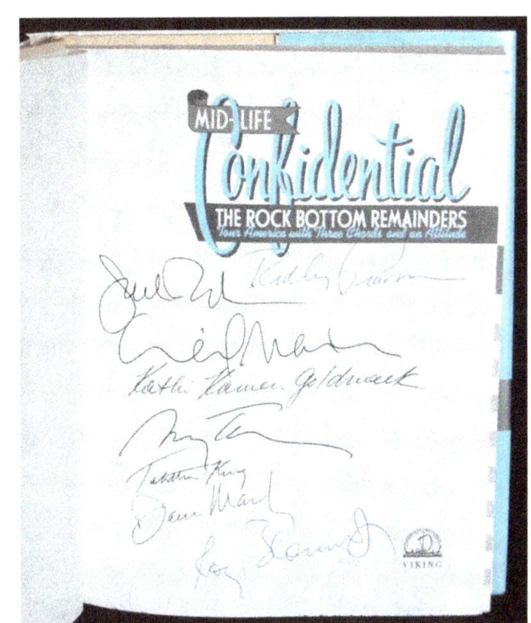

Mid-Life Confidential, Viking 1994

Answers:

Line 1: Joel Selvin; Ridley Pearson
Line 2: Greil Marcus
Line 3: Kathi Kamen Goldmark
Line 4: Amy Tan
Line 5: Tabitha King
Line 6: Dave Marsh
Line 7: Roy Blount, Jr.

MAY

5 MONDAY
Cinco de Mayo

6 TUESDAY

7 WEDNESDAY

SOLD MORE BOOKS THAN THE BEATLES!

ROCK BOTTOM REMAINDERS REVIEW – April 21, 2010, 9:30 Club.

Music reviewer for the Washington, D.C. area, Michael Darpino, published his account of seeing The Rock Bottom Remainders at the 9:30 Club and declared it "one of the weirdest concerts I have ever attended." He also said it was "one of the most unique and unlikely cover bands of all time." His obvious interest in the music scene, being a music reporter for the area, brought him to this very unlikely event with this group of heavy hitter authors there up on stage. Featuring Scott Turow, Amy Tan, Dave Barry, and Mitch Albom. He also noted that the Remainders MC, Roy Blount Jr. mentioned that "they are the only band that has sold more books that The Beatles."

Tuesdays with Morrie
Doubleday 1997

Who's going to debate that?

Mr. Darpino, who'd previously worked in a local bookstore, never imagined he'd actually see this band, much less locally. This was the

MAY

8 THURSDAY

9 FRIDAY

10 SATURDAY

11 SUNDAY

Mother's Day

2010 Wordstock Tour that had The Rock Bottom Remainders conducting a short East Coast tour to benefit World Vision's efforts on behalf of Haiti relief. The band also shared proceeds with local causes in the cities they performed in. In DC they gave to the Washington-based America's Promise Alliance; and We Give Books, donating 5 books per ticket-sold to DC Public Schools.

The Joy Luck Club 1989
G.P. Putnam's Sons

He also mentioned that "this band had a kind of mythical status as stories of their rare sightings were told by my co-workers as if they were akin to the Loch Ness Monster or Big Foot." Yes, I think we could all relate seeing these author's milling about in any of our locales would have been quite a pleasant surprise!

He also recounted that MC, Blount, told an anecdote of an old performance when during a Frank McCourt performance he was "singing one Beatles song while the band was playing another!" This is what happens at a concert where "some of

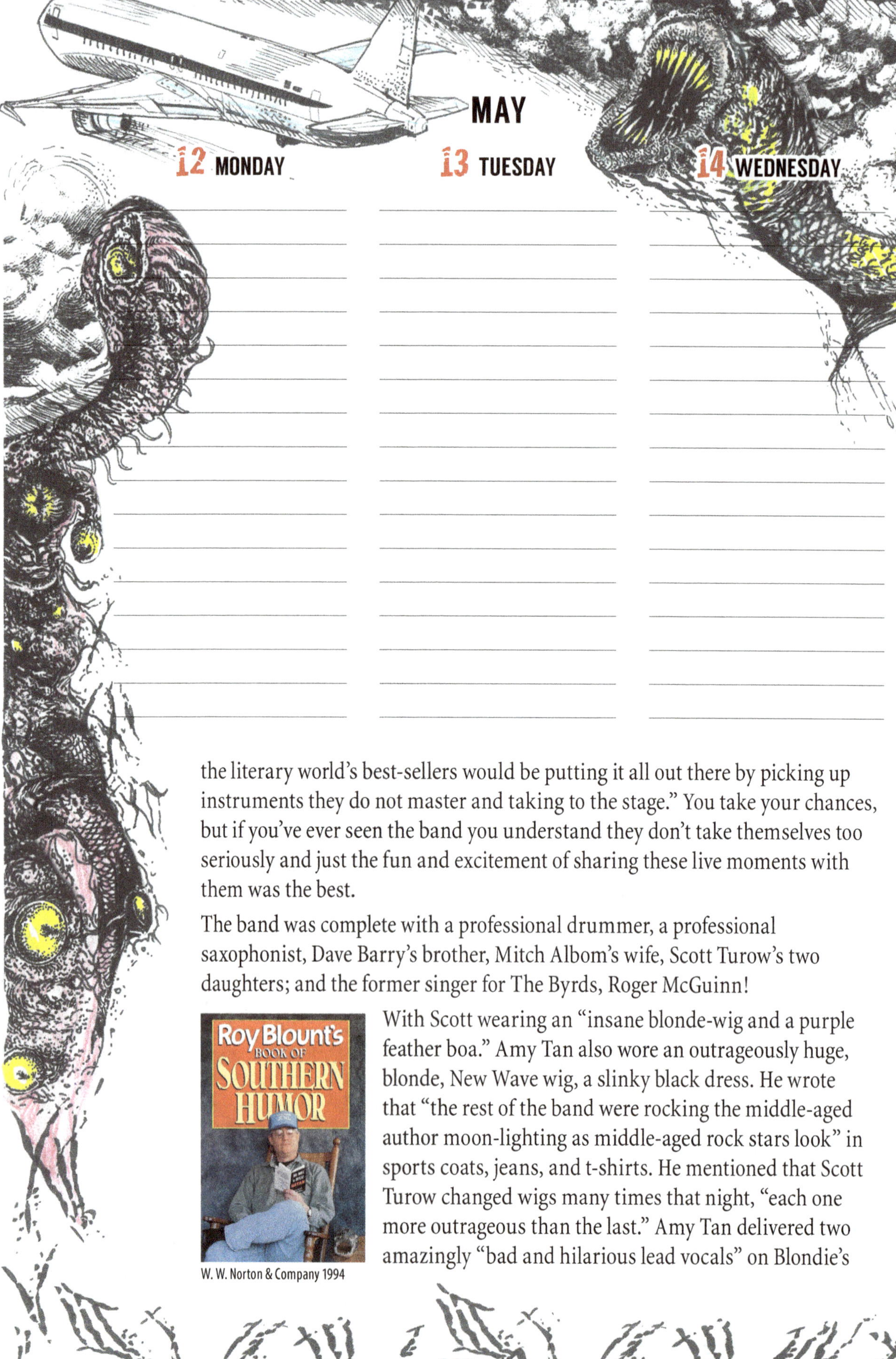

W. W. Norton & Company 1994

MAY

12 MONDAY

13 TUESDAY

14 WEDNESDAY

the literary world's best-sellers would be putting it all out there by picking up instruments they do not master and taking to the stage." You take your chances, but if you've ever seen the band you understand they don't take themselves too seriously and just the fun and excitement of sharing these live moments with them was the best.

The band was complete with a professional drummer, a professional saxophonist, Dave Barry's brother, Mitch Albom's wife, Scott Turow's two daughters; and the former singer for The Byrds, Roger McGuinn!

With Scott wearing an "insane blonde-wig and a purple feather boa." Amy Tan also wore an outrageously huge, blonde, New Wave wig, a slinky black dress. He wrote that "the rest of the band were rocking the middle-aged author moon-lighting as middle-aged rock stars look" in sports coats, jeans, and t-shirts. He mentioned that Scott Turow changed wigs many times that night, "each one more outrageous than the last." Amy Tan delivered two amazingly "bad and hilarious lead vocals" on Blondie's

'One Way Or Another', wearing slit-glasses, and The Shangri-La's 'Leader of the Pack', her husband as the motorcycle rebel. Mitch Albom delivered an incredible two-song Elvis tribute with a gold-jacket era Elvis, complete with an Elvis wig and sunglasses. During 'Jail House Rock', Albom then "turned his back to the crowd and hip swiveled right down to his t-shirt and boxer shorts!"

Roger McGuinn was the band's special guest and Roy Blount Jr. noted, that McGuinn was invited to "remind the audience what good music sounds like". He played The Bryds' hits 'Mr. Tambourine Man' and 'Turn! Turn! Turn!', along with three more.

It's obvious the night was special and a really good time for some very good causes. Michael Darpino wrote "these literary titans turned tongue-in-cheek rock-gods in concert was something I never expected to have the opportunity to experience… it was a funny, surreal evening and I am very glad that I was there." A unique show for anyone who's experienced it as I have in Atlanta, back in 1993.

– Dave Hinchberger

Dave Barry's Book of Bad Songs

Andrews McMeel Publishing 2000

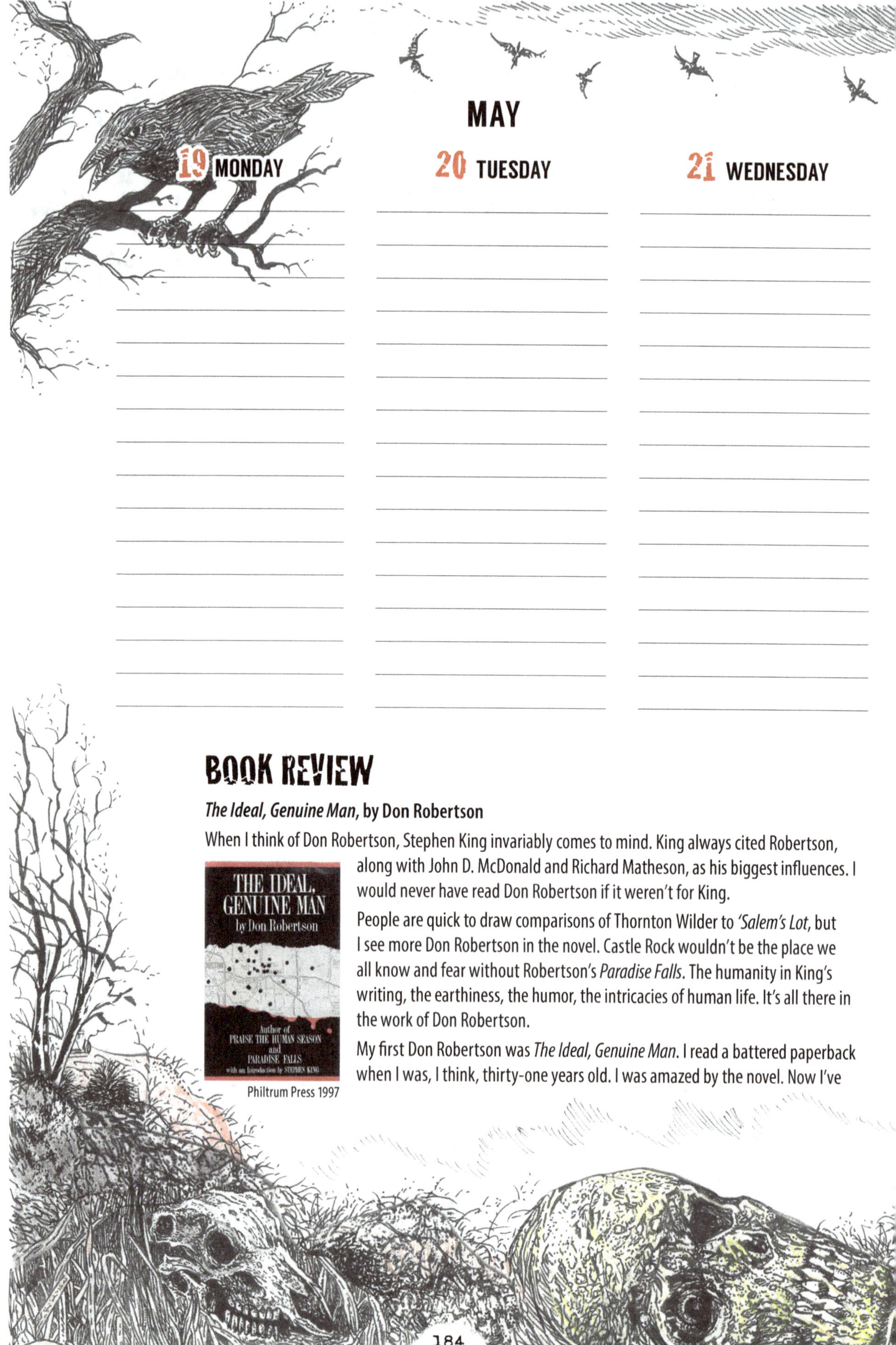

MAY

19 MONDAY

20 TUESDAY

21 WEDNESDAY

BOOK REVIEW

***The Ideal, Genuine Man*, by Don Robertson**

When I think of Don Robertson, Stephen King invariably comes to mind. King always cited Robertson, along with John D. McDonald and Richard Matheson, as his biggest influences. I would never have read Don Robertson if it weren't for King.

Philtrum Press 1997

People are quick to draw comparisons of Thornton Wilder to *'Salem's Lot*, but I see more Don Robertson in the novel. Castle Rock wouldn't be the place we all know and fear without Robertson's *Paradise Falls*. The humanity in King's writing, the earthiness, the humor, the intricacies of human life. It's all there in the work of Don Robertson.

My first Don Robertson was *The Ideal, Genuine Man*. I read a battered paperback when I was, I think, thirty-one years old. I was amazed by the novel. Now I've

MAY

22 THURSDAY

23 FRIDAY

24 SATURDAY

25 SUNDAY

re-read the book. It's a very different experience now. *The Ideal, Genuine Man* will affect a sixty-one-year-old man much more than one half his age.

The Ideal, Genuine Man is a deep look into the mind of Herman Marshall. Marshall is a typical Texas man from the mid twentieth Century. He drove a truck for years and years. He fought in the big war. Marshall has a wife, he loves Shiner beer, but it's all coming apart.

Herman Marshall's life is mostly behind him. He is old. His wife is slowly dying from cancer. His mind is filled with memories. Painful ones haunt him. Guilt and remorse plague his brain. There are sweet memories as well, but they bring him more unhappiness. All the good times are over. Now there's nothing left but hurt and a haunted mind.

Marshall killed men in the war, and he found he liked it. It was his duty, by God, and it never bothered him. He had numerous extramarital affairs, but what's a man to do when he is on the road all the time? He loves his wife, despite a humiliating confession she made. Their son died an agonizing death before he really even touched manhood.

DON ROBERTSON

THE IDEAL, GENUINE MAN

With a foreword by Stephen King

Bangor, Maine
PHILTRUM PRESS
1 9 8 7

Signed title page, 1988.

MAY

26 MONDAY
Memorial Day

27 TUESDAY

28 WEDNESDAY

Marshall washes all these and more memories down with endless bottles of Shiner. When his wife finally dies, the man is overcome with the futility of life and the indignity of old age.

The Ideal, Genuine Man is a meditation on aging. The novel examines the life of a man. Not necessarily a good man, nor a bad one. Just a normal southern man with the usual prejudices and values. But Herman Marshall is also a powder keg with a rapidly burning fuse.

Signet paperback 1989

This is a sad, profane, reflective story of a fading life. Until the final pages, when *The Ideal, Genuine Man* turns into the kind of nightmare Jack Ketchum might have dreamed up.

You've probably read a lot of books, but I doubt you've ever read anything like *The Ideal, Genuine Man*. It's a stunning novel. Just ask Stephen King. He not only admires the book, it is one of the very few publications from King's own Philtrum Press.

I have to make a note on the language in *The Ideal, Genuine Man*. It could never be done by a major publisher today. Sensitivity editors would drop dead. Herman Marshall is a man of his time, and his thoughts and vernacular are of his era. He isn't even hateful

MAY

29 THURSDAY

30 FRIDAY

31 SATURDAY

1 SUNDAY

about the words he uses. It's merely the way people thought and spoke then. Certainly, it was wrong, but we can't change the way people were. Nor was Don Robertson a hateful man. You only have to read *Praise the Human Season* or the *Morris Bird III* trilogy to see the humanity in his work. He was unflinchingly honest in his portrayals of people.

That wouldn't bother us, would it? We're horror fans. We go to the crucible to face hard truths every time we pick up a book or watch a movie.

– Mark Sieber,
horrordrive-in.com

Who is your favorite novelist of all time?

"Probably Don Robertson, author of *Paradise Falls, The Ideal, Genuine Man* and the marvelously titled *Miss Margaret Ridpath and the Dismantling of the Universe*. What I appreciate most in novels and novelists is generosity, a complete baring of the heart and mind, and Robertson always did that. He also wrote the best single line I've ever read in a novel: Of a funeral he wrote, "There were that day,
o Lord, squadrons of birds."

– Stephen King
The New York Times, June 4th, 2015

JUNE

2 MONDAY

3 TUESDAY

4 WEDNESDAY

BEST SEAT IN THE HOUSE

May 27th, 1993. Roxy Theater, Atlanta, Buckhead.

My introduction to Stephen King's work began later in my life than most other folks. It was back in 1984 when a co-worker clutched a hardcover copy of *IT* to her chest, like a Baptist going to church on Sunday. She read through it little by little, sharing with me what had scared the bejeezus out of her the previous night.

After lending me her copy, I was hooked and immediately dove into the archives and read everything I could get my hands on. Eventually I somehow discovered The Overlook Connection Bookstore, I think a friend had told me about this magical place where you can get your hands on all things King. I got my first copy of the Overlook Connection catalog and found a whole new world of fandom like I had never known. I became King obsessed. I simply HAD to have something more unique something signed, something rare, maybe even meeting the man one day?

JUNE

5 THURSDAY

6 FRIDAY

7 SATURDAY

8 SUNDAY

I became great friends with Dave Hinchberger at the Overlook. Here was a guy who not only had everything King you could imagine, but he had even met the man. Dave and I made a fast friendship.

We'd exchange notes and letters because the internet as we know it today was non-existent then. Soon we began casually conversing about the book biz and anything new about King (Dave was always known for having new tidbits on upcoming King things).

I think it was early on in 1993 that Dave let me know about this "thing" that was going to be happening in Atlanta. "Ed", Dave said "Steve's coming to Atlanta and this might be a good chance to see him".

I'm already totally in at this point, but yeah!, gimme some details.

The Shining
Vintage Trade
Paperback 2013

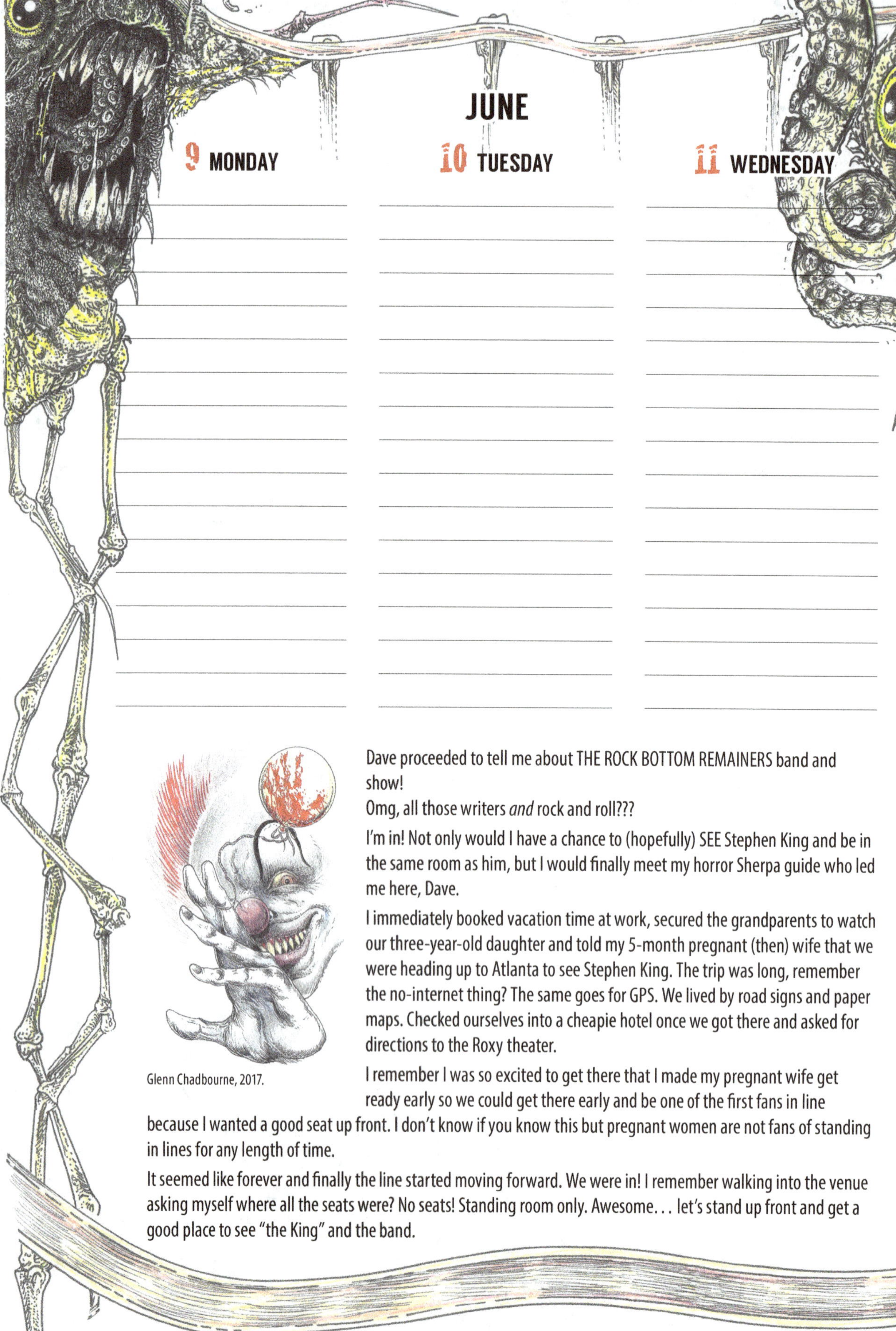

JUNE

9 MONDAY

10 TUESDAY

11 WEDNESDAY

Glenn Chadbourne, 2017.

Dave proceeded to tell me about THE ROCK BOTTOM REMAINERS band and show!

Omg, all those writers *and* rock and roll???

I'm in! Not only would I have a chance to (hopefully) SEE Stephen King and be in the same room as him, but I would finally meet my horror Sherpa guide who led me here, Dave.

I immediately booked vacation time at work, secured the grandparents to watch our three-year-old daughter and told my 5-month pregnant (then) wife that we were heading up to Atlanta to see Stephen King. The trip was long, remember the no-internet thing? The same goes for GPS. We lived by road signs and paper maps. Checked ourselves into a cheapie hotel once we got there and asked for directions to the Roxy theater.

I remember I was so excited to get there that I made my pregnant wife get ready early so we could get there early and be one of the first fans in line because I wanted a good seat up front. I don't know if you know this but pregnant women are not fans of standing in lines for any length of time.

It seemed like forever and finally the line started moving forward. We were in! I remember walking into the venue asking myself where all the seats were? No seats! Standing room only. Awesome... let's stand up front and get a good place to see "the King" and the band.

JUNE

12 THURSDAY

13 FRIDAY

14 SATURDAY

Flag Day

15 SUNDAY

Father's Day

My wife and I sat cross legged on the floor waiting. She's in *MISERY* (see what I did there?). I'm in my glory. Walking back up front to get us some refreshments, I see this larger-than-life gentleman dressed as good as any showman, talking to someone. I interrupted…

"Dave! Dave it's me Ed Yarb…"

"Fast Eddie! He replies (using my radio nickname, Dave's a huge fan of radio)

Dave doesn't shake hands he reaches out and pulls you in for a bear hug!

Now back into the show I cannot believe we have this kind of access to the stage. I walked up as the introduction s are made… Amy Tan, Dave Barry, blah blah blah… then finally, "and on guitar Mr. Steve King!" Spotlight on and the man walks out! There he is. He's real. He's moving around and I'm just a few feet away! Unreal. I can't tell you I remember a single song they played, I remember a surf anthem about a surfer lost at sea.

Stephen King, *The Shining*. ABC TV. 1997 Warner Bros

Well about three more songs go by and my wife is now swooning from pregnancy claustrophobia and… not feeling well, at all, and we have to go. All that planning, all that prep. Ugh!

But I can tell you I would do it all over again because Stephen King is a force to be around. There he was, large as life, right in front of me on stage. Best seats in the house I tell ya, best seats in the house.

I couldn't have done it without you Dave, even the half of *IT* I did get to do!

– Ed Yarb

JUNE

16 MONDAY

17 TUESDAY

18 WEDNESDAY

CUJO MEETS THE WOLVES

Living in New York, I've been close to a dozen Stephen King signings / events over the decades, but the one that stands out as the most memorable is the *Wolves of the Calla* event that took place at the Jacob Burns Film Center (formerly the Rome Theater) in Pleasantville, NY in the fall of 2003. The event consisted of a live interview of King conducted by New York Times literary critic Janet Maslin, audience Q&A, a screening of the film *Cujo*, and a meet and greet with Maslin and King.

Cujo theater poster, Warner Bros. 1983

I arrived about 5 hours early, as I wanted to get a good seat in the theater (this was general admission, as with most Stephen King appearances). Amazingly, I was the first person there, and over the next 90 minutes, others began to arrive. A number of us were members of the pre-Facebook Internet group, SKEMERs, met up in line and got to know one another. About an hour before doors opened, King's limo arrived, and he and his companions parked down the road and we watched him enter a coffee shop to have breakfast. Everyone wanted to respect his privacy and I don't recall anyone breaking out of line to go pester him for an autograph or a selfie.

About 15 minutes before the venue opened, King and his group arrived at the theater. I was wearing a custom-made t-shirt featuring artwork from the first edition of

JUNE

19 THURSDAY

Juneteenth

20 FRIDAY

21 SATURDAY

22 SUNDAY

The Stand and as King made his way to the theater entrance, he glanced at me and said, "Hey, cool shirt, man!" I could have gone home right then, and the day would have been worth it!

As we filed into the theater, each of us was given a small bag with a few goodies in it, including a paperback edition of *Cujo* and an event booklet.

Maslin was introduced and took the stage. She read a short and unnecessary bio of King, stumbling a few times, and King took the stage to a standing ovation. I could see that Maslin was a bit nervous, but King, clad in jeans and a t-shirt, very quickly put her at ease and as the interview progressed, King's informal down-to-earth and friendly disposition made the interview process flow naturally. His stories and answers to her questions were often humorous, and of course his continuing recovery from his somewhat recent accident (June 1999) was discussed at length.

Dark Tower V: Wolves of the Calla, Donald Grant 2003.

After the interview, King took questions from the audience, most of which dealt with the remaining "Dark Tower" novels and King's slowly improving health. After the questions were answered, King joined the audience for the screening of *Cujo*. He sat about halfway back on the left side of the auditorium and cracked the audience up during the film by loudly speaking to the screen ("Don't get out of the car, lady!").

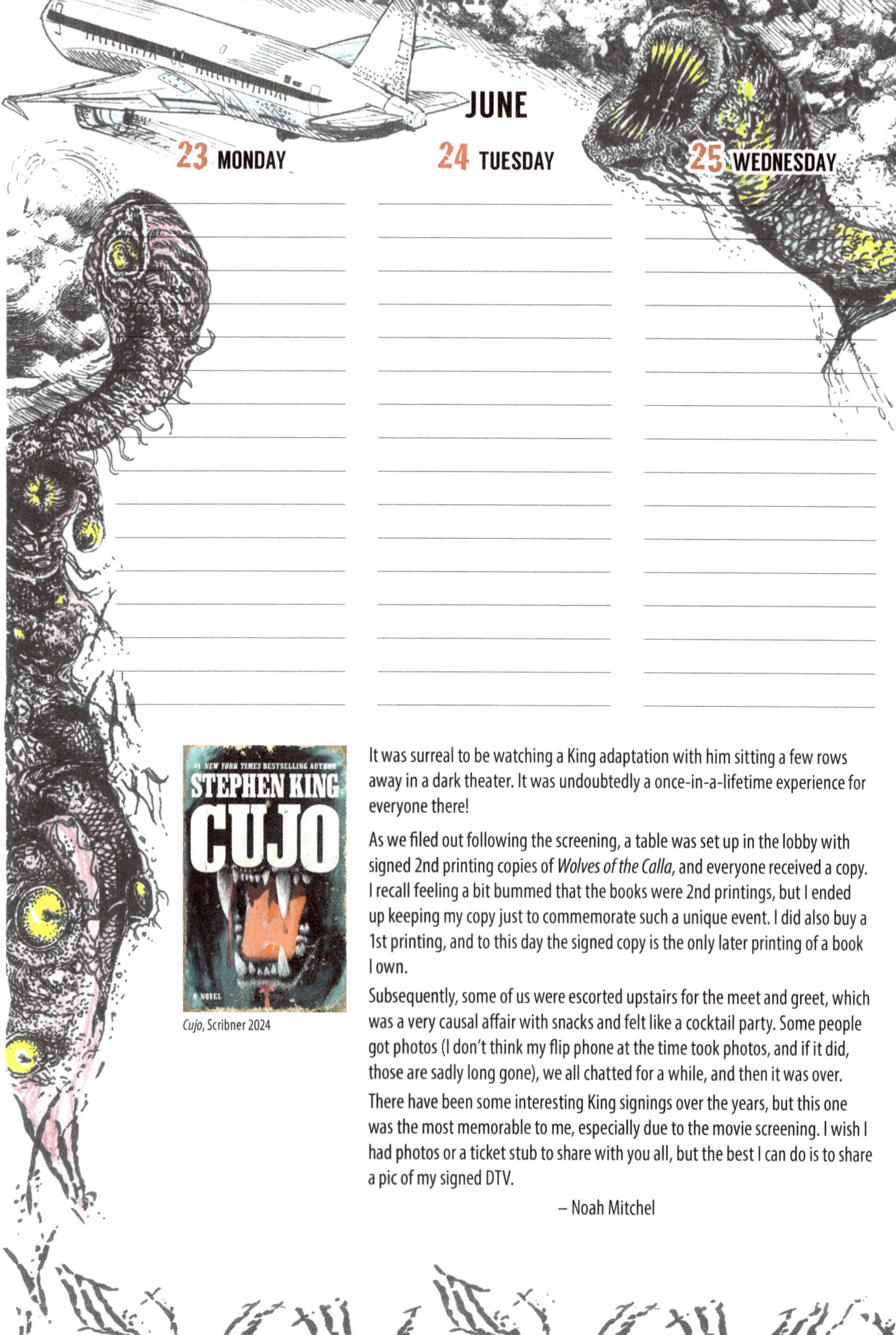

JUNE

23 MONDAY

24 TUESDAY

25 WEDNESDAY

Cujo, Scribner 2024

It was surreal to be watching a King adaptation with him sitting a few rows away in a dark theater. It was undoubtedly a once-in-a-lifetime experience for everyone there!

As we filed out following the screening, a table was set up in the lobby with signed 2nd printing copies of *Wolves of the Calla*, and everyone received a copy. I recall feeling a bit bummed that the books were 2nd printings, but I ended up keeping my copy just to commemorate such a unique event. I did also buy a 1st printing, and to this day the signed copy is the only later printing of a book I own.

Subsequently, some of us were escorted upstairs for the meet and greet, which was a very causal affair with snacks and felt like a cocktail party. Some people got photos (I don't think my flip phone at the time took photos, and if it did, those are sadly long gone), we all chatted for a while, and then it was over.

There have been some interesting King signings over the years, but this one was the most memorable to me, especially due to the movie screening. I wish I had photos or a ticket stub to share with you all, but the best I can do is to share a pic of my signed DTV.

– Noah Mitchel

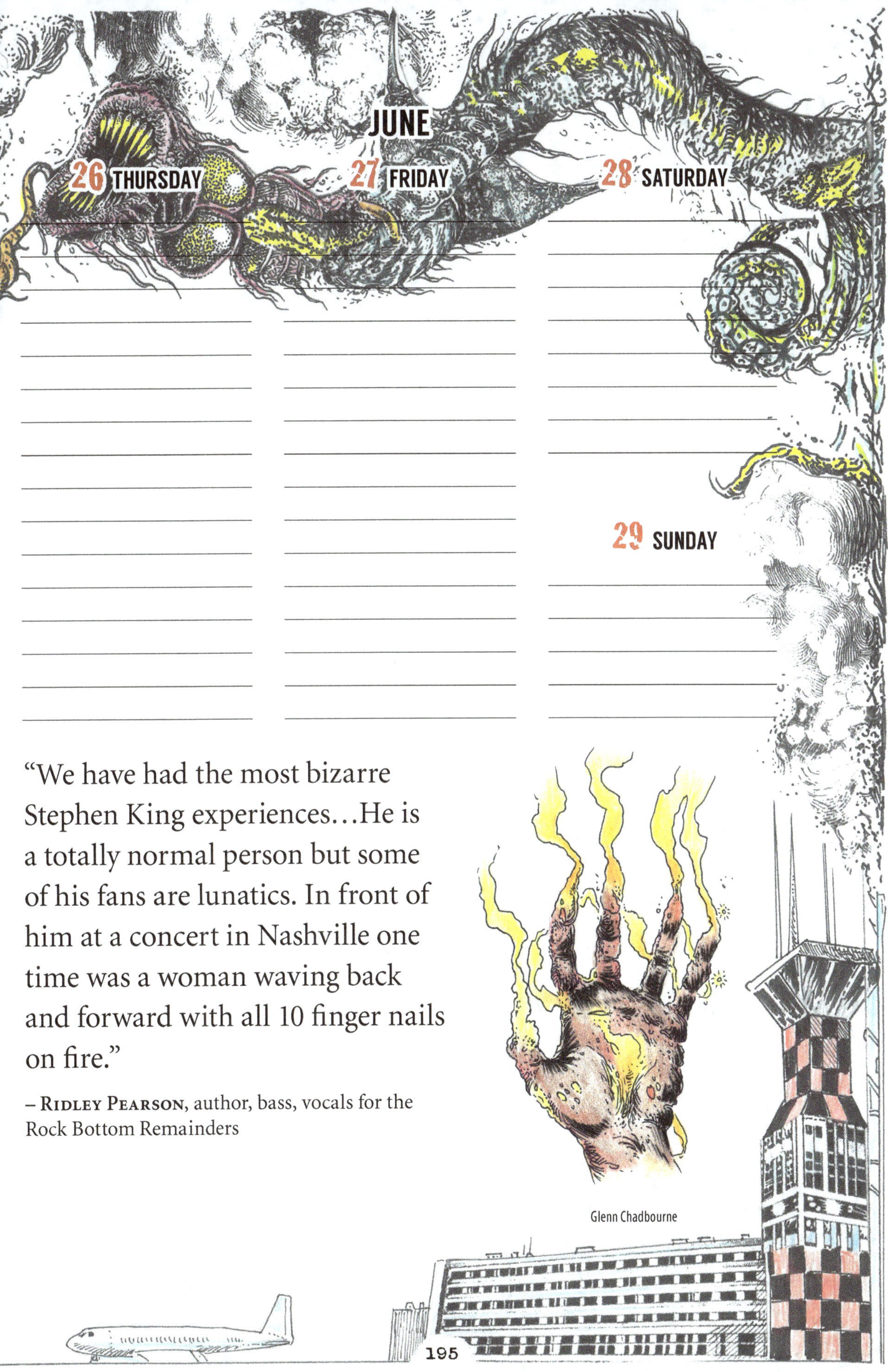

JUNE

26 THURSDAY

27 FRIDAY

28 SATURDAY

29 SUNDAY

"We have had the most bizarre Stephen King experiences…He is a totally normal person but some of his fans are lunatics. In front of him at a concert in Nashville one time was a woman waving back and forward with all 10 finger nails on fire."

– Ridley Pearson, author, bass, vocals for the Rock Bottom Remainders

Glenn Chadbourne

JULY

30 MONDAY

1 TUESDAY

2 WEDNESDAY

DON'T SLEEP ON IT!

I want to begin by saying, if you are indecisive about doing something... buy that ticket! Book that flight!

In 2017 I attended a *Sleeping Beauties* book tour event at J. Scheidegger Center for the Arts at Lindenwood University, in St Charles, Mo. I was raised in Missouri, from the age of 8 -18.

I'm like a bumper sticker that I read once: "I wasn't born in Texas, but I got here fast as I could!"

I have family in Missouri, so my trip was not so costly. My niece, Kara and her boyfriend, Seth, and I attended the event together. We arrived in St. Charles very early, so we decided to grab a bite to eat. But, first I suggested we do a drive by to see if there was a line forming yet. I told them if there was a line, to just drop me off and I would get in line. They could go eat, and bring me back something.

Photo: Marie Burns 2017

Yup!! There was a line formed already. We still ended up on the second row, center. While waiting in line, there was a reporter from the *St. Louis Post-Dispatch* interviewing attendees.

She stopped and talked to us, and I ended up in her article. So cool being mentioned in the same article as King. Every attendee received a copy of *Sleeping Beauties*. Only 400 attendees had a chance to receive a signed book. My niece and her boyfriend had already decided that if they got one, and I didn't, they would give it to me. It just so happened, we ALL three received one!

My only regret was not getting a photo of me with Stephen King in the background. My second trip to see him was a couple of years later. I traveled to Minnesota. Just so

JULY

3 THURSDAY

4 FRIDAY

Independence Day

5 SATURDAY

6 SUNDAY

happens, I have family in Minnesota. My cousin, Marina and I attended the events together. This trip was epic!

$116 round trip airfare. I know. I couldn't believe it either. I had to double check and make sure I booked it correctly. My cousin was a flight attendant, and she said it is cheap to fly from one big hub to another.

The Loft's WORDPLAY Opening Party featured The Rock Bottom Remainders at First Avenue.

The ticket for the concert was only $40. We got there early, and we were right up front. I got in early enough, that I was able to get Dave Barry to sign a CD that I had brought along, you know just in case!

They did a tribute to Prince, singing "KISS" while all dressed up in purple feather boas. Some staff members handed out some panties to the ladies up front, to toss onto stage. (Fyi, they still had tags.)

I waited until they were between songs. I sling shot mine at Stephen King's feet. He picked them up, raised his eyebrow, bit his bottom lip and nodded his head up and down. All while looking directly at me. Eeek! The closest I have come to meeting him. And being caught up in the moment, I still forgot to get a photo of me with him in the background!

The next day we went to a book festival to see him do an interview with Benjamin Percy.

Up front, again! The Wordplay Book Festival ticket was only $10. We were able to obtain a voucher to purchase a signed, *The Outsider* at book face value. That was their first annual book festival, so of course it was a learning curve for them. While in line to purchase the book, a woman was frustrated with how the line was organized. She asked if I wanted her voucher.

Well, you know the answer to that!

I was able to purchase not one, but two books! $60.00 for TWO signed Stephen King books.

Unheard of!! So, if I did the math right, my Minneapolis trip only cost $226.00. Enjoy life.

As Steve Jobs said, "The most important thing is to enjoy your life—to be happy—it's all that matters."

– Marie Burns

Photo: Marie Burns 2017

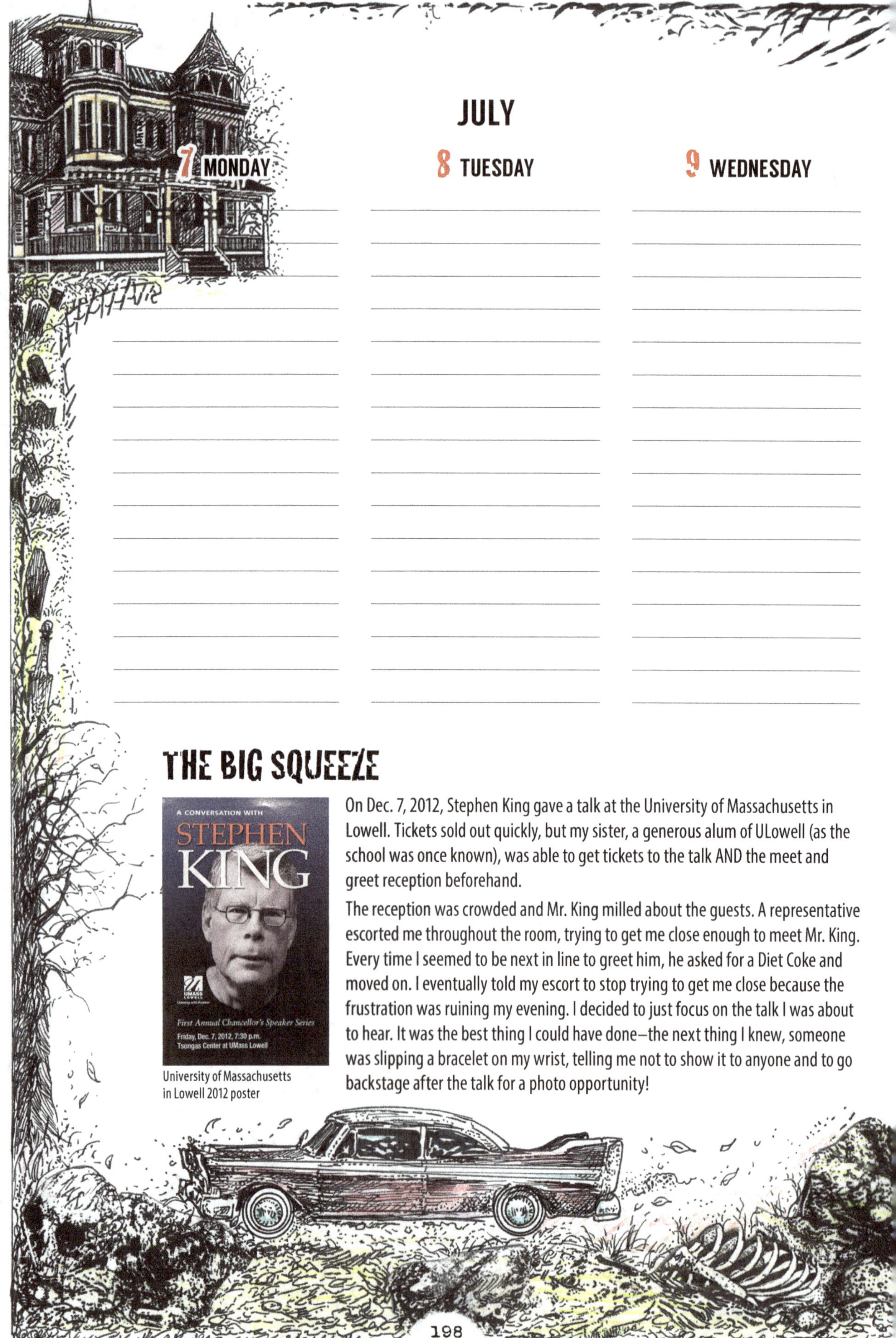

JULY

7 MONDAY

8 TUESDAY

9 WEDNESDAY

THE BIG SQUEEZE

University of Massachusetts in Lowell 2012 poster

On Dec. 7, 2012, Stephen King gave a talk at the University of Massachusetts in Lowell. Tickets sold out quickly, but my sister, a generous alum of ULowell (as the school was once known), was able to get tickets to the talk AND the meet and greet reception beforehand.

The reception was crowded and Mr. King milled about the guests. A representative escorted me throughout the room, trying to get me close enough to meet Mr. King. Every time I seemed to be next in line to greet him, he asked for a Diet Coke and moved on. I eventually told my escort to stop trying to get me close because the frustration was ruining my evening. I decided to just focus on the talk I was about to hear. It was the best thing I could have done—the next thing I knew, someone was slipping a bracelet on my wrist, telling me not to show it to anyone and to go backstage after the talk for a photo opportunity!

JULY

10 THURSDAY

11 FRIDAY

12 SATURDAY

13 SUNDAY

I enjoyed a third-row seat, listening to Stephen King and author and professor Andre Dubus III have an entertaining and informative conversation. I was happy to be there and didn't think the evening could have been better.

After the talk, I went backstage with my sister. We were supposed to have a quick photo and move on but I brought my battered book club edition *Christine*—the first Stephen King book I ever read—and Mr. King was gracious enough to sign it. I was able to tell him the significance of the book and how great my sister was to get me tickets to the event. My sister and I still recall how tightly he squeezed us during the photo. My sister won a copy of *11/22/63* that night, which she gifted to me.

Photo: Laurie Dupre 2012

The Stephen King Universe has continued to be very good to me. On 10/10/19, I attended An Evening With Joe Hill and Stephen King in Somerville, MA where they promoted *Full Throttle* and *The Institute* respectively. And in 2017 I had the opportunity to be an extra in Season One of *Castle Rock*.

– Laurie Dupre 10/8/24

JULY

14 MONDAY

15 TUESDAY

16 WEDNESDAY

MY LIFE WITH THE REMAINDERS or Why Didn't They Ask Dave Barry?

As the only non-writer in the band, I pleaded with the other Remainders to ghost-write this. "Forget it. You didn't let us lip-synch to Madonna tracks," they sang out in unison, slightly off-key. So, only the lonely...

In the fine rock & roll tradition, the Rock Bottom Remainders were conceived in a car. As a semi-pro musician with a day job in book publicity, I spend a lot of time driving touring authors around San Francisco. Some of them are so much fun to be with that conducting them from interview to interview doesn't feel like work. We'll start digging through my vast collection of tapes. I'll play weird food songs and they'll tell me about some Zairean Rockabilly group. Before I know it, another new friend is sitting in with my band, the Ray Price Club, at The

Kathi Kamen Goldmark and Stephen King

JULY

17 THURSDAY

18 FRIDAY

19 SATURDAY

20 SUNDAY

Blue Lamp. And he or she will get the sweetest, dreamiest look and tell me how lucky I am: "Writing is okay, but I was in a band in college and it was the most fun I ever had."

I decided to form a band of authors! We could burst upon the world at the 1992 American Booksellers Association convention in Anaheim!

As our debut approached, I became Remaindermom. Ridley Pearson, who plays in a real band and had some idea how bad we could be, made everyone a rehearsal tape. Amy Tan-with the help of a wig, shades, free weights and intensive karaoke work transformed herself into Ronnie Spector. Michael Dorris signed on as drummer, had to drop

Stranger Than Fiction CD. 1998 Don't Quit Your Day Job Records

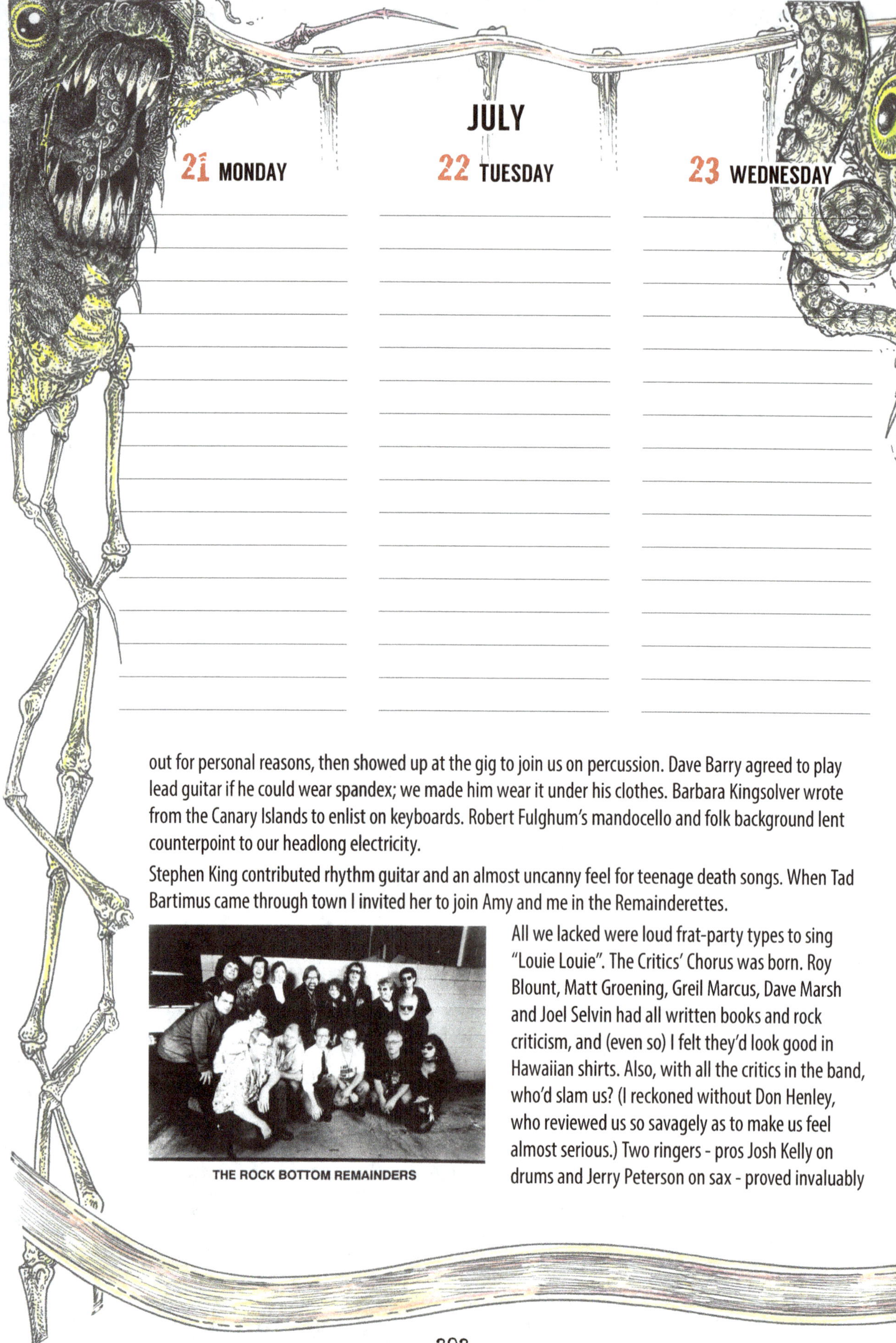

JULY

21 MONDAY

22 TUESDAY

23 WEDNESDAY

out for personal reasons, then showed up at the gig to join us on percussion. Dave Barry agreed to play lead guitar if he could wear spandex; we made him wear it under his clothes. Barbara Kingsolver wrote from the Canary Islands to enlist on keyboards. Robert Fulghum's mandocello and folk background lent counterpoint to our headlong electricity.

Stephen King contributed rhythm guitar and an almost uncanny feel for teenage death songs. When Tad Bartimus came through town I invited her to join Amy and me in the Remainderettes.

THE ROCK BOTTOM REMAINDERS

All we lacked were loud frat-party types to sing "Louie Louie". The Critics' Chorus was born. Roy Blount, Matt Groening, Greil Marcus, Dave Marsh and Joel Selvin had all written books and rock criticism, and (even so) I felt they'd look good in Hawaiian shirts. Also, with all the critics in the band, who'd slam us? (I reckoned without Don Henley, who reviewed us so savagely as to make us feel almost serious.) Two ringers - pros Josh Kelly on drums and Jerry Peterson on sax - proved invaluably

JULY

24 THURSDAY

25 FRIDAY

26 SATURDAY

27 SUNDAY

instrumental. And Al Kooper, of Blues Project fame, volunteered to be musical director. He added laid-back zest, rock & roll cynicism, and a distinguished ear. He cut Roy's song.

Amy Tan and Kathi Kamen Goldmark at The Electric Factory, April 22, 2010 Philadelphia

After three days' rehearsal in a secret location - assisted by my co-workers Carole and Lorraine, a volunteer crew and "spousal units" led by Tabby King - we hit the Cowboy Boogie club's stage. When our audience of booksellers and publishers began to scream, dance and throw underwear, we felt more like rock stars than we'd dared to hope (except for Marsh, whose standards are high). It was Fantasy Rock & Roll Camp. It raised money for the Homeless Writers' Coalition of Los Angeles, Literacy Volunteers of America and the Right To Rock Network, And we were so damn fine. In the words of emcee and weird food song collector Blount: "Ladies and Gentlemen, suspend your credibility for The ROCK...BOTTOM... RE-MAIN-DERS!"

– Kathi Kamen Goldmark (with secret help from Roy Blount Jr.)

JULY

28 MONDAY

29 TUESDAY

30 WEDNESDAY

GET A LEG UP!

I entered and won a competition run by the *Times* newspaper to get 2 x tickets to the Stephen King event at Battersea Park Events Arena, on Tuesday November 7, 2006 at 7.00 pm.

This was to be a talk and Q&A followed by a reading from *Lisey's Story*, and then a book signing by King.

At 1.00 pm on that day, King appeared at Borders Books and Music, Oxford Street, London for a book signing. He would sign for 2 hours only and each person was allowed two books to be signed. The books could be any book or whatever you wanted signed.

2006 Battersea flyer, Hodder & Stoughton, Waterstones

Problem. We live in the north of Scotland and would not be able to get to London in time to get a good place in the queue at Borders. I booked a hotel for me and my wife in Chelsea and a flight from Glasgow to London on the Tuesday morning.

I hit upon the idea of phoning up Borders Books and Music and telling them I was disabled and could they save me, and my wife a place in the queue.

I then looked out my medical boot and crutches which I still had from an accident, months previously. (I was fine now).

AUGUST

31 THURSDAY

1 FRIDAY

2 SATURDAY

3 SUNDAY

On the Tuesday morning, we flew down to London and arrived a little late. We had to run along the packed streets of London with me in crutches to get to Borders on time. When we got to Borders we asked for the manager who then ushered us upstairs to the signing area. King was already signing books by then. The manager asked us to wait until he could get us in the queue. I was waiting very close to King and eventually the manager moved us into the queue. Nobody seemed to mind. If it was me, I would be furious at someone queue jumping, which is worse than murder in the UK.

Lisey's Story signing, Alan Kyle 2006, Battersea

Stephen King, Battersea Borders, London

I presented my mint copy of "Twice the Power" to King who exclaimed, "what is this?" Then, when he opened it at the title page, he recognized it as a *Needful Things* proof. I got him to sign a copy of *Lisey's Story* as well. My wife got her two books signed after I did. I managed to get a few photos of King signing some books while I was waiting.

"Twice the Power"
Advance Proof,
Hodder & Stoughton
1991

After dinner, we made our way to the Battersea Park Events Arena where we noticed the *Lisey's Story* painted taxi. King did not arrive in that taxi. He had a limo. The taxi was just an advertisement. I had left my medical boot and crutches at the hotel as we had tickets for the event and plenty of time.

As competition winners we had good front and centre seats. The talk and Q&A was very good and King's reading was brilliant. He knows how to work an audience.

AUGUST

7 THURSDAY

8 FRIDAY

9 SATURDAY

10 SUNDAY

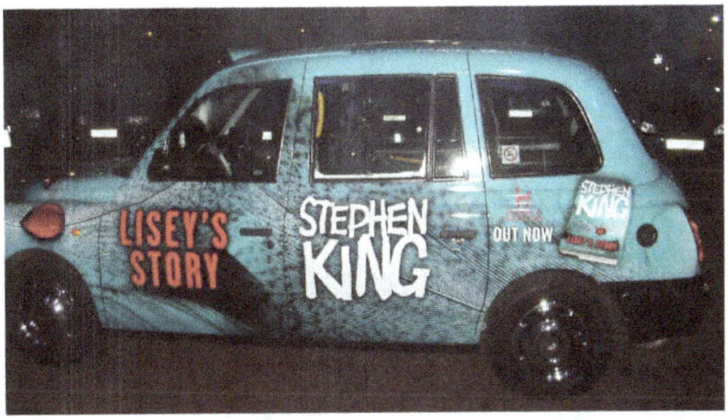

As he was finishing off his talk, a stampede for the signing area started. I spotted this happening and ran under the tape and bolted to the front. We ended up fifth in the queue with hundreds behind us. Once again King signed two books of any kind per person. I had brought a few unusual items and got them signed along with my wife's copies.

Promotional ad on a taxi for Stephen King's *Lisey's Story*, London, England 2006

On the way out we noticed a newspaper stand with dozens of *Times* newspaper supplements of King's visit to London and grabbed a few dozen for the other King fans we knew.

All together a great day out and between us we got eight rare King books signed. Some might say I was not very gentlemanly, but if you snooze… you lose.

– Alan Kyle (Mr. Rabbit Trick), United KIngdom

The Mist Limited Edition Lithograph Only 500 Signed Copies
17″ x 11″ Signed / Numbered by artist **Glenn Chadbourne**

Skeleton Crew: Unpublished Stephen King Anniversary Cover Lithograph Only 500 Signed Copies 17″ x 11″ Signed / Numbered by artist **Pete Von Sholly**

Search for LITHOGRAPH at **StephenKingCatalog.com**

2023 Overlook Connection Press. Sent Rolled.

AUGUST

11 MONDAY

12 TUESDAY

13 WEDNESDAY

A SIGNING IN JERSEY

Back in the early 1990's, I had a sales rep at Doubleday press in New York City for many years. His name was Sam, a lovely fellow, and always a big help to our mail-order bookstore, The Overlook Connection. Of course, our main subject was their author Stephen King, as they had all the early years, the magic years some might call it, touting such releases as *Carrie*, *'Salem's Lot*, *The Stand*, *The Shining*, *Night Shift*, and *Pet Sematary*.

During one conversation, Sam told me that he was working at a Barnes and Noble bookstore in New Jersey and they hosted Stephen King for a signing. One of the attendees who stepped up to King, getting his book signed, crouched down on a knee to speak with Stephen King for a moment. As it turns out, it was Pat DiNizio, co-founder and songwriter of the band, The Smithereens. Pat was able to convince King to do an interview right then and there, with his portable cassette player. As Sam tells the story, the interview was about 15-20 minutes.

You see, I was in the music business for years, working for a decade at Polygram Records, and then a short stint at Relativity records before I went full-time as a bookstore and press. I

AUGUST

14 THURSDAY

15 FRIDAY

16 SATURDAY

17 SUNDAY

was also operating my mail-order bookstore of Stephen King on the side. Sam knew this and thought I'd appreciate this story. Ah, when music and books collide. With this information in mind, I thought I had a good chance to get in touch with Pat and see if he still had this interview. Here he was all over MTV, the radio, with their hits "A Girl Like You", "Blood and Roses", etc. and here I was trying to get a Stephen King interview, from the eighties, from the leader of The Smithereens.

Smithereens 11, Capitol Records 1989

Fast forward to the mid-nineties, I was in New York City with Relativity Records for a conference. The record executives, and I, we were headed to a recording studio to visit with one of our bands there. Our van pulled up out front, we exited, when right in front of me, coming out of the same studio… Pat DiNizio and The Smithereens!

I was introduced to Pat, and I immediately took the opportunity. "Pat, do you remember doing an interview with Stephen King at Barnes and Noble?"

He was quite surprised at this question. He said yes, he did do an interview with Stephen King at a book signing. His question to me was, "How did you know this? Were you there?"

I explained how I came into this information about the interview, and said I would be very interested in publishing it in one of our newsletters or in some other form.

AUGUST

18 MONDAY

19 TUESDAY

20 WEDNESDAY

He said, "I do still have that cassette tape. It's buried in a bunch of stuff, but I will start looking for it because it would mean a lot for this to be published. Just the fact that anybody knows about this is amazing to me."

Email and the internet? Was not a thing yet, so Pat and I exchanged a couple of letters and we spoke on the phone. He said he'd been performing these living room concerts, and he'll eventually have one in Atlanta and he would give me a call, and keep the discussion going, especially talking about Stephen King's work. Maybe in all this he'd run across this "misplaced" Stephen King interview.

So, time marched on, I began working full-time on my bookstore and publishing and things trailed off, as they do. Life takes over when you're raising a family, working on the business, etc. every corner filled. Such is life.

It occurred to me, many years later, that I had never heard from Pat about that Atlanta living room concert. I just assumed he had stopped performing those concerts and never made it to town. So, I started looking for information about him (now that the internet was here and all-knowing), and the band and

AUGUST

21 THURSDAY

22 FRIDAY

23 SATURDAY

24 SUNDAY

what was currently happening, so we could possibly reengage on this Stephen King interview. After all these years he may have found it!

It was not to be. It turns out I was too late. Pat had passed away, not more than six months previously, in 2017, at age 62. My heart sunk. I'm 62 as I write this and as far as I'm concerned I'm going to be around as long as the universe lets me. That was too young. I'm very sorry he's gone.

Doubleday

And, we'll never discover this lost Stephen King interview by Pat, which may still be sitting in some box, in some closet, or storage, somewhere with his family in New Jersey, where he lived. I just want to say thanks to Pat, wherever he's landed in the universe, for at least trying and taking the time with me on this. I wish I could tell Sam, who, unbeknownst to him, began this adventure and how we had a chance meeting. We haven't been in touch in decades.

I can just imagine the smile Sam would be wearing if he ever heard that I'd made contact.

Pat was obviously a big fan of Stephen King. I'll never forget when I mentioned the interview to him, there on that sidewalk in sunny July, in New York City, his face beamed, came alight, his eyes widened and he said...

... "Yeah, I'm a huge Stephen King fan."

– Dave Hinchberger

AUGUST

25 MONDAY

26 TUESDAY

27 WEDNESDAY

BEST BIRTHDAY, EVER!

I heard Stephen and Owen King were going out on a book tour for *Sleeping Beauties*. My son said he would buy the tickets for me for my birthday. So, I started looking for tickets. Sold out! But I found 2 tickets on Craigslist! They were $50 each and that included a hard cover copy of *Sleeping Beauties* and random copies were autographed by Stephen and Owen King.*

My son Nathan, my youngest daughter Breanna, and I planned our trip for September 27, 2017 to Annandale-on-Hudson (New York). This was the day after my oldest daughter's birthday, Chelsea (sorry couldn't forget her in my story). The signing is a little over 4 hours away from my home in Dekalb Junction, New York. My husband Matt always did the driving but he couldn't go so it was up to me.

Nathan and I were going to go to the event and Breanna was going to be our "getaway driver". She was going to drop us off and pick us up so we could avoid the long line of traffic.

AUGUST

28 THURSDAY

29 FRIDAY

30 SATURDAY

31 SUNDAY

SOLD OUT!
Event date:
Wednesday, September 27, 2017 - 7:00pm
Event address:
Fisher Center for the Performing Arts at Bard,
60 Manor Ave, Annandale-on-Hudson, NY 12504
Presented by Oblong Books & Music and
the Richard B. Fisher Center for the Performing
Arts at Bard College
Tickets: $40
Includes one copy of SLEEPING BEAUTIES*

I was very nervous that I was going to get all the way there and the person I bought the tickets from was not going to be there but I had to take the chance. I had always wanted to meet Stephen King in person and this was my best shot.

On the day of the event the 3 of us headed out. My vehicles' air conditioner decided not to work but we made a quick stop at the auto parts store for a recharge and we were good to go.

We arrived at our destination early so we stopped at a pizza place for dinner. Then we headed to the venue. I messaged my ticket seller and we met to complete our transaction. As luck would have it they had an extra ticket which I bought for my daughter. This ticket put me just 5 rows from Stephen King! OMG!

We were not allowed to take pictures or record during the event.

SEPTEMBER

1 MONDAY
Labor Day

2 TUESDAY

3 WEDNESDAY

However I did sneak a pic of my seat and my kid's seats before the show. Breanna snuck a pic of me and I had a smile from ear to ear but I can't find it.

So here is where it gets good. Stephen and Owen came on stage and they allowed questions from the audience. I raised my hand and I was the first person picked. Eeeeek! So, you may be asking yourself what did I ask Mr. King? Most people ask him about his writing and where he gets his ideas from, but not me. I asked him why he doesn't bring Molly, a.k.a. "the thing of evil," on tour? This was after I told him he was awesome or something fan girlish like that. His response, after he told everyone who Molly was, he said "she would get all of the attention." For maybe a minute I had his full undivided attention and at that moment there was only 2 people in the room, not 800. I didn't think I would ever stop smiling.

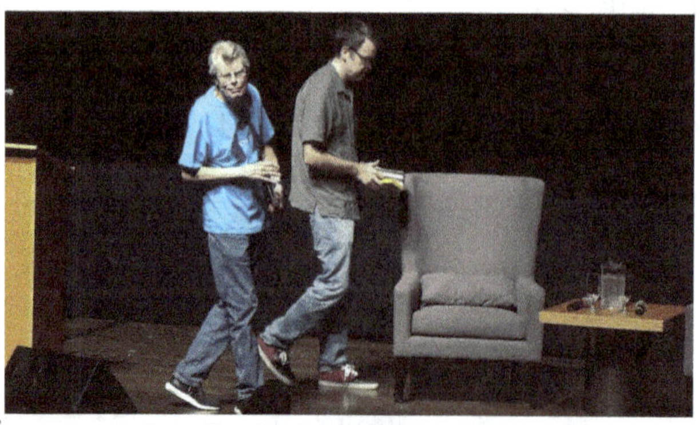

Stephen and Owen King, Bards College, Photo John Meore 2017

But wait it gets even better.

So we finished the event and on the way

SEPTEMBER

4 THURSDAY

5 FRIDAY

6 SATURDAY

7 SUNDAY

out we got to grab our books. My son, my daughter and I all grabbed one and peeked to see if we were one of the lucky ones to get an autographed copy. No, no and no. So, I was of course disappointed but still on a high from my encounter with the great one.

We make our way to the car to head home. All-of-a-sudden I thought, would my kids know to look at several of the pages? They did not. So, we all checked again.

Then, my daughter says OMFG! It's signed! Its signed!

She hands it to me, and it is in fact signed. Then she gives it to me says "happy birthday Mom."

One of my best days ever.

– Beverly Robinson, New York.

*As a special bonus, a limited number of attendees will randomly receive a signed copy / This event includes an audience Q&A but will not include a public book signing.

SLEEPING BEAUTIES

Glenn Chadbourne

SEPTEMBER

8 MONDAY

9 TUESDAY

10 WEDNESDAY

DON'T PLAY SO LOUD: 2004 WANNAPALOOZA TOUR

A note from Dave Barry and the Rock Bottom Remainders:

Teacher Man by Frank McCourt. Scribner 2005

"The World Famous (in certain places) Rock Bottom Remainders are getting ready to rock the Midwest this October. We're going on a four-city tour that will take us to St. Louis, the Rock and Roll Hall of Fame in Cleveland, the House of Blues in Chicago, and Detroit. We'll be traveling by bus, just like real rock stars, except of course that many real rock stars have actual talent. We may not have that, but we DO have a bunch of famous authors, including Amy Tan, Mitch Albom, Ridley Pearson, Scott Turow, Greg Iles, Roy Blount, Jr., and Kathi Kamen Goldmark, who founded the band. And – for the first time – Frank "The Harmonica King" McCourt.

Also performing with us once again will be Roger McGuinn, legendary co-founder of the Byrds, who really DOES have talent,

SEPTEMBER

11 THURSDAY

12 FRIDAY

13 SATURDAY

14 SUNDAY

and who has been giving the band valuable musical tips to improve our sound, such as "Don't play so loud."

We are going to rock the nation's Heartland so hard that there could be bruising as far away as the nation's Spleenland, and possibly even the nation's Kidneyland.

It's all for a great cause. So, get your tickets now, and tell your friends. If you have no friends, make some, because they will not want to miss this event."

– Dave Barry, Lead Guitar, Vocals

And Roger McGuinn says.... "Touring with the Rock Bottom Remainders has been a blast! This will be my 4th tour with them. Dave Barry has always said that touring with them would surely ruin my career, but so far it's hard to tell if that's true. Maybe it takes a while."

The Byrds *Turn Turn Turn*, Columbia 1965

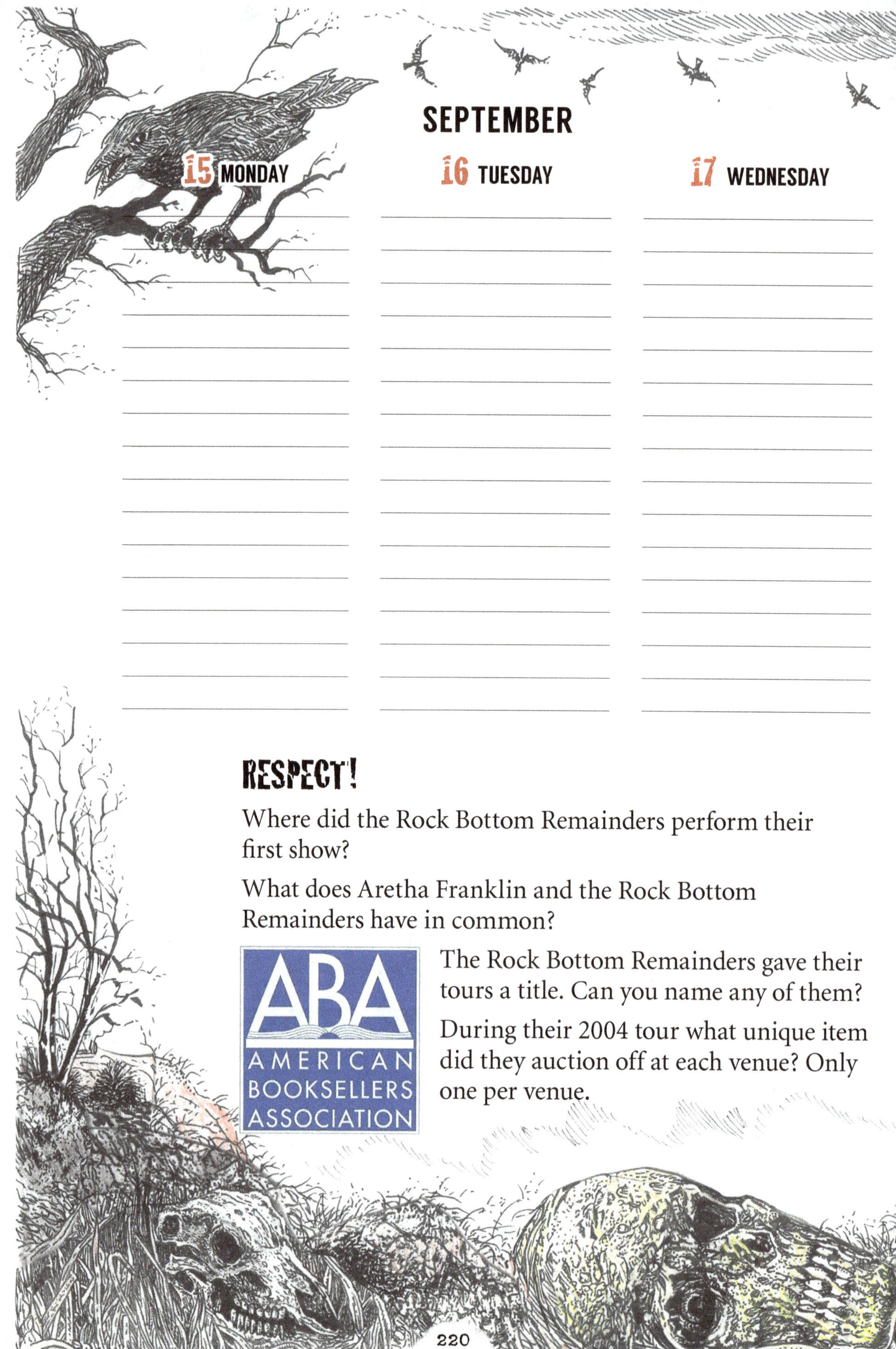

SEPTEMBER

15 MONDAY

16 TUESDAY

17 WEDNESDAY

RESPECT!

Where did the Rock Bottom Remainders perform their first show?

What does Aretha Franklin and the Rock Bottom Remainders have in common?

The Rock Bottom Remainders gave their tours a title. Can you name any of them?

During their 2004 tour what unique item did they auction off at each venue? Only one per venue.

SEPTEMBER

18 THURSDAY

19 FRIDAY

20 SATURDAY

21 SUNDAY

Answers:

A1: Premiered at the American Booksellers Association trade show in Anaheim, California, 1992.

A2: The Rock Bottom Remainders used the tour bus that was previously Aretha Franklin's.

A3: **WannaPalooza 2004** October 26-30 covered, St. Louis – Chicago – Cleveland – Detroit.

Wordstock 2010 tour includes gigs on April 20–24 in several East Coast cities, April 20-21: Washington D.C., April 21: The 9:30 Club, April 22: Philadelphia, Electric Factory April 22: New York, Nokia Theatre, April 24: Boston, The Royale.

The Past Our Bedtime tour June 22nd, 2012. A Tour in honor of former bandmate Kathi Goldmark had two shows. The 22nd was at the El Rey Theater, Los Angeles.

The June 23rd concert in Anaheim is at the American Library Association conference and open to registered attendees only.

A4: A guitar signed by everyone in the band was auctioned off at each concert.

Signed King guitar, Raptis Rare Books, raptisrarebooks.com

SEPTEMBER

22 MONDAY

23 TUESDAY

Rosh Hashanah

24 WEDNESDAY

IS STEPHEN KING. . . WORTH IT?

I discovered this question on the internet from 2014 about seeing Stephen King in person. This was for his six-city tour for his then new release, *Revival*. The tour began in New York City and continued through Washington DC, Kansas City, Wichita, Austin, and South Portland.

Have any of you been to a Stephen King book signing/event? Is it worth it?

REVIVAL

BOOK TOUR · FALL 2014

He's coming to my city soon. Tickets are $30. That gets you in the door, and a first edition hard copy of his new book (*Revival*). Signed copies will be distributed randomly, so no guarantees. Have any of you done it? Is it worth the price of admission?

– thearmadillo, reddit

SEPTEMBER

25 THURSDAY

26 FRIDAY

27 SATURDAY

28 SUNDAY

RESPONSES:

Dude, it's Stephen King! Do it! – Account deleted, reddit

"Yes, it's worth it. I've seen him twice. The first time was at a signing to promote *Four Past Midnight*, and I had to stand in line for three hours. Even after all that time, he was as nice as could be when my turn came to get my books signed. The second time I saw him was during his motorcycle tour for *Insomnia*. He spoke to a packed house for 90 minutes, and was incredibly entertaining. So, do it!

Thirty dollars is a deal." – dwenglish, reddit

"I stood in line (overnight! was #36 in line) to see Stephen King when he was doing his book tour for *Under the Dome*. Didn't cost me a cent to see him either. However, they did not allow anyone to bring any books to have signed other than *Under the Dome*, and it was required that you purchase the book at the store where he did the signing.

I would not have traded the experience of seeing one of my favorite authors in person for anything though. Even though I was up all night, the people in the line were super nice! One person brought hot chocolate, and someone else had several trays of mini cupcakes to share. Definitely go, if you have a chance to see ANY author in person! Especially Stephen King."

– Sms231, reddit

Glenn Chadbourne

SEPTEMBER

29 MONDAY

30 TUESDAY

1 WEDNESDAY

"MY FIRST STADIUM AUDIENCE!"

– Stephen King, UMass at Lowell

Stephen King took the stage at UMass at Lowell, December 7, 2012 to a packed audience at the Tsongas Center there. "A Conversation with Stephen King" was moderated by Andre Dubus III, best-selling author, and professor in UMass Lowell's English Department. There were thousands in attendance at the Tsongas Center which can seat 6,496. Floor seats were $50 and general admission in the stands was $30. Admission was free to UMass students who applied for a ticket. Stephen King also held a special master class for UMass Lowell creative writing majors during his visit to the university. Five dollars of every ticket was donated to help endow a new scholarship fund in his and his wife, Tabitha's name. King's appearance marked the debut of the new UMass Lowell Chancellor's Speaker Series, which later featured Oprah Winfrey and Meryl Streep.

Stephen King at Umass 12-7-2012

UMASS LOWELL

Stephen King took questions from the audience after his talk. Here's a couple I thought were memorable:

OCTOBER

2 THURSDAY
Yom Kippur

3 FRIDAY

4 SATURDAY

5 SUNDAY

A young man walks up to the microphone:
"Hi, hi, I'm talking to Stephen King!" The crowd laughs.

SK: "How old are you?"

YM: "I'm eleven-years old."

SK: "You go on with your bad self! What's your question?"

YM: "What was one of your best writing moments when you had your best idea and it just came to you?"

SK: "Oh man, what a great question that is. There have been a lot of times, you know, the thing is, I'm so lucky to be able to do this. Because you know, the thing is, like there are certain people in life where everybody else says we have to grow up, you stay a kid and play in

Stephen King at Umass 12-7-2012. Signing one of two chairs auctioned off at the event.

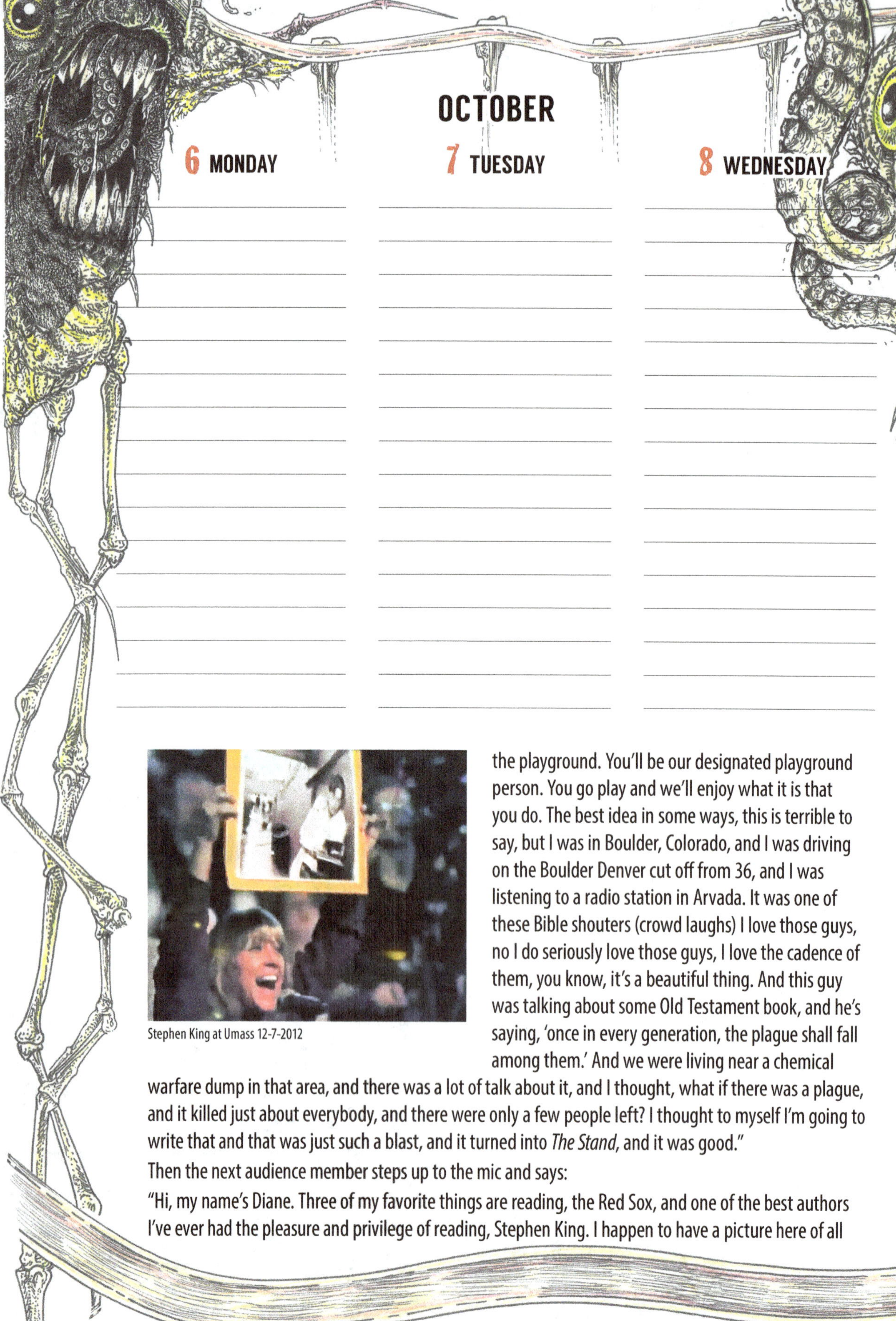

OCTOBER

6 MONDAY

7 TUESDAY

8 WEDNESDAY

Stephen King at Umass 12-7-2012

the playground. You'll be our designated playground person. You go play and we'll enjoy what it is that you do. The best idea in some ways, this is terrible to say, but I was in Boulder, Colorado, and I was driving on the Boulder Denver cut off from 36, and I was listening to a radio station in Arvada. It was one of these Bible shouters (crowd laughs) I love those guys, no I do seriously love those guys, I love the cadence of them, you know, it's a beautiful thing. And this guy was talking about some Old Testament book, and he's saying, 'once in every generation, the plague shall fall among them.' And we were living near a chemical warfare dump in that area, and there was a lot of talk about it, and I thought, what if there was a plague, and it killed just about everybody, and there were only a few people left? I thought to myself I'm going to write that and that was just such a blast, and it turned into *The Stand*, and it was good."

Then the next audience member steps up to the mic and says:

"Hi, my name's Diane. Three of my favorite things are reading, the Red Sox, and one of the best authors I've ever had the pleasure and privilege of reading, Stephen King. I happen to have a picture here of all

OCTOBER

9 THURSDAY

10 FRIDAY

11 SATURDAY

12 SUNDAY

three of these, which is a very young Stephen King, leaning against the wall of a vomitorium in Fenway Park, reading a book. I'm wondering if you remember what book you were reading in this picture."

Stephen King and Andre Dubois III at Umass 12-7-2012

SK: "Hand it down here." The picture-poster was handed up to Stephen King and moderator Andre Dubus III both examined the photo to take a closer look. The audience starts yelling for them to "turn it over," which they do and see the words "please sign this" written in large letters. Stephen King promptly pulls out a pen and signs the poster, while the audience applauds in unison at his generosity. Andre Dubus III takes the poster back down to Diane and says "you're wicked smahht!" while Diane does a dance holding the poster above her head, running down the aisle. I agree, she was a genius, she was "smahht!"

Do you know this photo of Stephen King at Fenway Park, reading a book? What is the book?

Stephen and Andre answer together:

SK: "It's The Friends of Eddie Coyle by George V. Higgins."

OCTOBER

13 MONDAY
Columbus Day
Indigenous Peoples' Day

14 TUESDAY

15 WEDNESDAY

NIRVANA

Stephen King premiered a new short story by reading it to a sold-out audience of over 6,000 at UMass in Lowell Massachusetts in 2012. What is the name of this story?

Where did it first appear in print?

It eventually appeared in Stephen King's own book. What title?

What was the genesis of this story?

Artwork by
Glenn Chadbourne

OCTOBER

16 THURSDAY

17 FRIDAY

18 SATURDAY

19 SUNDAY

Answers:

A1: "Afterlife"

A2: First published in the June 2013 edition of *Tin House*, an American literary magazine and publisher.

A3: *The Bazaar of Bad Dreams: Stories*.

A4: The story was later collected and re-introduced in the November 3, 2015 anthology *The Bazaar of Bad Dreams*, in which King revealed that the idea came from his own musings on mortality as he grew older.

Artwork by Glenn Chadbourne
From the New Stephen King Cover Series No. 9
Available from StephenKingCatalog.com

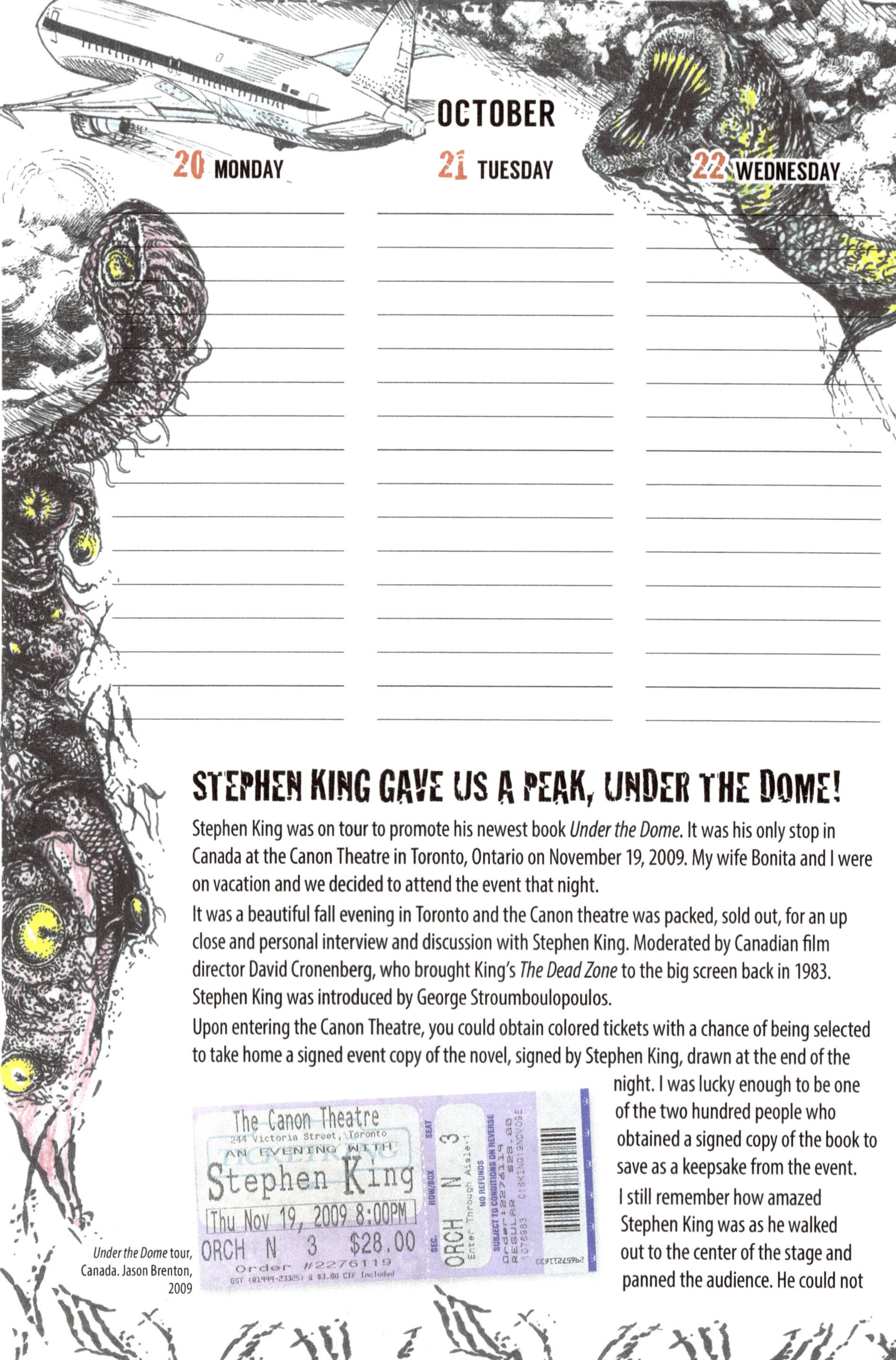

OCTOBER

20 MONDAY

21 TUESDAY

22 WEDNESDAY

STEPHEN KING GAVE US A PEAK, UNDER THE DOME!

Stephen King was on tour to promote his newest book *Under the Dome*. It was his only stop in Canada at the Canon Theatre in Toronto, Ontario on November 19, 2009. My wife Bonita and I were on vacation and we decided to attend the event that night.

It was a beautiful fall evening in Toronto and the Canon theatre was packed, sold out, for an up close and personal interview and discussion with Stephen King. Moderated by Canadian film director David Cronenberg, who brought King's *The Dead Zone* to the big screen back in 1983. Stephen King was introduced by George Stroumboulopoulos.

Upon entering the Canon Theatre, you could obtain colored tickets with a chance of being selected to take home a signed event copy of the novel, signed by Stephen King, drawn at the end of the night. I was lucky enough to be one of the two hundred people who obtained a signed copy of the book to save as a keepsake from the event. I still remember how amazed Stephen King was as he walked out to the center of the stage and panned the audience. He could not

Under the Dome tour, Canada. Jason Brenton, 2009

OCTOBER

23 THURSDAY

24 FRIDAY

25 SATURDAY

26 SUNDAY

believe the number of people in the audience and the first words out of his mouth was "Holy Shit." He claimed it was the largest audience that he had ever addressed at a book event.*

Stephen read the first chapter of his new novel, *Under the Dome*, and he discussed several of his older works. He then continued discussing *Under the Dome*. Every time he mentioned a title of one of his books the crowd cheered, and he seemed to get a charge out of it and continued to do it throughout the remainder of the event.

YouTube video, King & Cronenberg 2009

One of the highlights from the event was the announcing of a possible new book to follow up on *The Shining* called *Doctor Sleep*. The follow up book would focus on Danny Torrence, now in his forties as an orderly traumatized by the childhood events depicted in the first novel.

It was an amazing evening and a night that I will never forget for the rest of my life. If you ever get a chance to see King in person I highly recommend it.

– Jason Brenton, Canada

*The Canon theater seating capacity is 2,300.

OCTOBER

27 MONDAY

28 TUESDAY

29 WEDNESDAY

PLEASE. . . DON'T SIGN THE BOOKS

Stephen King, even on his early tours, I'm sure never received this request from a bookstore. In fact, I'd never heard of a situation like this before I ran across this story. Did you know that the author of *The Exorcist,* William Peter Blatty, was requested not to sign his books?

The Exorcist, a cross stitch

The beginnings of how *The Exorcist* came to be published happened at a party. William Peter Blatty, already an established screenwriter with films *A Shot in the Dark* with Peter Sellers, and *Darling Lili* with Julie Andrews, among others. His manuscript for *The Exorcist,* a retelling of a supposed exorcism from 1949, of a young boy, and the desperate family trying to get help. He'd discovered this story while attending Georgetown University. Blatty wasn't getting any takers. While attending a party in 1968, he met Max Jeff, an editor for Bantam books, who asked what he was working on (like any good publisher would), and Blatty told him. The editor said he'd publish it

OCTOBER

30 THURSDAY

31 FRIDAY
Halloween

1 SATURDAY

2 SUNDAY
Day of the Dead
Daylight Saving Time End

and paid him a $25,000 advance. That chance meeting was a stroke of luck for *The Exorcist*. *The Exorcist* became a book that to date has sold over 13 million copies in the USA alone have been translated into over a dozen languages.

In the beginning it hardly sold a copy. When Blatty was on his initial book tour, nobody was buying the book. Nobody. So, when he would go into the bookstores, the managers would ask if he wouldn't sign any of the unsold books, because if you sign them, they can't return them to the publisher. That must have been crushing.

He went back to New York City, visiting with his agent at the Four Seasons Hotel. Then the Dick Cavett show called and had an immediate open slot and asked if he'd be a guest. Apparently Robert Shaw, who was starring in *Jaws* at the time, was in the green room and couldn't go on. Blatty ran six blocks to the studio. Dick Cavett said he hadn't read the book, wasn't religious, and had Blatty tell him about *The Exorcist*. William Blatty had forty minutes to talk about *The Exorcist*, and the following week it went to number one on the New York Times bestseller list, and from there it began a history making run from book to film.

I wonder how many did get an *Exorcist book* signed back then.

William Peter Blatty passed away, January 12th, 2017.

"RIP William Peter Blatty, who wrote the great horror novel of our time. So long, Old Bill."

– Stephen King, Twitter

The Exorcist
First Print Hardcover
Harper & Row, New York, 1971

NOVEMBER

3 MONDAY

4 TUESDAY

Election Day (Go Vote!)

5 WEDNESDAY

MILK, BREAD... STEPHEN KING!... CHECK!

Yes, I met Stephen King at Tesco* store, Lakeside, Essex, England. during the *Lisey's Story* promotion tour.

King photo, Cliff Masters 2006.

A few weeks before, I was grocery shopping there and I noticed a poster for *Lisey's Story*. Being a Constant Reader it immediately had my attention. I could not believe my eyes, my favourite author was coming to my local supermarket!!!

The week before I spent planning what I would

NOVEMBER

6 THURSDAY

7 FRIDAY

8 SATURDAY

9 SUNDAY

say to him during those few golden seconds and I settled on "you're like a best friend I've never met" (I know, I know).

As we queued we were told "don't speak to him."
The hell with that and I took my opportunity.
Stephen replied "Thanks, how you doing fella?"
And it was over. . . just like that!

TESCO

A brief encounter to be forever cherished and never forgotten.
I have attached my photo just to show that I didn't dream this wonderful day!

– Cliff Masters, England

*TESCO has over 5,000 stores, mostly in the UK, and other countries. TESCO's superstores in the UK are comparable to the Walmart superstores in the US.

NOVEMBER

10 MONDAY

11 TUESDAY

Veterans Day

12 WEDNESDAY

Only 200 posters printed of the Rock Bottom Remainders 1998 Bangor, Maine appearance

ROCK BOTTOM BANGOR

Report from the Rock Bottom Remainders' Concert, May 8th, 1998

A dense fog hangs in the air of the Bangor Auditorium. Those in the audience may be inclined to first think of Stephen King's "The Mist," or perhaps of the remnants of one of Dave Barry's exploding animals. Then, a jet of the stuff spurts from a machine behind the well-equipped concert stage, and the audience forgets for a moment the literary aspects of the evening. That's a fog machine, those are real instruments, and this, just maybe, will be a real concert.

Suddenly, the house lights go down, and a spotlight from behind picks out the form of Roy Blount, Jr., a member of the Critic's Chorus section of the Remainders, who doubles as emcee for the band. In a clipped Southern accent burbling with good humor, he announces the members of the band as they appear on stage.

First up is Dave Barry, an immensely funny humor columnist, at present wearing a T-shirt which reads Poupon U. He explains, "It's from a mustard company!" As usual, Dave is two jokes ahead of the rest of us. He's also on lead guitar, strumming and tuning away.

In rapid succession, Roy brings out the rest of the Critic's Chorus. Joel Selvin ("If you rearrange the letters of his last name it almost spells 'Elvis!'"), Dave Marsh (who has become a cross-dressing legend amongst the band) and two locals: Joni Averill of the Bangor Daily News and Ric Taylor, meteorologist for WVII-TV in Bangor.

Another Maineiac (and part of the Remainderettes this evening), the multitalented Tess Gerritsen, who not only writes medical thrillers and is an actual medical doctor (Stephen King: "She's the only one of us who can prescribe Viagra!"), but also plays a mean electric violin. Rounding out the Remainderettes are Amy Tan, a well-respected author specializing in multigenerational family novels (seen now in leopard

NOVEMBER

13 THURSDAY

14 FRIDAY

15 SATURDAY

16 SUNDAY

skin and leather), and Kathi Goldmark, the "Band Mom" and media escort who began the Remainders and have been with them every step of the way.

Two band members have had some previous musical experience: radio host Mitch Albom (author of *Tuesdays with Morrie* and Elvis Presley impersonator) and Ridley Pearson (author of *Undercurrents* and Buddy Holly channeler) lend vocals and guitars to this already crowded lineup.

In a coup of stunt casting, the group has wrangled Warren Zevon, an actual rock and roll guy who's had songs on the charts. He seems very much an excitable boy on the stage, constantly grinning as if in mixed joy and disbelief. Drummer Jim Christie and sax man Erasmo Paolo also lend some musical credence.

The last person Roy brings on stage needs no introduction, especially here in Bangor. Stephen King appears and the crowd goes insane. He's a towering six foot two, in a cutoff Maine T-shirt. All eyes are on him, for it is Stephen King, and Stephen King alone, many are here tonight to see.

Then, the Remainders begin to play, and any such singularity promptly disappears. How they did it is a mystery, but it becomes immediately clear: The Rock Bottom Remainders really rock!

Undercurrents. RosettaBooks 2014

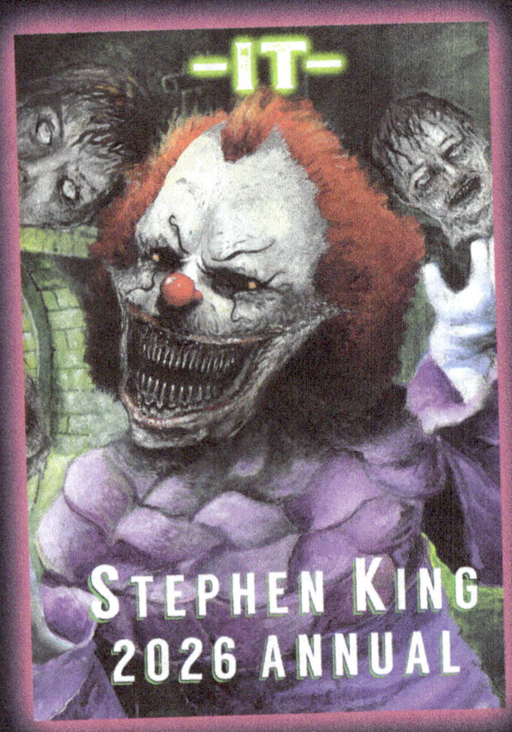

2026 STEPHEN KING ANNUAL: *IT*

The 2026 Annual celebrates Stephen King's novel, *IT*!

The Annual is full color and is 250 pages!

We delve into everything *IT* and Pennywise, the book, the films, merchandise, and everything in-between. Pennywise the clown, a malevolent entity, has become an iconic character the world over. The kids of *IT*, the heroes of this story, are members of The Losers' Club, a group of seven outcast children who are terrorized by Pennywise as *IT* emerges from the sewer.

Expect the usual photos, illustrations, informative articles, interviews, and reviews that are featured in every Stephen King Annual. The Annual also includes the *Stephen King Calendar* with facts, trivia, and art.

THE STEPHEN KING CALENDAR 2026

The 2026 Calendar Features Stephen King's novel, *IT*, All Year Long!

The *Stephen King Calendar* is also in color with 136 pages!

It's overflowing with trivia, facts, illustrations, photos, and with original border art by Glenn Chadbourne throughout the year. The *Stephen King Calendar* is now available separately for those that would like a calendar to use all year long!

If you're familiar with our Stephen King Calendars, then you know what to expect, and they are featured in full-color!

Both the ANNUAL and CALENDAR feature original cover and interior art by Glenn Chadbourne, this year featuring images from *IT* and Pennywise throughout.

Both are available for pre-order at **StephenKingCatalog.com**

Written and Edited by Dave Hinchberger
Also features Artwork by Glenn Chadbourne

Coming Fall 2025

Published by
Overlook Connection Press

Previous Stephen King Annuals Available!

STEPHEN KING and CREEPSHOW

2023 STEPHEN KING ANNUAL

Written and Edited by
Dave Hinchberger

Cover/interior art by
Glenn Chadbourne

Featuring Paul R. Gagne on the 1982 *Creepshow* set. Kelley Jones first time in print comic of Stephen King's "The Raft", New Adrienne Barbeau interview. Fairy Tale review, Stephen King's "Pinfall", interview with Stephen King and Richard Chizmar, more! Trivia, quotes, facts, and articles. Featuring, artists, director, actors, writers, et el. Art on every page! Special guests Bev Vincent, Tyson Blue, Stephen Spignesi, Anthony Northrup, Andrew Rausch, and Kevin Quigley.

STEPHEN KING and THE GREEN MILE

2022 STEPHEN KING ANNUAL

Written and Edited by
Dave Hinchberger

Cover/interior art by
Glenn Chadbourne

This Stephen King Catalog Annual theme for 2022 features *The Green Mile*. With trivia, quizzes, quotes, facts, and informative articles covering the novel / film, featuring Stephen King, artists, director, actors, writers with quotes on *The Green Mile*. Art on every page! Special guests Bev Vincent, Tyson Blue, Stephen Spignesi, *Green Mile* artist Mark Geyer, James Cole, Andrew Rausch, Kevin Quigley, and interview with Rodney Barnes "Standing in Line for Coffey".

STEPHEN KING and THE STAND

2020 STEPHEN KING ANNUAL

Written and Edited by
Dave Hinchberger

Cover/interior art by
Glenn Chadbourne

Featuring Stephen King, *The Stand* director, Mick Garris, Stand actors Rob Lowe, Miguel Ferrer, and many other guests. *The Stand* Annual also features trivia, quizzes, quotes, Did You Know facts, and informative articles covering the novel and the original film. Many collectible items and promotional items are featured, many never seen before! Directed by Mick Garris and screenplay written by Stephen King. You'll be pleasantly surprised what you find within these pages in one of Stephen King's most popular novels… *The Stand*.

STEPHEN KING GOES TO THE MOVIES

2021 STEPHEN KING ANNUAL

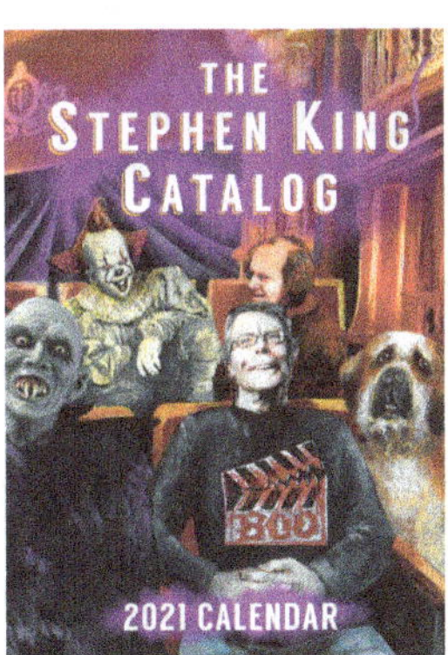

Written and Edited by
Dave Hinchberger

Cover/interior art by
Glenn Chadbourne

This Stephen King Catalog Annual theme for 2021 features STEPHEN KING GOES TO THE MOVIES. Covering the many theatrical films produced of Stephen King's work. Trivia, quizzes, quotes, facts, artwork, rare images, and informative articles covering the novel and the original films, featuring in depth articles, quotes from directors, actors, writers on their works. Revisit the films that brought Stephen King, and all of us, to the theaters for decades! From *Carrie* to *IT* (2017)!

The online Store Dedicated to EVERYTHING STEPHEN KING!

Order at StephenKingCatalog.com

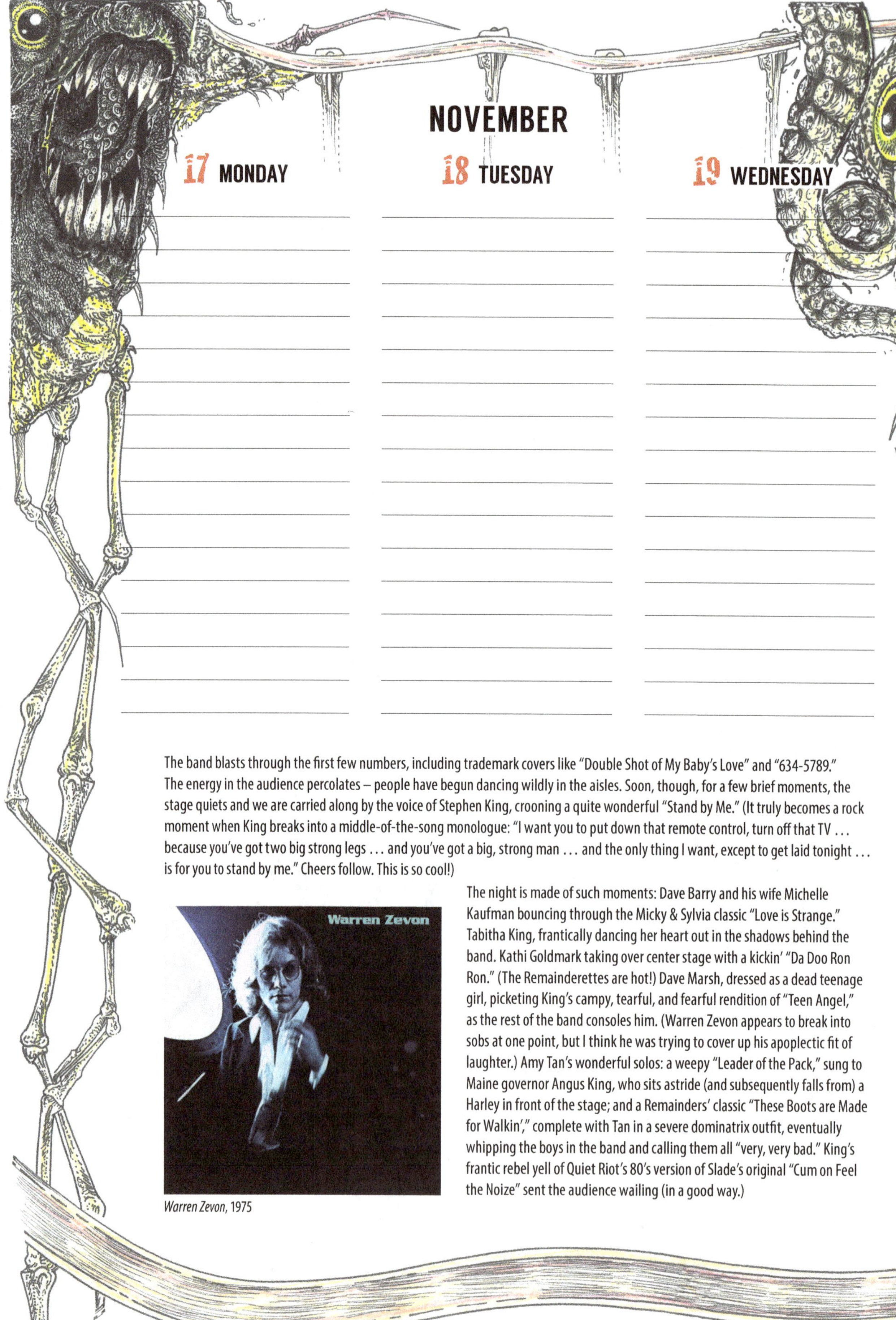

NOVEMBER

17 MONDAY

18 TUESDAY

19 WEDNESDAY

The band blasts through the first few numbers, including trademark covers like "Double Shot of My Baby's Love" and "634-5789." The energy in the audience percolates – people have begun dancing wildly in the aisles. Soon, though, for a few brief moments, the stage quiets and we are carried along by the voice of Stephen King, crooning a quite wonderful "Stand by Me." (It truly becomes a rock moment when King breaks into a middle-of-the-song monologue: "I want you to put down that remote control, turn off that TV . . . because you've got two big strong legs . . . and you've got a big, strong man . . . and the only thing I want, except to get laid tonight . . . is for you to stand by me." Cheers follow. This is so cool!)

Warren Zevon, 1975

The night is made of such moments: Dave Barry and his wife Michelle Kaufman bouncing through the Micky & Sylvia classic "Love is Strange." Tabitha King, frantically dancing her heart out in the shadows behind the band. Kathi Goldmark taking over center stage with a kickin' "Da Doo Ron Ron." (The Remainderettes are hot!) Dave Marsh, dressed as a dead teenage girl, picketing King's campy, tearful, and fearful rendition of "Teen Angel," as the rest of the band consoles him. (Warren Zevon appears to break into sobs at one point, but I think he was trying to cover up his apoplectic fit of laughter.) Amy Tan's wonderful solos: a weepy "Leader of the Pack," sung to Maine governor Angus King, who sits astride (and subsequently falls from) a Harley in front of the stage; and a Remainders' classic "These Boots are Made for Walkin'," complete with Tan in a severe dominatrix outfit, eventually whipping the boys in the band and calling them all "very, very bad." King's frantic rebel yell of Quiet Riot's 80's version of Slade's original "Cum on Feel the Noize" sent the audience wailing (in a good way.)

NOVEMBER

20 THURSDAY

21 FRIDAY

22 SATURDAY

23 SUNDAY

Dave Barry wrote an original song for this show: "Proofreading Woman," which is hilarious and actually a good song (the chorus: "She's got a big dictionary / real good grammar / she never says 'between you and I.'")

The show closes with a slam-bang double-shot. The Remainders buzz through the infamous "FBI version" of "Louie Louie" (the only reprintable line is in the chorus, "Get her way down low.") At the end of this, a surprisingly nimble Joel Selvin jumps around the stage in the rapture of a "scream solo" which lasts at least thirty seconds. The finale, King's take on Zevon's famous "Werewolves of London," is terrific fun; if nothing else, the entire night would have been worth it to see Stephen King howl.

The show proper ends and people are getting up from their seats, when a frenzy of light and sound jumps out from the stage. The Remainders retake the room with their encore of Them's "Gloria" (Dave Barry never sounded better). It's one of the truly transcendent moments of the night. You can literally lose yourself in the power of rock and roll.

The Rock Bottom Remainders are not primarily musicians. They are a group of mainly writers with separate ideas and agendas, individuals who shape the world individually. But tonight, together, they formed something larger than themselves, something grand, something cohesive.

They were a band, they were magic, and they were sure as hell born to run.

Rock on, Remainders.

– Kevin Quigley

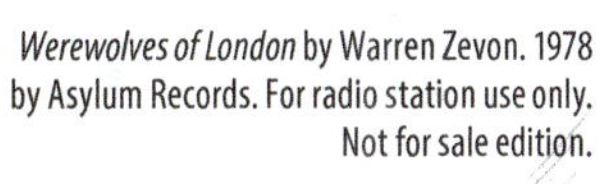

Werewolves of London by Warren Zevon. 1978 by Asylum Records. For radio station use only. Not for sale edition.

NOVEMBER

24 MONDAY

25 TUESDAY

26 WEDNESDAY

THE KING'S GO TO CHURCH

On September 28th, 2017, I was lucky enough to score two tickets to see Stephen King and his son Owen King sit down to speak to their fans about co-authored book *Sleeping Beauties* at the beautiful First Baptist Church in Newton, Massachusetts.

First Baptist Church, Newton, Massachusetts On April 15, 1982, it was listed in the National Register of Historic Places.

I called my friend Paul, another constant reader, with the good news. As the date approached we we texted each other with our game plan. Paul was going to slide off work a bit early that day with a bit of a sore throat. I took the whole day off to excited to focus on my job. I swung by Paul's house and tooted the horn with three loud blares until he appeared rushing down the front steps to my car.

Photo: Ron Naimo

I was sporting my *'Salem's Lot* t-shirt. A gift from last Christmas. Paul had on this Red Sox cap and a pretty cool *Creepshow* tee he bought for the occasion. Off we drove and suffered through notorious Boston traffic that late

NOVEMBER

27 THURSDAY
Thanksgiving

28 FRIDAY

29 SATURDAY

30 SUNDAY

Thursday afternoon inching our way along Route 128 towards Newton Centre.

Finally arriving we made our way in and got as close to the altar / stage as we could to get the best view. The stage was lit up and the shiny organ pipes stood out in all their magnificence. As we took a few pictures a familiar face turned to his right. Paul and I knew right away it was actor Chris Cooper! Chris played Al Templeton in the adaption of *11/22/63*. To say we were floored is an understatement. Glad to know even movie stars are fans. Stephen and Owen came out on stage soon after to discuss their co-creative craft and read from their new book.

Actor, Chris Cooper

Photo: Ron Naimo

The price of admission entitled us both to copies of the book and lucky ole me did in fact happen to receive a signed copy, with signatures from both Stephen and Owen. I still have the book and proudly display it on my ever-growing bookshelf with the King family of authors.

I hope maybe to see Stephen and maybe Owen again sometime.

I hope that maybe they will collaborate on a new book together soon.

I hope I never get too old to stop reading their works.

I hope...

– Ron Naimo, Boston

DECEMBER

1 MONDAY

2 TUESDAY

3 WEDNESDAY

NO SLEEP 'TIL PARIS

My wife and I visited Paris for 3 days in November 2013 to coincide with Stephen King's visit to MK2 Bibliotheque store, Paris on 13 November 2013 for the *Dr. Sleep* tour.

MK2 Bibliotheque bookstore. Paris, France 2013. Photo: Alan Kyle

We booked a hotel near the venue the day before and visited the store to have a look around. The MK2 Bibliotheque shop was all set up for the King signing the next day.

At dinner we decided it would be a good idea to go

DECEMBER

4 THURSDAY

5 FRIDAY

6 SATURDAY

7 SUNDAY

to the venue early and wait in line. We walked the short distance to the MK2 Bibliotheque around midnight and found many fans already waiting in line. More and more people started to arrive after us and the fans first in line decided to get organized. She gave the first hundred people in line a number corresponding to their place in the line. I was number 89.

It was pretty cold that night and we were finally warmed when the sun came up in the morning. We saw King arriving and the excitement started to build in the line.

While in Germany he was given a Porsche to drive.

The first 100 fans were allowed inside and

Stephen King Arrives in a Porsche
Paris, France 2013 Photo: Alan Kyle

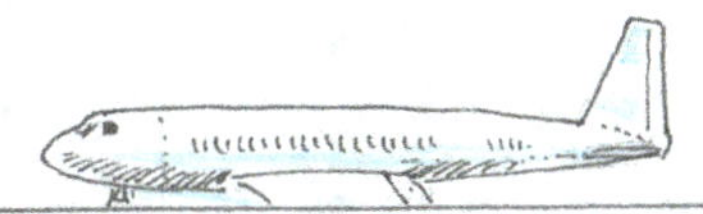

DECEMBER

8 MONDAY

9 TUESDAY

10 WEDNESDAY

Paris, France 2013. Photo: Alan Kyle

the security people informed us that King would only sign one item per person. They were very strict about this as there would be hundreds of fans outside who would not get in.

I decided to chance my luck and put my "The New Lieutenant's Rap" proof inside my *The Shining* UK trade edition to see if he would sign both. When he saw the NLR proof he was excited and he not only signed it, he added a peace sign doodle. I was able to film him signing both. I also

DECEMBER

11 THURSDAY

12 FRIDAY

13 SATURDAY

14 SUNDAY

managed to get him to sign my *'Salem's Lot* UK trade edition.

Before we left the store I was able to blag some swag off a French store worker for a few euros. Can't get enough souvenirs. As we left, there was several hundred unfortunate people still waiting in line.

Alan Kyle Photo, Paris, France 2013

After his visit to Paris, King moved on to the US Ramstein Air Base in Rheinland-Pfalz Germany on 18-Nov-23, Zirkus Krone in Munich on 19-Nov-23, and CCH in Hamburg on 20-Nov-23. I was not able to go to any of these events. Next tour!

– Alan Kyle, Paris, France

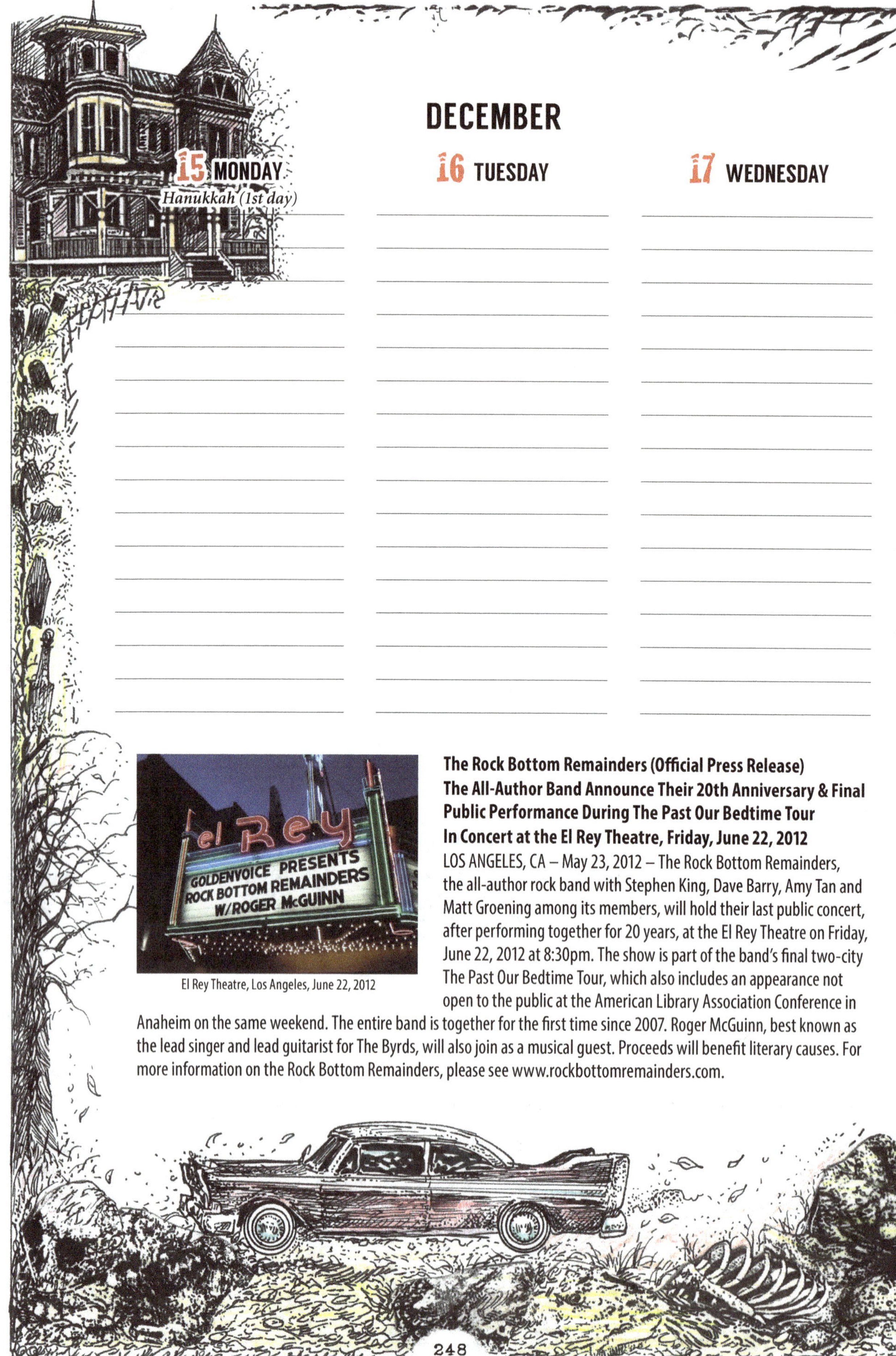

DECEMBER

15 MONDAY

Hanukkah (1st day)

16 TUESDAY

17 WEDNESDAY

El Rey Theatre, Los Angeles, June 22, 2012

The Rock Bottom Remainders (Official Press Release)
The All-Author Band Announce Their 20th Anniversary & Final Public Performance During The Past Our Bedtime Tour
In Concert at the El Rey Theatre, Friday, June 22, 2012

LOS ANGELES, CA – May 23, 2012 – The Rock Bottom Remainders, the all-author rock band with Stephen King, Dave Barry, Amy Tan and Matt Groening among its members, will hold their last public concert, after performing together for 20 years, at the El Rey Theatre on Friday, June 22, 2012 at 8:30pm. The show is part of the band's final two-city The Past Our Bedtime Tour, which also includes an appearance not open to the public at the American Library Association Conference in Anaheim on the same weekend. The entire band is together for the first time since 2007. Roger McGuinn, best known as the lead singer and lead guitarist for The Byrds, will also join as a musical guest. Proceeds will benefit literary causes. For more information on the Rock Bottom Remainders, please see www.rockbottomremainders.com.

DECEMBER

18 THURSDAY

19 FRIDAY

20 SATURDAY

21 SUNDAY

> ***"We play music about as well as Metallica writes novels"***
> *- Dave Barry*

Doors open at 7:30pm. Tickets are $40-$200 and go on sale Thursday, May 24, 2012 via TheElRey.com and Ticketmaster. $200 VIP ticket includes pre-show reception and "meet & greet" from 6:30pm to 7:30pm. This is an all-ages show. The historic El Rey Theatre is located in the preserved art deco Miracle Mile district at 5515 Wilshire Blvd., Los Angeles, CA 90036 (323-936-6400). Valet, lot and street parking are available.

On the upcoming concert, popular horror and science fiction writer Stephen King, who plays rhythm guitar says, "A few years ago, Bruce Springsteen told us we weren't bad, but not to try to get any better otherwise we'd just be another lousy band. After 20 years, we still meet his stringent requirements. For instance, while we all know what 'stringent' means, none of us have yet mastered an F chord."

The Band –

By day, they're authors. Really famous authors. But once a year, they shed their pen-and-pencil clutching personas and become rock stars, complete with roadies, groupies and a wicked cool tour bus. Most of them are both amateur musicians and popular English-language book, magazine, and newspaper authors. Their self-mocking band name was taken from the publishing term "remaindered book," a work of which the unsold remainder of the publisher's stock of copies is sold at a reduced price.

Confirmed for the concert are Stephen King, who hasn't performed with the band since 2007, as well as Amy Tan (vocals & whip), Dave Barry (co-lead guitar),

DECEMBER

22 MONDAY

23 TUESDAY

24 WEDNESDAY
Christmas Eve

Matt Groening (cowbell), Mitch Albom (keyboards), Scott Turow (vocals), James McBride (sax), Greg Iles (co-lead guitar), Ridley Pearson (bass), Roy Blount, Jr. (the crowd), and Sam Barry (harmonica).

King adds, "I'm looking forward to reuniting with all my bandmates. We're older but not dead. Some of us can remember all of the words; all of us can remember some of the words; but NONE of us can remember all of the music. That's why they call it rock and roll."

Barry chimes in, "It's not that we had a 'creative differences' issue, or some in the band wanted to launch solo music careers, but the fact is that we can no longer play an entire set without having to pee." Barry adds, "We realize the Rolling Stones are celebrating 50 years this year, but we don't want to reach the point where our stage moves involve motorized scooters."

The ROCK BOTTOM REMAINDERS

1992 May 25th Program booklet, Cowboy Boogie, Anaheim, CA

Material – The band has two original songs and mostly performs covers. Audiences are likely to be treated to some combination of the following classic tunes performed with The Remainders' unique sensibility, as well as backing up Roger McGuinn on several Byrds classics.

• "Gloria" • "High School Sweater" • "If the House is a Rockin'. . ." • "In the Midnight Hour" • "Louie Louie" • "Paperback Writer" • "Rockaway Beach" • "Stand By Me" Ben E King version • "Steamroller Blues" • "These Boots Are Made for Walkin" • "Wild Thing" • "You Ain't Goin' Nowhere" • "You Can't Judge a Book by its Cover" • "You May Be Right"

Causes – Since the band's founding, they have raised over $2 million for various literacy causes. Proceeds from the Anaheim show support the

DECEMBER

25 THURSDAY
Christmas Eve

26 FRIDAY
Kwanzaa

27 SATURDAY

28 SUNDAY

American Library Association's scholarship program for graduate students in library and information studies. Proceeds from the El Rey show in Los Angeles will benefit The Midnight Mission, the Los Angeles Downtown Women's Center and a new Emerging Author Series at Live Talks Los Angeles to be launched in January 2013. "Kathi founded the Remainders as a one-night stand, and the fling turned us into family who have had 20 years of fun. We promised Kathi she would be on stage with us for our 20th and final year, and so we have.
We dedicate these last two shows to our instigator and Remainderette." – Amy Tan

Villard Books, T-shirt

"We play music as well as Metallica writes novels." – Dave Barry

"The Rock Bottom Remainders? Who the hell are they?" – Kirk Hammett, Metallica

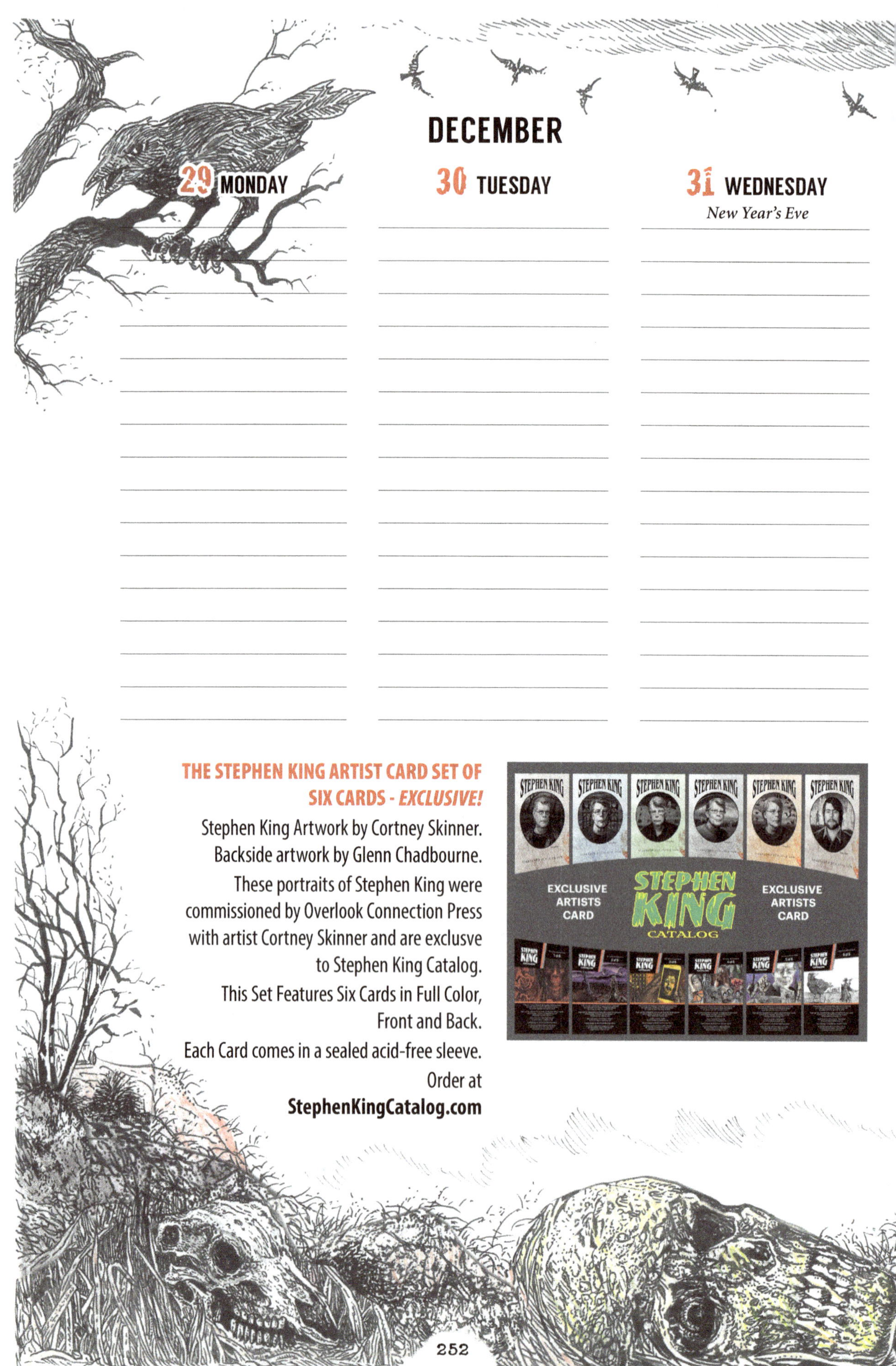

DECEMBER

29 MONDAY

30 TUESDAY

31 WEDNESDAY
New Year's Eve

Dedicated to
Stephen King and Stephen Spignesi

Every Stephen King Annual is dedicated to the writer that brought us all together here… Stephen King. He toured the United States, and the world, for over forty years. He was always willing to promote his work, meet folks and sign books. As you've read within, Stephen King would appear at afternoon movie theaters, visit colleges, and bookstores, independent and corporate. He was happy to tour speaking to large crowds and small. Authors do tour, but not all of them. I attended the only tour that Ray Bradbury, at the age of 70, took across the US. He stopped in Atlanta at Mark Stevens' store, The Science Fiction and Mystery Bookshop. I asked him if he'd done many tours (I hadn't heard of any previously) and he said "this is the only tour I've ever done." When you look at the history of King's touring, and traveling that span of years, I'd bet that Stephen King's appearances must set a record of some sort, for authors that is. What a gift to his Constant Readers.

Maybe we should get on the horn to the Guiness World Records?

In the 1980's I met author Stephen J. Spignesi, who had written about pop culture. He was then working on *The Shape Under the Sheet: The Stephen King Encyclopedia.* It was a five-year project that became one massive tome on Stephen King. During those lean years, with no internet, no email, we communicated by mail (carrier pigeon) or by phone (land lines). Photos were still being processed from a roll of film that was taken with a camera, and we had to wait weeks for the processing. I had no idea then, but we were living in the stone age of publishing, but we made it happen. Upon our discovery of a mutual obsession (Stephen King), we became fast friends and exchanged information and rare King stories that were only available by xerox, many from typescripts as they hadn't been published (later we published his, *The Lost Work of Stephen King*). Our friendship has endured for almost forty years. A friendship that I am grateful for, a brother-from-another-mother I've had the good fortune to know these decades. In all these years, in all these books he's written about Stephen King (and so much more), he's never actually met King, has never seen him speak live. It's difficult to fathom that fact. This just led me to the obvious conclusion that this 2025 Annual: Stephen King On Tour is warmly dedicated to Stephen Spignesi. Of all the worlds I've encountered, there has been no one more influential, and knowledgeable, in my world of Stephen King. Steve, you made a difference in so many ways. Steve, this one's for you, my friend, and deservedly so.

Steve… I can't thank you enough… for everything.

Thank you.

Every Stephen King Annual is a lot of work, work that I look forward to every year.

Thank you to the diligence and dedication of our writing team to help bring this publication to fruition.

A thank you to my long-time partner in so many projects, the featured artist, Glenn Chadbourne.

Our graphic designer, Bryan McAllister, who creates the magic and wizardry to whip up our Annuals every year, and to his lovely wife Laura, son Ian (who may be visiting from college), and daughter Maggie, who patiently lets him work away for hours at a time. You might want to check on him from time to time… with a sandwich and a drink. 😊

This edition is also lovingly dedicated to Cordelia and Kyler, who arrived since last year's edition.

To my wife, LeeAnn, who makes life a joy to share with, on every level, every day.

CONTRIBUTORS:

Dave Hinchberger I devour everything: movies or comic books, novels or theater, Rock n' Roll to Jazz. Before I was in "books" I managed record stores and then marketing at Polygram and Relativity Records for 15 years. Growing up it was The Beatles, and rock music. In the 70's, at night, we'd tune into the CBS Mystery Theater on the car radio with my family on long car trips. The family huddled behind mom and dad in the station wagon, as the fateful sound of the drum roll theme came echoing out of the tinny car speakers. Hairs raised on our necks. Experiencing Planet of the Apes in the theater with my dad, at the wide-eyed age of six. These are the sparks that have led me here. I've been operating The Overlook Connection Bookstore and Press, since 1987, and created The Stephen King Catalog to dedicate this area to everything King. I'm never bored. There isn't enough time for me to see, read, and experience what the creative world has to offer, but... I'm damn sure gonna try.

Glenn Chadbourne This amazing artist is well known in the horror world of writers, artists, and even in film (if you look close in Stephen King's *The Mist*, directed by Frank Darabont, you'll see Glenn's work). "Artist to the stars," we all call him. Illustrator of many novels and short story collections, but especially Stephen King special editions. He created a beautiful two-volume set, *The Secretary of Dreams*, an illustrated Stephen King short story collection. Glenn is also the artist for the New Stephen King Cover Series that gives every Stephen King book a new cover (see ad within). You can see a whole category with hundreds of items from Glenn Chadbourne at StephenKingCatalog.com and you can visit with him at **glennchadbourne.com**.

Bryan McAllister has been bringing the visual design of OCP projects to life since 2002. A lifelong sci-fi fan, he honed his artistic abilities early, absorbing the gorgeous craftsmanship of Star Wars. Today, the man behind graphic design and illustration studio, Fine Dog Creative. He's also a devoted caver and serves on the board of directors of the Missouri Caves and Karst Conservancy, is a Life Member and Fellow of the National Speleological Society - to which he was named Fellow in 2016. Inspired by the 70's TV series The Land of the Lost as a kid (remember those scary Sleestaks?) he has discovered, mapped, and surveyed caves across the United States including portions of Mammoth Cave (the longest known cave in the world). He lives in St. Louis with his lovely wife, Laura, their two children, Maya the wonder dog and two comical cats.

Bev Vincent, is the author of *Stephen King: A Complete Exploration of his Work, Life and Influences*, *The Road to the Dark Tower*, *The Dark Tower Companion* and *The Stephen King Illustrated Companion*. Over 100 short stories, with appearances in *Doctor Who: Destination Prague*, *The X-files: The Truth Is Out There*, *Ellery Queen's*, *Alfred Hitchcock's* and *Cemetery Dance* magazines. He has been nominated for the Stoker (twice), Edgar, Ignotus and ITW Thriller Awards. In 2018, he co-edited the anthology *Flight or Fright* with Stephen King. He collaborated with Brian Keene on *Dissonant Harmonies*. More at **bevvincent.com** and Twitter @ BevVincent.

CONTRIBUTORS:

Joseph Pittman worked as an editor at New American Library/Signet Books with Elaine Koster, the president and publisher of NAL, and supervised many Stephen King novels during those years, working closely with the author. He also worked in the managing editorial department at Viking/Penguin. He's also the author of many books with his first novel being *Tilting at Windmills*. Under his pseudonym, Adam Carpenter, he wrote a series of novels in The Jimmy McSwain Files.

Jim Argendeli is a lifelong horror reader. Author F. Paul Wilson once described me as a friend to the genre. I have been a CNN.COM book reviewer, written book copy for small press publishers, been a freelance writer for Turner Classic Movies and am a published writer. I have felt fortunate to grow up reading horror fiction in all the different elements the genre offers. The friends I have made with writers and publishers (Hi Dave) is something that if you told the teenage me what would happen to being involved with these amazing talented artists, and becoming published within fiction and non-fiction, this Canadian would have been in disbelief.

Stephen Spignesi is a retired Practitioner in Residence from the English Department at the University of New Haven and the author of more than 65 books. He is considered an authority on the work of Stephen King, the *Titanic*, the Beatles, and other pop culture and historical topics. His latest books are *Stephen King, American Master*, *Elton John: Fifty Years On*, and *Robin Williams, American Master*. He lives in New Haven, Connecticut.

Tyson Blue, a true *eminence grise* in the world of King scholarship, is one of the world's primary authorities on King's work and the media projects based thereon. He was a Contributing Editor for *Castle Rock: the Stephen King Newsletter* from 1985-1989, and his work has appeared in *Twilight Zone*, *Cemetery Dance*, *Midnight Graffiti* and many other magazines worldwide. He is the author of *The Unseen King*, and most recently edited *Hope and Miracles: The Shawshank Redemption* and *The Green Mile: Two Screenplays* by Frank Darabont, published in 2021 by Gauntlet Press. He lives near Rochester, NY with his wife, Janice, and Hank, their golden retriever.

Andrew J. Rausch is a popular culture writer and the author of nearly 50 books, including *The Stephen King Movie Quiz Book*, *The Wit & Wisdom of Stephen King*, and *Perspectives on Stephen King*. He lives in Independence, Kansas. He can be found at **authorandyrausch.wordpress.com**

Kevin Quigley is known for his monographic work on Stephen King (*The Stephen King Illustrated Movie Trivia Book*, *Chart of Darkness*, *Stephen King Limited*). He is the author of the novels *Meatball Express*, *I'm On Fire*, and *Roller Disco Saturday Night*, as well as the short story collections *Damage & Dread* and *This Terrestrial Hell*. His stories have appeared in the *Cemetery Dance* anthologies *Halloween Carnival* and *Shivers*, the bestselling *Shining in the Dark* anthology, the thriller collection *Death of a Bad Neighbour*, and Lawrence Block's upcoming *Playing Games*. He lives in Boston, Massachusetts with his husband, Shawn.

CONTRIBUTORS:

Anthony Northrup is the author of *Stephen King Dollar Baby: The Book*, *Stephen King Dollar Baby: The Sequel* (Bear Manor Media), Currently adapting his story "Yardwork" as a screenplay for film director Rob Darren. Entertainment writer for the *Tri-County Sun* for over a decade, earning him two writer's awards. His "All Things King" Stephen King Fan Page (Facebook) of ten years is acknowledged in *Stephen King American Master*, by author Stephen Spignesi. Host/Co-Host of Stephen King Dollar Baby Film Fests: Crypticon MN, (2014/15) SK Rules: DB1 Worldwide Online (2021), SKR: DB2 Alternating Currents, Davenport, IA (2022), "Long Live the King" DBFF Brazil (2022) Anthony currently resides in North Dakota with his wife Gena.

Ariel Bosi was born and lives in Buenos Aires, Argentina. He's the author of *Todo sobre Stephen King* (2016, Penguin Random House) and *Edición limitada* (2020, RdlM Ediciones). A Constant Reader since 1996, he has worked in the publishing field, focusing on Stephen King promotional campaigns for the Spanish publisher since 2010. Currently, he hosts *La Corte del Rey*, a podcast about Stephen King's works and life for Penguin Random House. *Los Tesoros del Rey*, a newsletter about King's works, all available in Spanish for Constant Readers in Spain / Latin America. He's attended red carpet events and press junkets of Stephen King adaptations as an influencer and has personally met his favorite author on several occasions. His published work: *Todo sobre Stephen King:* penguinlibros.com/ar/biografias/135313-libro-todo-sobre-stephen-king-9788401346958 and *Edición limitada:* restaurantdelamente.com/4227-edicion-limitada-nueva-edicion-a-bosi-y-p-tarantino.html

L.L. Soares is a marooned time traveler from the year 2317, trying to find a way home. In the meantime, he tells stories. His books include the novels *Life Rage* (2012 Bram Stoker Award-winner for First Novel), *Rock 'n' Roll*, *Hard*, *Buried in Blue Clay*, and *Teach Them How to Bleed*, and a new career-spanning story collection, *Something Blue and Other Colorful Deaths*. His short fiction has appeared in dozens of magazines and anthologies, including *Gothic.net*, *Cemetery Dance*, *Zippered Flesh Vol. I-III*, and *Wicked Sick*. For more than a decade, he co-wrote the Stoker-nominated movie review column *Cinema Knife Fight*. He lives in the Boston area with his wife and their pet iguana, Osiris, King of the Dead. To keep up on his endeavors (and to find out if he ever gets back to this own time), please go to **www.llsoares.com**

Hank Wagner lives in northwestern New Jersey with his beautiful wife, Nancy. A respected critic and interviewer, his work has appeared in numerous genre publications such as *Deadly Pleasures*, *Dead Reckonings*, *Cemetery Dance*, *Mystery Scene* and *Crimespree*. Wagner is a co-author of *The Complete Stephen King Universe* and *Prince of Stories: A Guide to the Many Worlds of Neil Gaiman*. He also co-edited *Thrillers: 100 Must Reads with David Morrell*, an Edgar, Anthony, and Macavity Award finalist. He tries to conceal this part of his past, but he was known to review for a seedy newsprint type publication/catalog called The Overlook Connection, many decades ago. He may also have spent way too many hours on the road over the years with reprobates like Dave and LeeAnn Hinchberger.

Hans-Åke Lilja has been reading Stephen King for over 40 years. Since 1996, he has run the website Lilja's Library – The World of Stephen King and has published six books related to Stephen King that has been translated into 17 languages. Hans-Åke has met Stephen King three times, interviewed him twice and has lectured regularly about him since 2017. Visit **liljas-library.com**

CONTRIBUTORS:

Noah Mitchell has been reading King since 1980 and collecting since 1985. He has an extensive King collection that includes first US and UK editions, signed limited and lettered editions, and first appearances of short stories. He has an enormous home library that includes impressive collections of many other writers such as Joe Hill, Clive Barker, Dean Koontz, Ed Gorman, Jack Ketchum, Shirley Jackson, Robert McCammon, Peter Straub, Dan Simmons, F Paul Wilson, and others. Facebook friends from across the country have traveled to New York to tour his home library.

Diana Petroff has been an avid Stephen King reader for decades, and, while relatively new to the rare collecting world, has dedicated years to learning the idiosyncrasies of rare book collecting with a concentration on Stephen King. This love of rare books has led her into the world of publishing. She currently works with Alex Berman, the founder of Phantasia Press in the production and design of limited editions. Phantasia marked Stephen King's entry into the signed/limited market in 1980 with one of the most coveted collectibles: the lettered "asbestos" *Firestarter*, which of course is highlighted in this year's edition.

Bibliography, End Notes, Images

PAGE 1: Rock Bottom Remainders 1/200 Poster release. Design by DJ McGee, © 1998.

PAGE 4: Stephen King, George Mason University Award, 9-23-11. Photo by Glen Reitz © 2011.

PAGE 6: Stephen King at SCAD, 2-19-2012, Trustees Theater, Georgia. Photo Glen Reitz © 2012.

PAGE 10: Stephen King, *The Tommyknockers*, Putnam © 1987.

PAGE 10: Don Robertson, *Ideal Genuine Man*, Philtrum Press © 1987.

PAGE 10 Timeline: Stephen King, *Carrie*, Doubleday © 1974. *The Texas Chain Saw Massacre*, Bryanston Dist. Company 1974.

PAGE 11: Stephen King & Don Robertson, "Walkin' Dudes" River Oaks Bookstore 1-29-88, Photo © 1988 Sam Houston

PAGES 11-12: Stephen King & Don Robertson, River Oaks Bookstore 1-29-88, Photos Bev Vincent © 1988.

PAGE 11 Timeline: 1970s TV antenna, Fall of Saigon 1975, Roy Scheider in *Jaws*, Universal Pictures © 1975, Stephen King, *'Salem's Lot*, Doubleday © 1975.

PAGE 12 Timeline: 1970s mainframe computer punch card, Dungeons & Dragons, TSR, © 1974.

PAGE 13 Timeline: Wall home telephone, *Carrie* film, United Artists © 1976, Mars Viking Lander, 1970s disco ball, 1970s pinball machine.

PAGE 14: Stephen King, *Wizard and Glass: Dark Tower IV*, Donald Grant © 1997, Dave McKean cover art.

PAGE 14: Stephen King, and Peter Straub, *The Talisman*, Viking © 1984.

PAGE 14 Timeline: Stephen King, *The Shining*, Doubleday © 1977, *Close Encounters of the Third Kind*, Columbia Pictures © 1977, 1970s 8-tracks.

PAGE 15: Stephen King, *IT*, Viking © 1986 and *Needful Things*, Viking © 1991.

PAGE 15 Timeline: *Star Wars*, 20th Century Fox, © 1977, Atari CX40 joystick © 1977, Stephen King, *Night Shift*, Doubleday © 1978, 1970s roller skates.

PAGE 16: Stephen King, original *Dark Tower* story appearances, *Fantasy & Science Fiction* © 1978, © 1980, 3 issues ©1981.

PAGE 16 Timeline: Stephen King, *The Stand*, Doubleday © 1978, *Halloween* movie mask, Compass Int. Pictures © 1978, 1970s CB Radio, Jonestown cult mass suicide.

PAGE 17: Stephen King, *Bag of Bones*, Scribner © 1998.

PAGE 17 Timeline: Punk rock, Space Invaders video game, Taito © 1978.

PAGES 18-19: Photos Ariel Bosi © 2025.

PAGE 18 Timeline: Three Mile Island disaster, *Alien* film, 20th Century Fox, © 1979.

PAGE 19: Stephen King holding *The Monkey* film popcorn bucket, Stephen King © 2025.

PAGE 19 Timeline: Stephen King, *The Dead Zone*, Viking © 1979, Phantasm film poster, New Breed Productions © 1979, late 1970s skateboard.

PAGE 20: Stephen King, *Insomnia*, Ziesing © 1993 limited edition.

PAGE 20: *Maximum Overdrive* one-sheet movie poster, De Laurentiis Entertainment Group © 1986.

PAGE 20 Timeline: late 1970s cassette tape, *The Amityville Horror*, American International Pictures, © 1979.

PAGE 21: AC/DC "Who Made Who" tour poster, Pace Concerts © 1986.

PAGE 21: "Gramma", *The Twilight Zone*, CBS © 1986.

PAGE 21 Timeline: World Fantasy Convention logo, *When a Stranger Calls*, Columbia Pictures © 1979, *Star Trek: The Motion Picture*, Paramount Pictures © 1979.

PAGE 22: *Fangoria* No. 56, © 1986.

PAGES 22-23: *Maximum Overdrive* press photos, Stephen King, De Laurentiis Entertainment Group © 1986.

PAGE 22 Timeline: 5.5" floppy computer disc, CNN debuts 1980, *Prom Night*, AVCO Embassy Pictures © 1980.

PAGE 23 Timeline: Pac-Man, Namco © 1980, Missile Command video game, Atari © 1980, Stephen King, *Firestarter*, Viking © 1980.

PAGE 24 Timeline: China begins loaning giant pandas to zoos around the world 1980, Jason's mask from *Friday the 13th* film, Paramount / Warner Bros. © 1980.

PAGE 25: Stephen King & Dave Hinchberger, Hard Rock Cafe Atlanta, May 27, © 1993 Dave Hinchberger.

PAGE 25 Timeline: *The Fog*, Avco Embassy Pictures © 1980, *Dark Forces*, Edited by Kirby McAuley, Viking © 1980, John Bonham, drummer for Led Zepplin, dies 1980.

PAGE 26: Rock Bottom Remainders signed photo, © 1993.

PAGE 26 Timeline: World Fantasy 6 convention book 1980, Jack Nicholson image from *The Shining* film, Warner Bros. © 1980.

PAGE 27: The Rock Bottom Remainders tour t-shirt, © 1993.

PAGE 27 Timeline: Anarchy graffiti 1980s, *Dallas* TV show 'Who shot J.R.?" episode 1980.

PAGE 28: The Rock Bottom Remainders tour Crew t-shirt, © 1993.

PAGE 28 Timeline: John Lennon image. Stephen King, *Danse Macabre*, Everest House © 1981.

PAGE 29 Timeline: *Ghost Story* film poster, Universal Pictures, © 1981, NASA Space Shuttle, MTV Logo, Paramount media.

PAGE 30: *UMass at Lowell* Magazine for Alumni and Friends, Spring 2013, Stephen King speaks photo, *UMass at Lowell* © 2013.

PAGE 30 Timeline: Vans shoes 1981, Stephen King, *Cujo*, Viking © 1981.

PAGE 31: Stephen King (as Richard Bachman), *The Long Walk*, Signet © 1979.

PAGE 31 Timeline: Rubiks Cube, Rubik's Brand Ltd © 1980, Stephen King, Different Seasons, Viking © 1982, Wayfarer sunglasses 1982.

PAGE 32: Stephen King, "The New Lieutenant's Rap", Philtrum Press chapbook © 1999.

PAGE 32: Glennon Reitz with Stephen King at UMASS Lowell, Photo *UMass at Lowell Magazine*, Spring 2013, (photo date) 12-7-12.

PAGE 32 Timeline: *Creepshow* film, Warner Bros. © 1982, *The Thing* film, Universal Pictures © 1982, *E.T.* figure, Universal Pictures© 1982.

PAGE 33: *UMass at Lowell* Magazine for Alumni and Friends, Spring, cover and photos *UMass at Lowell* © 2013.

PAGE 33 Timeline: The "boombox" portable radio, VHS tapes, Stephen King, Bernie Wrightson, *Creepshow* trade paperback, Plume © 1982.

PAGES 34-37: Photos by Donna Girard © 2024.

PAGE 34 Timeline: Stephen King, *Christine*, Viking, © 1983, Swatches 1980s.

PAGE 35 Timeline: Disney Channel launches on basic cable 1983, Apple IIe computer debuts, *The Twilight Zone* movie poster, Warner Bros © 1983.

PAGE 36: Collage of photos of Stephen King, © 2024 Donna Girard.

PAGE 36 Timeline: Sally Ride, the first woman astronaut 1983, Stephen King, *Pet Sematary* Doubleday © 1983, *The Dead Zone* film poster, Paramount Pictures © 1983.

PAGE 37 Timeline: Eddie Van Halen's "Frankenstrat" guitar, Sony Walkman © 1984, Apple Macintosh commercial 12-31-83.

PAGE 38 Timeline: George Orwell book *1984*, Big Brother sign 1984.

PAGE 39: Stephen King, *Under the Dome*, Scribner © 2009.

PAGE 39 Timeline: *Children of the Corn* film, Universal Pictures © 1984, Stephen King, *Skeleton Crew*, Putnam © 1985.

PAGES 39-40: Headline News, Robin Meade, Stephen King, CNN © 2009.

PAGE 40: Stephen King, Barnes & Noble Bookstore, Buckhead, Atlanta, 11-13-09. B&N Bookstore photo © 2009.

PAGE 40 Timeline: *Firestarter* film, Universal Pictures, © 1984, *Ghostbusters* film logo, Columbia Pictures © 1984, PG-13 rating begins July 1984.

PAGE 41: Ryman Auditorium poster, 200 unnumbered copies printed / sold at the event. Printed by Hatch Show Print © 2016.

PAGE 41 Timeline: *A Nightmare on Elm Street*, New Line Cinema © 1984, Michael Jackson "Thriller" video 12-2-83, *Cat's Eye* film, MGM/UA © 1985, *Back to the Future* film Dolorean time machine, Universal © 1985.

PAGE 42 Timeline: The 'brick' first cell phone 1983, The Compact Disc is introduced, Stephen King, *Bachman Books*, NAL © 1985.

PAGE 43: Stephen King, *Under the Dome*, Scribner © 2009, *Under the Dome* slipcase, Overlook Connection Press © 2009.

PAGE 43 Timeline: Semi monster truck, *Maximum Overdrive*, De Laurentiis Entertainment Group © 1986, Stephen King, *IT*, Viking © 1986.

PAGE 44: Stephen King, *Under the Dome* limited edition, Scribner © 2009.

PAGE 44 Timeline: *Creepshow 2* film poster, New World Pictures © 1987, Lunar Prospector is launched 1988.

PAGE 45: Stephen King, *Under the Dome*, Scribner © 2009, signed Atlanta appearance copy.

PAGE 45 Timeline: Don Robertson, *Ideal Genuine Man*, Philtrum Press, © 1988, computer 3.5" diskettes 1980s, Parental Advisory label introduced 1988.

PAGE 46: Stephen King, *The Green Mile 2: The Mouse on the Mile*, Signet © 1996.

PAGE 46: Edgar Allen Poe Gravesite. Photo by Kevin B. Moore.

PAGE 46 Timeline: *The Satanic Verses*, Salmon Rushdie, Viking Penguin UK © 1988, Oil drenched pelican from the Exxon Valdez oil spill, Tiananmen Square protests and massacre.

PAGE 47 Timeline: Baseball, Fall of the Berlin Wall 1989.

PAGE 48: Stephen King in front of the King's West Broadway house, Bangor, Maine © 1982, Photo by Carroll Hall, *Bangor Daily News*.

PAGE 48 Timeline: Baseball player catching, *Twin Peaks* TV series premieres, ABC © 1990.

PAGE 49: The front of the King's West Broadway house, Bangor, Maine, © 2022. Stephen King House-View of the house_©httpsunusualplaces.orgstephen-king-house

PAGE 49: Stephen King, *Maleficio (Thinner)*, Spanish edition, Emece' Editores © 1986.

PAGE 49 Timeline: *Misery* film poster, Columbia Pictures © 1990, Stephen King, *Needful Things*, Viking © 1991, Super Nintendo © 1991.

PAGES 50-52: Stephen King in Hamburg / Munich, Germany, photos Udo Erhart © 2013.

PAGE 50 Timeline: Rodney King was beaten by L.A. Police officers, sparking the start of race riots 1991, Stephen King, *The Dark Tower III: The Waste Lands*, Grant © 1991.

PAGE 51: Stephen King artwork by Stephan Behrndt, © 2013.

PAGE 51 Timeline: *Sleepwalkers* film poster, original story by Stephen King, Columbia Pictures © 1992, *The Lawnmower Man* film poster. Stephen King had his name removed from the production as it had no resemblance to the story. New Line Cinema © 1992.

PAGE 52 Timeline: *The Dark Half* film poster, Orion Pictures, © 1993, *Jurassic Park* film released, Universal Pictures © 1993, Stephen King, *Nightmares & Dreamscapes*, Viking © 1993.

PAGE 53: Stephen King flyer for Umass 12-7-2012 event, Umass at Lowell © 2012.

PAGE 53 Timeline: OJ Simpson and the Ford Bronco Los Angeles chase, *The Stand* ABC Series © 1994, Stephen King, *Insomnia*, Viking © 1994.

Bibliography, End Notes, Images

PAGE 54 Timeline: various color CDs holder, Ty Beanie Babies premiere © 1993/© 1994.

PAGE 55 Timeline: *The Shawshank Redemption* film poster, Columbia Pictures © 1994, Rollerblades.

PAGES 54-56: Stephen King at USO by U.S. Air Force, Photos Airman First Class, Jordan Castelan, © 2013.

PAGE 56 Timeline: John Travolta & Samuel L. Jackson, *Pulp Fiction* film, Miramax © 1994, "I want to believe" poster from The X-Files, 20th Cent. Fox © 1993.

PAGES 55-56: Photos of Stephen King and Robin Amstutz, *Doctor Sleep*, and event ticket, Robin Amstutz © 2013.

PAGE 57: George Mason Photos by Glen Reitz, © 2011.

PAGE 57 Timeline: Portable CD Player. Serial killer, Jeffrey Dahmer, imprisoned 1992, *Dolores Claiborne* film poster, Columbia Pictures © 1995.

PAGES 58-59: Lilja's Corner photos, Hans-Åke Lilja © 2013.

PAGE 58 Timeline: Bombing of the Alfred P. Murrah Federal Building in Oklahoma City on April 19, 1995, *The Langoliers* TV series, Laurel Entertainment © 1995, Wireless home phone.

PAGE 59 Timeline: Jerry Garcia of The Grateful Dead dies, Stephen King, *Rose Madder*, Viking © 1995, 1990s computer mouse and cursor.

PAGE 60: Stephen King at the Ryman ticket photo, Dave Hinchberger © 2016.

PAGE 60 Timeline: Theodore "Ted" Kaczynski, the Unabomber, apprehended © 1996, Stephen King, *Desperation* (Viking) and *The Regulators* (Dutton) both in © 1996, *Thinner* film, Paramount Pictures © 1996.

PAGE 61: Stephen King Live! At the Ryman Auditorium, Ryman website ad, © 2016.

PAGE 61: Tweet "What can I say, Driving people…", Twitter, Stephen King © 5-12-16.

PAGE 61 Timeline: Garry Kasparov loses chess match to super computer Deep Blue, 1997, Stephen King, *Six Stories* collection, Philtrum Press © 1997.

PAGE 62: Email communication with Stephen King , Dave Hinchberger © 2016.

PAGE 62 Timeline: Heaven's Gate cult mass suicide, 1997, *Austin Powers International Man of Mystery* film, New Line Cinema © 1997, *Quicksilver Highway* film poster, Fox Network © 1997, *Men In Black* film, Columbia Pictures © 1997.

PAGE 63 Timeline: Pathfinder Sojourner rover lands on Mars 1997, *Contact* film, Warner Bros. © 1997, Stephen King, *Everything's Eventual* © 2002, *The Night Flier* film, New Line Cinema © 1997.

PAGES 63-67: Ryman and Nashville photos, Dave Hinchberger © 2016.

PAGE 64 Timeline: *Sphere* film, Warner Bros. © 1998, *The Big Lebowski* film, Gramercy Pictures © 1998, Frank Sinatra's death May 14th, 1998.

PAGE 65 Timeline: *Deep Impact* film, Paramount Pictures © 1998, *The X-Files: Fight the Future* film, 20th Century Fox © 1998, Stephen King, *Bag of Bones* (UK), Hodder & Stoughton © 1998.

PAGE 66 Timeline: Apple introduces the iMac G3 1998, Blockbuster Video's popularity grows 1998.

PAGES 64-66: Stephen King quoted from Ryman, Nashville appearance, June 11, 2016.

PAGES 68-73: Stephen King, quoted from Rock Bottom Remainders interview, BMG VHS © 1992.

PAGE 67: Tweet "Thanks to everyone who came out . . .", Twitter, June, Stephen King © 2016.

PAGE 67 Timeline: 1990s pager, Google premieres, Tamagotchi virtual pets are popular 1998.

PAGES 68-73: Kathi Kamen Goldmark, quoted from Rock Bottom Remainders interview, BMG VHS © 1992.

PAGE 68: Rock Bottom Remainders image, Gretchen Schields and Chris Morris © 1992

PAGE 68 Timeline: Puff Daddy and Jimmy Page perform "Come With Me", based on Led Zepplin's "Kashmir" song, 1990s CD player/boombox.

PAGE 69 Timeline: Korn, *Follow the Leader*, Immortal/Epic ©1998, Lauryn Hill, *The Miseducation of Lauryn Hill*, Ruffhouse Records ©1998, MpMan mp-f60, the first commercially available MP3 player 1998.

PAGE 70 Timeline: The Internet Corporation for Assigned Names and Numbers (ICANN) is formed 1998, *Urban Legends* film, Tri-Star © 1998.

PAGE 71: Rock Bottom Remainders poster, *The Simpsons* "The Book Job" S23 E6.

PAGE 71 Timeline: Furby talking toy, Tiger Electronics © 1998, *Apt Pupil* film, Sony Pictures © 1998.

PAGE 72 Timeline: John Glenn flies on Space Shuttle Discovery, age 77, The United Nations Framework Convention on Climate Change is formed 1998, Voyager 1 overtakes Pioneer 10 as the most distant spacecraft from Earth 1998.

PAGE 73 Timeline: Disposable cameras are popular, Cher, *Believe*, WEA, Warner Bros. © 1998.

PAGES 74-75: Rock Bottom Remainders in Miami, photos Glen Reitz © 2024.

PAGE 74 Timeline: The Sega Dreamcast system debuts, *Vampires* film, Columbia © 1998, *The Matrix* film, Warner Bros. © 1999.

PAGE 75 Timeline: Stephen King hit by a van accident 1999, 'Missing' flyer from *The Blair Witch Project*, Artisan Entertainment © 1999, Ebay launched 1999, *The Green Mile* film, Warner Bros. © 1999.

PAGE 76: Stephen King, *Firestarter*, Signet © 1981.

PAGE 76 Timeline: Year 2,000 glasses, *American Psycho* film, Lions Gate Films © 2000, Scooters are popular.

PAGE 77: Stephen King, *The Dead Zone*, Signet © 1980, *Different Seasons*, Viking, © 1982.

PAGE 77 Timeline: SpongeBob Squarepants popular, Nickelodeon © 1999, Stephen King, *On Writing*, Scribner © 2000, Presidential election hanging chad 2000.

PAGE 78: Tabitha King, *The Caretakers*, MacMillan, © 1983.

PAGE 78: Stephen King, *Cycle of the Werewolf*, Signet, © 1983.

PAGE 78 Timeline: Wikipedia is launched 2001, Stephen King, *Dreamcatcher*, Scribner © 2001, America Online purchases Time Warner 2001.

PAGE 79: Stephen King, *The Dark Tower the Gunslinger*, Plume © 1988.

PAGE 79 Timeline: Sport watches gaining popularity 2001, 9-11-01 World Trade Center attack, Stephen King, *Hearts in Atlantis*, Scribner © 2001.

PAGE 80: Stephen King, *Dolores Clairborne*, Signet © 1993.

PAGE 80 Timeline: Apple introduces the iPod 2001, Stephen King & Peter Straub, *Black House*, Random House 9-14-01, *Spiderman* film, Sony Pictures © 2002.

PAGE 81: Stephen King, *Insomnia*, Viking © 1994. Released with two covers.

PAGE 81 Timeline: *Signs* film, Buena Vista Pictures © 2002, Stephen King, *From a Buick 8*, Scribner © 2002.

PAGE 82: Stephen King, *The Green Mile 1: The Two Dead Girls*, Signet © 1996.

PAGE 82 Timeline: Netflix gaining popularity 2002, ENRON goes bankrupt.

PAGE 83: Stephen King, *The Green Mile 2: The Mouse on the Mile*, Signet, © 1996.

PAGE 83 Timeline: Bluetooth headsets popular 2002, LinkedIn and Crocs debut.

PAGE 84: Stephen King, *The Green Mile 3: Coffey's Hands*, *The Green Mile 6: Coffey on the Mile*, Signet © 1996.

PAGE 84 Timeline: *Dreamcatcher* film, Warner Bros. © 2003, *DTV: Wolves of the Calla*, Grant © 2003.

PAGE 85: Stephen King, *The Green Mile 4: The Bad Death of Eduard Delacroix*, *The Green Mile 5: Night Journey*, Signet, © 1996.

PAGE 85 Timeline: Stephen King, *DTVII The Dark Tower*, Grant © 2004, *Riding the Bullet* film, Innovation Film Group © 2004.

PAGE 86: Stephen King (as Richard Bachman), *The Regulators*, Dutton © 1996, *Desperation*, Viking © 1996.

PAGE 86 Timeline: *Saw* film franchise debuts, Lions Gate Films © 2004, Stephen King, *The Girl Who Loved Tom Gordon*, Scribner © 1999, Stephen King and Stewart O'Nan, *Faithful*, Scribner © 2004.

PAGE 87 Timeline: Stephen King, *Lisey's Story*, Scribner © 2006, Lance Armstrong wins 7th consecutive Tour de France 2005 (later losing all medals in doping scandal), Guitar Hero released.

PAGE 88: Peter Straub, *Koko*, Dutton © 1988.

PAGE 88 Timeline: Hurricane Katrina 2005, YouTube founded © 2005, Disney buys Pixar Studios © 2006.

PAGE 89: Joseph Pittman, *The Original Crime: Remembrance*, E-reads © 2013.

PAGE 89 Timeline: Stephen King, *Cell*, Scribner © 2006, Gnarls Barkley, *Crazy*, Warner Bros. © 2006, Blu-ray discs first released 2006, *Idiocracy*, 20th Century © 2006.

PAGE 89: Bentley Little, *The Mailman*, Signet © 1991.

PAGE 90: Bentley Little, *The Walking*, Signet © 2000.

PAGE 90 Timeline: FIFA 2006 begins. Mars Reconnaissance Orbiter spacecraft reaches Mars 2006, Twitter social site begins © 2006, *Desperation* film, ABC TV © 2006.

PAGE 91: Stephen King, *The Dark Tower: The Drawing of the Three*, Plume © 1989.

PAGE 91 Timeline: *Nightmares & Dreamscapes* anthology series, TNT, © 2006, Pluto demoted as a planet 2006, Facebook opens to anyone 13 or older with a valid email address 2006.

PAGE 92: *The Shining*, ABC TV © 1997.

PAGE 92: Joseph Pittman, *Tilting at Windmills*, Atria © 2001.

PAGE 92 Timeline: *Silent Hill* film, Alliance Atlantis © 2006, Yelp gains in popularity 2006.

PAGE 93: Joseph Pittman, author photo © 2025.

PAGE 93 Timeline: *Borat* film, 20th Century © 2006, Microsoft Office © 2007, Heelys, shoes with wheels, are popular.

PAGE 94 Timeline: The UK K2 red telephone box, Big Ben is the nickname for the Great Clock of Westminster in London.

PAGE 95: Photo of Phantasia Press publisher, Alex Berman © 2024.

PAGE 95 Timeline: Grenadier Guards / King's Guards for Buckingham Palace, London, The AEC Regent III RT or the red double-decker bus, Firefox 2.0 introduced 2006.

PAGE 96 Timeline: Nintendo's Wii video game console debuts, Dictator General Augusto Pinochet assumes full responsibility for his actions and then dies 2006, *Time* magazine's 'Person of the Year' is You 2006.

PAGE 97 Timeline: Smart phones debut, 1408 film, MGM © 2007, Rock Band video game debuts, MTV Games © 2007.

PAGE 98: Photos of *Firestarter* limited edition, Phantasia Press © 1980.

PAGE 98 Timeline: J.K. Rowling, *Harry Potter and the Deathly Hallows*, Arthur A. Levine Books © 2007, Amateur drone sales take off, *The Mist* film, Dimension Films © 2007, Beats headphone by Dr. Dre gains popularity 2008, *Fela'* Musical on Broadway debuts.

PAGE 99: Photos of *Firestarter* lettered edition, Phantasia Press © 1980.

PAGE 99 Timeline: Barack Obama is elected 44th President © 2008, Stephen King, *Just After Sunset*, Scribner © 2008, Snuggie is popular 2008, Flight 1549 lands on the Hudson River.

Bibliography, End Notes, Images

PAGE 100: Stephen King, *Dark Tower 1: Gunslinger*, Grant © 1982, *Dark Tower 7: Dark Tower*, Grant © 2004.

PAGE 100 Timeline: *Drag Me to Hell* film, Universal. *Orphan* film, Warner Bros. © 2009, *Dolan's Cadillac* film G2 Pictures © 2009, Usain Bolt breaks the world record for the 100 meter dash at 9.58 seconds 2009, *The Road* film, Dimension © 2009.

PAGE 101: *Firestarter* painting for Phantasia Press limited edition, by Michael Whelan © 1980.

PAGE 101 Timeline: *Book of Blood* film, Matador Pictures © 2009, Alice Cooper in *Suck*, Capri Films © 2009, *Zombieland*, Sony © 2009, 'Balloon Boy' fiasco 2009, Stephen King, *Under the Dome*, Scribner © 2009.

PAGE 102 Timeline: Bitcoin debuts. Anonymous hacker group, U2 360 tour debuts © 2009, U2 360 DVD, Interscope © 2010.

PAGE 103 Timeline: Silly Bandz are all the rage 2009, AC/DC's "Black Ice World Tour" grossed $135.2 million from 76 shows 2009, Susan Boyle, *I Dreamed a Dream*, Syco Music © 2009.

PAGES 103-104: Photos by Robert Jackson © 2024.

PAGE 104 Timeline: ZhuZhu Pets are popular 2009, *Up in the Air* film, Paramount Pictures © 2009.

PAGE 105: *Sleeping Beauties* Deluxe hardcover, IDW © 2024.

PAGE 105 Timeline: Angry Birds make their debut © 2009, *Avatar* film, 20th Century Fox, © 2009, Apple iPad debuts 2009.

PAGE 106: *Sleeping Beauties* Deluxe hardcover, IDW © 2024.

PAGE 106: Stephen King and Owen King, *Sleeping Beauties*, Scribner © 2017, *Sleeping Beauties* Issue No. 1, IDW © 2020.

PAGE 106 Timeline: WikiLeaks launched, Shutter Shades are popular 2010, The Deepwater Horizon BP Oil Spill 2010.

PAGE 107: Stephen King and Owen King, *Sleeping Beauties*, IDW Issue No. 4, No. 5, No1 Peach Momoko Virgin variant, No. 1 Retailer Incentive variant.

PAGE 107 Timeline: *The Walking Dead* debuts/logo, AMC © 2010, Stephen King, *Full Dark, No Stars*, Scribner © 2010, Osama Bin Laden dies 2011, *Hellgate* film, IFC films © 2011.

PAGES 108-109: Stephen King *Insomnia* tour, Nashville, Photos George Walker IV © 1994.

PAGE 108 Timeline: Muammar Gaddafi is assassinated, Stephen King, *11-22-63* released, Scribner © 2011.

PAGE 109 Timeline: *Gangnam Style* song by Psy 2011, Nyan Cat meme becomes huge 2011, *Hugo* film debuts, Paramount © 2011, UK 'Keep Calm' poster and variations of it become popular 2011.

PAGE 110: Stephen King and Mike Flanigan photo, Warner Bros, © 2019.

PAGE 110 Timeline: *Bag of Bones* mini-series, A&E © 2011, 'Planking' becomes an exercise trend 2011.

PAGE 111: *Doctor Sleep* advance movie poster, Warner Bros. © 2019.

PAGE 111 Timeline: *Avengers* movie debuts, Paramount Pictures, Walt Disney Pictures, Walt Disney Studios Motion Pictures © 2012, Stephen King & John Mellencamp, *Ghost Brothers of Darkland County* premieres © 2012, Sandy Hook School massacre 2012.

PAGE 112 Timeline: The Chelyabinsk meteor in Russia © 2013, Edward Snowden leaks U.S. information © 2013, Stephen King, *Joyland*, Hard Case Crime © 2013.

PAGE 113 Timeline: Stephen King at the Mortensen Hall Mark Twain House, Dumb Ways to Die video goes viral 2013, Stephen King, *Doctor Sleep*, Scribner, © 2013.

PAGE 114 Timeline: Selfie sticks and taking selfies are all the rage 2013, selfie photo by Glen Reitz © 2012. *Breaking Bad* series finale 2013.

PAGE 115 Timeline: Katy Perry album, *Prism*, debuts, Capitol Records, © 2013, Candy Crush App game becomes a sensation 2013, Dabbing is all the rage 2013.

PAGE 116: Douglas E. Winter, *Stephen King the Art of Darkness*, NAL © 1984.

PAGE 116 Timeline: Mars MAVEN Orbiter spacecraft was launched 2013, Doge dog becomes a meme sensation 2013.

PAGE 117: Stephen King, *Carrie*, Doubleday © 1974, and *Christine*, Viking © 1983.

PAGE 117 Timeline: *Oldboy* movie, Show East © 2014, Nelson Mandela dies, *A Good Marriage* film, USA Media © 2014, Mercy film, Blumhouse © 2014.

PAGE 118: Stephen King, *'Salem's Lot*, Doubleday © 1975, Kevin Quigley, *Chart of Darkness*, CD Publications © 2021.

PAGE 118 Timeline: Malaysia Air Flight 370 goes missing 2014, The ALS Ice Bucket Challenge 2014, *Guardians of the Galaxy* film, Walt Disney Studios Motion Pictures © 2014, The Rosetta orbiter/lander begins orbiting comet 67P/Churyumov–Gerasimenko 2014.

PAGES 119-125: Photos from *I Know What You Need*, © 2024 Julia Marchese.

PAGE 119 Timeline: Robin Williams dies 2014, Stephen King, *Revival*, Scribner © 2014.

PAGE 120 Timeline: The Umbrella Revolution, Hong Kong 2014, The process of normalizing relations between Cuba and the United States formally begins 2014.

PAGE 121 Timeline: Marriage Equality with the Supreme Court decision in Obergefell v. Hodges 2015, Stephen King, *Finders Keepers*, Scribner © 2015, *De Palma* movie, A24 © 2015.

PAGE 122 Timeline: *11.22.63* mini-series, Hulu © 2016, David Bowie's last album *Blackstar*, released two days before his death, ISO Columbia Sony © 2016, *10 Cloverfield Lane* movie, Paramount Pictures © 2016, *Hush* movie, Netflix © 2016.

PAGE 123 Timeline: Prince dies 2016, *Can't Stop the Feeling* by Justin Timberlake, RCA © 2016, Muhammad Ali dies 2016, Stephen King, *End of Watch*, Scribner © 2016.

PAGE 124 Timeline: U.S. total ban on commercial trade in African elephant ivory goes into effect, *Warcraft* movie, Universal Pictures © 2016.

PAGE 125 Timeline: The Pulse nightclub mass shooting 2016, Facebook unveils emoticons 2016.

PAGE 126 Timeline: Water bottle flipping is all the rage 2016, Solar Impulse 2 plane circumnavigates the globe as the first piloted, fixed-wing aircraft using only solar power 2016, Vine app debuts 2016.

PAGE 127: Photos by Bob Ireland.

PAGE 127 Timeline: Anton Yelchin dies 2016, Virtual reality goggles flood the market 2016, Glastonbury Festival of Contemporary Performing Arts 2016, Pokémon Go app is introduced 2016.

PAGE 128: Photo by Mickie Roberston, © 2025.

PAGE 128 Timeline: *Stranger Things* TV show begins streaming, Netflix © 2016, *Cell* movie debuts, Saban Films © 2016, *The Accountant* movie, Warner Bros. Pictures © 2016.

PAGE 129 Timeline: Lady Gaga album *Joanne* debuts, Interscope © 2016, Stephen King, *Hearts In Suspension*, University of Maine Press © 2016, *Watership Down* author Richard Adams dies 2016, *Mr. Mercedes*, David E. Kelley Productions, © 2016.

PAGE 130 Timeline: Women's March 2017, Cassini-Huygens orbiter mission concludes on September 15 when it's trajectory takes it into Saturn's upper atmosphere and it burns up 2017, Tossing paper towels rolls at hurricane victims in Puerto Rico 2017, *IT Chapter One* movie, Warner Bros. © 2017, *1922* film, Netflix © 2017.

PAGE 131 Timeline: Stephen King and Owen King, *Sleeping Beauties*, Scribner 2017, Fidget spinners fad takes over 2017, Snapchat app puppy filter is all the rage 2017.

PAGE 132 Timeline: *Gerald's Game* movie, Netflix © 2017, Fortnite game takes over 2017, Las Vegas Strip mass shooting at Route 91 Harvest music festival 2017.

PAGE 133: Stephen King, *The Plant* ebook, Philtrum Press © 2000.

PAGE 133 Timeline: Glitter everything becomes a thing 2017, National Academies of Science, Engineering, and Medicine (NASEM) issued a report on human gene editing recommending that clinical trials should be permitted within a regulatory framework 2017, Making homemade slime takes over 2017.

PAGE 134 Timeline: *The Shape of Water* movie, Fox Searchlight Pictures © 2017, *Castle Rock* TV series, Hulu © 2018, *Hamilton* musical takes over the country 2018.

PAGE 135 Timeline: *The Outsider* TV series, HBO © 2019, Stephen King, *The Institute*, Scribner © 2019, Joe Hill, *Full Throttle*, William Morrow © 2019, *Doctor Sleep* movie debuts, Warner Bros. Pictures © 2019.

PAGE 136: *The Life of Chuck*, Neon © 2025.

PAGE 136 Timeline: Covid-19 virus decimates the world, killing millions 2020, Stephen King, *If It Bleeds*, Scribner © 2020, Black Lives Matter protests across U.S. 2020, Eddie Van Halen dies 2020.

PAGE 137: *Derry* image, HBO/Max © 2025, Stephen King, *The Institute*, Hodder & Stoughton UK Waterstones release, © 2019, Stephen King, *The Running Man*, NEL.

PAGE 137 Timeline: Jan. 6th Insurrection 2021, Ukraine invaded by Russia 2022, Taylor Swift *Eras* world tour dominates 2023, *'Salem's Lot* movie, Max © 2024, *The Monkey* film, Neon © 2025.

PAGES 232-233: William Peter Blatty, wikipedia.com

PAGES 144-145: Cheltenham Literacy Festival © 2022.

PAGES 154-155: "Hitting Rock Bottom", excerpts from *On Writing* by Stephen King, Scribner © 2000.

PAGE 161: Photo of Earl Hamner on *The Waltons* TV show set in © 1976, public domain.

PAGE 162: Rock Bottom Remainders poster image, *The Simpsons* Ep 492 "The Book Job" aired 11-20-11.

PAGES 168-169: "Conversation with Stephen King", John F. Kennedy Sixth Floor Museum, Majestic Theatre, Dallas, Texas November 10, 2011. YouTube video.

PAGE 177: Rock Bottom Remainders concert photo, rockbottomremainders.com

PAGES 180-183: Michael Darpino, excerpts from Rock Bottom Remainders Review, April 21, © 2010.

PAGE 187: Stephen King, *Who is your favorite novelist of all time?* NY Times 6-4-© 2015.

PAGES 184-187: Mark Sieber, Book Review: *The Ideal Genuine Man* © 2024.

PAGE 195: Ridley Pearson, quote from Andrew Rausch interview © 2024.

PAGE 200: Kathi Kamen Goldmark, "My Life With the Remainders", BMG gatefold flap copy, VHS © 1992.

PAGE 202: The Rock Bottom Remainders first press photo, © 1993.

PAGE 212: Pat DiNizio press photo.

PAGE 214: *Sleeping Beauties* release banner, StephenKing.com, Scribner's cover art © 2017.

PAGE 219: Roger McGuinn, © 2004 RockBottomRemainders.com

PAGE 220: American Booksellers Association logo.

PAGES 224-227: Stephen King at Umass, video screen shots 12-7-2012.

PAGE 235: Logo, © Tesco.

PAGES 248-251: Rock Bottom Remainders official press release, June 12, © 2012.

PAGES 25, 37, 63, 64, 65, 66, 67: photos by Dave Hinchberger © 2024.

Unless otherwise listed, all artwork, calendar border art, and cover is by Glenn Chadbourne, © 2024.

Layout, design, and border re-creations (of Glenn Chadbourne art)
by Bryan McAllister, Fine Dog Creative.

Published © 2024 by Overlook Connection Press. PO Box 1934, Hiram, Georgia 30141

OverlookConnection.com StephenKingCatalog.com

First Printing ISBN: 9781623307073

www.ingramcontent.com/pod-product-compliance
Lightning Source LLC
Chambersburg PA
CBHW081138300726
48982CB00006B/1003

* 9 7 8 1 6 2 3 3 0 7 0 7 3 *